IF TH

Virginia Andrews,
USA, studied art a
worked as a fashi
and later as a portrait painter.

Flowers in the Attic, based on a true story, was her first novel and became an immediate best-seller. Published in 1979, it received tremendous acclaim on both sides of the Atlantic, and was made into a feature film. It was followed by three more books about the Dollanganger family – *Petals on the Wind*, *If There be Thorns* and *Seeds of Yesterday* – as well as by the prequel to *Flowers in the Attic*, *Garden of Shadows*. In addition to these novels, she is also the author of *My Sweet Audrina*, and the novels in the Casteel family saga – *Heaven*, *Dark Angel*, *Fallen Hearts*, *Gates of Paradise* and *Web of Dreams* – set in Virginia Andrews' home country, West Virginia, and in Boston.

Virginia Andrews died in December 1986, but left a considerable amount of unpublished work.

By the same author

FLOWERS IN THE ATTIC
PETALS ON THE WIND
MY SWEET AUDRINA
SEEDS OF YESTERDAY
HEAVEN
DARK ANGEL
GARDEN OF SHADOWS
FALLEN HEARTS
GATES OF PARADISE
WEB OF DREAMS

VIRGINIA ANDREWS

If There be Thorns

HarperCollins*Publishers*

HarperCollins*Publishers*
77–85 Fulham Palace Road,
Hammersmith, London W6 8JB

www.fireandwater.com

This paperback edition 1994

Previously published in paperback by Fontana 1981
Reprinted thirty times

First published in the USA by
Pocket Books 1981

ISBN 0 00 777366 8

Set in Ehrhardt

Printed and bound in Great Britain by
Bookmarque Ltd, Croydon, Surrey

PROLOGUE

In the late evening when the shadows were long, I sat quiet and unmoving near one of Paul's marble statues. I heard the statues whispering to me of the past I could never forget, hinting slyly of the future I was trying to ignore. Flickering ghostly in the pale light of the rising moon were the will-o-the-wisp regrets that told me daily I could and should have done differently. But I am what I have always been, a person ruled by my instincts. It seems I can never change.

I found a strand of silver in my hair today, reminding me soon I might be a grandmother, and I shuddered. What kind of grandmother would I make? What kind of mother was I? In the sweetness of twilight I waited for Chris to come and join me and tell me with the true blue of his eyes that I'm not fading; I'm not just a paper flower but one that's real.

He put his arm about my shoulder and I rested my head where it seemed to fit best, both of us knowing our story is almost over and Bart and Jory will give to both of us, either the best or the worst of what is yet to be.

It is their story now, Jory's and Bart's, and they will tell it as they knew it.

PART ONE

JORY

Whenever Dad didn't drive me home from school, a yellow school bus let me off at an isolated spot where I would recover my bike from the nearest ravine, hidden there each morning before I stepped on to the bus.

To reach my home I had to travel a winding narrow road without any houses until I came to the huge deserted mansion that invariably drew my eyes, making me wonder who had lived there? Why had they deserted it? What had been its story? When I saw that house I automatically slowed down, knowing soon I'd be home.

An acre from that house was our home, isolated and lonely on a road that had more twists and turns than a puzzle maze that led the mouse to the cheese. We lived in Fairfax, Marin County, about twenty miles north of San Francisco. Dense woods were on the other side of the mountains, and the ocean too. Ours was a cold place, sometimes dreary. The fog would roll in great billowing waves and often shrouded the landscape all day, turning everything cold and eerie. The fog was spooky, but it was also romantic and mysterious.

As much as I loved my home, I had vague disturbing memories of a southern garden full of giant magnolia trees dripping with Spanish moss. I remembered a tall man with dark hair turning grey; a man who called me his son. I didn't remember his face nearly as well as I remembered the nice, warm and safe feeling he gave me. I guess one of the saddest things about growing bigger and older, was that no one was large enough, or strong enough to pick you up and hold you close, and make you feel that safe again.

My own father died before I was born; his name was Julian Marquet, and everyone in the ballet world knew about him. But hardly anyone outside of Clairmont, South Carolina knew about Dr Paul Scott Sheffield who had been my mother's second husband. In that same southern state in the town of Greenglenna lived my paternal grandmother, Madame Marisha.

She was the one who wrote me a letter each week, and once a summer we visited her. It seemed she wanted, almost as much as I did, for me to become the most famous dancer the world had ever known. And thus I would prove to her, and to everyone that my father had not lived and died in vain.

By no means was my grandmother an ordinary little old lady. Once she'd been very famous, and not for one second did she let anyone forget this. It was a rule I was never to call her Grandmother when others could overhear and possibly guess her age. She'd whispered to me once that it would be all right if I called her *Mother*, but that didn't seem right when I already had a mother whom I loved very much. So I called her Madame Marisha, or Madame M just as everyone else did.

Our yearly visit to South Carolina was long anticipated during the winter and quickly forgotten once we were back and safely snuggled in our little valley where our long redwood house nestled. 'Safe in the valley where the wind doesn't blow,' my mother said often. Too often really – as if the wind blowing greatly distressed her.

I reached our curving drive, parked my bike and went inside the house. No sign of Bart or Mom. Heck! I raced into the kitchen where Emma was preparing dinner. She spent most of her time in the kitchen, and that accounted for her 'pleasingly plump' figure. Nevertheless she had a long dour face unless she was smiling. Fortunately she smiled most of the time. She could order you to do this, do that, and with her smile take the pain from the ordeal of doing things for yourself. That was something my brother Bart refused to do. I suspected Emma waited on Bart more than me because he spilled when he tried to pour his own milk. He dropped when he carried a glass of water. There wasn't anything he could hold on to, and nothing he could keep from bumping into. Tables fell, lamps toppled. If an extension flex was anywhere in the house Bart would be sure to snag his sneaker toes underneath and down he'd go – or the blender, the mixer, or the radio would crash to the floor.

'Where's Bart?' I asked Emma who was peeling potatoes to put in with the roast beef she had in the oven.

'I tell you, Jory, I'll be glad when that boy stays in school just as long as you do! I hate to see him come in the kitchen. I have to stop what I'm doing and look around and anticipate just what he might knock off or bump into. Thank God he's got that wall to sit on! What is it you boys do on that wall anyway?'

'Nothing,' I said. I didn't want to tell her how often we stole over to the deserted mansion beyond the wall and played there. The estate was off-limits to us, but parents weren't supposed to see and know everything. Next I asked, 'Where's Mom?' Emma said she'd come home early, after cancelling her ballet class, which I already knew. 'Half her class has colds,' I explained. 'But where is she now?'

'Jory, I can't keep my eyes on everybody and still know what I'm doing. A few minutes ago she said something about going up to the attic for old pictures. Why don't you join her up there and help her search?'

That was Emma's way of saying I was in her way. I headed for the attic stairs which were hidden in the far end of our large walk-in linen cupboard in the back hall. Just as I was passing through the family room, I heard the front door open and close. To my surprise I looked to see my dad standing stock still in the foyer, a strange look of reflection in his blue eyes, making me reluctant to call out and break into his thoughts. I paused, undecided.

He headed for his bedroom after he put down his black doctor's bag. He had to pass the linen cupboard with its door slightly ajar. He stopped, listening as I was to the faint sound of ballet music drifting down the stairs. Why was my mother up there? Dancing there again? Whenever I asked why she danced in such a dusty place, she explained she was compelled to dance up there, despite the heat and dust. 'Don't tell your father about this,' she'd warned me several times. After I questioned her, she'd stopped going up there – and now she was doing it again.

This time I was going up. This time I was going to listen to the excuses she gave him. For Dad would catch her!

On tip-toes I trailed him up the steep, narrow stairs. He paused directly under the bare electric bulb that hung down from the apex of the attic. He riveted his eyes upon my Mom who kept right on dancing as if she didn't see him there. In one hand she held a dustmop and playfully she swiped at this or that, miming Cinderella and certainly not Princess Aurora from 'The Sleeping Beauty', which was the music she had on the ancient record player.

Gosh. My stepfather's heart seemed to jump right up into his eyes. He looked scared and hurt, and I sensed she was hurting him just by dancing in the attic. How odd. I didn't understand what went on between them. I was fourteen, Bart was nine, and we were both a long, long way from being adults. The love they had for each other seemed to me very different from the love I saw between the parents of the few friends I had. Their love seemed more intense, more tumultuous, more passionate. Whenever they thought no one was watching they locked eyes, and they had to reach out and touch whenever they passed one another.

Now that I was an adolescent, I was beginning to take more notice of what went on between the most meaningful models I had. I wondered often about the many different facets my parents had. One for the public to view; another for Bart and me, and the other, most fervent side which they showed only one to the other. (How could they know two sons were not always discreet enough to turn away and leave like they should?).

Maybe that's the way all adults were, especially parents.

Dad kept staring as Mom whirled in fast *pirouettes* that fanned her long blonde hair out in a half circle. Her leotards were white, her *pointes* white too, and I was enthralled as she danced, wielding that dustmop like a sword to stab at old furniture that Bart and I had outgrown. Scattered on the floor and shelves were broken toys, toy cars and scooters, dishes she or Emma had broken, which she meant to glue back together one day. With each swipe of her dustmop she brought zillions of golden dustmotes into play. Frenzied and crazy they struggled to settle down before she attacked again and once more drove them into flight.

'Depart!' she cried as a queen to her slaves. 'Go and stay away! Torment me no more!' – and round and round she spun so fast I had to turn to follow her with my eyes, or end up dizzy just from watching. She whipped her head, her legs doing *fouettes* with more expertise then I'd seen on stage. Wild and possessed she spun faster and faster, keeping time to the music, using the mop as part of her action, making housework so dramatic that I wanted to kick off my shoes, jump in and join her, and be the partner my real father had once been. But I could only stand in the dim purplish shadows and watch something I sensed I shouldn't be watching.

My dad swallowed over the lump which must have risen in his throat. Mom looked so beautiful, so young and soft. She was thirty-seven, so old in years, but so young in appearance, and could so easily be wounded by an unkind word. Just as easily as any sixteen-year-old dancer in her classes.

'Cathy!' cried Dad, jerking the needle from the record so the music screeched to a halt. 'STOP! What are you doing?'

She heard, and fluttering her slim pale arms in mock fright, flittered towards him, using the tiny even steps called *bourrées*. For a second or so only, then she was off again spinning in a series of *pirouettes* around him, encircling him and swiping at him with her dustmop.

'Stop it!' he yelled, seizing hold of her mop and hurling it away. He seized her by her waist, pinioning her arms to her side as a deep blush rose to stain her cheeks. He released his hold enough to allow her arms to flutter like broken birdwings so her hands could cover her throat. Above those crossed pale hands, her blue eyes grew larger and very dark. Her full lips began to quiver, and slowly, slowly, with awful reluctance she was forced to look where Dad's finger pointed.

I looked too and was surprised to see two twin beds set up in the portion of the attic that was soon to be under construction. Dad had promised her we'd have a recreation room up here. But twin beds in all this junk? Why?

Mom spoke then, her voice husky and scared. 'Chris? You're home? You don't usually come home this early . . .'

He'd caught her and I was relieved. Now he could straighten her out, tell her not to dance up here again in the dry dusty air that could make her faint. Even I could see she was having trouble coming up with some excuse.

'Cathy, I know I brought those bedsteads up, but how did you manage to put them together?' Dad shot out. 'How did you find the mattresses?' Then he jolted for a second time, spying then the picnic hamper between the beds. 'Cathy,' he roared, glaring at her, 'does history have to repeat itself? Can't we learn and benefit from the mistakes of others? *Do we have to do it all over again?*'

Again? What was he talking about?

'Catherine,' Dad went on in the same cold hard voice, 'don't stand there and try to look innocent, like some wicked child caught stealing. Why are those beds here, all made up with clean sheets and new blankets? Why the picnic hamper? Haven't we seen enough of those baskets to last us our whole lives through?'

And here I was thinking she'd put the beds together so she and I could have a place to fall down and rest after we danced, as we had a few times. And a picnic hamper hamper was, after all, just another basket.

I drifted closer, then hid behind a strut that rose to the rafters. Something sad and painful was between them; something young, fresh, like a raw wound that refused to heal. My mother looked ashamed and suddenly awkward. The man I called Dad stood bewildered; I could tell he wanted to take her in his arms and forgive her. 'Cathy, Cathy,' he pleaded with anguish, 'don't be like *her* in every way!'

Mom jerked her head high, threw back her shoulders and with arrogant pride glared him down. Next she flipped her long hair back from her face and smiled to charm him. Was she doing all of that just to make him stop asking questions she didn't want to answer?

I felt strangely cold in the musty gloom of the attic. A chilling shiver chased down my spine, making me want to run and hide. Making me ashamed too for spying – that was Bart's way, not mine.

How could I escape without attracting their attention? I had to stay in my hidden place.

'Look at me, Cathy. You're not the sweet young *ingénue* any more, and this is not a game. There is no reason for those beds to be there. And the picnic basket only compounds my fears. What the hell are you planning?'

Her arms spread wide as if to hug him, but he pushed her away and spoke again: 'Don't try to appeal to me when I feel sick to my stomach. I ask myself each day how I can come home and not be tired of you, and still feel as I do after so many years, and after all that has happened. Yet I go on year after year loving you, needing and trusting you. Don't take my love and make it into something ugly!'

Bewilderment clouded her expression. I'm sure it clouded mine too. Didn't he truly love her? Was that what he meant? Mom was staring at the beds again, as if surprised to see them there.

'Chris, help me!' she choked, stepping closer and opening her arms again. He put her off, shaking his head. She implored, 'Please don't shake your head and act like you don't understand. I don't remember buying the basket, really I don't. I had a dream the other night about coming up here and putting the beds together, but when I came up today and saw them, I thought you must have put them there.'

'Cathy! I did not put the beds there!'

'Move out of the shadows. I can't see you where you are.' She lifted her small pale hands, seeming to wipe away invisible cobwebs. Then she was staring at her hands as if they'd betrayed her – or was she really seeing spiderwebs tying her fingers together?

Just as my Dad did, I looked around again. Never had the attic been so clean before. The floor had been scrubbed, cartons of old junk were stacked neatly. She had tried to make the attic look homely by hanging pretty pictures of flowers on the walls.

Dad was eyeing Mom as if she were crazy. I wondered what he was thinking, and why he couldn't tell what bothered her when he was the best doctor ever. Was he trying to decide if she was only pretending to forget? Did that dazed troubled look in her terrified eyes tell him differently? Must have, for he said softly, kindly, 'Cathy, you don't have to look scared. You're not swimming in a sea of deceit any more, or helplessly caught in an undertow. You are not drowning. Not going under. Not having a nightmare. You don't have to clutch at straws when you have me.' Then he drew her into his arms as she fell towards him, grasping as if to keep from drowning. 'You're all right, darling,' he whispered, stroking her back, touching her cheeks, drying her tears that began to flow. Tenderly he tilted her chin up before his lips slowly lowered to hers. The kiss lasted and lasted, making me hold my breath.

'The grandmother is dead. Foxworth Hall has been burned to the ground.'

Foxworth Hall? What was that?

'No it hasn't, Chris. I heard her climbing the stairs a short while ago, and you know she's afraid of small confined places – how could she climb the stairs?'

'Were you sleeping when you heard her?'

I shivered. What the devil were they talking about? Which grandmother?'

'Yes,' she murmured, her lips moving over his face. 'I guess I did drift into nightmares after I finished my bath and lay out on the bedroom patio. I don't even remember climbing the stairs up here. I don't know why I come, or why I dance, unless I am losing my mind! I feel I am her sometimes, and then I hate myself!'

'No, you're not her. Momma is miles and miles away where she can never hurt us again. Virginia is three thousand miles from here, and yesterday has come and gone. Ask yourself one question whenever you are in doubt – if we could survive the worst, doesn't it stand to reason we should be able to bear the best?'

I wanted to run, wanted to stay. I felt I too was drowning in a sea of deceit even when I didn't understand what they were talking about. I saw two people, my parents, as strangers whom I didn't know, younger, less strong, less dependable.

'Kiss me,' Mom murmured, 'wake me up and chase away the ghosts. Say you love me and always will, no matter what I do.'

Eagerly enough he did all of that. When he had her convinced, she wanted him to dance with her. She replaced the needle on the record and again the music soared.

Shrivelled up tight and small, I watched him try to do the difficult ballet steps that would have been so easy for me. He didn't have enough skill or grace to partner someone as professional as my Mom. It was embarrassing to even see him try. Soon enough she put on another record where he could lead.

'Dancing in the dark,
'Til the tune ends, we're dancing in the dark . . .'

Now Dad was confident, holding her close, his cheek pressed to hers as they went gliding around the floor.

'I miss the paper flowers that used to flutter in our wake,' she said softly.

'And down the stairs the twins were quietly watching the small black and white TV set in the corner.' His eyes were closed, his voice soft and dreamy. 'You were only fourteen, and I loved you even then, much to my shame.'

Shame? Why?

He hadn't even known her when she was fourteen. I frowned, trying to think back to when and where they'd first met. Mom and her younger sister, Carrie, had run away from home soon after Mom's parents were killed in a car accident. They'd gone south on a bus and a kind black woman named Henny had taken them to Dr Paul Sheffield who had generously taken them in, and given them a good home. My Mom had started ballet classes again and there she met Julian Marquet, the man who was my father. I was born shortly after he was killed. Then Mom married again. And Daddy Paul was Bart's father. It had been a long, long time before she met Chris, who was Daddy Paul's younger brother. So how could he have loved her when she was fourteen? Had they told us lies? Oh gosh, oh gosh . . .

But now the dance was over, the argument began again: 'Okay, you're feeling better, yourself again,' Dad said. 'I want your solemn promise that if anything ever happens to me, be it tomorrow, or years from now, you swear that you will never, so help you God, hide Bart and Jory in the attic so you can go unencumbered into another marriage!'

Stunned, I watched my Mom jerk her head upwards before she gasped: 'Is that what you think of me? *Damn you for thinking I am so much like her!* Maybe I did put the beds together. Maybe I did bring the basket up here, but never once did it cross my mind to . . . to . . . Chris, you know I wouldn't do that!'

Do what, what?

He made her swear. Really forced her to speak the words while her blue eyes glared hot and angry at him all the while.

Sweating now, hurting too, I felt angry and terribly disillusioned in my Dad who should know better. Mom wouldn't do that. She couldn't. She loved me. She loved Bart too. Even if she did look at him sometimes with shadows in her eyes, still she would never, never hide us away in this attic.

My dad left her standing in the middle of the attic as he strode forward to seize the picnic hamper. Next he unlatched and pushed open the screen, and hurled the basket out of the open window. He watched it fall to the ground before he turned once more to confront my Mom angrily:

'Perhaps we are compounding the sins of our parents by living together as we are. Perhaps in the end both Jory and Bart will be hurt – so don't whisper to me tonight about adopting another child. We cannot afford to involve another child in the mess we've made. Don't you realize, Cathy, when you put those beds up here you are unconsciously planning what to do in case our secret is exposed?'

'No,' she objected, spreading her hands helplessly. 'I wouldn't. I couldn't do that . . .'

'You have to mean that,' he snapped. 'No matter what happens, we will not, or you will not put your children in this attic to save yourself, or me.'

'I hate you for thinking I would!'

'I am trying to be patient. I am trying to believe in you. I know you still have nightmares. I know you are still tormented by all that happened when we were young and innocent. But you have to grow up enough to look at yourself honestly. Haven't you learned yet the subconscious often leads the way for the reality?'

He strode back to cuddle her close, to soothe and kiss her, to soften his voice as she clung to him desperately. (And why did she have to feel so desperate?)

'Cathy, my heart, put away those fears instilled by the cruel grandmother. She wanted us to believe in hell and its everlasting torments of revenge. There is no hell but that which we make for ourselves. There is no heaven but that which we build between us. Don't chip away at my belief, my love, with your unconscious deeds. I have no life without you.'

'Then don't go to see your mother this summer.'

He raised his head and stared over hers, pain in his eyes. I slid silently down to the floor, to sit and stare at them, speechless, utterly bewildered.

What was going on? Why was I suddenly so afraid?

BART

'And on the seventh day God rested,' read Jory as I finished patting the earth nice and firm over the pansy seeds that were meant to honour my Aunt Carrie and Uncle Cory's birthday, May fifth. Little aunt and uncle I'd never seen. Both been dead a long, long time. Dead before I was born. People died easy in our family. (Wonder why they liked pansies so much? Silly little nothing flowers with pudding faces.) Wish Momma didn't think honouring dead people's birthdays was so darn important.

'You know what else?' asked Jory, like nine was a dumb age, and he was an adult. 'In the beginning, when God created Adam and Eve, they lived the Garden of Eden without wearing any clothes at all. Then one day an evil talking snake told them it was sinful to walk around naked, so Adam put on a fig leaf.'

Gosh . . . naked people who didn't know naked was wicked. 'What did Eve put on?' I asked as I looked around, hoping to see a fig leaf. He went on reading in a sing-song way that took me to olden times when God was looking out for everyone – even naked people who could talk to snakes.

'Jory, where d'you find fig leaves?'

'Why?'

'If I had one, I'd take off all my clothes and wear it.'

Jory laughed. 'Good golly, Bart, there's only one way for a boy to wear a fig leaf – and you'd be embarrassed.'

'I would not!'

'You would too!'

'I'm never embarrassed!'

'Then how do you know what it's like? Besides, have you ever seen Dad wear a fig leaf?'

'No . . .' but I figured since I'd never seen a fig leaf, how could I know whether or not I had? I said this to Jory.

'Boy, you'd know!' he answered with another laugh to mock me.

Then he was grinning, jumping up to leap up all the marble steps in one long bound that I couldn't help but admire. Me, I had to trail along behind. Wish I was graceful like him. Wish I could dance and charm everybody into likin' me. Jory was bigger, older, smarter – but wait a minute. Maybe I could make myself smarter if not bigger. My head was big. Had to have a big brain inside. I'd grow taller by and by, catch up with Jory, bypass him. Why I'd grow taller than Daddy; taller than the giant in *Jack and the Beanstalk* – and that giant was taller than anybody!

Nine years old . . . wish I was fourteen.

There was Jory sitting on the top step, waitin' for me to catch up. Insulting. Hateful. God sure hadn't been kind to me when he passed out co-ordination. Remembered five years ago when I was four and Emma gave each of us a baby chick all soft yellow fuzz, making chirps and cheeps. Never felt nothin' so good before in my whole life. There I was lovin' it, holdin' it, sniffin' its baby smell before I put it kindly on the ground – and darn if that chick didn't fall over dead.

'You squeezed,' said Daddy who knew about stuff like that. 'I warned you not to hold it too tight. Baby chicks are fragile and you have to handle them with care. Their hearts are very near the surface – so next time, gentle hands, okay?'

Thought God might strike me dead then and there, even though most of it wasn't my fault anyway. Wasn't my fault He didn't make my nerve endings go all the way to the surface of my skin. Wasn't my fault I couldn't feel pain like everybody else. Then I'd shivered, fearful He might do somethin'. But when he was forgivin' I went an hour later to the little pen where Jory's live chick had been walkin' around lonesome. I picked him up and told him he had a friend. Boy, we had a good time with me chasin' him and him chasin' me – when all of a sudden, after only two hours of havin' fun – that chick keeled over dead too.

Hated stiff cold things. Why'd it give up so easily? 'What's the matter with you?' I shouted. 'I didn't squeeze! My hands didn't hold you! I was careful – so stop playin' dead and get up or my Daddy will think I killed you on purpose.' Once I'd seen my Daddy haul a man out of the water, and save his life by pumpin' out the water and blowing in air, so I did the same things to the chick. It stayed dead. Next I massaged its heart, then I prayed, and still it stayed dead.

I was no good. No good for nothing. Couldn't stay clean. Emma said clean clothes on me were a waste of her good time. Couldn't hold on to a dish when I dried it. New toys fell apart soon after they came my way. New shoes looked old in ten minutes after knowing my feet. Weren't my fault if they scuffed up easily. People just didn't know how to make good unscuffable shoes. Never saw a day when my knees weren't scabby or covered with plasters. When I played ball I tripped and fell between bases. My hands didn't know how to catch right so my fingers bent backwards and twice I'd had fingers broken. Three times I'd fallen from trees. Once I broke my right arm, once my left. Third time I only got bruises. Jory never broke anythin'.

No wonder my Mom kept tellin' me and him not to go next door to that big old house with so many staircases, 'cause sooner or later she knew I'd fall down steps and break all my bones.

'What a pity you don't have much co-ordination,' mumbled Jory. Then he stood up and yelled, 'Bart, stop running like a girl. Lean forward, use your legs like pumps. Put your heart in it and let go! Forget about falling. You won't if you don't expect to. And if you catch me I'll give you my super-speed ball!'

Boy, wasn't nothin' I wanted in this whole wide world more than I wanted that ball of his. Jory could throw it with a curve. When he pitched at tin cans setting on the wall, he'd hit 'em one after another. I never hit anything I aimed for – but I did hit a lot I didn't even see, like windows and people.

'Don't want your old speed-ball!' I gasped, though I did want it. It was a better ball than mine; they were always givin' him better things than me.

He looked at me with sympathy, making me want to cry. I

hated pity! 'You can have it even if you don't win the race, and you can give me yours. I'm not trying to hurt your feelings. I just want you to stop being afraid of doing everything wrong, and then maybe you won't – sometimes getting mad enough helps you win.' He smiled and I guess if my Momma had been around she would have thought his flash of white teeth was charming. My face was born for scowling. 'Don't want your old ball,' I repeated, refusing to be won over to someone handsome, graceful and fourteenth in a long line of Russian ballet dancers who'd married ballerinas. What was so great about dancers? Nothing, nothing. God had smiled on Jory's legs and made them pretty, while mine looked like knobby sticks that wanted to bleed.

'You hate me, don't you? You want me to die, don't you?'

Jory gave me a funny long look. 'No, I don't hate you and I don't want you to die. I kinda like you for my brother even if you are clumsy and a squealer.'

'Thanks heaps.'

'Yeah . . . think nothing of it. Let's go look at the house.'

Every day after school we went to the high white wall and sat up there, and some days we went over the wall and inside the house. Soon school would be over and we'd have nothing to do all day but play. It was nice to know the house was there, waitin' for us. Spooky old house with lots of rooms, jagged halls, trunks full of hidden treasures, high ceilings, odd-shaped rooms with small rooms joining, sometimes a row of little rooms hiding one behind the other.

Spiders lived there and spun webs on the fancy chandeliers. Mice ran everywhere, having hundreds of babies to put droppings all over. Garden insects moved inside and climbed the walls and crept on the wood floors. Birds came down the chimneys and fluttered about madly as they tried to find a way out. Sometimes they banged against walls, windows, and we'd come in and find them dead and pitiful. Sometimes Jory and I would arrive in the nick of time and throw open windows and doors so they could escape.

Jory figured someone must have abandoned the old house

quickly. Half the furniture was there, dusty and mouldering, giving off smelly odours that made Jory wrinkle his nose. I sniffed it and tried to know what it was saying. I could stand real still and almost hear the ghosts talking, and if we sat still on a dusty old velvet couch and didn't talk, up from the cellar would come faint rustlings like the ghosts wanted to whisper secrets in our ears.

'Don't you ever tell anybody ghosts talk to you, or they'll think you're crazy,' Jory had warned. We already had one crazy person in our family – our Daddy's mother who was in an nut house way back in Virginia. Once a summer we went East to visit her and old graves. Momma wouldn't go in the long brick building where people in pretty clothes strolled over green lawns, and nobody would have guessed they were crazy if attendants in white suits hadn't been there too.

Every summer Momma would ask when Daddy came back from seeing his mother, 'Well, is she better?' And Daddy would look sad before he'd say, 'No, not really much progress . . . but there would be if you would forgive her.'

That always shook Momma up. She acted like she wanted that grandmother to stay locked up forever.

'You listen to me, Christopher Doll!' my Momma had snapped, 'it's the other way around, remember! We're the ones she should go down on her knees and plead with – she should ask for our forgiveness!'

Last summer we hadn't gone East to visit anybody. I hated old graves, old Madame Marisha with her black rusty clothes, her big bun of white and black hair – and I didn't care even now if two old ladies back East never had a visit from us again. And as for them down in those graves – let them stay there without flowers.

Too many dead people in our lives, messing it up.

'C'mon Bart!' called Jory. He had already scaled the tree on our side of the wall, and he was sitting up there waiting for me. I managed the climb, then settled down next to Jory who insisted I have the tree trunk behind me – just in case. 'You know what,' said Jory wistfully, 'some day I'm gonna buy Mom a house just as big. Every once in a while I overhear her and Dad talking about big houses, so I guess she wants one larger than the one we've already got.'

'Yeah, they sure do talk a lot about big houses.'

'I like our house better,' said Jory, while I set about drumming my heels against the wall which had bricks under the crumbling white stucco. Momma had mentioned once she thought the bricks showing through added interesting texture contrast. I did what I could to make the wall more interesting.

But, it was sure true that in a big house like that one over there you could get lost in the dark and ramble on and on for days on end. None of the bathrooms worked. No water. Crazy sinks with no water and stupid fruit cellar with no fruit, and wine cellar with no wine.

'Gee, wouldn't it be nice if a big family moved in over there?' Jory said, wishing like me we could have lots and lots of nearby friends to play with. We didn't have anybody but each other once we came home from school. 'And if they had two boys and two girls it would be just perfect,' he went on dreamily. 'Sure would be neat to have all girls living next door.'

Neat, sure. I'll bet he was wishing Melodie Richarme would move in over there. Then he could see her every day and hug and kiss her like I'd seen him do a few times. Girls made me sick. 'I hate girls, I want all boys!' I grouched. Jory laughed, saying I was only nine and soon enough I'd like girls more than boys.

'What makes Melodie's arms rich?'

'Do you realize how dumb that makes you sound? That's her last name and doesn't mean anything.'

Just when I wanted to say he was the dumb one for all names had to mean something – two trucks pulled up in the long driveway of the mansion. Wow! Nobody ever went over there but us.

We sat on and watched the workmen running around, doing this and that. Some went up on the orange roof Momma said was called 'pantile', and began to check it over. Others went inside the house with ladders and cans that looked like they held paint.

Some had huge rolls of wallpaper under their arms. Others checked over the windows, and some looked at the shrubs and trees.

'Hey!' said Jory, very upset, 'Somebody must have bought that place. I'll bet they'll move in after it's fixed up.'

Didn't want no neighbours who would disturb Momma and Daddy's privacy. All the time they were talking about how nice it was not to have close neighbours to disturb their privacy.

We sat on until it grew dark, then went into our house and didn't say a word to our parents – for when you said something out loud, that meant it was really true. Thoughts didn't count.

Next day it was Sunday and we went on a picnic at Stinson Beach. Then came Monday afternoon and Jory and I were sitting on the wall, staring over at all that activity. Was foggy and rainy, but we could see just well enough to be bothered. We couldn't go over there and have a place of our own any more. Where would we play now?

'Hey, you kids!' called a burly man on another day when we were only watching, 'What are you doing up there?'

'Nothing!' said Jory. (I never talked to strangers. Jory was always teasing me for not talking to anybody much but myself.)

'Don't you kids tell me you're not doing nothing when I see you over here! This house is private property – so stay off these grounds or you'll hear from me!'

He was real mean, and fierce-looking; his workclothes were old and dirty. When he came closer I saw the biggest feet in my life, and the dirtiest boots. I was glad the wall was ten feet high and we had the advantage over him.

'Sure we play over there a little,' said Jory who wasn't scared of anybody, 'but we don't hurt anything. We leave it like we found it.'

'Well, from now on stay off altogether!' he snapped, glaring first at Jory, then at me. 'Some rich dame has bought this place and she won't want kids hanging around. And don't you think you can get by with anything because she's an old lady living alone. She's bringing servants with her.'

Servants. Wow!

'Rich people can have everything their own way,' muttered the giant on the ground as he moved off. 'Do this, do that, and have it done yesterday. Money – God, what I wouldn't do to have my share.'

We had only Emma, so we weren't really rich. Jory said Emma was like a maiden aunt, not really a relative or a servant. To me she was just somebody I'd known all my life, somebody who didn't like me nearly as much as she liked Jory. I didn't like her either so I didn't care.

Weeks passed. School ended. Still those workmen were over there. By this time Momma and Daddy had noticed, and they weren't too happy about neighbours they didn't intend to visit and make welcome. Both me and Jory wondered why they didn't want friends coming to our house.

'It's love,' whispered Jory. 'They're still like honeymooners. Remember Chris is our Mom's third husband, and the bloom hasn't worn off.'

What bloom? Didn't see any flowers.

Jory had passed on to the junior year of high school with flying colours. I sneaked into the fifth grade by the skin of my teeth. Hated school. Hated that old mansion that looked like new now. Gone was all the spooky eerie times when we'd had lots of fun over there.

'We'll just bide our time until we can sneak over there and see that old lady,' Jory whispered so all those gardeners trimming the shrubs and snipping at the trees wouldn't hear.

She owned acres of land, twenty or more. That made for lots of clean-up jobs since the workmen on the roof were letting everythin' fall. Her yard was littered with papers, spills of nails, bits of lumber left over from repair jobs, plus trash that blew through the iron fence in front of the driveway that was near what Jory called 'lover's lane'.

That hateful construction boss was picking up beer cans as he headed our way, scowling just to see us when we weren't doing a thing bad. 'How many times do I have to tell you boys?' he bellowed. 'Now don't force me to say it again!' He put his huge fists on his hips and glared up at us. 'I've warned you before to stay off that wall – now scat!'

Jory was unwilling to move from the wall when it wasn't any harm to just sit and look.

'Are the two of you deaf?' he yelled again.

In a flash Jory's face turned from handsome to mean. 'No, we are *not* deaf. We live here. This wall is on the property line, and just as much ours as it is hers. Our Dad says so. So we will sit up here and watch just as long as we like. And don't you dare yell and tell us to scat again!'

'Sassy kid, aren't yah?' and off he wandered without even looking at me who was just as sassy – inside.

INTRODUCTIONS *Jory*

It was breakfast time. Mom was telling Dad about one of her ballerinas. Bart sat across the table from me, poking at his cold cereal and scowling. He didn't like to eat much of anything but snack foods which Dad said were bad for him.

'Chris, I don't think Nicole is going to pull out of this,' Mom was saying with a worried frown. 'It's awful that cars hurt so many people, and she's got a little girl only two years old. I saw her a few weeks ago. Honestly, she reminded me so much of Carrie when she was two.'

Dad nodded absently, his gaze still fixed on the morning newspaper. The scene in the attic between them still haunted me, especially at night when I couldn't sleep. Sometimes I'd just sit alone in my room and try and remember what was hidden way back in the dark recesses of my mind. Something important. But I couldn't remember.

Even as I sat and listened to them talk about Nicole and her daughter, I kept thinking of that attic scene, wondering what it meant, and just who was the grandmother they were afraid of. And how could they have known each other when Mom was only fourteen?

'Chris,' implored Mom, her tone trying to force him to put down the sports page. 'You don't listen when I talk. Nicole has no family at all – did you hear that? Not even an uncle or an aunt to care for Cindy if she dies. And you know she has never been married to that boy she loved.'

'Hmmm,' he answered before biting into his toast. 'Don't forget to water our garden today.'

She frowned, really annoyed. He wasn't really listening as I was. 'I think it was a huge mistake to sell Paul's home and move here. His statues just don't look right in this kind of setting.'

That got his attention.

'Cathy, we have vowed never to have regrets about anything. And there are more important things in life than having a tropical garden where everything grows rampant.'

'Rampant? Paul had the most manicured garden I've ever seen.'

'You know what I mean.'

Silent for a second, she spoke again about Nicole and the two-year-old girl who would go into an orphanage if her mother died. Dad said someone was sure to adopt her quickly if she did. He stood up to pull on his sports jacket. 'Stop looking on the darkest side. Nicole may recover. She's young, strong, basically healthy. But if you're so worried, I'll stop by and have a talk with her doctors.'

'Daddy,' piped up Bart who'd scowled darkly all morning. 'Nobody here can make me go East this summer! I won't go and nobody can make me!'

'True,' said Dad, chucking Bart under the chin and playfully rumpling his already unruly dark hair. 'Nobody can make you go – I'm just hoping you'd rather go than stay home alone.' He leaned to kiss Mom goodbye.

'Drive carefully,' Mom had to say this every day just as he was leaving. He smiled and said he would, and their eyes met and said things I understood, in a way.

'There was an ole lady who lived in a shoe,' chanted Bart, 'she had so many children she didn't know what to do.'

'Bart, do you have to sit there and make a mess? If you aren't going to finish your meal, excuse yourself and leave the table.'

'Peter, Peter Pumpkin Eater, had a wife and couldn't keep her, put her in a pumpkin shell, there he kept her very well.' He grinned at her, got up and left the table – that was his way of excusing himself.

Great golly, almost ten and he was still chanting nursery rhymes. He picked up his favourite old sweater, tossed it over his shoulder and in so doing he knocked over a carton of milk. The milk puddled to the floor where Clover was soon lapping it up like a cat. Mom was so enthralled with a snapshot of Nicole's little girl, she didn't notice the milk.

It was Emma who wiped up the milk and glared at Bart who stuck out his tongue and sauntered away. 'Excuse me, Mom,' I said, jumping up to follow Bart outside.

Again on the top of the wall, we sat and stared over, both of us wishing the lady would hurry and move in. Who knows, maybe she'd have grandchildren.

'Missing that old house already,' complained Bart. 'Hate people who move in our place.'

We both fiddled away the day, planting more seeds, pulling up more weeds, and soon I was wondering how we were going to pass a whole summer without going next door even once.

At dinner Bart was grouchy because he too missed the house. He glared down at his full plate. 'Eat heartily, Bart,' said Dad, 'or else you may not have enough strength to enjoy yourself in Disneyland.'

Bart's mouth fell open. 'Disneyland?' His dark eyes widened in delight. 'We're goin' there really? Not goin' East to visit old graves?'

'Disneyland is part of your birthday gift,' explained Dad. 'You'll have your party there, and then we'll fly to South Carolina. Now don't complain. Other people's needs have to be considered as well as yours. Jory's grandmother likes to see him at least once a year, and since we skipped last summer, she's doubly anticipating our visit. Then there's my mother who needs a family too.'

I found myself staring at Mom. She seemed to be smouldering. Every year she was like this when the time came to visit his mother. I thought it a pity she didn't understand why mothers were so very important. She'd been an orphan so long maybe she'd forgotten – or maybe she was jealous.

'Boy, I'd rather have Disneyland than heaven!' said Bart. 'Can never, never get enough of Disneyland.'

'I know,' said Dad in a dry way.

But no sooner did it sink in that Bart was getting his heart's desire when he started complaining again about having to go East. 'Momma, Daddy. I am not going! Two weeks is too long for visiting old graves and old grandmothers.'

'Bart,' said Mom sharply, 'you show such disrespect for the dead. Your own father is one of those dead people whose grave you don't want to visit. Your aunt Carrie is there too. And you are going to visit their graves, and Madame Marisha too, whether or not you want to. And if you open your mouth again, there will be no trip to Disneyland.'

'Momma,' now a subdued Bart wanted to make up. 'Why did your daddy who's dead in Gladstone, PA . . . '

'Say Pennsylvania, not PA.'

'How come the picture of him looks so much like the daddy we have now?'

Pain flashed in her eyes. I spoke up, hating the way Bart had of grilling everyone. 'Gee, Dollanganger is sure some whopper of a name. Bet you were glad to get rid of it.'

She turned to stare at a large photograph of Dr Paul Sheffield, then quietly said, 'Yes, it was a wonderful day when I became Mrs Sheffield.'

Then Dad was looking upset. I sank deeper into the cut velvet plush of a dining chair. All about me in the air, creeping on the floor, hiding in the shadows, were pieces of the past that they remembered and I didn't. Fourteen years old, and still I didn't know what life was all about. Or what my parents were about either.

Finally the day came when the mansion was completed. Then came the cleaning ladies to work on the windows, and scrub the floors. Gardeners came to rake, mow, trim again, and we were there all the time, peeking into windows, then running swiftly back to the wall and skimming up a tree, to the top of the wall. There we sat quietly as if we'd never disobey any rule made by our parents. 'She's coming,' whispered Bart, very excited. 'Any moment, that old lady, she's coming!'

The house was fixed up so grand we expected to see a fancy

film actress, a president's wife, somebody important. One day when Dad was at work, Mom was shopping, and Emma was still in the kitchen like always, we saw a huge long black limousine turn slowly into the long drive next door. Another car followed, older but still a snazzy-looking car. Two weeks ago that driveway had been cracked and buckled concrete, now it was smooth black asphalt. I nudged Bart to calm his excitement. All about us the leaves made a fine concealing canopy, and still we could see everything.

Slowly, slowly, the chauffeur pulled the long luxury car to a stop, then he got out and circled the car to let out the passengers. We breathlessly watched. Soon we'd see her – that rich, rich woman who could afford anything!

The chauffeur was young and had a jaunty air. Even from a distance we could tell he was handsome, but the old man who stepped from the limo wasn't handsome at all. He took me by surprise. Hadn't that workman told us a lady and servants? 'Look,' I whispered to Bart, 'what he's wearing, that must be livery. I never knew butlers rode in the same car as their employer.'

'Hate people who move in our house!' grumbled Bart.

The feeble old butler stretched out his hand to help an old woman out of the back seat. She ignored him and took the arm of the chauffeur instead. Oh gosh! She wore all black, from head to toe covered over like an Arab woman. A black veil was over her head and face. Was she a widow? A Moslem? She looked so mysterious.

'Hate black dresses that drag on the ground. Hate old ladies who want black veils over their heads. Hate spooks.'

All I could do was watch, fascinated, thinking that woman moved rather gracefully beneath the black robe, and even from our hidden place, I could tell she felt nothing but scorn for the feeble old butler. Gee, intrigue.

She looked around at everything. For the longest time she stared our way, at the white wall, at the roof of our house. I knew she couldn't see very much. Many a time I'd stood where she

...ooking homeward, and I'd seen only our roofpeak and the ...imney. Only when she was inside on her second floor could she ...ee into some of our rooms. I'd better tell Mom to plant some more big trees near the white wall.

It occurred to me then why two workmen might have chopped down a number of her large eucalyptus trees. Maybe she wanted to look over at our house and be nosey. But it was more likely she didn't want those trees growing so near her house.

Now the second car drew up behind the first. Out of this one stepped a maid in a black uniform with a fancy white apron and cap, following her came two servants dressed in grey uniforms. It was the servants who rushed about, carrying in many suitcases, hatboxes, live plants and such, all while the lady in black stood stock-still and looked at our chimney. What she was seeing?

A huge yellow moving-van drew up and began to unload elegant furniture, and still that lady stayed outside and let the maids decide where to put each piece. Finally, when one maid kept running to her and obviously asking questions, she turned away and disappeared into the mansion. All the servants vanished with her.

'Bart, would you look at that sofa those men are carrying in! Have you ever seen such a fancy sofa?'

Long ago he'd lost interest in the movers. He was now staring intently at the yellow and black caterpillar undulating along a thin branch not far below his dirty sneakers. Pretty birds were singing all around. The deep blue sky was full of fluffy white clouds. The air felt fresh, cool, fragrant with pine and eucalyptus – and Bart was staring at the one ugly thing in view. A blessed horny caterpillar!

'Hate ugly things that creep with horns on their heads,' he mumbled to himself. I knew he always had a desire to know what was inside. 'Bet you got sticky green goo under all that pretty coloured fuzz. You mean little dragon on the branch, stop coming my way. Get too close and you're dead.'

'Quit that silly talk. Look at that table those men are taking in now. Boy, I'll bet that chair came from a castle in Europe.'

'Just one more inch and something ugly is going to get it!'

'You know what, I'll bet that lady who's moving in is kinda nice. Anybody who has such good taste in furniture must be real quality.'

'One more inch . . . and you're dead!' Bart told the caterpillar.

As the sun set the sky turned rosy and wide streaks of violet came to make the early evening even more beautiful.

'Bart, look at the sunset. Have you ever seen more glorious colours? Colours are like music to me. I can hear them singing. I'll bet if God struck me deaf and blind this very moment I'd go right on hearing the music of colours, and seeing them behind my eyes. And in darkness I'd dance and never know it wasn't light.'

'Crazy talk,' mumbled my brother, his eyes still on the fuzzy worm coming closer and closer to that deadly sneaker held above him. 'Blind means black as pitch. No colours. No music. No nothing. Dead is silence.'

'Deaf . . . d-e-a-f – not dead.'

Just then Bart smashed down his sneaker on the caterpillar. Then he jumped from the tree to the ground and there he wiped the sticky green goo on the lady's new lawn.

'That was a mean thing you did, Bart Winslow! Caterpillars go through a stage called metamorphosis. The kind you just killed makes the most beautiful butterfly of all. So you didn't kill a dragon but a fairy king or queen – the sweetest lover of roses.'

'Stupid ballet talk,' was his opinion, though he did manage to look slightly scared. 'I can make up for it,' he said uneasily, looking around nervously. 'I'll set a trap, catch a caterpillar alive. Keep it for a pet, and wait until it turns into a fairy king, and then I'll let it go.'

'Hey, I was just joking, but from now on, don't kill any insect that isn't on the roses.'

'If I find some on the roses can I kill 'em all?'

Puzzling the way Bart needed to kill all insects. Once I'd

caught him pulling off a spider's legs one by one before he squashed it between his thumb and forefinger. Then the black blood held his interest. 'Do bugs feel pain?'

'Yeah,' I said, 'but don't let it worry you. Sooner or later you'll feel pain too. So don't cry. It was only a fuzzy worm, not a fairy king or queen. Let's go home now.' I was feeling sorry for him because I knew he was sensitive about not being able to feel pain like I did, though gosh knows he should be glad.

'No! I don't wanna go home! I want to see inside that house next door.'

Just then Emma came out to ring her dinner bell, making us scamper home quickly.

Next day we were right back on the wall. The movers had finished up after we'd gone to bed. No more trucks coming and going. I'd spent most of my morning and early afternoon in Mom's ballet class, while Bart stayed home and played alone. And summer days were long. He smiled, happy to have me with him again. 'Ready?' I asked.

'Ready!' he agreed. Having decided on our course of action earlier, we slipped over the wall and down to the other side. It was ground we'd been forbidden to step on, but rightly or wrongly it was ground we considered ours, for it had belonged to us first. Like two shadows, we slithered along. Bart looked at the shrubs that had been trimmed into shapes of animals. How weird. A strutting rooster beside a fat hen on a nest. Neat, really neat. Who would have guessed that old Mexican man was so clever with those snippers?

'Don't like shrubs that look like animals,' complained Bart. 'Don't like green eyes. Green eyes are mean eyes. Jory – they're watchin' us!'

'Sssh, don't whisper! Watch where you put your feet. Step only where I step.' I glanced over my shoulder to see the sky had changed to a dark plum colour streaked with crimson that looked like freshly spilled blood. Soon night would descend and the moon wasn't always a friendly face.

'Jory,' came Bart's whisper as he tugged on my shirt tail, 'didn't Momma tell us to be home by dark?'

'It's not dark yet.' But almost. The creamy white of the mansion in daylight was bluish white in the dusk and scary-looking.

'Don't like bony-looking old house made to look like new.'

Bart and his ideas.

'Sure must be time to be getting home now.'

I resisted his tugs. Since we'd come this far we might as well go all the way. I put my finger to my lips, whispered, 'Stay where you are,' and by myself I stole to the only window that was bright in a huge house of many windows.

Instead of staying where I'd told him, Bart followed at my heels. Again I cautioned him, then I climbed a small oak tree just strong enough to bear my weight. I climbed high enough to peek into the house. At first I couldn't see anything but a huge dim room cluttered with cartons as yet unpacked. A tall and fat lamp blocked my view so I had to lean away from the tree to see around it. Fuzzily I could make out a black-robed figure seated in a hard wooden rocker that looked very uncomfortable, when I'd seen such soft luxurious couches and chairs carried inside. Was that a woman under that black veil? Was it the same one I'd seen from outside?

Arab men wore dresses so that could be the feeble butler, but then I saw a pale slim hand with many sparkling rings and I knew it was the mistress of this manor. Shifting my weight I sought a better viewing position and as I did, the branch supporting my weight cracked! The woman inside lifted her head and stared my way.

Her eyes were wide and frightened looking. I told myself people in a bright room couldn't look out in darkness and see. My heart throbbed in triple time as I held my breath. Little winged night insects buzzed around my head and began to nibble on my skin. Everywhere they touched I needed to scratch.

Below me Bart was growing impatient. He shook my frail tree. I tried to hang on and at the same time signal to Bart to stop.

Fortunately at that moment a maid opened the door and came in with a large silver tray laden with many covered dishes.

'Hurry up!' grouched scaredy cat. 'I want to go home!'

What was he afraid of? I was the one about to fall from the tree. The clatter of the dishes and silverware being taken from the tray and placed on a small table covered the noise Bart was making. No sooner was that maid out of the room than the veiled woman lifted her hands to take off the veil.

She began to eat. All alone, she picked at her food. Just when I felt sure she hadn't heard any noise to warn her someone was spying – the weak branch of my tree made a splitting sound!

When she turned her head I saw she wasn't wearing the black veil. I saw her. Really saw her. But I didn't really see her nose, her lips, her eyes, I saw only the jagged rows of scars on each side of her face. Had a cat scratched her and made those scars? I felt suddenly sorry for an old woman who had to sit alone at a table without enough appetite to enjoy anything. It didn't seem fair to live such a lonely, unloved life. Not fair either for fate to show me how age could steal the beauty of someone who might have been just as lovely as my mother – once.

'Jory . . .?'

'Sssh . . .'

She kept on staring, then quickly lowered the veil over her face. 'Who's out there?' she called. 'Go away whoever you are. If you don't I'll call the police!'

That did it. I jumped to the ground, seized Bart by his hand and took off. He stumbled and fell, as usual holding me back. I jerked him upright and ran on, forcing him to run faster than he could have without my help. He gasped, 'Jory! Not so fast! What did you see? Quick, tell me – was it a ghost?'

Worse than that. I'd seen how my mother might look thirty years from now, if she lived long enough to be ravaged by time.

'Where've you two been?' Mom blocked our way as we tried to slip by unseen into the bathroom to wash up before she had a chance to notice our dishevelled clothes.

'We came from the garden in back,' I answered, feeling guilty. Immediately she saw my guilt and grew suspicious. 'Where were you really?'

'Just out back . . '

'Jory, are you going to grow evasive like Bart?'

I threw my arms about her and pressed my face against the softness of her breast. I was too old to do this, but I had the sudden need to feel safe and comforted.

'Jory darling, what's wrong?'

Nothing was wrong. I didn't know what bothered me, not really. I'd seen old age before, my own grandmother Marisha, but she'd always been old.

That night Momma came in my dreams and was a lovely angel who put an enchanted spell over all the world to stop people from growing older. I saw two-hundred-year-old ladies as young and pretty as when they'd been twenty – all but one old woman in black, all alone, rocking in her chair.

Towards morning, Bart slipped into my bed and cuddled up behind my back, watching with me the grey fog that rolled in great billowing pillows of mist, obliterating the trees, erasing the golden grass, smothering all signs of life and making the world out there seem dead.

Bart rattled on to himself: 'Earth is full of dead people. Dead animals and plants too. Makes all that stuff Daddy calls mulch.'

Death. My half-brother Bart was obsessed by death, and I pitied him. I felt him cuddle closer as we both stared out at the fog that was so much a part of our lives.

'Jory, nobody ever likes me,' he complained.

'Yes, they do.'

'No, they don't. They like you better.'

'That's because you don't like them and it shows.'

'Why do you like everybody?'

'I don't. But I can put on a smile and pretend even when I don't. Perhaps you'd better learn to put on a false face sometimes.'

'Why? It's not Hallowe'en.'

He troubled me. Like those beds in the attic troubled me. Like that strange thing between my parents that rose up every so often reminding me that they knew something that I didn't.

I closed my eyes and decided everything always worked out for the best.

GONE HUNTING *Bart*

They looked at me but they didn't see me. They didn't know who I was. To them I was just a thing to sit at their table and try to swallow the stuff they put on my plate. My thoughts were all around, but they didn't read my mind, couldn't figure me out at all. I was going next door to the mansion to where I'd been invited. And when I went, I'd remember to pronounce my 'ings' – they were always tellin' me to say them. I'd do it right, everything, for the old lady next door.

Gonna go alone and not tell Jory. Jory didn't need new friends anyway. He had his ballet classes with pretty girls all around and that was enough. With Melodie, more than enough. Me – I didn't have nobody but parents who didn't understand. Soon as I was excused from breakfast I'd make it quickly to our garden while Jory was still inside eating his stack of pancakes with melted maple sugar poured all over. Pig, that's what he was . . . a darn hog!

Day was hot. Sun was too bright. Shadows long on the ground. White wall rose up so dratted high – had that wall known in advance I was coming, and I'd be clumsy, and 'they' wanted to make it difficult? Tree I climbed wasn't so bad.

Yard was so big it tired my short legs. Wish I had long pretty legs like Jory. Always fallin', always hurtin' myself, but never felt no pain. Daddy had been amazed when first he found that out. 'Bart, because your nerve endings don't reach your skin you will have to be doubly careful of infections! You could seriously hurt yourself and not even know it. So always wash all your minor cuts and scratches with soap and water, then tell your mother and me so we can put on disinfectant.'

Washing with soap kept away germs. Wonder where they went? Up to heaven, down to hell? Wonder what a germ looked like? Monsters, Jory had said, ugly itty-bitty monsters. A billion of them could sit on the point of a pin. Wish I had eyes like a microscope.

I gave her yard another long look, then jumped, closing my eyes so I couldn't see the ground smack me. Landed square in a clump of her rose bushes. More cuts and scratches to add to my collection. More germs too. Didn't care. Crouched down low, squinted my eyes against the sun, and tried to spot all the dangerous wild animals that lurked in dark mysterious places – like this.

Look over there! Behind that big bush – a tiger! I raised my rifle and took careful aim. It swished its long tail and sparked its yellow eyes, then licked its chops, thinking it would soon have me for lunch. I squeezed hard on the trigger. Bang! Bang! Dead as a doornail.

Slinging my rifle over my shoulder I wended a careful way along all the dangerous jungle paths. Ignoring an orange and white kitten that mewed plaintively. (Plaintively was one of the new words I had to use. One new word each day, and Daddy gave a list of seven words to both Jory and me, insisting we use today's word at least five times in our conversation. Didn't need a bigger vocabulary. Knew how to talk good enough already.)

A tune popped in my head. Came from a movie I saw last night on TV about West Point.

'There's something about a soldier . . . something about a soldier . . .'

Marching to the tune in my head I carried my rifle smartly on my shoulder, my chest out, my chin in. Straight up to her front door I marched. Then I banged hard, using the brass knocker that was a lion's head with a loose jaw.

My perfect military bearing was so admirable I just knew that old lady would be impressed. Doctors weren't so special. Dancers either. But a five-star general – that was impressive. Nobody had a name longer than mine, General Bartholomew Scott Winslow Sheffield. Even Jory Janus Marquet Sheffield was not so long, not so good sounding. Just wait until the enemy knew who was in charge of the war.

Should have been that creepy old butler who opened the door, but it was the old lady herself. I'd seen her a few times in her yard. She held the door open a slot and stingily allowed a long wedge of sunlight to shine on her floor. 'Bart . . .?' she whispered, her voice surprised and happy. Was she really so glad to see me? Gee, and she didn't even know me yet.

'Bart, how wonderful! I was hoping you'd come.'

'Step aside, Madame!' I commanded, 'My men got you surrounded.' Made my voice deep, gruff, to scare the living lights out of her. 'No use resistin'. Better to give up and raise your white flag. The odds are all against you.'

'Oh, Bart,' she said with silly giggles. 'It's so sweet of you to accept my invitation. Sit down and talk to me. Tell me about yourself, your life. Tell me if you're happy; if your brother is happy, if you like where you live, and love your parents. I want to know everything!'

Forcefully I kicked the door to behind me, as all good generals did. Bang! To see her blue eyes smiling while her lips were covered by that dratted black veil was very weird. My tough military composure vanished. Why'd she have to wear that scary veil? 'Lady,' I said weakly, feeling young and timid again; 'you did call over the wall yesterday. You said you wanted me to come over when I was lonely. I sneaked over . . .'

'Sneaked?' she asked in an odd voice. 'Do you have to slip away from your parents? Do they punish you often?'

'Naw,' I said, 'Wouldn't do them no good. Couldn't hurt me with spankin's; couldn't starve me for I don't like food anyway.' I hung my head and whispered, 'Momma and Daddy told me not to pester rich old ladies who live in big spooky houses next door.'

'Oh!' she said with a sigh, 'Do you have a great many spooky big houses next door with rich old ladies inside?'

'Heck no, ma'am,' I drawled, then sauntered over to a window in a pretty parlour where I could look out and see who was coming, who was going. I slouched against the wall and took the makings for a good smoke from my pocket and rolled my own as she sat down in a rocker to watch. She kept watching me blow smoke rings in her air, faintly smiling as they wreathed around her head. Stupid veil puffed in and out as she breathed. Wonder if she slept with that thing over her head and face?

'Bart, often I hear you and your brother talking in your yard. I use a stepladder sometimes to look over the wall – I hope you don't mind.' Wouldn't answer. Blew smoke rings right in her face. 'Please talk, Bart . . . sit down and relax, feel comfortable, feel at home. I want my house to feel like your home, open to you and Jory. My own life is so lonely and to have a real family living next door is so comforting. You can say anything you want to me, anything at all.'

Wasn't nothin' to say – but here was an adult who wanted to listen – what could we talk about? 'People shouldn't spy on me and my brother.'

'I wasn't spying,' she said in a hurry, 'just taking care of my roses that climb the wall and need pruning – and I can't help if I overhear, can I?'

Spy. That's what she was. Ground out the butt of my cigarette with my dusty boot heel. Sun was getting in my eyes again, making me tilt the brim of my hat. Ole Devil sun was making me thirsty. 'Ma'am, ya'll asked me over and here ah is . . . so get t'point.'

'Bart, if you take a chair, we'll have refreshments soon. See that bell-pull? My maid will bring in ice-cream and cake. It is a long time until lunch, so your appetite shouldn't be spoiled.'

Might as well stay a bit longer. Fell into a soft chair and fixed my eyes on her feet which could barely be seen. Was she wearing high heels – fancy sandals – painted toenails? Then, in the door came a pretty Mexican maid with a tray full of goodies! Wow wow! The maid smiled at me, nodded to the lady, then disappeared. I politely accepted what she gave me – not enough of anything, and set to. Didn't like food that was good for me; it tasted so bad. I stood up to go as soon as I polished off my treats.

'Thank you, ma'am, for takin' kindly to an ole cowpoke who

just ain't used to your kind of hospitality. I've got to be amblin' on now . . .'

'All right, if you have to go,' she said sadly, and I felt sorry for her living with servants only, no kids like me. 'Come back tomorrow if you want, and bring Jory with you. I'll have whatever you want . . .'

'Don't want to bring Jory!'

'Why not?'

'You're my secret! He gets to do everything . . . I never get to do nothin'! Nobody ever likes me.'

'I like you.'

Gee, she made me feel good. I peeked at her face, but couldn't see anything but her blue eyes.

'Why do you like me?' I asked with so much wonder – nobody else did.

'I don't just like you, Bart Winslow,' she said queerly, 'I love you.'

'Why?' I didn't believe her. Ladies fell on first sight for Jory, never for me.

'Once I had two sons, now I don't,' she said with her eyes cast down, and her voice sad and tight, 'and then I wanted to have another son by my second husband, and I couldn't.' She looked up and met my eyes. 'So I want *you* to take the place of the third son I couldn't have. I'm very rich, Bart. I can give you anything you want.'

'My heart's desire – my real heart's desire?'

'Yes, anything that can be bought with money, I can give you.'

'Can't everything be bought?'

'Sadly, it can't. I used to think it could, but now I know money can't buy the most important things. Things I used to take for granted and treated lightly – oh, if I had my life to live over, how different I would be! I've made so many mistakes, Bart. I want to do everything right for you, with you and if you have to keep me as your secret, perhaps one day . . . well, let's save that for later. You will come again?'

She sounded so pitiful and made me feel so uneasy. I shuffled my feet about and decided I'd better get away quick before she tried to kiss me. 'Ma'am, gotta get back to camp. My men will be wonderin' if I'm wounded or dead. But remember this – I got you surrounded and you cannot win this war!'

'I know,' she said, her voice so sad-sounding. 'I've never won any games I've tried to play. I've always gone down in defeat even when I thought I held the winning cards.'

Just like me! Made me feel sorry for her. 'Lady, you play your cards right and I'll come over every day and pay you a visit – or even two or three.'

'Thank you, Bart. You just tell me what cards to play and I'll have them on the table waiting for you.'

Had me an idea then. Lots and lots of things I wanted and never got. Didn't want books, games, toys or other ordinary stuff. One thing I had to have, and hopefully I stared at her . . . maybe she'd be the one to give it to me. 'What's your name?'

'Come again and I'll tell you.'

I'd be coming again. Darn if I could stay away now.

Went home and nobody even noticed I was there. Momma went right on talking about that baby girl she had to have if her favourite student Nicole died. God, don't let Nicole die I silently prayed.

'Jory, let's play ball.'

'Can't. Mom's driving me to afternoon class. Melodie's parents are taking me to dinner tonight, then to a movie.'

Nobody ever took me anywhere – except my parents. No friends. No pet of my own. Dratted Clover liked Jory better, squealing like he was hurt when I stepped on his tail by accident, or stumbled over him, and he was always underfoot.

A few days later I again headed for the back door. 'Where are you going?' asked Momma who had been staring at a picture of that little girl she wanted for her own. Weren't enough she had two boys – had to have a daughter too. Sissy, silly girl.

'Bart, answer me! Where are you going?'

'Nowhere.'

'Every time I ask you what you do, and where you go, you say you haven't been anywhere, and haven't done anything. Now I want to hear the truth.'

Jory laughed and hugged her. 'Gee, Mom, you oughta know him by this time. When Bart steps out the back door he's everywhere! You never saw a kid so crazy about pretending. He's this, he's that, and the only thing he never is . . . is himself.'

The power I poured into my mean piercing eyes should have shut Jory up – but he went right on. 'He prefers fantasy to reality, Mom, that's all.'

Weren't so. I was bored, that's all. Didn't get enough of what I wanted in real life and in my pretend games I did everything right – and got everything I wanted. Then he and Momma were laughing, and I was shut out, again. Mad. They were making me mad.

Drat everybody who made fun of me. But hating everybody made me feel bad, and pretending made me happy. What did I have to lose if I went over to her place? Nothing, nothing at all.

Risking my life in the darkest of dangerous jungles, I fought my way over to her place. Bravely I struggled onwards, facing death over and over just to get to her . . . climbing that slippery tree that wanted me to fall. Scaling that high wall to get to her. Through the wind and snow, through the sleet and rain, freezing my feet, blinding my eyes, I struggled onwards to her.

I stumbled to her house for the fifth time in three days. And there she was smiling beneath her veil, loving me as no one else did. I felt happy and warm all over as she called and opened her arms wide. I went flying into them, hugging her, eager to sit on her lap and be petted and pampered. She needed me. She wanted to love me like her own. Her lap didn't burn me as I was afraid it would. It didn't feel so awful to be kissed on my cheeks – but it did feel dry. Drat that veil!

Because she loved me, and I loved her now, she'd given me a room of my own to hold all the things she gave me. A miniature electric train with all the accessories, toy cars, trucks and games.

All this stuff for me to play with – in her house.

Time went by. I was getting to love her more and more each day. Then one Tuesday I found that creepy old butler in her favourite room, messing around with her things, muttering to himself about how a fool and her money being soon parted. Didn't like him touching her things! Didn't like him talking mean about her behind her back.

'You get out of here,' I said in my big man voice. 'You tell my lady I'm here, and tell your chef I want chocolate ice-cream today with Oreo cookies – not brownies.'

He was an awful sight. 'You can trust a few some of the time, and most none of the time. Feel lucky if you have even one to trust all of the time.'

What was that supposed to mean? I scowled and tried to draw away. Didn't like his false teeth that kept slipping so he had to push them back, and they clacked too, as if they didn't fit his mouth.

'You like her, don't you?' he asked, slyly smiling, nodding his head up and down, from side to side, so I could be confused if I wanted. 'When you want the full truth about who you are – and who she is, come to me.' The lady's steps on the stairs sent him scurrying off.

Creepy. He made me feel creepy and scared. I knew who I was – most of the time.

All alone now. Nothing to do. I sat down and crossed my legs like my Daddy did, then leaned back to light up an expensive cigar, which Daddy never did. (Momma didn't like men who smoked.) Nothing wrong with smoking as far as I could tell, I thought as I blew four perfect smoke rings into the air . . . and away they sailed towards the Pacific. They'd end up in Japan over Mt Fuji.

'Good morning, Bart darling. I'm so glad to see you.' She came in and sat in the rocker.

'You got my pony yet?'

Her voice sounded worried, 'Sweetheart, I know I promised

you a pony as your heart's desire, but I did that without knowing how much trouble a pony can be.'

'You promised!' I cried. Was I putting my trust in the wrong person? One who failed to deliver what she promised.

'Sweetheart, a pony needs a stall, and ponies make you smell bad. When you went home your parents and Jory would guess you had a pet over here.'

Instead of answering I began to cry. 'All my life I been wantin' a pony,' I sobbed, 'all my live-long life, and now I've got to grow old without havin' one . . .' Sobbed some more, then hung my head and headed for home – never to return.

'Bart . . . there is a beautiful big dog that won't smell and betray your secrets. A St Bernard – a dog so big you can ride it like a pony, and if you keep him clean and fluffy he won't betray you with his odours.'

Slowly I turned to glare at her. 'Ain't no dog as big as a pony!'

'Isn't there?'

'No! You're tryin' to make fun of me! I don't like you any more. I'm goin' home and never comin' back – not until you have a pony I can name Apple.'

'Darling, you can call your puppy Apple – but he won't eat them – and just think how jealous Jory would be if you have a dog more marvellous than his.'

Headed home. Disgusted.

'Only the super-rich can afford to feed a St Bernard, Bart!'

Like I was a pin and she was the magnet, I turned back to her unwillingly. She lifted me up on her lap and cuddled me there, and it wasn't so awful after all. 'You can call me Grandmother . . .'

'Grandmother.' Felt good to have a grandmother at last. I snuggled closer and waited for her to call me Baby, but she just went right on rocking and singing a lullaby. I put my thumb in my mouth. Nice to be hugged and kissed and made to feel helpless and loved. And she didn't smell like mothballs after all.

'Are you ugly under that veil?' I asked, always curious about what she looked like. The veil was almost transparent, but not enough.

'I guess you would think so, but once I was very beautiful – like your mother.'

'You know my mother?' I asked.

The door opened and my favourite pretty maid came in with a dish of ice-cream and hot brownies fresh from the oven. 'Now only eat one brownie, and let this little bit of ice-cream be enough so you can come over after lunch.' She went on to tell me not to shove in such huge mouthfuls because it was not good manners, and was also a shock to my digestive system.

I had good manners. My momma taught me all the time. I was angry enough to jump down from her lap, wondering just what it was the butler had to tell me. As I stumbled towards the door, all of a sudden John Amos was there in the hall, smiling at me spooky-like. He bowed a little and put a small red leather book in my hands. 'I sense you're not very confident about yourself,' he whispered, making lots of hissing sounds like a snake. (Loose teeth I guessed.) 'It's time you knew just who you really are. That lady who told you to call her grandmother – is really your true grandmother.'

Oh, good golly! I didn't know I had a true grandmother. I though all my grandmothers were dead.

'Yes, Bart, she's your grandmother, and not only that, once she was married to your father. Your real father.'

Didn't know what to think, except I was awful happy having a genuine true grandmother of my very own, just like Jory had his own. And she wasn't dead.

'Now you listen to me, boy, and you will never feel weak and ineffective again. You read a little of this book every day and it will teach you to be like your great-grandfather, Malcolm Neal Foxworth. Never on this earth did there live a man who was smarter than your own great-grandfather – the father of your grandmother who sits in that rocker and wears that ugly black veil.'

'She's pretty underneath!' I said. I didn't like what he was saying and the way he was looking, like he didn't love her as much as I did. 'Never have seen her face, but I can tell from her voice that's she's pretty – prettier than you!'

He sneered, then quickly changed his expression to smiling.

'All right, have it your way. But after you read this book written by your own dear great-grandfather you will understand that women are not to be trusted, especially pretty women. They have ways, cunning ways, of making men do what they want. You'll find that out soon enough when you become a man. A man as handsome as your own father was, and she took him and made him her slave, made him her lap dog like she's making you.'

Wasn't no lap dog, wasn't!

'He was her second husband, Bartholomew Winslow, and eight years younger than her, and he didn't know any better. He thought he could use her – but she used him. I want to save you from her so you won't end up like your father did – dead.'

Dead. Amost everybody was dead in our family. Wasn't really surprised by nothing he said, except I hadn't known women were that bad. Always suspected they were . . . but never really knew. I should warn Jory.

'Now if you want to save your everlasting soul from the fires of eternal hell, you will read this book and grow strong and powerful like your great-grandfather. Then women will never rule you again. You will rule them.'

I looked up in his long gaunt face, seeing his skinny moustache, his yellowish teeth through which he not only hissed but sometimes whistled. He was uglier than anyone I'd seen before. But I'd heard Emma say more than once that pretty was as pretty did. So I guessed I might as well give my powerful great-grandfather a try, and read his little red leather book with its sprawly handwriting.

Didn't take much to reading. Wasn't my kind of thing to do at all. But when I was in the barn near the stall that would some day be a home for my pony, I snuggled down in the hay. Wanted that pony so bad it hurt. Didn't really care if it smelled bad and was lots of trouble. I then opened the book which looked mighty old.

> I am beginning this journal with the most bitter day of my life, the day my beloved mother ran away and left me for another man. She left my father too. I remember how I felt when he told me what she'd done, how much I cried, how lost I felt without her. How lonely to go to bed and have no mother to kiss me goodnight and hear my prayers. I was five years old. And until she left, she'd always said I was the most important person in her life. How could she have left me, her only son? What evil thing possessed her so she could turn her back on a loving son?
>
> I was so innocent then, so unknowing. When I read the words of the Lord, I began to realize that ever since Eve women have betrayed men in one way or another, even Mothers. Corrine, Corrine, how I began to hate that name.

Funny. I felt strange as I lifted my eyes from that red journal with its small cramped handwriting that sometimes sprawled larger at the bottom of the page, as if he had to use every bit of space.

I too had always been scared my Momma might up and go for no reason except she didn't want to be near me any more. And I'd be left alone with a stepfather who couldn't possibly love me as much as if I'd been his own true son. Jory would be all right, for he had his dancing and that was all that really mattered to him.

'You like that book?' asked John Amos who had sneaked into the barn, and was standing still in the shadows and watching me with small glittery eyes.

'Sure, it's a good book,' I managed to say, though it made me feel bad inside, and so afraid Momma might run away too with some man who wasn't a doctor. All the time she was wishing Daddy wasn't a doctor and could stay home more.

'Now you keep reading that book each day,' advised John

Amos who might really like me, even though his face was mean, 'and you will learn all about women and how to control them.' I could listen better when I couldn't see him very good. 'And not only will you learn how to control women, but also all people. That small red book in your hands will save you from making the mistakes so many men make. You remember that when you grow tired of reading. You remember it is the God-given duty of men to dominate women who are basically weak and stupid.'

Gee, I hadn't guessed Momma was weak and stupid. I thought she was strong and wonderful. Just like my grandmother was generous and kind . . . and in some ways, much better than my own mother who always seemed too busy to bother with me.

'Malcolm was the kind of man other people looked up to, Bart. The kind of man everyone respected and feared. When you can inspire that kind of awe it makes you revered – like a god. You don't have to tell your grandmother about this book. It would be better if you didn't, and just went on pretending to love her as much as before. Never let women know what you're thinking. Keep your honest thoughts to yourself.'

Maybe he was right. Maybe if I read this book to the very end I'd end up smarter than Jory, and the whole world would look up to me.

I smiled that night in my bed, hugging the journal of Malcolm Foxworth close to my heart. Here I had the tool to use to make me the richest man in the world – just like Malcolm Neal Foxworth who used to live in a faraway place called Foxworth Hall.

I had two friends now. My lady in black grandmother and John Amos who talked to me more than my Daddy ever did. Boy, sure was funny how strangers came into my life and started giving me more than my parents.

SUGAR AND SPICE *Jory*

The ballet school that Mom had purchased still bore the name of the original owner. She adopted that name, *Marie DuBois School of Ballet*, and led her students to think she was Marie DuBois. She explained to me and Bart later, it was easier than changing the name of the school and more profitable too. Dad seemed to agree.

Her school was located on the top floor of a two-storey building in San Rafael, not far from where Dad had his medical office. Often they ate lunch together or spent the night in town so they could see a ballet, or go to movies and not have to drive back and forth. Emma was with us, so we didn't really mind too much, except sometimes I felt left out to see them come home so happy and glowing. It made me think we weren't as important to them as we liked to believe.

One night when I was restless, and couldn't sleep, I silently stole out of my bedroom with the idea of a midnight snack on my mind. The second my feet hit the hall near the living-room I could hear the sound of my parents' voices. They were arguing, and they seldom even spoke crossly to one another.

I didn't know what to do, to stay, or to return to my room. Then I remembered that scene in the attic, and for my protection and Bart's too, I felt I had to know what this was all about.

Mom still wore the pretty blue dress she'd worn out to dinner with Dad. 'I don't know why you keep objecting!' she stormed as she paced back and forth, throwing Dad furious looks. 'You know as well as I do that Nicole isn't going to get well. And if we wait until she's buried, then the state will have custody of Cindy, and we'll have a devil of a time getting her away from them. Let's move now. Possession is nine-tenths of the law, and that landlady doesn't want to be bothered any longer. Chris, please make up your mind!'

'No!' he said coldly. 'We have two children and that's enough. There are other young couples who will be delighted to adopt Cindy. Couples who don't have as much to lose as we do when the adoption agency starts to investigate . . .'

Mom threw her hands wide. 'That's what I'm saying! If we have Cindy before Nicole dies, the agency won't have any reason to investigate. I'll go tonight and tell Nicole what I plan. I'm sure she'll agree and sign whatever legal papers are needed.'

'Catherine,' said my stepfather in a firm voice, 'you can't have everything the way you want it. Nicole may very well recover in a few weeks, and even if she is permanently crippled, she'll still want her child.'

'But what kind of mother will she make?'

'That's not for us to decide!'

'She can't recover! You know it, and I know it – and what's more, Christopher Doll, I have already gone to the hospital and talked to Nicole, and she wants me to have her daughter! She signed the papers I took and I had Simon Daughtry with me. He's an attorney, and had his secretary along – so what can you do now to stop me?'

Appearing shocked, my stepdad put his hands to his face, while my mother railed on and on:

'Christopher, stop cringing behind your hands. Show your face, and recognize what you made me do. You were there the night Bart was born – there with your pleading eyes telling me Paul wouldn't be enough, and it would be you in the end who won. If you hadn't been there, pleading with those damned blue eyes, I wouldn't have let the doctors talk me into signing those papers and allowing the sterilization! I would have borne another child even if it did kill me! But you were there – and I gave in – for your sake, damn it! For your sake!'

Sobbing, she fell to the floor and lay curled up on her side, her fingers working in the deep shag of the carpet. Her long blonde hair spread like a golden fan on the carpet and cushioned her cheek as she cried on and on, berating him and herself for what they were doing.

What were they doing?

She rolled on to her back, spreading her arms wide. Dad uncovered his face and stared at her, looking deeply wounded.

'You're right, Christopher! You are always right! There's only been one time when I was right, but that single time might have saved Cory's life.' Sobbing, she jerked her head away from Dad who knelt beside her and tried to pull her into his embrace. She hit at him, making me gasp.

'You were right again when you told me not to marry Julian. I'll bet you gloated when our marriage turned out a miserable failure. I'll bet you were delighted when Julian sat back and allowed Yolanda Lange to destroy everything we owned. Everything happened just the way you predicted, making you so happy. Then Bart suffocated in the fire that burned Foxworth Hall to the ground. Were you laughing inside then too – glad to be rid of him? Did you think I'd run straight into your arms and forget about all I owed Paul? Did you doubt I loved Paul?' Her voice rose to a shrill shriek. 'When Paul and I were lovers I never thought of him as too old, until you kept harping on his age. Perhaps I wouldn't have paid any attention to Amanda and what she said, if you hadn't bugged me so much about marrying a man twenty-five years older.'

I shrank into a tighter ball. Ashamed to stay and listen; afraid to get up and go now that I'd overheard so much. Mom was wound up, as if she'd saved this for a long time, ready to throw it into his face at the right opportunity – and here it was. He recoiled from the viciousness of her attack.

'Remember the afternoon I married Paul,' she yelled. 'Remember? Think of the moment when you handed me the ring he put on my finger. You hesitated so long the minister had to urge you with a whisper. And all the time you were pleading with your eyes. I resisted you then, as I should have resisted you after he died. Did you wish for him to die soon so then you'd have your chance? A self-fulfilling wish, Christopher Doll. You win! You always win! You sit back and wait while you do what you can to mess up my life! Well here I am! Right where you wanted me – in your bed, acting as your wife. Are you enjoying yourself? Are you?' She choked, sobbed. She then slapped his face. Hard.

He reeled backwards but didn't say a word, not a word. She hadn't finished with him even then. 'Don't you realize I would never have gone to Bart in the first place if you hadn't always been hanging around, coming between Paul and me; making me ashamed of what Momma had done to you, to me? I had to take Bart away from her then – it was the only way I could punish her for what she did to us. And now, after all Paul did for us, you won't even have the decent generosity to take in a poor little girl who will soon be an orphan. Even when I have paved the way legally so there won't be any investigation by the authorities. Still you want me for yourself, thinking two sons are enough to get in the way of our privacy, and another child might bring down our house of cheating cards.'

'Cathy, please . . .' he moaned, trying to take her in his arms and smother with kisses all she was screaming out.

She hit at him with small balled fists, then yelled again, 'Perhaps you even told me it was all right for Paul to have sex just so he would have another heart attack!'

Then she sank back, gasping, panting, tears streaking her face while her watery blue eyes stared up at Dad, but he only stayed still, hunkered down on his heels as if frozen by all she'd said.

I wanted to cry, for him, for her, for Bart and for me. Though I didn't understand nearly enough.

My dad began to shiver uncontrollably, as if winter had come unexpectedly into our living-room. Had Mom told the truth? Was he the one who was behind all the deaths in our lives? I shivered too, scared, for I loved him.

'Great God, Catherine,' he said at last, rising to his feet and heading towards their bedroom, 'I'll pack my bags and move out before the hour is over, if that's what you want. And I hope you're satisfied. This time, you win!'

In one single graceful bound, she was on her feet and running after him. She caught hold of his arm and spun him around before she flung her arms about his waist and clung. 'Chris!' she cried out. 'I'm sorry! So sorry. I didn't mean a word I said. It was cruel, and I know it. I love you; I've always loved you: I lie. I cheat. I say anything I want to get my way. I'll put the blame on anyone. I can't bear it as my own. Don't look so hurt, so betrayed. You're right to deny me Nicole's daughter, for I do end up hurting everyone I love. I do destroy what I care most about – if I'd been the right kind of person I would have found the right words to say to Carrie, but I didn't say anything right to her then, and nothing right to Julian either.'

She still clung to him while he stood like a tall stick of wood in her embrace, doing nothing to return all the passion she lavished with her words, her kisses, her embraces. She took one of his limp hands and tried to slap her face with it, and failing, she slapped her own face with her free hand.

'Why don't you hit me, Chris? God knows I've given you reason enough tonight. And I don't have to have Cindy, not when I have you, and my sons . . .'

I could tell my stepdad felt impotent against all the anguish she displayed. Her histrionics had driven him into a corner and he wanted to stay there long enough to reason out his position. But she was at him, demanding of him, until she was yelling out again:

'What's the matter now, Christopher Doll? There you stand wooden, saying nothing, trying to judge me by your own ethics. Recognize the truth – that I don't have any ethics! You want to believe I am only an actress playing a role, like our mother played hers. Even now, after all these years, you can't tell when I'm acting and when I'm not. Do you know why?' Now her voice became nasty, cynical. 'Since you have never bothered to analyse my pathetic case, I'll do it for you. Christopher, you are afraid to look at me honestly. You don't want to know what I am really like, what I have become. If I'm not acting, and this side I'm showing you now is the real me – then you can't face up to being a fool. You would discover then you have based your great unselfish love on a woman who is ruthless, demanding and utterly selfish. Go on, see the truth! I'm not a divine goddess and never was, never will be! Chris, you've been a fool all your adult life trying to make me into something I'm not – so that makes you a liar too. Doesn't it?' She laughed as he paled.

'Look at me, Christopher. Who do I remind you of?' She pulled back and looked at him in silence for a long time as she waited. When he refused to answer she said, 'Come on, say it – I'm like her – right? This is the way she was that last night in Foxworth Hall when the guests were there swarming about the Christmas tree in the ballroom, and in the library she was screaming as I'm screaming now – yelling out how her father beat her and made her do what she did.'

Slowly, slowly, Dad was losing his temper. I was trembling, so afraid of what might happen next. I loved her and I loved him. I wanted to rush in and stop what was going on, but how could I? If he raised his hand to strike her I knew I'd rush to her defence. Never, never would I let him hit my mother – and never, never had I thought he would, until now.

Mom, please don't say anything more, please, please!

Did she hear my silent pleas? She did let go of him and slid silently down to the floor again. I cried unseen tears of fearful bewilderment, confused and dazed to see them fighting, really fighting. And who was this *her* Mom kept referring to? Why was she so important in their lives? Why was the name Foxworth Hall stirring up hidden fears?

Once more Dad knelt beside her. This time with great tenderness he gathered her into his arms, and I sighed in relief. I should have known he'd never harm her, never. His kisses rained on her pale face and tried to smother her words. 'Chris,' she sobbed, 'how can you keep on loving me when I'm such a bitch? How can you keep on understanding why I act as ugly as I do, when I don't understand? I'm just as much a bitch as she was – only I'd give my life to undo the harm she's done us.'

Without a word he locked eyes with her until their breathing began to come in short pants. Between them that passion that was always just below the surface ignited, caught fire, and something electric tingled my skin too.

Lest I see too much, I silently crawled back to my room with the embarrassing vision of them rolling about on the floor still on my mind. Over and over again turning, clutching at each other, both wild, and the last thing I heard was a zipper being pulled. His or hers, I didn't know. Though I wondered about it. Did a woman ever pull down a man's fly zipper of her own free will – even a wife?

I ran into the garden. In the dark, near the great white wall, near a pale nude statue of marble, I fell down on the ground and cried. Rodin's statue 'The Kiss' was the first thing I saw when I looked up. Just a copy, but it told me a whole lot about adults and their feelings.

I'd been a child believing my parents' intregrity was flawless, their love a brilliant smooth ribbon of unbroken satin. Now it was tattered, stained, and no longer shining. Had they argued many times and I just hadn't heard? I tried to remember. It seemed to me that they'd never had such a terrible argument before, only brief conflicts which had been soon resolved.

Too old to cry, I told myself. Fourteen was almost a man's age. Already I was sprouting a few hairs above my lips and other places. Sniffling, choking my sobs back, I ran to the white wall and climbed the oak tree. Once there on the wall I sat in my favourite place and stared at the huge white mansion which looked ghostly in the moonlight. I thought and I thought about Bart and who was his father, and why hadn't he been named after Daddy Paul? Surely a son should have his father's name. Why Bart instead of Paul?

As I watched, as I wondered, fog from the sea began to billow in great rolling mountains, curling back upon itself, enfolding the mansion until I couldn't see it. All about me spread the thick grey mists. Eerie, frightening, mysterious.

From the grounds next door came strange muffled noises. Was that someone crying over there? Great racking sobs that were punctuated by moans and short prayers that asked for forgiveness.

Oh, God! Was that pitiful old woman crying just like my mother had cried? What had she done? Did everyone have a shameful past to conceal? Would I be like them when I grew up?

'Christopher,' I heard her sob. Startled, I jerked and tried to find where she was. And how did she know my Dad's name? Or did she have a Christopher of her own?

I knew one thing. Something dark and threatening had come into our lives. Bart was acting stranger than usual. Something or someone had to be influencing him in subtle ways I couldn't quite put my finger on. Whatever was changing Bart didn't have anything to do with Mom and Dad. If I couldn't understand them, Bart wouldn't have a chance. But whatever it was between my parents, and whatever was going on with Bart, I felt I had the weight of the world on my shoulders, and they weren't that strong yet.

One afternoon I hurried home from ballet class early, deliberately. I wanted to find out what Bart did with himself when I was away. He wasn't in his room, he wasn't in the garden, so that left only one place he could possibly be. Next door.

I found him easily. Much to my surprise he was inside and sitting on the lap of the old woman who never wore any clothes that weren't black.

I sucked in my breath. The little rascal cuddled up cosily on her black lap. I stole closer to the window of the parlour she seemed to favour above the others. She was singing softly to him as he gazed up into her veil-shrouded face. His huge dark eyes were full of innocence before his expression suddenly changed to that of someone sly and old. 'You don't really love me, do you?' he asked in the strangest voice.

'Oh, yes I do,' she said softly. 'I love you more than I have ever loved anyone before.'

'More than you could love Jory?'

Why the devil should she love me?

She hesitated, glanced away, answered, 'Yes . . . you are very, very special to me.'

'You will always love me best of all?'

'Always, always . . .'

'You will give me everything I want, no matter what?'

'Always, always . . .'

'Bart, my dear love, the next time you come over you will find waiting for you – your heart's desire.'

'You'd better have it here!' said Bart in a hard way that surprised me. Until now he'd had the sweet little-boy voice that would have made a good tenor for church choir singing. All of a sudden he sounded years older. But he was always changing his way of talking, walking. Play-acting, always pretending.

I'd go home and tell Mom and Dad. Bart really needed friends his own age, not an old lady. It wasn't healthy for a boy not to have peers to play with. Then again, I wondered why my parents never asked any of their friends to our home the way other parents had their friends over occasionally. We lived all to ourselves, isolated from neighbours – until this one Moslem woman, or whatever she was, came to win my brother's affections. I should be glad for him. Instead I was uneasy.

Finally Bart got up and said. 'Goodbye Grandmother.' Just his ordinary little-boy voice – but what the heck did he mean by *grandmother?*

I waited patiently until I was sure Bart was in our yard before I circled the huge old house and banged hard on her front door. I expected to see that old butler come shambling down the long hall to the foyer, but it was the old lady herself who put an eye to the peephole and asked who it was.

'Jory Marquet Sheffield.' I said proudly, just as my Dad would.

'Jory,' she whispered. In another moment she had flung open the door. 'Come in,' she invited happily, stepping aside to admit me. Way back in the shadows I thought I glimpsed someone who quickly dodged out of sight. 'I'm so happy to have you visit. Your brother was here and has depleted our supply of ice-cream but I can offer you a cola drink and cake or cookies.'

No wonder Bart wasn't eating Emma's good cooking. This woman was feeding him junk food. 'Who are you?' I asked, angrily. 'You have no right to feed my brother anything.'

She stepped back, appearing hurt and humble. 'I try to tell him he should wait until after his meals, but he insists. And please don't judge me harshly without giving me a chance to explain.' Her gesture invited me to take a chair in one of her fancy parlours. Though I wanted to decline my curiosity was aroused. I followed her into what must have been the grandest room outside of a French palace! There was a concert grand piano and love seats, and brocade chairs, a desk, a long marble fireplace. Then I turned to look her over. 'Do you have a name?'

Floundering, she managed a small voice. 'Bart calls me . . . Grandmother.'

'You're not his grandmother,' I said. 'And when you tell him you are, you confuse him, and Lord knows, lady, if there is one thing my brother doesn't need it is more confusion.'

A slow redness coloured her forehead. 'I have no grandchildren of my own. I'm lonely, I need someone . . . and Bart seems to like me . . .'

Pity for her overwhelmed me so I could hardly say what I'd determined beforehand, but I managed nevertheless. 'I don't think coming over here is good for Bart, ma'am. If I were you I would try and discourage him. He needs friends his own age . . .' and here my voice dwindled away, for how could I tell her she was too old? And two grandmothers, one in a nut house, and the other a ballet nut, were more than enough.

The very next day Bart and I were told that Nicole had died in the night, and from now on her daughter, Cindy, would be our sister. My eyes met Bart's. Dad had his eyes on his plate but he wasn't eating. I looked around, startled, when I heard a young child crying. 'That's Cindy,' said Dad. 'Your mother and I were at Nicole's side when she died. Her last words were a request for us to take care of her child. When I thought about you two boys being left alone like Cindy, I knew I could die feeling more at peace knowing my children had a good home . . . so I let your mother say what she's been wanting to say ever since Nicole's accident.'

Mom came into the kitchen. In her arms she carried a small girl with blonde ringlets, large blue eyes almost the same colour as hers. 'Isn't she adorable, Jory, Bart?' She kissed a round rosy cheek while the big blue eyes looked from one to the other of us. 'Cindy is exactly two years and two months and five days old. Nicole's landlady was delighted to be rid of what she thought a heavy burden.' She gave us a happy smile. 'Remember when you asked for a sister, Jory? I told you then I couldn't have more children. Well, as you can see, sometimes God works in mysterious ways. I'm crying inside for Nicole who should have lived to be eighty. But her spine was broken and she had multiple internal injuries . . .'

She left the rest unsaid. It was terribly sad for someone as young and pretty as nineteen-year-old Nicole Nickols to die just so we could have the sister I'd only mentioned casually a long time ago.

'Was Nicole your patient?' I asked Dad.

'No, son, she wasn't. But since she was a friend, and your mother's student, we were notified of her failure to respond to medical treatment. We rushed to the hospital to be with her. I suppose neither of you heard the phone ring about four this morning.'

I stared at my new sister. She was very pretty in her pink pyjamas with feet. Her soft curls fluffed out around her face. She clung to my mother and stared at strangers before she ducked her head and hid from our eyes. 'Bart,' said Mom with a sweet smile, 'you used to do that. If you hid your face, just because you couldn't see us, you thought we couldn't see you.'

'Get her out of here!' he yelled, his face a red mask of anger. 'Take her away! Put her in the grave with her mother. Don't want no sister. I hate her, hate her!'

Silence. No one could speak after this outburst.

Then, while Mom stood on looking too shocked even to breathe, Dad reached to control Bart who jumped up to hit Cindy. Then Cindy was crying, and Emma was glaring at my brother.

'Bart, I have never heard anything so ugly and cruel,' said Dad as he lifted Bart up and sat him on his knee. Bart wriggled and squirmed and tried to get away but he couldn't escape. 'Go to your room and stay there until you can learn to have some human compassion for others. You would feel very lucky in Cindy's place.'

Grumbling under his breath, Bart stomped to his room and slammed his door.

Turning, Dad picked up his black bag and prepared to leave. He gave my mother a chastising look. 'Now do you see why I objected to adopting Cindy? You know as well as I that Bart has always had a very jealous streak. A child as lovely and young as Cindy wouldn't have been two days in an orphanage before some lucky couple scooped her up.'

'Yes, Chris, you are right, as always. If Cindy had been taken into legal custody she would have been adopted by others – and you and I would have gone daughterless all our lives. As it is I have a little girl who seems so much like Carrie to me.'

My father grimaced as if from sharp pain. Mom was left sitting at the table with Cindy on her lap, and for the first time since I could remember, he didn't kiss her goodbye. And she didn't call out, 'Be careful.'

In no time at all Cindy had me enchanted. She toddled from here to there, wanting to touch everything and then have a taste. A nice warm feeling rushed over me to see the little girl so well cared for, so loved and pampered. The two of them together looked like mother and daughter. Both dressed in pink, with pink ribbons in their hair only Cindy had on white socks with lace.

'Jory will teach you to dance when you're old enough.' I smiled at Mom as I passed her on my way to ballet class. Quickly Mom got up to hand Cindy over to Emma, then she joined me in her car that was still parked in our wide garage. 'Jory, I think Bart is learning to like Cindy a little more, don't you?'

I wanted to say, no he wasn't, but I nodded, not letting her know how worried I was about my brother. *Trouble trouble, boil and double . . .*

'Jory, what was that you just mumbled?'

Gee. I didn't know I said it aloud. 'Nothing, Mom. Just repeating something I overheard Bart saying to himself last night. He cries in his sleep, Mom. He calls for you, screaming because you've run away with your lover.' I grinned and tried to look lighthearted. 'And I didn't even know you play around.'

She ignored my facetious remark. 'Jory, why didn't you tell me before Bart has nightmares?'

How could I tell her the truth? – that she was much too taken up with Cindy to pay attention to anyone else? And never – never should she give anyone more attention than Bart. Even me.

'Momma, Momma!' I heard Bart cry out in his sleep that night. 'Where are you? Don't leave me alone. Momma, please don't leave me. Don't love him more than me! I'm not bad, really not bad . . . just can't help what I do sometimes. Momma . . . Momma . . .!'

Only crazy people couldn't help what they did. One crazy person in our family was enough. We didn't need another living under our roof.

So . . . it was up to me to save Bart from himself. Up to me to straighten out something crooked that had begun a long time ago. And way back in the shadowed recesses of my brain, there were vague unsettling memories of something that had troubled me years ago when I was too young to understand. Too young to put the jigsaw pieces together.

Trouble was, I'd been doing too much thinking about the past that now it was waking up, and I could remember a man with dark hair, a man Mom used to call Bart Winslow – and those were my half brother's first and second names.

MY HEART'S DESIRE *Bart*

Wicked little girl, that Cindy. Didn't care who saw her naked. Didn't care who saw her sit on the potty. Didn't care about being decent or clean. Took my toy cars and chewed on them.

Summer wasn't so good no more. Nothing t'do. Nowhere to go but next door. Old lady kept promising that pony and it never did show up. Leading me on, teasing me. I'd show her. Make her sit over there all alone, wouldn't visit. Punish her. One night I heard Momma telling Daddy how she saw that old lady in black standing on a ladder propped against the wall. 'And she was staring at me, Chris. Really staring!'

Daddy had laughed. 'Really, Cathy. What harm can her stares do? She's a stranger in a strange land. Wouldn't it have been friendly of you to wave and perhaps introduce yourself?' I snickered to myself. Grandmother wouldn't have answered. She was shy around all strangers but me. I was the only one she trusted.

Another day of being mean to Cindy had everywhere named off-limits to me. But I was clever and stole outside and snuck quickly away to next door, to where people liked me.

'Where's my pony?' I screeched when I saw the barn still empty. 'You promised me a pony – so if you don't give me one I'll tell Momma and Daddy you are trying to steal me away!'

She seemed to shrink inside her ugly black robe while those pale thin hands of hers fluttered to the neckline so she could tug out a heavy rope of pearls she usually kept hidden.

'Tomorrow, Bart. Tomorrow you get your heart's desire.'

Met John Amos on the way home. He led me into his secret cubby-hole and whispered of 'man-doings'. 'Women like her are born rich and they never need brains,' said John Amos, his watery eyes hard and slitlike. 'You listen to me, boy, and never fall in love with a stupid woman. And all women are stupid. When you deal with women you have to let them know who is boss right from the start – and never let them forget it. Now, your lesson for today. Who is Malcolm Neal Foxworth?'

'My great-grandfather who is dead and gone but powerful even so,' I said, not really understanding even as I said it.

'What else was Malcolm Neal Foxworth?'

'A saint. A saint deserving of a lordly place in heaven.'

'Correct. But tell it all, leave nothing out.'

'Never was there a man born smarter than Malcolm Neal Foxworth.'

'That's not all I've taught you. You should know more about him from reading his journal. Are you reading it daily? He wrote in that book faithfully all his life. I've read it a dozen or more times. To read is to learn and to grow. So never stop reading your great-grandfather's journal until you are just as clever and smart as he is.'

'Is clever the same as being smart?'

'No, of course not. Clever is not letting people suspect just how smart you are.'

'Why didn't Malcolm like his Momma?' I asked, though I knew she'd run away, but would that make me hate my Momma?

'Like his mother? Lord God above, boy, Malcolm was wild about his mother until she ran off with her lover and left Malcolm with his father who was too busy to pay him any attention. If you read on, boy, you'll find out soon just what turned Malcolm against all women. Read on and increase your knowledge. Malcolm's wisdom will become yours. He will teach you never to trust a woman to be there when you need her.'

'But my Momma is a good Momma,' I defended weakly, not so sure any more that is was true. Life was so devious. (New word for today, 'devious'. It means departing from the shortest way; crooked and unfair – D-E-V-I-O-U-S.)

'Now I'm going to leave you alone so you can read more of

Malcolm's words,' said John Amos before he shuffled off, bent slightly forward and to the side.

I opened the book to the page where the leather bookmark was.

Today I just wanted to try a little of my father's tobacco, so I filled his pipe with what I found in his office, then stole outside and smoked behind the garage.

I don't know how he found out unless one of the servants told on me, but he knew. Fire came in his hard eyes and he ordered me to strip down to naked. Cringing, I cried when he whipped me, and then he put me in the attic until I could learn the ways of the Lord and redeem my sins. While I was up there I found old photographs of my mother when she was just a girl. How beautiful she was, so innocent and sweet looking. I hated her! I wanted her to die that very moment wherever she was in the world. I wanted her to be suffering as I was, with cuts bleeding down my back, while I nearly suffocated in that airless hot attic.

I found things in that attic, corsets with laces so a woman swelled out in front, deceiving men into believing she had more than what came naturally. I knew I would never be deceived by any woman, no matter how beautiful. For it was beauty that put me in the attic, and beauty that used the whip on my back, and it wasn't really my father's fault what he did. He was hurting too, like I was.

Now I knew what he'd said all the time was true; no woman could be trusted. And most especially those with beautiful faces and seductive bodies.

Lifting my eyes I stared into space, not seeing the barn and all the hay, but the sweet and beautiful face of my mother. Was *she* devious? Would she one day run away with her lover and leave me to fend for myself with a stepfather who didn't love me nearly as much as he loved Jory and Cindy?

What would I do then? Would my grandmother take me in? I asked her later on. 'Yes, my love, I will take you in. I will care of you, fight for you, do what I can for you, for you are the true son of my second husband, Bart Winslow. Haven't I told you that before? Trust me, believe in me, *and stay away from John Amos.* He is not the kind of friend you should have.'

Son of her second husband, did that mean my Momma had been married to him too? All the time marrying somebody! I closed my eyes and thought about Malcolm who was long gone in his grave. Rock, rock, rock went her chair. Thud, thud, thud went the dirt on my grave. Dark now. Smothery. Cramped and cold. Heaven . . . where was heaven?

'Bart, your eyes are glassy.'

'Tired, Grandmother, so tired.'

'Soon you will have your heart's desire.'

Money, wanted money, piles and piles of greenbacks. At that moment someone banged on the front door. I jumped off her lap, and quickly hid.

Jory ran in ahead of John Amos who had admitted him. 'Where is my brother?' he asked, looking around the room. 'I don't like what's happening to him, and I think it has something to do with coming over here – '

'Jory,' said my grandmother, putting out her hand with the sparkling jewelled fingers. 'Don't glare at me. I don't harm him. I only give him a little ice-cream after his meals. Sit down and talk for a while – I'll send for refreshments.'

Ignoring her, with the nose of a bloodhound Jory raced straight to me and yanked me out from behind the potted palms. 'No thank you, lady,' he said coldly. 'My Mom gives me all I need to eat – and what you're doing over here is changing him, so please don't let him come again.'

Her barely visible lips clamped together and I saw tears in her eyes as I was pulled away. Jory shook me in our back yard. 'Don't you ever go back there again, Bart Sheffield! She is not your grandmother. You look at her as if you like her more than Mom!'

There were some who said Bart Winslow Scott Sheffield was not as tall as other boys at nine. But I knew as soon as I hit ten I'd shoot up like a weed in the summertime. Soon as I was in Disneyland again, I'd be inspired enough to grow as tall as a giant.

'Why are you looking so solemn, darling?' asked Grandmother when I was snuggled on her lap again the next day. The pony still hadn't come.

'Not coming to see you no more,' I said grumpily. 'Daddy will give me a pony for my birthday when I tell him again I want one. Won't need yours.'

'Bart, you haven't told your parents about me, have you?'

'No, ma'am.'

'If you lie God will punish you.'

Sure, why not? Everybody else did. 'Never tell nobody nothing,' I mumbled. 'Momma and Daddy don't like me no way. They got Jory. Now they got Cindy too. That's enough for them.'

She took a quick glance around, paying special attention that doors were closed and latched tight, then she whispered: 'Bart, I've seen you talking to John. I've asked you to stay away from him. He's an evil old man who can be very cruel. Keep that in mind.'

Gee, who could I trust? He said the same thing about her. Once I'd thought everyone in my family could be trusted. Now I was learning people weren't always what they seemed to be on the surface. Weren't loving, never cared enough, especially when it came to me. Maybe it was only Grandmother who really cared – and John Amos. Then I was bewildered again. Was John Amos my true friend? If he was then my grandmother couldn't be. Had to choose. Which to choose? How did I made big decisions like that? Then, when Grandmother had her arms about me, my face held to her soft breast, her kisses on top of my head, I knew. She was the one who loved me best. She was my own true-for-a-fact grandmother.

But . . . what if she wasn't?

I'd seen my grandmother a dozen or more times. John Amos

had been my friend for only five days. Maybe if he waited for me seven times in a row that would tell me he was lucky and good for me. Seven times of anything meant good luck. Five times of talking to me in his spooky place had taught me already that women were sneaky and devious.

'Bart, my darling,' whispered my granny, putting her dry lips on my cheek near my ear, 'don't look so afraid, just leave John Amos alone, and don't believe anything he tells you.' She stroked my face, then I felt her smile. 'Now, if you run down to the barn, and take a look inside, you will find something any boy would love to have, and those who don't will envy you.'

She started to say something else, but I jumped from her lap and raced from her room and ran all the way to the barn. Oh gosh, oh gee, every day I carried an apple in my pocket, just hoping. Every day I carried lumps of Momma's sugar, just hoping. Prayed every night for that pony I just had to have. This pony was going to love me more than anybody! I ran to the barn and didn't fall once. Then I pulled up short and stared. *That wasn't a pony!*

It was only a dog. A big hairy dog who stood with his tail wagging, and his eyes looking at me adoringly already, and I hadn't done one thing to win his love. I wanted to cry. It was leashed and tied by a rope to a stump in the barn dirt floor. The dog wriggled all over, as if happy to see me – and I hated that dog.

Behind me she came running up, all breathless and panting. 'Bart darling, don't be disappointed! I really wanted to give you a pony, but as I told you, if I did, you would go home reeking of horses, and Jory and your parents would find out, and never let you come back to visit me.'

I sank down on my knees and bowed my head. I wanted to die. I'd eaten all that ice-cream, suffered through all those kisses and hugs . . . and still she hadn't given me a pony. 'You lied to me.' I choked with tears in my eyes. 'You've made me waste all my days visitin' you when I could have done somethin' better.' And there I went, dropping my g's again. Not so grown up after all.

'Bart darling, you don't understand about St. Bernards at all,' she said, gathering me up in her arms. 'This dog is still just a puppy, and see how big he is. He will grow up to be as big as a pony. You can saddle him and ride him around. And did you know in the mountains they use this breed of dog to rescue people who have been lost in the snow? A keg of brandy is tied around the dog's neck, and all by himself, a dog like this can find a lost man and save his life. A St Bernard is the world's most heroic dog.'

I didn't believe her. Still, I had to stare at the puppy with more interest – that was a puppy? He strained at his leash, trying to get to me, and I liked him a little more for doing that. 'Will he really grow up to be as big as a pony?'

'Bart, he's only six months old, and already he's almost as big as some ponies!' She laughed and caught my hand and pulled me inside the barn. 'See,' she said, pointing to a red saddle with bit and bridle, and then to a little two-wheeled red cart. 'You can ride him, or hitch him to the cart – and have an all-purpose dog or pony, whatever you want. All you have to do is use your imagination.'

'Will he bite me?'

'No, of course not. Darling, look at him, how happy he is to see a boy. Put out your hand and let him sniff your palm. Treat him kindly, feed him well, and keep his hair free of briars and tangles, and you will not only have the most beautiful dog in the world, but the best friend of your life.'

Fearfully I inched my hand away from my body – and the puppy licked it like ice-cream! Slurpy kisses! I laughed because it tickled. 'Go way, Grandmother,' I ordered.

She backed away reluctantly while I knelt in front of the pony so I could tell it what it was. 'Now you look here,' I said firmly, 'and you remember what I say. You are not a dog but a pony. You are not meant to carry brandy in kegs to people who are lost and snowed in – you are meant for carrying me only. You are my pony, and mine alone.'

He looked at me as if bewildered, cocking his big shaggy head to one side as he sat on his haunches. 'Don't you sit like that!' I yelled. 'Ponies don't sit, only dogs.'

'Bart,' came my grandmother's soft voice, 'be kind, remember.'

I ignored her. Women didn't count in man-doings like this. John Amos had told me that. Men ruled the world, and women had to sit back and keep quiet.

I had to cast a spell and make a puppy over into a pony. Mean witches on stage knew how to do that. I thought and thought about every stage witch I'd seen in ballets and finally I thought I knew just how it was done.

Needed a long hooked nose and a jutting long chin, and hollowed-out eyes and bony long fingers with black nails two inches long. Only thing I had right was mean black piercing eyes – maybe that would do the trick. Knew how to make eyes real good.

I flung my arms overhead, curled my fingers into claws, hunched my back and cast my spell: 'I chrisss-sen thee Apple! With this magic potion I give, and with this spell I put upon thee, I make you into a pony.' I gave him the magic potion which was an apple. 'Now, you are mine, all mine. Never will you eat or drink if I am not the one to give you the food and water. Never will you love anyone but me. You will run to me and die when I do. Mine Apple, mine! Now and forevermore . . . mine!'

The power of my magic spell had Apple sniffing at the fruit I offered. He whimpered unhappily and turned his nose away, showing more interest in the sugar I was saving for later. 'Now don't you whinny and try to eat everything,' I scolded, biting into the apple myself to show him how it was done. Again I held the apple out for my pony to eat. Again he turned away his giant white and golden head. Some of his fur was reddish gold and sorta pretty. I bit into the apple again and chewed, showing him what good food he was missing.

'Bart,' called Grandmother with a choke in her voice, 'perhaps I made a mistake. I'll take the puppy back to the pet shop and buy you that pony you wanted.'

I looked from her to my new pet, then towards my home, considering. They'd be sure to smell a horse, if ponies smelled horsy. And dog smells would seem natural; they'd be convinced Clover had finally learned to trust me – when he never would let me near him. 'Grandmother, I'm going to keep this here puppypony. I'll teach him all about how to play horse. If he doesn't learn before I go to Disneyland you can take him back – and never can I come to visit you again.'

Laughing and happy then, I fell on to the hay and frolicked with my puppypony, the only puppypony in the whole wide world. And his big warm body felt good in my arms, real good.

I looked at her then, and I knew John Amos was wrong. Women were not evil and devious, and I was so relieved to have found out at last that it was John Amos who was devious, and Momma and my grandmother were the best things in my whole life – next to Apple.

'Grandmother, are you truly my real grandmother, and my real Daddy was your second husband?'

'Yes, it's true,' she said with her head bowed. 'But it's a secret just between us. You must promise not to tell anyone.' She seemed to droop, to look sad, but I was so happy inside I wanted to burst. A puppypony, a real grandmother who had been married to my real father, gosh, I was getting lucky at last.

And there I was saying my 'ings'. That's what loving Apple and my grandmother did for me, taught me how to pronounce the 'ings' with a G. And in only one day they succeeded, when Momma and Daddy had been trying for years and years.

Soon I found out eating had lots to do with loving. The more food I gave Apple, the more he loved me. And without the help of more spells, he was mine, all mine. When I came in the mornings he raced to me, jumping up and spinning in circles, wagging his tail, licking my face. When I hitched him to the new pony cart he bucked just like a real horse! Tried his best to rid himself of the small saddle I put on his back too. Boy, just wait until Jory got a load of the kind of magic I could work.

'Gonna be eleven soon,' I said to grandmother one day, in

hopes of giving her a few ideas. 'Ten,' she corrected. 'You will be ten on your next birthday.'

'Eleven!' I shouted, insisting. 'All year I've been going on ten. I have to be eleven by now.'

'Bart, don't start wishing your life away. Time goes by quickly enough. Hold on to your youth, stay as you are.'

I went on stroking Apple's head that rested on my lap. 'Granny, tell me about your little boys.'

She looked sad again, not from her face I couldn't see, but from the way her shoulders drooped. 'One went to heaven,' she whispered hoarsely, 'the other ran away.'

'Where did the other go?' I asked, thinking maybe I'd go there too.

'South,' she said simply, drooping more.

'I'm going south too. Hate that place – full of old graves and full of old grandmothers. One is locked up in a loony bin. The other is a mean-faced old witch. You're my best grandmother,' for by now I knew she couldn't be Daddy's crazy mother, but the mother of my real Daddy. And women changed names when they changed husbands, so that's . . . and then I knew I didn't even know her last or first name.

'Corrine Winslow,' she said when I asked, her head still bowed. I could see a little of her face where her nose lifted the black veil from her cheeks. A bit of her hair showed too. Grey hair with streaks of gleaming gold, soft hair. I pitied her. She was really going to suffer when I was gone.

'Going to Disneyland, Grandmother. Gonna stay there one week and have a party with more gifts from Momma and Daddy and Jory and Emma, and then we'll all fly East and spent two rotten weeks just visiting – '

'I know,' she interrupted with a smile in her voice, 'two weeks wasted by visiting old graves and old grandmothers. But you have a good time anyway.' She leaned to kiss and hug me tight. 'And while you're gone I'll take good care of Apple.'

'No!' I screamed, terrified Apple would love her more than me when I came back. 'You leave my pet alone. He's mine.

Don't you go feedin' him and makin' him more yours than mine.'

She agreed to do what I wanted. I told her next I was gonna find a way to go to Disneyland, then sneak back to take care of Apple. How I was gonna do this wasn't really clear in my mind – and from the way she looked, it wasn't clear in hers either.

Later I was in the barn with Apple. John Amos stood tall and skinny above, as I sprawled on the hay. He lectured again on how evil women were, and how they made man sin.

'Nobody does anything for nothing,' he said. 'Don't you think for one second she doesn't have wicked plans for you, Bart Winslow.'

'Why'd you call me that?'

'It's your name, isn't it?'

I grinned, really proud to tell him I had the longest name ever.

'That's not important,' he said with no patience. 'Be attentive, boy. You asked me yesterday about sin, and I wanted to tell you exactly, but I had to plan the wording. Sin is what men and women do together when they close their bedroom door.'

Gee, what was so bad about closing a door?

'What's so bad about sin?'

He scowled, showing his teeth, and I shrank back into the hay, wishing he'd go away and leave me and Apple alone.

'Sin is what women use to make a man weak. You've got to face up to certain facts. Inside of every man there is a weak spineless streak and women know how to find it by taking off their clothes and using earthly pleasure to sap a man's strength by desire. Watch your own mother, see how she smiles at your father, how she paints her face and nails, and wears skimpy clothes, and see your stepfather's eyes light up – both are on their way to sinning when you see that.'

I swallowed, kinda hurting inside. Didn't want my parents to do bad things to make God punish them.

'Now hear the words of Malcolm again. "I cried and cried for five years after my mother went away and left me with my father who hated me for being hers. He told me all the time she was married to him she was unfaithful, deceiving him with many lovers. And then he couldn't love me. Couldn't stand for me to be near him, and it grew so lonely shut up in that big house with no one who cared. Time and again Father told me he'd never be able to remarry because of me. None of his paramours liked me. But they did fear me. You can bet I let them know what I thought. I knew they'd burn over the eternal fires of hell."'

'What's a paramour?' I asked, bored sometimes with Malcolm.

'A derelict soul on its way to hell!' He burned his eyes into me. 'And don't you think you can go away on a vacation and leave the care of Apple to another. When you accept the love of an animal, that animal is your responsibility for its entire life! You feed him, water him, groom and exercise him – or God will see that you suffer!'

I shivered and looked at my puppypony who was chasing his tail.

'There is power in your dark eyes, Bart. The same kind of power Malcolm had. God has sent you to carry out an unfinished duty. Malcolm will never rest easy in his grave until all the Devil's spawn are sent down to roast over the fires of hell!'

'Fires of hell,' I repeated dully.

'Two are there already . . . three more to go.'

'Three more to go.'

'Evil seeds reproduce and multiply over and over.'

'Over and over.'

'And when you have done your duty, Malcolm will rest easy in his grave.'

'Rest easy in my grave.'

'What's that you said?'

I was confused. Sometimes I pretended *I* was Malcolm. John Amos smiled for some reason and seemed pleased. I was allowed to go home then.

Jory came on the run to question me. 'Where've you been? What do you do over there? I see you talking to that old butler. What does he tell you?'

He made me feel like a mouse facing up to a lion. Then I

remembered Malcolm's book and how he handled situations like this. I put a cold mask on my face. 'John Amos and I have secrets that are none of your damn business!'

Jory stared. I strode off.

Under a huge spreading tree Momma was pushing Cindy in her babyswing. Sissy girls had to be strapped in to keep from falling out. 'Bart,' she called, 'where have you been?'

'Nowhere,' I snapped.

'Bart, I don't like facetious answers.'

I didn't like long words I didn't understand. I stopped and decided I'd do like Malcolm and wither her small with my mean glare – instead I saw to my amazement she wore a skimpy blue haltertop that didn't meet the top of her white shorts that showed her bellybutton. She was showing bare skin. Sin was connected to bare skin! In the Bible the Lord had commanded Adam and Eve to put on clothes and cover their wicked flesh. Was my Momma just as sinful as that wicked Corrine who had run off with her paramour?

'Bart, don't stare like you don't know who I am.'

Into my mind popped one of the lines from the Bible John Amos was always quoting. Bit by bit I was learning what God expected from the people he created. 'Be warned, Momma, the Lord will see when I do not, and He will punish.'

Momma almost jumped. Then she swallowed and in a dry voice asked, 'Why did you say that?'

Look at her tremble, I thought. I turned my head to glare at all the naked statues in this evil garden of sin. Wicked naked people made Malcolm rest uneasy in his grave.

But I loved her; she was my mother; sometimes she came and kissed me goodnight and stayed to hear my prayers. Before Cindy came she was better, and spent more time with me. And she didn't appear to be in love with a paramour.

Didn't know what to do. 'Sleepy, Momma,' I said and then drifted away, feeling at odds with myself and the rest of the world. What if what Malcolm wrote, and John Amos quoted, was true? Was she evil and sinful, luring men to be like animals?

Was it bad to be like animals? Apple wasn't bad, or sinful. Not even Clover was, and he didn't like me.

Inside Jory's room I paused before his thirty-gallon aquarium. The air made a steady stream of tiny bubbles that burbled to the surface like the champagne Momma had let me sip once. Pretty fish wouldn't live in my tank. Fish in Jory's tank never died. My empty tank held nothing but water, and a toy pirate ship spilled out fake jewels on the fake ocean floor. Jory's tank grew seaweed that snaked in and out of a small castle. His fish darted in and out of coral reefs.

Jory did everything better than me. I didn't like being Bart any more. Bart had to stay home and forget about Disneyland now that he had responsibilities.

A pet could be a heavy, heavy burden.

I fell on my bed and stared up at the ceiling. Malcolm didn't need his power and strength any more, or his clever brain that was smart too. He was dead and his talents were wasted. Nobody ever made Malcolm do anything he didn't want to after he grew up. Didn't want to be a boy any more. Wanted to be a man, like Malcolm the powerful, the financial wizard.

I was gonna make people jump when I spoke. Tremble when I looked. Cower when I moved. The day was coming. Felt it.

'Jory,' said Mom as we picked up our bags and headed for her car, 'I can't understand what's happening to Bart this summer. He's not the same child. What do you think he does outside alone all the time?'

I felt uncomfortable. I wanted to protect Bart and let him have the old lady next door for his friend, but I couldn't tell Mom that woman was saying she was Bart's grandmother. 'Don't you worry about Bart, Mom,' I assured her. 'You just keep on having fun with Cindy. She's sure a cute kid, like you must have been.'

She smiled and kissed my cheek. 'If my eyes aren't deceiving me, there's another cute kid you admire too.'

I felt a blush heat up my cheeks. I couldn't help but look at Melodie Richarme, she was so darn pretty with her hair that wasn't quite the same colour of blonde as Mom's, but a deeper honey shade. But her blue eyes were just as soft and shining. I thought I'd never love any girl who didn't have blue eyes. Just then Melodie showed up, running to her father's car, making me stare at the way she was turning into a woman. Gosh, it was miraculous the way flat-chested little girls showed up one day with bosoms, tiny waists and swelling hips, and suddenly they were ten times more interesing.

The minute we hit home Mom had me hunting up Bart. 'If he's over in that other yard, you tell me. I don't want you children bothering an old recluse, though I wish to heaven she'd stop climbing that ladder and staring at me over the wall.'

Climbing, jumping, calling, I searched until I found Bart in the old barn that had once been what was called in olden times 'a carriage house', but now it had empty stalls where horses used to live and in one was Bart. I stared, disbelieving my eyes. With him was a St Bernard puppy. The dog was almost as big as he was. It was easy enough to tell it was only a puppy for it had kiddish ways, frolicking and making puppy noises.

Bart threw down his rake and scolded the dog. 'You stop jumping around like that, Apple! Ponies don't jump anything but hurdles – now you eat that hay or I won't give you clean hay tomorrow.'

'Bart . . ." I called softly, leaning against the barn wall and smiling to see him jump. 'Dogs don't eat hay.'

His face flamed. 'You go away. You get out of here. You don't belong!'

'Neither do you.'

'You get out of here,' he sobbed, hurling down his rake and pulling the huge puppy into his arms. 'This is my dog; he was supposed to have been a pony – so I'm making him both a puppy and a pony. Don't you laugh and think I'm crazy.'

'I don't think you're crazy,' I said, a lump in my throat to see him so upset. It really was a shame I had more affinity for animals than he did. They seemed to know he'd step on their tails or trip over them. In fact even I wasn't too comfortable lying on the floor when Bart was around.

'Who gave you the puppy?'

'My grandmother,' Bart said with so much pride in his eyes. 'She loves me, Jory, really loves me more than Momma does. And she loves me more than your old Madame Marisha loves you.'

That was the trouble with Bart. No sooner did I feel close to him than he slapped me in my face, making me regret I'd ever let him under my skin.

I didn't pat the beautiful puppy on his head, though he was making up to me. I let Bart have his way; maybe this time he'd make a friend after all.

He smiled at me happily as we headed for home. 'You're not mad at me?' he asked. Of course I wasn't. 'You won't tell on me, Jory? It's important not to tell Momma or Daddy.'

I didn't like to keep secrets from my parents, but Bart was insistent, and what would it hurt anyway if a kind lady gave Bart a few gifts and a new puppy – she was making him feel loved and happy.

In the kitchen Emma was spooning cereal into Cindy's open mouth. Cindy had been dressed by Mom in new baby-blue coveralls with a white blouse embroidered with pink rabbits in a gay field of dainty flowers. Mom had done that embroidery work herself. Cindy's hair had been brushed until it gleamed like silvery gold; a blue satin ribbon held her ponytail high on the back of her head. She was so clean and fresh I wanted to hug her but I only smiled. I knew better than to be demonstrative when Bart was around to get jealous. Strangely, it was Bart who fascinated Cindy far more than me. Perhaps because he wasn't so much larger than she was.

My brother hurled himself down into a kitchen chair that almost toppled over backwards from the force. Emma looked his way and frowned. 'Go wash your hands and face, Bart Winslow, if you expect to eat at my table.'

'Not your table,' he grouched as he headed for the bathroom. He pulled his dirty hands along the walls to leave long smudges.

'Bart! Take your filthy hands off the walls!' called Emma sternly.

'Not her walls,' he mumbled. It took him forever to wash his hands, and when he was back only his palms were clean. He stared with disgust at the soup and sandwiches Emma had prepared.

'Eat up, Bart, or you'll fade away to nothing,' said Emma.

Already I was on my second sandwich, my second bowl of home-made vegetable soup, and ready for dessert while Bart still nibbled on one half of his sandwich, his soup as yet untouched.

'What do you think of your new sister?' asked Emma, wiping Cindy's messy mouth, taking off the soiled bib. 'Isn't she a living doll?'

'Yeah, she's sure cute,' I agreed.

'Cindy's not our sister!' flared Bart. 'She's just another messy little baby that nobody but our mother would want!'

'Bartholomew Winslow . . . don't you ever let me hear you talk like that again.' Emma gave him a long chastising look. 'Cindy is a lovely child who resembles your mother so much she could be her own daughter.'

Bart continued to scowl at Cindy, at me, at Emma, even at the wall. 'Hate blonde hair and red lips that are wet all the time,' he mumbled under his breath before he stuck out his tongue at Cindy who laughed. 'If Momma didn't fuss around with her so much, curling her hair and buying her new clothes, she'd be ugly.'

'Cindy will never be ugly,' denied Emma, looking at the little girl with admiration. Then she leaned to kiss the child's pretty small face.

That kiss drew another of Bart's darkest frowns.

I sat there, up-tight, frightened. Each morning I woke up knowing I'd have to face a brother who was growing more and more strange. And I loved him; I loved my parents, and darn if I wasn't beginning to love Cindy too. Somehow I knew I had to protect everyone – but from what I didn't know, or couldn't even guess.

CHANGELING CHILD *Bart*

Drat Jory and Emma, I was thinking as I slipped through the hot Arizona desert. Good thing I had Apple to love me as well as my grandmother, or I'd be in a sorry state. There stood my lady in black with her arms wide open to welcome me and I was kissed and hugged much more than Cindy ever was.

She served me a bowl of soup. It was so good, with cheese on top. 'Why can't I tell my parents how much I like you, and how much you love me? That would be so neat.' I didn't tell her I thought she wasn't really my own true grandmother, but only said that to please me. In a way that made her love better, for families had to love each other. Strangers didn't.

Square in the middle of one of her tables she put a large dumptruck before she answered my question. Odd she seemed so sad, and in a way scared, when a moment ago she'd seemed happy enough.

'Your parents hate me now, Bart,' she whispered thinly. 'Please don't tell them anything about me. Keep me your secret.'

My eyes widened. 'Did you know them once?'

'Yes, a long, long time ago, when they were very young.'

Gee. 'What did you do to make them hate you?' Everybody hated me, almost, so I wasn't surprised someone might hate her.

Her hand reached for mine. 'Bart, sometimes even adults make mistakes. I made a terrible mistake that I'm paying for dearly. Every night I pray for God to forgive me; I pray for my children to forgive me. I find no peace when I look in a mirror, so I hide my face from myself, from others, and sit in uncomfortable rockers so I'll never forget for one second all the harm I did to those I loved most.'

'Where did your children go?'

'Have you forgotten?' she sobbed, tears in her eyes now. 'They ran away from me. Bart, that hurts so much. Don't you ever run away from your parents.'

Gosh, I hadn't intended to run. World out there was too big. Too scary. Safe, had to stay where it was safe. I ran to embrace her, then turned to play with my truck, and that's when John Amos limped into the room, his watery eyes angry.

'Madame! You do not develop strength in young children by indulging their every whim. You should know that by now!'

'John,' she said haughtily, 'don't you ever come in this room again without knocking – stay in your place.'

Tough. My grandmother was tough. I smiled at John Amos who backed away, mumbling under his breath about how she wasn't giving him any place, or not the place he deserved. I forgot him the moment he was out of sight as I fell under the spell of my enchanting new dumptruck and why it worked like it did. Soon I'd find out – and maybe my curiosity was the same thing as being mean, for everything given to me ended up broken within an hour.

My grandmother sighed and looked unhappy as my truck came apart.

Long summer days passed slowly, with John Amos teaching me lots of important things about being powerful and fearsome like Malcolm, who knew all about being sneaky and clever. In his own kind of way John Amos was fascinating, just watching him with his queer shuffling walk, his skinny legs more knobbly than mine, his whistling breath, his hissing words, his stringy moustache and bald head where one white hair grew. One day I was gonna pull it out. I wondered why my grandmother didn't like him? She was the boss, she could fire him, and yet she didn't. Something hard and mean was between them.

I was happy living between them, blessed on one side with all her nice gifts, her hugs and kisses, and on the other side John Amos, who was teaching me how to be a powerful man who could make women do his bidding. Now that I had someone who loved me for myself, no matter how mean or clumsy I was, I began to feel that special kind of magic that Momma and Jory shared. I thought I too could hear the music of sunset colours. I had Apple, my puppypony. And best of all Disneyland was waiting for me and my birthday was coming up soon.

Now that I was getting brilliant like Malcolm, I tried to figure out a way to keep Apple's love, while I went away for three weeks. It woke me up at night. Worried me all day. Who would feed Apple and steal his love while I was gone? Who?

Deep in the throes of my problems, I went back to the wall and checked on a peach pit that hadn't sprouted any roots as yet. It was supposed to be in the throes (my new vocabulary word) of growing – and it wasn't growing. Next I checked my sweetpea seeds. Dumb things were just lying there, not in the throes of anything either.

Cursed. I was cursed. I glared at the part of the garden Jory cared for. All his flowers were in full bloom. Even flowers wouldn't grow for me. I crawled to where Jory's hollyhocks grew. My knees crushed petunias, squashed portulaca. What would Malcolm do if he was me? He's rip up all Jory's flowers, dig holes with his thumbs in his own garden, and stick in the blossoms.

One by one I filled my thumb holes with Jory's hollyhocks. They refused to stand up straight, but I arranged them so they could lean against one another – and now I had blooming flowers in my garden too. Clever. Devious and smart too.

Glanced down at my filthy knees and saw I'd ripped my new pants on the doghouse I'd started building for Clover. It was my way of asking forgiveness for tripping over him so often. Right now he was up on that veranda keeping a keen eye on me, afraid to sleep while I was in sight. I didn't need his love now. Once I had, but now I had a better pet.

Bugs were biting my face. I rubbed at my eyes, not caring if my hands were covered with grease from fooling around in my dad's garage workshop. Emma wouldn't like seeing my new white tanktop that had grease all over, and even Momma couldn't repair the nailrip from neck to shirt-tail. I chewed on my lip thoughtfully.

Saturdays were for having fun and I wasn't having any. Nothing special to do like Jory. I wasn't born to dance, only to be dirty and have scratches. Momma had Cindy. Daddy had patients. Emma had cooking and cleaning. Nobody cared if I was bored. I threw Clover a hateful look. 'I gotta better dog than you!' I yelled. Clover backed up closer to the house, then hid under a chair. 'You're just a miniature French poodle!' I screamed. 'You don't know how to save people lost in the snow. You don't know how to wear a red saddle or eat hay either.' Every day I was giving Apple a little more hay that I mixed up in his dogfood just so he'd get to like hay better than meat.

Clover looked ashamed. He inched himself under the chair more and gave me another of his sad looks that got on my nerves. Apple never did that.

I sighed, got up, brushed off my knees, my hands. Time to visit Apple. On my way over I got distracted by the white wall which needed more texture. Picking up a stone I began to pound on the wall in order to chip off more of the white stucco. Gosh, what if this wall went on forever? It might even end up in China, keeping out the Mongol hordes. Wonder what Mongols were? Apes? Yeah, sounded like apes – mean kind of big apes that ate people who were in the 'throes' of something. Would be nice to be as huge as King Kong so I could step on things I hated.

I'd step on teachers first, schools next – and step over churches. Malcolm respected God and I didn't want to make God mad with me. I'd pluck the stars from the sky and stick them on my fingers for diamond rings, like my grandmother's. I'd wear the moon for my cap. I'd leave the sun alone for it might burn my hand – but if I picked up the Empire State Building I could use it as a bat and swat that sun right out of our universe! Then everything would go black as tar. There'd be no daytime and only forever night. Black was like being blind, or dead.

'Bart,' came a soft voice, making me jump.

'Go away!' I ordered. I was having fun all by myself. And what was she doing up on that ladder again? Spying on me? I sat on the ground again and poked at it with a stick.

'Bart,' she called again, 'Apple is waiting for you to feed him, and he needs fresh water. You promised to be a good master. Once you make an animal love and trust you, you are obligated to it.'

Today her eyes weren't covered over, the veil only covered from her nose downwards. 'I want cowboy boots, a new genuine cowboy saddle of real leather, not fake, and a hat, buckskins, chaps, spurs, and beans to cook over campfires.'

'What is that you just dug up?' She poked her head up higher to see better. She looked funny, like a head on the wall with no body underneath.

Gosh . . . look what was buried in the dirt. Dead bones. Where had the fur gone? And the soft white ears?

I began to tremble, very scared as I tried to explain. 'Tiger. There I was helpless the other night, wearing only my pyjamas when out of the dark came this man-eating tiger with the green eyes. He snarled then jumped me. He meant to eat me. But I grabbed up my rifle in the nick of time and shot him through his eye!'

Silence. Silence meant she didn't believe me. Pity was in her voice when she spoke. 'Bart, that's not the skeleton of a tiger. I see a bit of the fur. Is that the kitten I used to have? The stray one I took in and cared for? Bart, why did you kill my kitten?'

'No!' I yelled. 'I wouldn't kill a kitty! Wouldn't ever do that! I like kitties. This is a tiger, a not so big one. Old bones been here a mighty long time, way before I was born.' Yet, they looked like kitty bones, they did. I rubbed at my eyes so she wouldn't see the tears.

Malcolm wouldn't cry like this. He'd be tough. Didn't know what to do. Old John Amos over there kept telling me to be like Malcolm, and hate all women. I decided it was better to act like Malcolm than like me who was a sorry thing. Wasn't no good trying to be King Kong, Tarzan, or even Superman. Being

Malcolm was better, for I had his book of instructions on how to do it right.

'Bart, it's growing very late. Apple is hungry and waiting for you.'

Tired, so tired. 'I'm coming,' I said wearily. Gee, pretending to be an old man was tiring. Bad to act so old, better to be a boy again. Old meant no time from work and trying to make money with no fun at all. Took all my time getting there now that I made my legs walk slow. Foggy all around. Summer wasn't so hot when you were old. *Momma, Momma, where are you? Why don't you come when I need you? When I call why don't you answer? Don't you love me any more, Momma? Momma, why aren't you helping me?*

I stumbled on, trying to think. Then I found the answer. Nobody could like me, for I didn't belong here, and I didn't belong there. I didn't belong anywhere.

PART TWO

TALES OF EVIL *Jory*

I gobbled down my bacon, scrambled eggs with sour cream and chives, and a third slice of toast as Bart nibbled on and on as if he didn't have any teeth at all. His toast grew cold – waiting for Bart to sip orange juice as if it were poison. An old man on his death bed could have had more appetite.

He shot a hostile glance my way before he fixed his eyes on Mom. I was jolted. I knew he loved her – how could he look like that?

Something weird was going on in Bart's head. Where was the shy, introverted little brother I used to have? Gradually he was changing into an aggressive, suspicious, cruel boy. Now he was staring at Dad as if he'd done something wrong – but it was Mom who drew most of his scathing looks.

Didn't he know we had the best mother alive? I wanted to shout this out, make him go back to the way he used to be, mumbling to himself as he stumbled around hunting big game, fighting wars, riding herd on cattle. Where had all his love and admiration for Mom gone? Soon as I had the chance I backed Bart up against the garden wall. 'What the heck is wrong with you, Bart? Why do you look so mean at Mom?'

'Don't like her no more.' He crouched over, put out his arms horizontally and turned himself into a human aeroplane. That was normal for Bart. 'Clear the way!' he ordered. 'Make way for the jet taking off for far-away places! It's kangaroo shootin' time in Australia!'

'Bart Sheffield, why do you always want to kill something?'

His wings fluttered; his plane stalled; his engine died and he was staring at me in confusion. The sweet child he'd been at the beginning of summer came fleetingly to his dark brown eyes. 'I'm not gonna kill real kangaroos. Just gonna capture one of those little ones and put it in my pocket and wait for it to grow big.'

Dumb. Dumb! 'First of all you don't have a pocket with a nipple for the baby to suck.' I sat him down hard on a bench. 'Listen, it's time you and I had a man-to-man talk. What's troubling you, fella?'

'In a big bright house setting on a high-high hill, while the night was on and the snow came down, the flames of red and yellow shot up higher, higher! Snowflakes turned pink. And in that big old house was an old-old lady who couldn't walk and couldn't talk and my real daddy who was an attorney ran to save her! He couldn't – and he burned – burned – burned!'

Spooky. Crazy! I pitied him. 'Bart,' I began carefully, 'You know that isn't the way Daddy Paul died.' Why had I put it like that? Bart had been born only a few years before Daddy Paul died. How many years? Almost I could remember my thoughts back then. I could ask Momma, but somehow I didn't want to trouble her more, so I led Bart towards our house. 'Bart, your real daddy died while he was sitting on his front veranda reading the newspaper. He didn't die in a fire. He had heart trouble that led to a coronary thrombosis. Dad told us all that, remember?'

I watched his brown eyes grow darker, his pupils dilated before he raged with a terrible temper: 'I don't mean that Daddy! Talking about my *real* Daddy! A big strong lawyer Daddy who never had a bad heart!'

'Bart, who told you that lie?'

'Burning!' he screamed, whirling around like a man blinded by smoke as he tried to find his way outside. 'John Amos told me how it was! All the world was on fire, one Christmas night when the tree burned up. People screamed, ran, stepped on the ones who fell down – and the biggest, grandest house of them all snared my true father so he died, died, died!'

Boy, I'd heard enough. I was going straight into the house and telling my parents. 'Bart, you hear this. Unless you stop going next door and listening to lies and crazy stories I'm telling Mom and Dad about you – and them next door.'

He had his eyes squinted shut, as if trying to see some scene scorched on his brain. He seemed to be looking inwards as he described it in more detail to me. Then his dark eyes flew wide open. His look was wild and crazy. 'Mind your own damn business, Jory Marquet, if you don't want yours.' He swooped to pick up a discarded baseball bat, then took a wild swing that might have splattered my brains if I hadn't ducked. 'You tell on me and grandmother and I'll kill you while you sleep.' He said it loud, cold and flat, his eyes challenging mine.

Swallowing, I felt fear raise the hackles on my neck. Was I scared of him? No. I couldn't be. As I watched, he suddenly lost his bravado and began to gasp and clutch at his heart. I smiled, knowing his secret, this way of backing out of a real encounter. 'All right, Bart,' I said coldly, 'now I'm going to let you have it. I'm going next door and I am going to speak to those old people who fill your head with garbage.'

His old man act was quickly abandoned. His lips gaped apart. He stared at me pleadingly, but I whirled on my heel and strode off, never thinking he'd do anything. Wham! Down flat on my face I fell with a weight on my back. Bart had tackled me. Before I could congratulate him for being fast and accurate for a change, he began to pummel my face with his fists.

'You won't look so pretty when I finish.' I warded him off as best I could before I noticed he was delivering his blows with his eyes squeezed shut, punching blindly, childishly, sobbing as he did. And I swear, as much as I wanted to I couldn't punch my kid brother.

'Got you scared, huh?' He pulled back his upper lip and snarled, looking pleased with himself. 'Guess you know now who's boss, huh? Ain't got nearly the guts you thought you had, do you?'

I shoved him hard – he fell backwards, but darn if I could fight a baby like him, who was strong only when he was angry. 'You need a good spanking, Bart Sheffield, and I might be just the one to give it to you. The next time you pull any stunt on me think twice – or you might be the one left without guts.'

'You're not my brother,' he sobbed, all the fight gone out of him, 'you're only a half brother and that's as good as none.' He choked on his own emotions and ground his fists into his eyes as he wailed louder.

'You see! That old woman is putting nutty ideas in your head – and one thing you don't need is more nuts in the belfry. She's turning you against your own family – and I'm going to tell her exactly that.'

'Don't you dare!' He shrieked, his tears gone, his rage back. 'I'll do something terrible. I will, I swear I will! If you go you'll be sorry.'

My smile was wry. 'You and who else is gonna make me sorry?'

'I know what you want,' he said, all child again, 'you want my puppypony. But he won't like you, he won't. You want my grandmother to love you more, but she won't! You want to take everything from me – but you can't.'

I felt sorry for him, but I'd neglected my duty long enough. 'Aw, go suck your baby bottle!' and with that I was off. He screamed behind me, yelling out how he'd make me sorry by hurting something that couldn't fight back. 'And you'll cry, Jory!' he warned, 'you'll cry more than you have before!'

The road was dappled with sunlight and shadows, and soon enough Bart and his temper were far behind me. The sun burned down hot on top my head, and behind me little feet came running. I turned to see Clover racing to catch up. Waiting, I knelt to catch him as he leaped into my arms, licking my face with the same devoted adoration he'd given me since I was three.

Three years old. I remembered where Mom and I had lived then, in the Blue Ridge Mountains of Virginia, in a little cottage nestled down near the mountains. I remembered a tall man with dark eyes had given me not only Clover, but a cat named Calico, and a parakeet we called Buttercup too. Calico had roamed off in the night and never came back. And Buttercup had died when I was seven.

'Would you like to be my son?' I heard the man's voice in my memory. That man who was called . . . what was his name? Bart? Bart Winslow? Oh, golly, was I just beginning to understand something that had slipped over my head until now? Was my half-brother Bart the son of that man, and not Daddy Paul? If not, why would Mom name her baby for a man not her husband?

'You gotta go back home now, Clover,' I said, and he seemed to understand. 'You're eleven years old and not up to frisking around in the noonday sun. Go back and find your favourite cool place and wait for me, okay?'

Wagging his tail, he turned obediently and headed home, looking back often to see if I'd turn away and he could follow again. I watched until he was out of sight around the bend in the road. Then I headed once more for the huge old mansion. In my head the distant past beat like muffled drums, reminding me of events I'd forgotten. The ballet on Christmas Eve night, and the handsome man who gave me my first electric train. I shut off memories, wanting to keep my mother sacred, my love for Daddy Paul intact, my respect for Chris intact too. No, I wasn't going to let myself remember too much.

Lovers came and went in everyone's life, I told myself, if ballets were just true stories exaggerated a bit. And like my Dad would, I strode boldly up to the iron fence and demanded into the box to be let in. The iron gates swung silently open, like jail bars to beckon me forward. I almost ran up the curving drive until I was before the double front doors, and there I jabbed at the doorbell, then banged the brass knocker as loud as I could.

Impatiently I waited for that crotchety old butler to show up. Behind me the iron gates had closed. I felt like I was walking into a trap. Gee, just like Bart and his imagination, I used my ballet background to write this script. I felt like some wretched unwanted prince who didn't possess the magic password. Only Bart knew that.

Confusion and regrets brewed and unsettled my determination. This didn't seem the castle of some wicked fairy queen, only the big outdated home of a lonely old woman who needed Bart just as much as he needed her. But she couldn't be his grandmother, she just couldn't be. That grandmother was way back in Virginia, locked up for something terrible she'd done once.

Quiet was all around me, smothering me, making me feel old. My home was full of noises from the kitchen, music, Clover barking, Cindy squealing, Bart shouting, and Emma bossing. Not even a squeak came from this house. Nervously I shuffled my feet about, thinking I might give up my idea of confronting her. Then I glimpsed a dark shadow behind one of the windows draped with sheer curtains. I shivered. Almost left. But just then the door opened a crack, enough to allow the butler to put a squinty watery eye to the slit. 'You can enter,' he said inhospitably, 'but don't you stay too long. Our lady is frail and tires easily.'

I asked her name, tired of thinking of her as old woman, or woman in black. My request was ignored. The butler intrigued me with his shuffling gait, his suggestion of a limp, his ebony cane that tapped on the hard parquet, his bald pate that was pink and shiny. His thin white moustache hung in long strands on either side of his grim lips. But as old as he was, and as weak as he appeared, he still managed to convey a scarey, sinister air.

He beckoned me onwards, but I hesitated. Then he smiled cynically, showing his too large, too even and too yellow teeth. I squared my shoulders and followed him bravely, thinking I could set everything straight and our lives would be as happy as they'd been before they came to live in this house that used to be ours alone.

I didn't know suspicions were in my head. I thought it was only curiosity.

The room she always used surprised me again. Though I couldn't say exactly why. Maybe it was because she kept her curtains drawn together on such a beautiful summer day. Behind the curtains, the shutters were closed, making bars of light on the window covering. The shutters and the curtains held the heat outside at bay, making her parlour unexpectedly chill. There was no real need for air-conditioning in our area. The nearby Pacific kept our weather cool, making sweaters in the evenings a real necessity, even in the middle of summer. But this house was unnaturally cold.

Again she was in that wooden rocker staring at me. Her thin hand made some welcoming gesture to draw me closer. I knew instinctively she was a threat to my parents, to my own security, and most of all to Bart's mind.

'You don't have to be afraid of me, Jory,' she said in a sweet voice. 'My home belongs to you as much as to Bart. I will always welcome you here. Sit down and chat for a while. Will you share a cup of tea with me, and a slice of cake?'

'Beguiled' was our word yesterday to add to our growing vocabulary Daddy insisted upon. 'The world belongs to those who know how to speak well, and fortunes are made by those who write well,' he'd said. And I admit, she beguiled me, that woman in her hard rocker, sitting so old and yet so proud. 'Why don't you open your shutters, pull your curtains and let in some light and air?' I asked.

Her nervous gestures brought into play the sparkling rays of the many gems she wore. Rubies, emeralds and diamonds on her fingers, each colour spectrum trying to enchant me more. Her jewels seemed so out of place when she had to wear that plain black dress, and cover her head with several layers of black chiffon – but today her eyes were revealed, her blue-blue eyes. Such familiar blue eyes.

'Too much light hurts my eyes,' she explained in a faint husky whisper when I kept staring.

'Why?'

'Why does the light hurt my eyes?'

'Yes.'

Her sigh was small. 'For a long time I lived locked away from the world, shut up in a small room, but even worse than that, locked up within myself. When you are forced to encounter yourself for the first time in your life, you draw back from the shock. I recoiled when first I looked deep into myself, staring into a mirror they had in my room, and I was frightened. So now I live in rooms full of mirrors but I cover my face so I can't see too much. I keep my rooms dim as I no longer admire the face I used to adore.

'Then take down the mirrors.'

'How easy you make it. But you are young. The young always think everything is easy. I don't want to take down the mirrors. I want them there to remind me constantly of what I've done. The closed windows, the stuffy atmosphere are my punishments, not yours. If you want, Jory,' she went on as I sat silently, 'open the windows, spread the shutters; let in the sunlight and I will take off my veils and let you look at the face I hide from, but you won't find it pleasant. My beauty is gone but it is a small loss compared to everything else that has come and gone, all the things I should have held on to valiantly.'

'Valiantly?' I asked. That was a word not too familiar to me in any meaningful way, just a word suggesting bravery.

'Yes, Jory, valiantly I should have protected what was mine. I was all they had, and I let them down. I thought I was right, they were wrong. I convinced myself each day I was right. I resisted their pitiful pleas, and even worse, at the time I didn't even think they were pitiful. I told myself I was doing all I could because I brought them everything. They grew to distrust me, dislike me, and that hurt, hurt more than any pain I've ever felt. I hate myself for being weak, so cowardly, so foolishly intimidated when I should have stood my ground and fought back. I should have thought only of them and forgotten what I wanted for myself. My only excuse is that I was young then, and the young are selfish, even when it comes to their own children. I thought my needs were greater than theirs. I thought their time would come and then they could have their way, I felt it was my last chance at happiness. I had to grab for it quick, before middle-age made me unattractive, and there was a younger man I loved. I couldn't tell him about them.'

Them? Who was she talking about?

'Who?' I asked weakly, for some reason wishing she wouldn't tell me anything – or at least not too much.

'My children, Jory. My four children, fathered by my first husband whom I married when I was only eighteen. He was forbidden to me, and yet I wanted him. I thought I would never find a man more wonderful . . . and yet I did find one just as wonderful.'

I got up to leave. I'd said what I came to say. I didn't want to hear her story. She pleaded for me to stay. I sat again on the edge of one of her fine chairs.

'So,' she continued, 'I put my fear out in front, allowed my love for a man to blind me to their needs, and I ignored what they wanted – their freedom – and now, as the result, I cry myself to sleep every night.'

What could I say? I didn't understand what she was talking about. I reasoned she must be crazy, and no wonder Bart was acting just as nutty. She leaned forward to peer at me more closely.

'You are an exceptionally handsome boy. I suppose you know that already.'

I nodded. All my life I'd heard remarks about my good looks, my talent, my charm. But talent was what counted, not looks. In my opinion looks without talent were useless. I knew too that beauty faded with the passing years, but still I loved beauty.

Looking around I saw this woman loved beauty as much as I did, and yet . . . 'What a pity she sits in the dark and refuses to enjoy all that's been done to make this place beautiful,' I murmured without thought.

She heard and replied tonelessly, 'The better to punish myself.'

I didn't reply, only sat on in the chair while she rambled on and on about her life as a poor little rich girl who made the mistake of falling in love with her half-uncle who was three years older, and for this she was disinherited. Why was she telling me her life history? I didn't care. What did her past have to do with Bart? He was my reason for being here.

'I married for a second time. My four children hated me for doing that.' She stared down at her hands folded on her lap, then began to twist the sparkling gems one by one. 'Children always think adults have it so easy. That's not always true. Children think a widowed mother doesn't need anyone but them.' She sighed. 'They think they can give her enough love, because they don't understand there are all kinds of love, and it's hard for a woman to live without a man once she's been married.'

Then almost as if she'd forgotten me, she interrupted herself, 'Oh! I've been a poor hostess. Jory, what would you like to eat and drink?'

'Nothing, thank you. I came only to tell you that you must not encourage Bart to come over here any more. I don't know what you tell him, or what he does here, but he comes home with weird ideas, and acting very disoriented.'

'Disoriented? You use large words for a boy so young.'

'My father insists we learn one new word each day.'

Those nervous hands of hers flitted up to her throat to play with her string of large pearls with a diamond butterfly clasp. 'Jory, if I ask you a hypothetical question, would you give me an answer – a truthful answer?'

I got up to go. 'I'd rather not answer questions . . .'

'If your mother, or your father ever disappointed you, failed you in some way, even a major way – could you find it in your heart to forgive them?'

Sure, sure, I thought quickly enough, though I couldn't imagine them ever failing me, Bart or Cindy. I backed to the door that would allow me to leave while she was waiting for my answer. 'Yes, Madame. I think I could forgive them anything.'

'Murder?' she asked quickly, standing too. 'Could you forgive them for that – not premeditated murder, but accidental?'

She was crazy! Just like her butler. I wanted to get out of there and fast. I cautioned her one more time to send my brother home. 'If you want Bart to stay sane, leave him alone!'

Her eyes filled with tears before she nodded and inclined her head. I'd hurt her, I knew that. I had to harden my heart not to say I was sorry. Then, just as I was leaving, a delivery man was banging on the door, and I opened it to allow him to carry in a huge oblong crate. It took two men to rip off the nailed cover.

'Don't go, Jory,' she begged. 'Stay! I'd like you to see what's inside this crate.'

What difference did it make? But I stayed, having the same curiosity as most people about the contents of a closed box.

The old butler came tapping down the hall but she shooed him away. 'John! I didn't ring for you. Please stay in your part of the house until you're sent for.'

He gave her a smouldering look of resentment and hobbled into his hole, wherever that was.

By this time the crate was open, and the two men were pulling out packing straw. Then they lifted a huge thing wrapped in a grey quilt from its nest in the crate.

It was like waiting for a ship to be launched. I grew sort of breathless in anticipation, even more so because she had such a look on her face . . . as if she couldn't wait for me to see the contents. Was she giving me a gift, like she gave Bart anything he wanted? He was the greediest little boy ever born, needing double the amount of affection most people required.

I gasped then and stepped backwards.

It was an oil painting the men unwrapped.

There stood my beautiful mother in a formal white gown, pausing on the next to the bottom step, with her slender hand resting on a magnificent newel post. Trailing behind her lay yards and yards of the shimmering white fabric. The curving stairs behind her rose gracefully and faded into swirling mists through which the artist had cleverly managed to give the impression of gold and glittering jewels, hinting at a palace-like mansion.

'Do you know whose portrait that it?' she asked when the men had it hung in place, in one of the parlours she didn't seem to use often. I nodded, dumbfounded and speechless.

What was she doing with my mother's portrait?

She waited for the two men to go. They smiled, thrilled with the tip she gave them. I was panting, hearing my heavy breathing and wondering why I felt sort of numb. 'Jory,' she said softly, turning again to me, 'that's a portrait of me my second husband commissioned shortly after we were married. When we moved to Greenglenna, South Carolina, to his family home, he sent for the portrait, and it hung in our living-room there. I was thirty-seven when I posed for that.'

In the portrait the woman looked just like my mother looked today. I swallowed and wanted to run, suddenly needing the bathroom badly, but still I wanted to stay, I wanted to hear her explain, even though I was paralysed with the fear of what she might tell me.

'My second husband who was younger was named Bartholomew Winslow, Jory,' she said quickly as if to make sure I heard before I got up and ran. 'Later on, when my daughter was old enough, she seduced him, stole his love away from me, just so she could hurt me with the child she gave him. The child I couldn't have. Can you guess who that child is, can you?'

I jumped up and backed away. Holding out my hands to ward off any more information I didn't want to hear.

'Jory, Jory, Jory,' she chanted, 'don't you remember me at all? Think back to when you lived in the mountains of Virginia. Think of that little post office, and the rich lady in the fur coat. You were about three then. You saw me and smiling, you came to stroke my coat, and you told me I was pretty – remember?'

'No!' I cried more stoutly than I felt. 'I have never seen you before in my life, not until you moved here. All blondes with blue eyes look somewhat alike.'

'Yes,' she said brokenly, 'I suppose you're right. I just thought it would be amusing to see your expression. I shouldn't have played a trick on you. I'm sorry, Jory. Forgive me.

I couldn't look in those blue-blue eyes. I had to get away.

I felt miserable as I slowly trudged home. If only I hadn't stayed. If only the portrait hadn't been delivered while I was there. Why did I have to sense that woman was more a threat to my mother than to my stepfather? What had I accomplished? Was it you, Mom, who stole her second husband's love? Was it? Didn't it make good sense when Bart had the same name as him? Everything she'd said confirmed the suspicions that had been sleeping in my mind for so many years. Doors were opening, letting in a fresh assault of memories that almost seemed like enemies.

I climbed the stairs of the veranda Mom jokingly called 'Paul's kind of southern veranda.' Certainly it wasn't the customary California patio.

There was something different about the patio today. If I had been less troubled, perhaps I would have spotted immediately what was missing. As it was it took me minutes to realize. Clover wasn't there. I looked around, distressed, calling him.

'For heaven's sake, Jory,' called Emma from the kitchen window, 'Don't yell so loud. I just put Cindy down for a nap and you'll wake her up. I saw Clover a few minutes ago heading into the garden, chasing a butterfly.

Of course. I felt relieved. If one thing brought out the puppy in my old poodle, it was a fluttery yellow butterfly. I joined Emma in the kitchen and asked, 'Emma, I've been wanting to ask for a long time, what year did Mom marry Dr Paul?'

She was leaning over, checking inside the refrigerator, grumbling to herself. 'I could swear there was some fried chicken in here, left over from last night. Since we're having liver and onions tonight I saved what was left of the chicken for Bart. I thought your finicky brother could eat the leftover thighs.'

'Don't you remember the year they were married?'

'You were just a little one then,' she said, still rummaging through covered dishes.

Emma was always vague about dates. She couldn't remember her own birthday. Maybe deliberately. 'Tell me again how my mother met Dr Paul's younger brother . . . you know, the stepfather we have now.'

'Yes, I remember Chris then, he was so handsome, tall and

tan. But not one bit better looking than Dr Paul was in his own way . . . a wonderful man, your stepfather Paul, so kind, so soft-spoken.'

'It's funny Mom didn't fall for a younger brother instead of an older one – don't you think it's odd?'

She straightened and put a hand to her back which she said hurt all the time. Next she wiped her hands on her spotless white apron. 'I sure hope your parents aren't late tonight. You run and hunt up Bart before it's too late for him to take a bath. I hate for your mother to see him so filthy.'

'Emma, you haven't answered my questions!'

Turning her back she began to chop green bellpeppers. 'Jory, when you need answers, you go to your parents and ask. Don't come to me. You may think of me as a family member but I know my place is that of a friend – so run along and let me finish dinner.'

'Please, Emma, not just for my sake, but Bart's too! I've got to do something to straighten out Bart, and how can I when I don't have all the facts?'

'Jory,' she said, giving me a warm smile, 'just be happy you have two such wonderful parents. You and Bart are very lucky boys. I hope Cindy grows up to realize how blessed she was the day your mother decided she had to have a daughter.'

Outside the day was growing old. Search as I would I couldn't find Clover. I sat on the back steps and stared unhappily at the sky turning rosy with bright streaks of orange and violet. I felt overwhelmingly sad and burdened, wishing all this mystery and confusion would go away. Clover, where was Clover? I never knew until this moment how very much he added to my life, how much I'd miss him if he was gone for good. Please don't let him be gone for good, God, please.

One more time I looked around our yard, then decided I'd better go in the house and call the newspapers. I'd offer a reward for a missing dog – such a big reward somebody would bring Clover back. 'Clover!' I yelled, 'Chow time!'

My call brought Bart stumbling out of the hedges; his clothes torn and filthy. His dark eyes were strangely haunted. 'Why are you yellin'?'

'I can't find Clover,' I answered, 'and you know he never goes anywhere. He's a home dog. I read the other day about people who steal dogs and sell them to science labs for experimentation. Bart, I'd want to die if somebody did something so awful to Clover.'

He stared at me, stricken looking. 'They wouldn't do that . . . would they?'

'Bart, I've got to find Clover. If he doesn't come back soon, I'll feel sick, really sick enough to die too. Suppose he's been run over?'

I watched my brother swallow then begin to tremble. 'What's wrong?'

'Shot me a wolf back there, I did. Shot me a big bad wolf right through his mean red eye. He came at me lickin' his chops, but I was smarter and moved quick and shot him dead.'

'Oh, come off it, Bart!' I said impatiently, really getting irritated with somebody who could never tell the truth. 'There aren't any wolves in this area, and you know it.'

Until midnight I searched all around our neighbourhood, calling for Clover. Tears kept clogging my voice, my eyes. I had the worst premonition that Clover would never come home again.

'Jory,' said Dad who'd been helping me hunt, 'let's hit the sack and look again in the morning if he doesn't come home by himself. And don't you lie in your bed and worry. Clover may be an old dog, but even the elderly can feel romantic on a moonlit night.'

Aw heck. That didn't make much sense. Clover had stopped chasing female dogs a long time ago. Now all he wanted was a place to lie where Bart wasn't likely to stumble over him, or step on his tail.

'You go to bed, Dad, and let me look. I don't have to be in ballet class until ten, so I don't need my sleep as much as you do.'

He briefly embraced me, wished me luck, and headed for his room. An hour later, I decided it was fruitless effort. Clover was dead. That's the only thing that would keep him away.

I decided I had to tell my parents what I suspected.

I stood beside their bed looking down at them. Moonlight streamed through the windows and fell over their bodies. Mom was half-turned on her side so she could cuddle up close to Dad who was on his back. Her head was on his bare chest, while his left arm encircled her so his hand lay on her hip. The covers were pulled up just high enough to shield their nudity which made me back away, feeling very guilty. I shouldn't be here. Sleep made them look vulnerable, younger, moving me but giving me a deep sense of shame too. I wondered why I felt ashamed. Dad had taught me the facts of life a long time ago, so I knew what men and women did together to make babies or just for fun.

I sobbed and turned to go.

'Chris, is that you?' asked my mother, half-asleep and rolling over on her back.

'I'm here, darling. Go back to sleep,' he mumbled sleepily, 'the grandmother can't get us now.'

I froze, startled. What a strange thing to say. They both sounded like children. And that grandmother again.

'I'm scared, Chris, so afraid. If they ever find out what will we say? How can we explain?'

'Sssh,' came his whisper, 'life will be good to us from now on. Hold fast to your faith in God. We have both been punished enough, he won't punish us more.'

Run, run. I had to run fast to my room and hurl myself down. I felt hollow inside, emptiness all around instead of the confidence and love I used to feel here. Clover was gone. My dear little harmless poodle who had never done even one bad thing. And Bart had shot a wolf.

What would Bart do next? Did he know what I did? Was that why he was behaving so strangely, turning his mean glare on Mom like he wanted to hurt her? Tears rose in my eyes again, for memory couldn't be denied forever. I knew now that Bart was not the son of Dr Paul. Bart was the son of that old lady's second husband with the same name as my half brother – that tall lean man who sometimes haunted my dreams along with Dr Paul and my own real father whom I'd only seen in photographs.

Our parents had lied to both of us. Why hadn't they told us the truth? Was the truth so ugly they couldn't tell us? Did they have such little faith in our love for them?

Oh God, their secret must be something so dreadful we could never forgive them!

And Bart, he could be dangerous, I knew he could be. Day by day it was beginning to show more and more. In the morning I wanted to run up to Mom, to Dad and tell them. But when morning came I couldn't say anything. Now I knew why Dad insisted that we learn one new word each day. It took special words to put across subtle ideas, and as yet I wasn't as educated as I needed to be to express my troubled thoughts that wanted to reassure them. And how could I reassure them when Bart was before me, his dark eyes hard and mean?

Oh, God, if you're up there somewhere, looking down, hear my prayer. Let my parents have the peace they need so they don't have to dream of evil grandmothers at night. Right or wrong, whatever they've done, I know they've done the best they could.

Why did I put it like that?

Safe was a word that no longer had substance. Like dead people who were only shadows in my memory, nothing as concrete as Bart's hate that was growing larger day by day.

LESSONS *Bart*

July. My month. 'Conceived in fire, born in heat,' said John Amos when I told him it would soon be my tenth birthday. Didn't know what he meant and didn't care either. Disneyland would see me in a few days. Hip-hip-hooray! Drat Jory for not looking happy, spoiling my fun with his long sad face just because some silly little old dog wouldn't come home when he called.

I was making plans that would see Apple through until I could steal back to him after seeing Disneyland. John Amos grabbed me when I went over, and hauled me up to his room. I looked around, thinking it smelled sour and old, like medicine.

'Bart, you sit down in that chair and read aloud to me from Malcolm's journal. For the Lord will punish you if you say you're reading his book, when you are not.'

I didn't need John Amos as much as I used to, so I looked at him with scorn. With the kind of scorn Malcolm would show for a bent and lame old man who couldn't speak without hissing, whistling, or spitting. But I sat and I read from Malcolm's red journal:

> My youth had been squandered in earthy pleasures, and as I approached thirty I realized what was missing in my life was a purpose other than money. Religion, I needed religion, and redemption for all my sins, for despite the vows of my childhood, I had regressed into desiring women, and the more wicked they were, the more they seemed to please me. There was no sight more pleasurable to me than to see some haughty beautiful woman, humbled and made to do obscene things that went against the rules of decency. I took pleasure in beating them, putting red welts on their fair unbroken skins. I

saw blood, their blood and it made me excited. That's when I knew I needed God. I had to save my everlasting soul from hell.

I looked up, tired of trying to figure out all those long words that didn't mean much to me. Except I sure was learning how women could corrupt men.

'Do you see what Malcolm is telling you, boy? He's telling you no matter how much you hate women, still there is pleasure to be had from them – but at a cost, boy, at a dear, dear cost. Unfortunately God built into mankind sensual desires – you must try to smother yours as you approach manhood. Plant it in your mind so deep it can never be removed – women will be your destruction in the end. I know. They have destroyed me and kept me a servant when I could have been far more.'

I got up and walked away, sick of John Amos. I was going to my grandmother who loved me more than God ever would. More than anyone ever would! She loved me for myself. She loved me so much she even made up lies, like me, to tell me she was my own true grandmother when I knew that just couldn't be so.

Saturday was the best day of the week. My stepfather stayed home and made Momma happy. She hired some dumb assistant to help out on Saturdays in her ballet class now that she had to spend so much time dolling up Cindy – like anybody cared how she looked. Jory had to go to ballet class on Saturdays too so he could see his stupid girlfriend. By noon he'd be home to mess up all my plans. Had lots of plans to fill my time. Take care of Apple. Sit on my grandmother's lap and let her sing to me. Why, mornings could pass quicker than a wink with all I had to do.

John Amos gave me more lessons on how to be like Malcolm, and darn if it wasn't working. I was feeling his power growing bigger and stronger.

That afternoon Cindy was in a brand new plastic swimming pool. The old one wasn't good enough for her. Bratty kid had to have everything new, even a bathing suit with red and white stripes, and little red straps that tied over her shoulders to keep the thing up. Little bows she was trying to undo!

Jory jumped up and rushed into the house for his camera, then ran back to take Cindy's picture. He tossed the camera to Momma who caught it. 'Take my picture with Cindy,' he said.

Sure, she was happy to take his picture with Cindy. Didn't bother to ask about me. Maybe once too often I'd made a face, ducked my head, or stuck out my tongue. Everyone was always saying Bart sure did know how to ruin a perfectly good shot.

Dratted bushes were all around me, scratching my legs, arms. Bugs crawled on me. I slapped at them as I narrowed my eyes to see that sissy girl splashing the water, having more fun than I ever had in a pool.

When they tried to take me East from Disneyland, I'd sneak away and catch a ride and come home and take care of Apple – that's what Malcolm would do. Dead people wouldn't miss me. They wouldn't care if I wasn't there to put flowers on their graves. Jory's nasty grandmother would be glad I wasn't there.

I ran to where I could climb the tree, the wall, and on to the barn to visit with Apple who was growing huge. I shoved a doggy biscuit in Apple's mouth. It vanished in a second. He jumped and made me fall down. 'Now you eat this carrot so it will be like a toothbrush to clean your teeth.' Apple sniffed at the carrot, wagged his tail. Then he jumped and swiped at the carrot with his paw. Apple still didn't know how to play pony games at all.

Soon I had Apple hitched up to my new pony cart and we flew all over the place! 'Giddy-up!' I yelled. 'Catch those rustlers over yonder! Run faster, you durn horse, if yer gonna get me home before chow is served!' I saw a movement in the hills. Twisted 'round and spied Indians comin' lickity-split – scalpin' Indians! Indians gave us a mad chase until we lost them in the hills that soon became a desert. Tired and thirsty my mount and I looked for an oasis. Saw a mirage.

There she was, the woman of the oasis mirage. Wearing her fluttering black rags, her bare feet sandy, glad to welcome us both back to the land of the livin' . . .

'Water,' I gasped. 'Need cold clear water.' I sprawled in a fancy chair and spread out my long thin legs that ended in dusty, worn boots. I reached to flick sand from my chaps. 'Make it a beer,' I said to the saloon girl. She brought me beer, all foamy and brown, and cold, too cold. Hit my stomach like a rattler, making me hunch over and give her the eye. 'What's a nice girl like you doing in a rotten place like this?'

'I'm the local schoolmarm, Snapping Sam, don't you remember?' Behind her veil she cast down her eyelids, fluttered her lashes. 'But when hard times come, a lady must do what she can to survive.' She was playing my game. Nobody ever played my games with me. It felt so good to have a playmate.

I smiled, real friendly like. 'Took good care of Apple. He's so clean he can't die.'

'Darling, you play too hard. And it's not healthy to think so much about dying. Come sit on my lap and let me sing you a song.'

Nice. I liked being treated like a baby. Cosy on her soft lap, with my face on her breast, and her singing in my ears. Each rock of the chair put me more and more in a trance. I looked up and tried to see through her veils. Was I getting to love her more than Momma? I saw then her veils were attached to little combs she caught in her hair, for today she had left her hair uncovered. Most of it was silver-coloured with streaks of gold . . .

I didn't want Momma to grow old and have grey hair. Already she was leaving me each day she cared for Cindy; leaving me for others to take over. Why did Cindy have to come and spoil my life?

'More please,' I whispered when she stopped rocking. 'Do you love me more than Madame M. loves Jory?' I asked. If she said yes, much much more, I might move in.

'Does Jory's grandmother love him a great deal?' Was that envy in her voice? I felt mad, mean – and she saw this and began to cover my face with kisses, dry kisses on account of that veil.

'Granny, got to tell you somethin'.'

'Fine . . . but remember to sound your g's. Tell me anything, I've got the rest of my life to listen.' She stroked my hair back from my face and tried to make it neat.

'Two days before my birthday we're heading for Disneyland. A week there and we fly to where the graves are. Gotta visit cemeteries, buy flowers, put the flowers in the sun where they can die too. I hate graves. Hate Jory's grandmother who don't like me 'cause I can't dance.'

Again she kissed me, 'Bart – tell your parents there have been too many graves in your life. Tell them again how it unhappy it makes you feel.'

'Won't listen,' I said dully. 'They don't ask what I want like you do. They just tell me what I have to do.'

'I'm sure they'll listen if you tell them about your dreams of being dead. They'll know then they have taken you too many times into cemeteries. Just tell them the truth.'

'But . . . but . . .' I sputtered unhappily. 'I want Disneyland!'

'You tell them like I said, and I'll take care of Apple.'

I felt frantic. Once I turned the care of Apple over to anyone he'd never be all mine again. I sobbed because life was so impossible. And my plan to escape had to work, it would, it had to . . .

We rocked on and on, and she said we were on a sailing ship riding choppy waters to a beautiful island called peace. I lost my land legs, so when I reached there I couldn't stand or find my balance. She disappeared. Alone, all alone. Like on Mars – and way back on Earth, Apple was waiting for me to show up. Poor Apple. In the end he'd have to die.

I woke up, I think – where was I? Why was everyone so old? Momma . . . why have you got your face covered with black?

'Wake up, sweetheart. I think you'd better hurry home before your parents become alarmed. You've had a nice nap so you must feel better.'

Next morning I was in the yard trying to finish up that doghouse I was building for Clover. Poor Clover should have had his own house all along, and then he wouldn't have run away looking for one. From Daddy's toolshed I took a hammer, nails, saw, wood, and lugged them out into the yard. I set to. Dratted saw didn't know how to cut straight. Gonna have a crooked house. If Clover complained I'd give him a kick. I picked up my jaggedly sliced board and put in on the roof. Dratted nail! It didn't stand still, and the hammer hit my thumb. Stupid hammer didn't see my fingers. I went right on hammering. Good thing I couldn't feel little pains or I'd be crying. Then I smashed my thumb hard and it hurt. Gosh, I was feeling pain like any normal boy.

Jory dashed out of the house yelling at me: 'Why are you building a house for Clover when he's been gone two weeks? Nobody has answered our ads. He's no doubt dead by now, and if he does come home he will sleep on the foot of my bed, remember?' Dumb. Dumb, that's what he meant, and Clover might come back. Poor Clover.

I sneaked a glance and saw Jory swipe at the tears in his eyes. 'Day after tomorrow we're leaving for Disneyland, and that should make you happy,' he said hoarsely. Did it make me happy? My swollen thumb began to ache a little. Apple was gonna die from loneliness.

Then I had an idea. John Amos had told me that prayers brought about miracles, and God was up there in his heaven looking out for dumb animals down here and people too. And Daddy had always told me not to ask for things in my prayers, only blessings for other people, not myself. So, as soon as Jory was gone I threw down my hammer and raced to where I could kneel and pray for my puppypony, and for Clover too. Next I went to Apple, rolling with him on the golden grass, me laughing, him trying to whinnybark. His tongue slurped my face with wet kisses. I kissed him back. When he lifted his leg and aimed at the roses – I took off my pants and let go too. We did everything together.

It came to me then just what to do. 'Don't you worry none, Apple. I'll only spend one week in Disneyland before I come back to you. I'll hide your puppypony biscuits under the hay and leave the water tap dripping in your pail. But don't you dare eat or drink anything John Amos gives you, or my grandmother either. Don't you let anybody bribe you with goodies.'

'Time for your lessons, Bart,' called John Amos from the barn, his bald head gleaming in the sunlight. I felt captured as I lay on the hay and stared at him towering over me. He smelled old and stale.

'Are you reading Malcolm's journal faithfully?' he asked.

'Yes, sir.'

'Are you teaching yourself the ways of the Lord and saying your prayers dutifully?'

'Yes, sir.'

'Those who follow in His footsteps will be judged accordingly, as will those who don't. Let me give you an example. Once there was a beautiful young girl who was born with a silver spoon in her mouth, and she had everything money could buy – but did she appreciate all she had? No, she didn't. When she grew older she began to tempt men with her beauty. She'd flaunt her half-nakedness before their eyes. She was high and mighty, but the Lord saw and He punished her, though it took him some time. The Lord, through Malcolm, made her crawl and cry and pray for release, but Malcolm bested her in the end. Malcolm always bested everyone in the end – and so must you.'

Boy, he sure could tell boring stories. We had naked people in our garden and I wasn't tempted. I sighed, wishing he had more subjects to talk about than God and Malcolm . . . and some darn beautiful girl.

'Beware of beauty in women, Bart. Beware of the woman who shows you her body without clothes. Beware of all those women who lie in wait to do you in, and be like Malcolm, clever.'

Finally he let me go. I was glad to be done with pretending I was like Malcolm. All I had to do to feel good was to crawl sneakily on the ground, listening to the jungle noises in the dense foliage where wild animals lurked. Dangerous animals ready to gobble me down. I bolted upright! No! That couldn't be what I thought it was. Just wasn't fair for God to send a dinosaur. Taller than a skyscraper. Longer than a train. I had to jump up and run off to find Jory and tell him what we had living in our backyard.

A noise in the jungle ahead – I stopped short, gasping for breath.

Voices. Talking snakes?

'Chris, I don't care what you say. It is not necessary for you to visit her again this summer. Enough is enough. You've done what you can to help her and you can't. So forget her and concentrate on us, your family.'

I peeked around a bush. Both my parents were in the prettiest part of the garden, where the larger trees grew. Momma was on her knees, mulching the ground around the roses. Green thumb she had, and he did too.

'Cathy, must you stay a child forever?' he asked. 'Can't you ever learn to forgive and forget? Perhaps you can pretend she doesn't exist, but I can't. I keep thinking we are the only family she has left.' He pulled her to her feet then put his hand over her mouth when it opened to interrupt. 'All right, hold on to your hatred, but I'm a doctor sworn to do what I can for those in distress. Mental illnesses can be more devastating than physical ailments. I want to see her recover. I want her to leave that place – so don't glare at me and tell me again that she was never insane, that she was only pretending. She'd have to be crazy to do what she did. And for all we know the twins might never have grown tall anyway. Like Bart. He's not of normal height for a boy his age.'

Oh, wasn't I?

'Cathy, how can I feel good about myself, or anything, if I neglect my own mother?'

'All right!' stormed Momma, 'go on and visit her! Jory, Bart, Cindy and I will stay on with Madame Marisha. Or we could fly on to New York so I can visit with some old friends, until you're ready to join us again.' She gave him a crooked smile. 'That is, if you still want to join us.'

'Where else would I go but to you? Who cares if I live or die but you and our children? Cathy, think about this – the day I turn my back on my mother, will also be the day when I turn my back on all women, including you.'

She fell into his arms then and did all that mushy loving stuff I hated to see. I backed away, still on my hands and knees, wondering about what Momma had said, and why she hated his mother so much. I felt sick in my stomach. What if my grandmother next door really was my stepfather's mother and she was loving me only because she had to? What if John Amos was telling the truth?

It was so hard to figure out. Was Corrine Malcolm's real daughter like John Amos had told me? Was she the one who had 'tempted' John Amos or was that Malcolm who hated someone pretty and half-naked too. Sometimes I got confused after reading Malcolm's book. He'd skip back to his childhood, and write about his memories even after he was grown up, like his childhood was more important than his adult life. How odd, I couldn't wait to grow up.

I heard them again, coming at me. Quickly I crawled under the nearest hedges.

'I love you, Chris, as much as you love me. Sometimes I think we both love too much. I wake up at night if you're not there. I want you not to be a doctor, but a man who stays home every night. I want my sons to grow up but each day brings them nearer to learning our secret, and I'm so afraid they'll hate us and won't understand.'

'They'll understand,' he said. How could he know I would understand when I wasn't good at understanding even simple things? Much less something so bad it woke Momma up at night.

'Cathy, have we been bad parents? Haven't we done the best we could? After living with us from their childhood, how can they help but understand? We'll tell them how it was, give them all the facts, so they will see it as we lived it, and in so doing, they'll wonder, as I often wonder, how we survived without losing our minds.'

Oh, John Amos was right! They had to be sinning or they wouldn't be so afraid we wouldn't understand! And what secret? Whatever were they hiding?

I stayed under the hedges long after my parents went into the house. I had favourite caves I'd made deep in the hedges, and when I was inside them, I felt like some small animal of the woods, scared of everything human that would kill me if possible.

Malcolm was on my mind, him and his brain that was so wise and cunning. I thought of John Amos who was teaching me about God, the Bible and sinning – but it wasn't until I thought of Apple and my grandmother that I felt good. Not real good, only a little good.

'Jory! Bart!' called Momma from the open kitchen door. 'Dinnertime!'

I fell on the ground and began to sniff around, trying to find something I'd buried last week, or a month ago. I looked in the little fish pond Dad wanted us to have so we could watch how little fish were born. I'd seen. Tiny fish came out of eggs, and the parents swam like crazy to gobble down their children!

I peered into the water. There was my face all funny looking, with jagged edges, hair up in points, not curly and pretty like Jory's. Something dark red was on my face – an ugly face that didn't belong in a pretty garden where the little birds came to bathe in a fancy bath. I was bleeding tears. I dipped my hands into the fishwater and washed my face. Then sat back to think. That's when I saw the blood on my leg – lots of blood that was drying in a big dark clot on my knee. Didn't really matter for it didn't hurt too much.

How did it get there? I retraced my crawl with my eyes. That board with the rusty nail – had I driven that in my knee? Just because I was doing a kind deed for Clover. I crawled over to the board and felt the blood sticky on its end. Dad called nail holes in skin 'punctures' and I guess I had one. 'Now it's very important that a puncture bleeds freely,' he explained. Mine wasn't bleeding freely.

I put my finger in the puncture and stirred up the blood so it would run. Freaky people like me could do awful things like that, while sissy people like Momma would look sick. Blood in my wound felt hot and thick. Maybe I wasn't so freaky after all for all of a sudden I was beginning to feel real pain. Mean pain.

'Bart!' bellowed Daddy from the back veranda. 'You get in this house instantly! Unless you want a spanking.'

When they were in the dining room they couldn't see me sneak in the sliding door of the family room and that's just what I did. In the bathroom I washed my hands, put on my PJs to hide my bad knee, and quiet and meek I joined my family at the table.

'Well, it's about time,' said Momma, who looked pretty.

'Bart, why do you insist on causing trouble every time we sit down to eat?' asked Daddy. I hung my head, not feeling sorry, just not feeling well. My knee was really throbbing with pain, and what John Amos said about God punishing those who disobeyed must be right. I was being judged and a knee puncture was my own hellfire.

Next day I was back in the garden, hiding in one of my special places. All day I sat there and enjoyed my pain that meant I was normal, not a freak. I was being punished like all others sinners who'd always felt pain. I wanted to miss dinner. Had to go and see Apple. Couldn't remember if I'd been over there or not. Drank a little water from the fishpond, lap, lap, lap like a cat.

Momma had been packing all day, smiling even early this morning when she put my clothes in a suitcase first. 'Bart, try to be a good boy today for a change. Come to your meals on time and then Daddy won't have to spank you before bedtime. He doesn't like punishing you, but he does have to have a way to discipline you. And do try to eat more. You won't enjoy Disneyland if you feel sick.'

Sunset changed the blue sky to pretty colours. Jory ran outdoors to watch the colours he said were like music. Jory could also feel colours: they made him glad, sad, lonely, mystical too.

Momma was another one who could feel colours. Now that I was getting the knack of feeling pain, maybe soon I'd learn to feel colours too.

Real night started coming. Darkness could bring out the ghosts. Emma tinkled her little crystal bell to call me in to dinner. I wanted so badly to go, but couldn't do it.

Something rotting was in the hollow tree behind me. I turned and crawled out of my cave and peeked into the dark hole in the tree. Rotten eggs inside! Phew! I put my hand in slowly, feeling around for what I couldn't see. Something stiff and cold and covered with fur. Dead thing had a collar around its neck with points that cut my hand – was that barbed wire? Was that rotten dead thing Clover?

I sobbed, wild with fear.

They'd think I'd done it!

They were always thinking I did everything that was bad! And I'd loved Clover. I had. Always wanted him to like me more than Jory. Now poor Clover would never live in that wonderful doghouse I'd finish some day.

Jory came down the main garden path, calling and searching for me. 'Come out from where you are, Bart! Don't make waves now that we're all ready to leave!'

Found me a new place he didn't know about and lay flat on my stomach.

Jory left. Next came my mother. 'Bart,' she called, 'if you don't come inside . . . Please, Bart. I'm sorry I slapped you this morning.' I sniffed away my tears of self-pity. I had only accidentally dumped a whole box of detergent in the dish-washer thinking I could help. How was I to know one small box could make a whole ocean of suds? Foamy suds that filled the kitchen.

This time it was Daddy, 'Bart,' he called in a normal voice, 'come in and eat your dinner. No need to sulk. We know what you did was an accident. You are forgiven. We realize you were trying to help Emma. So come in.'

On and on I sat, feeling guilty for making them suffer more.

Panic had been in Momma's voice as if she really did love me, and how could she when I never did anything right? Wasn't fit for her to love.

Worse. The pain in my knee was much worse. Maybe I had lockjaw. Kids at school had told me all about how it made your jaws lock together so you couldn't eat, making doctors knock out your front teeth so they could put a tube in your mouth and you could suck in soup. Soon the ambulance would come screaming down our street, and with me inside it, would sound its siren all the way to Daddy's nearest hospital. They'd rush me to the emergency room and a masked surgeon would shout: 'Off with his rotten stinking leg!' They'd hack it off short, and I'd be left with a stump full of poison that would put me in my coffin.

Then they'd put me in that cemetery in Clairmont, South Carolina. Aunt Carrie would be at my side, and at last she'd have someone small like her to keep her company. But I wouldn't be Cory. I was me, the black sheep of the family – so John Amos had called me once when he was mad with me.

On my back, with my arms crossed over my chest. I lay just like Malcolm Neal Foxworth, staring upwards as I waited for winter to come and go and summer to bring Momma, Dad, Jory, Cindy and Emma to my grave. Bet they wouldn't bring me pretty flowers. Down in my grave I'd stiffly smile, not letting them know I liked the killer Spanish moss much better than I liked the smelly roses with prickly thorns.

My family would leave. I'd be trapped in the ground, in the dark, forever and ever. When at last I was in the cold-cold ground, and the snow lay all around, I wouldn't have to pretend to be like Malcolm Neal Foxworth. I pictured Malcolm when he was old. Frail, with thin hair and a limp like John Amos, and only a little better looking than John Amos, who was very ugly.

Just in the nick of time, I was solving all of Momma's problems and Cindy could live on and on in peace.

Now that I was dead.

WOUNDS OF WAR *Jory*

Dinner came and went. Bedtime was drawing nearer and still Bart didn't come into the house. We had all searched, but I was the one who kept it up longest, I was the one who knew him best.

'Jory,' said Mom, 'if you don't find him in ten more minutes I'm calling the police.'

'I'll find him,' I said, not nearly as confident as I tried to sound. I didn't like what Bart was doing to our parents. They were trying to do the best they could for us. They weren't getting any big kick out of visiting Disneyland for the fourth time. That was Bart's treat, and he was too dumb to understand.

He was bad too. Dad and Mom should punish him severely, not indulge him like they did, then he'd know at least they cared enough to punish him for his wicked ways.

Yet when I'd mentioned this to them once or twice, both had explained they'd learned in the worst way about parents who were strict and cruel. I'd thought it odd at the time that both of them had come from the same kind of heartless parents, but my teacher often said that likes were attracted to one another more than opposites. All I had to do was look at them to know this was true. Both had the same shade of blond hair, the same colour blue eyes, and the same dark eyebrows and long black curling lashes – though Momma used mascara which made Dad tease her, for he didn't think she needed any.

No, they wouldn't punish Bart severely even when he was wicked, for they had found out first-hand what harm it could do.

Boy, did Bart love to talk about wickedness and sin. A new kind of talk, like he'd been reading the Bible and taking from it the kind of talk that some preachers screamed out behind the pulpits. Why, he could even quote passages from the Bible – something from the Song of Solomon, and a brother's love for his sister.

Gee, I didn't even like to think about that kind of thing. Made me feel so uneasy, even more uneasy than when Bart spoke of how he hated graves, old ladies, cemeteries, and almost everything else. Hate was an emotion he felt often, poor kid.

I checked his little cave in the shrubs and saw a bit of cloth torn from his shirt. But he wasn't there now. I picked up a board meant for the top of the doghouse Bart was building, and stared at the rusty, bloody end of the nail.

Had he hurt himself with this nail, and crawled off somewhere to die? Dying was all he talked about lately, excluding talk of those already dead. He was always crawling around, sniffing the ground like a dog, even relieving himself like a dog. Boy, he was some mixed-up little kid.

'Bart – it's Jory. If you want to stay out all night, I'll let you, and won't tell our parents . . . just make some noise so I can know you're alive.'

Nothing.

Ours was a big garden, full of shrubs and trees and blooming bushes Mom and Dad had planted. I circled a camellia bush. Oh, golly – was that Bart's bare foot?

There he was, half under the hedge with only his legs stretched out. I'd overlooked him before because this was not his usual place to hide. It was really dark now, the fog making it even more difficult to see.

Gently I eased him out from the shrubs, wondering why he didn't complain. I stared down at his flushed hot face, his murky eyes staring dully at me. 'Don't touch me,' he moaned. 'Almost dead now . . . almost there.' I picked him up and ran with him in my arms. He was crying, telling me his leg hurt . . . 'Jory, I really don't want to die, I don't.'

By the time Dad picked him up and put him in his car, he was unconscious. 'I don't believe this,' said Dad. 'That leg of his is swollen three times larger than it should be. I only pray he doesn't have gas gangrene.'

I knew about gangrene – it could kill people.

In the hospital Bart was put to bed immediately, and other doctors came to check over his leg, trying to force Dad to leave the room since it was professional ethics for doctors not to treat someone in their own family. Too emotionally involved I guessed.

'No!' stormed Dad, 'he's my son, and I'm staying to see what's done for him!' Mom cried all the time, kneeling and holding on to Bart's slack hand. I was sick inside too, thinking I hadn't done nearly enough to help Bart.

'Apple. Apple,' whimpered Bart whenever his eyes opened. 'Gotta have Apple.'

'Chris,' said Mom, 'can't he have an apple?'

'No. He can't eat in his condition.'

What a terrible state he was in. Sweat beaded on his forehead and his small thin body, soaking the sheets. Mom began to really sob. 'Take your mother out of this room,' ordered Dad. 'I don't want her to watch all of this.'

As Mom cried in the waiting room down the hall, I stole back inside Bart's private room and watched Dad shoot penicillin into Bart's arm. I held my breath. 'Is he allergic to penicillin?' asked another doctor. 'I don't know,' said Dad in a calm way, 'he's never had a serious infection before. But at this point there isn't much else we can do but take a chance. Get everything ready in case he reacts.' He turned to see me crouched in the corner, trying to stay out of the way. 'Son, go to your mother. There's nothing you can do to help here.'

I couldn't move. For some reason, perhaps guilt for neglecting my brother, I had to stay and see him through. Soon enough Bart was in worse trouble. Dad frowned, signalled a nurse, and two more doctors came. One of them inserted a tube in Bart's nostril. Next something so dreadful happened I couldn't believe my eyes. All over his body, Bart was breaking out in huge swollen welts. Red as fire, and they itched too for his hands kept moving from one patch of fire to another. Next Dad was lifting Bart and putting him on a stretcher so orderlies could wheel him away.

'Dad!' I cried, 'where is that stretcher going? They're not going to take off his leg, are they?'

'No, son,' he said calmly. 'Your brother is having a severe allergic reaction. We have to move fast and perform a tracheotomy before his throat tissues become inflamed and cut off his air passage.'

'Chris,' called the doctor pushing one side of the stretcher, 'it's okay. Tom has cleared an air passage – no trache necessary.'

A day passed and still Bart was no better. It seemed likely Bart would scratch himself raw, and he'd die from another kind of infection. With fascinated horror I stayed on until dawn watching his stubby swollen fingers work convulsively in useless efforts to relieve the torment of his body that itched all over. His entire body was scarlet. I could tell his condition was serious from Dad's face, from the attitudes of the other professionals all around his bed. Then Bart's hands were bandaged so he couldn't scratch. Next his eyes puffed up so much they looked like two huge red goose eggs. His lips swelled and protruded three inches beyond normal.

I couldn't believe all this could happen just on account of an allergic reaction.

'Oh!' cried out Mom, clinging tightly to Dad, her tired eyes glued on Bart. He'd been sick forever or so it seemed. Two days passed and still Bart was no better. He'd spent his tenth birthday on a hospital bed, delirious and raving. His fourth trip to Disneyland was cancelled, and our trip back to South Carolina put off for another year.

'Look,' said Dad, pointing with a glow of hope on his tired face, 'the hives are diminishing.'

The second hurdle cleared. I thought now Bart would get well fast. Wasn't so. His leg grew ever larger and soon he proved allergic to every antibiotic they had! 'What are we going to do now?' cried Mom with so much anxiety I feared for her health.

'We're doing everything we can,' was all Dad would say.

'Oh, Lord, why has thou forsaken me?' mumbled Bart in his

delirium. Tears streamed down my face and fell on my shirt like rain.

'The Lord has not forsaken you,' said Dad. He knelt by Bart's bed and prayed, holding fast to his small hand while Mom slept on a cot put in the room for her to use. She didn't know the pills Dad had given her were tranquillizers, not aspirin for her headache. She'd been too upset to even notice the colour.

Dad touched my head. 'Go home and sleep, son. There's only so much you can do, and you've done that.' Slowly I got up, stiff from sitting for so long, and headed for the door. When I gave Bart one more long last glance, I saw him tossing restlessly as my father fitted himself on the cot behind my mother.

The next day Mom had to rush to the hospital from ballet class, leaving me to warm up to piano music. 'Life goes on, Jory. Forget your brother's problems for a while, if you can, and join us later on.' No sooner was she out of sight than something dawned on me. Apple! Of course. Bart didn't want an apple . . . he wanted his dog. His puppypony!

In ten minutes I was out of my leotards and in a telephone booth calling my father. 'How's Bart?' I asked.

'Not very good, Jory, I don't know how to tell your mother, but the specialist working on Bart wants to amputate his leg before the infection has a chance to weaken him more. I can't let him do that – and yet, we don't want to lose Bart.'

'Don't you let them amputate!' I almost screamed. 'You tell Bart – and make him hear – that I'm going home to take care of Apple.' Please let Bart keep both his legs. God knows, Bart would feel even more inferior if he lost one.

'Jory, your brother lies on his bed and refuses to co-operate. He isn't trying to recover. It seems he wants to die. We can't give him any kind of antibiotic and his temperature is steadily rising. But I'm with you. There must be something we can do to bring down that fever.'

For the first time in my life I hitched a ride home. Once Bart knew Apple was okay he'd get well. He was punishing himself, just the way he beat his fists against the rough bark of a tree when he broke something. I sobbed with the realization my kid brother was more important to me than I'd known before. Nutty little kid who didn't like himself very much. Hiding in pretend games, telling tall tales so everyone would be impressed. Dad had told me a long time ago to indulge him in his pretence. But maybe we'd indulged too much.

I gasped when I saw Apple in the barn of the mansion. He was chained to a stake driven in the ground of the floor. A dish of moist dogfood was placed just beyond his reach. His thick shaggy fur told the story of his hunger. He was ragged, panting, looking at me with pleading eyes. Who had done this? He'd clawed the ground in his futile efforts to dig free, and now, still only an overgrown puppy, he lay and panted in the barn which had been closed and shuttered cruelly.

'It's all right, boy,' I soothed, as I set about getting him fresh water. He lapped it up so thirstily I had to take it away. I knew a little about doctoring. Dogs, like people, had to drink sparingly after a long thirst. Next I set him free and went to his shelf of supplies and took, from a long row of cans, what looked best to me. Apple was starving in the midst of plenty. I could feel his ribs when I ran my hands over his pitiful shabby coat which had been so beautiful.

When he'd eaten and had his fill of water too, I curry-combed his thick mat of hair. Then I sat on the dirt floor and held his huge head on my lap. 'Bart's coming home to you, Apple. He'll have two good legs too, I promise. I don't know who did this to you and why, but you can bet I'll find out.' What worried me most was the awful suspicion that the very person who loved Apple most might be the very one who'd starved and punished his pet. Bart had such an odd way of reasoning. To his way of thinking, if Apple really suffered when he was gone, Apple would be ten times more grateful to see him.

Could Bart be that heartlessly cruel?

Outside the July day was mildly hot. As I approached the great mansion I heard the low voices of two people. That old woman in black, and the creepy old butler, both of them seated on a cool patio lush with colourful potted palms, and ferns planted in huge stone urns.

'John, I feel I should go down again and check on Bart's puppy. He was so happy to see me this morning, I couldn't understand why he was so hungry. Really, do you have to keep him chained up like that? It seems so cruel on a day like this.'

'Madame, it is not a hot day,' said the mean-looking butler, as he sipped a beer and sprawled in one of her chaise-longues. 'When you insist on wearing black, naturally you feel hotter than anyone else.'

'I don't want your opinion on how I dress. I want to know why you keep Apple chained.'

'Because the dog might run off to look for his young master,' said John sarcastically. 'I guess you didn't think of that.'

'You could lock the barn door. I'm going down to look at him again. He seemed so thin, so desperate.'

'Madame, if you have to concern yourself, make it worthy of the bother. Be concerned for your grandson who is about to lose his leg.'

She'd half risen from her chair, and at this announcement sank back on the pillows. 'Oh. He's worse? Did Emma and Marta talk again this morning?'

I sighed, knowing Emma liked to gossip and she shouldn't. Though I honestly didn't think she'd say anything important. She never told me any secrets. And Mom never had time to listen.

'Of course they did,' grouched the butler, 'did you ever hear of a woman who didn't? Those two use stepladders every day to gab away. Though to hear Emma talk, the doctor and his wife are perfect.'

'John, what did Marta find out about Bart? Tell me!'

'Well, Madame, it seems that kid has managed to drive a rusty nail in his knee and now he has gangrene – the kind of gangrene that demands amputation of the limb or the patient dies.'

I stared from my hidden place at the two who sat and talked, the one very upset, the other totally unconcerned, almost amused with the reaction of his mistress.

'You're lying!' screamed the woman, jumping to her feet. 'John, you tell me lies just to torture me more. I know Bart will be fine. His father will know what to do to help him recover. I know he will. He has to . . .' and then she broke into tears. She took off the veil then and wiped at her tears and I glimpsed her face, and didn't notice the scars so much this time, only her look of suffering. Did she really care so much for Bart? Why should she care? Could she really be Bart's grandmother? – She couldn't be. His grandmother was in a mental institution in Virginia.

I stepped forward then to let my presence be known. She appeared surprised to see me, then remembered her bare face and hastily put on her veil again.

'Good morning,' I said, addressing myself to the lady and ignoring the old man I couldn't help but detest. 'I heard what your butler said, ma'am, and he's right only to a certain extent. My brother is very ill, but he does not have gas gangrene. And he will not lose his leg. My father is much too good a doctor to let that happen.'

'Jory, are you sure Bart will be all right?' she asked with so much concern. 'He's very dear to me . . . I can't tell you how much,' she choked and bowed her head and worked her thin ringed hands convulsively.

'Yes, ma'am,' I said. 'If Bart wasn't allergic to most of the drugs the doctors give him, they would have destroyed the infection – but that won't matter in the long run, for my dad will know what to do to help him. My father always knows just what to do.' I turned then towards the butler and tried to put on adult authority. 'As for Apple, he does not need to be kept chained in a hot barn with all the windows shuttered over. And he doesn't need to have his food and water placed just out of his reach. I don't know what's going on in this place, and why you want to make a nice dog like that suffer – but you'd better take good care of him if you don't want me to report you to the humane society.' I whipped about and started towards home.

'Jory!' called the lady in black. 'Stay! Don't leave yet. I want to know more about Bart!'

Again I turned to look at her. 'If you want to help my brother, there's only one thing you can do – leave him alone. When he comes back – you tell him some nice reason why you can't be bothered – but don't you hurt his feelings.'

She spoke again, pleading for me to stay and talk, but I strode on, thinking I'd done something wonderful to protect Bart. To protect him from what, I didn't know.

That very night Bart's fever raged higher: his doctors ordered him to be wrapped in a thermal blanket that worked like a refrigerator. I watched my father, I watched my mother, I saw them look at each other, touch each other, giving each other strength, and strangely both turned to pick up cubes of ice that they rubbed on Bart's arms and legs, then his chest. Like one person with no need to speak. I choked up and bowed my head feeling moved by their kind of love and understanding. I wanted then to speak up and tell them about the woman next door, but I'd promised Bart not to tell. He had the first friend in his life, the first pet that could tolerate him; yet the longer I withheld what I knew, the more my parents might be hurt in the long run. Why did I have to think that? How could that old lady hurt my parents?

Somehow I knew she could. Some day I knew she would. I wished I were a man with the abilities to make right decisions.

As I grew sleepier, I remembered the expression Dad used so often: 'God works in mysterious ways his wonders to perform.'

The next thing I knew Dad was shaking me awake. 'Bart's better,' he cried, 'Bart's going to keep his leg and recover.'

Slowly, day by day that hideous swollen leg diminished in size. Gradually it turned to a normal colour, though Bart seemed listless and uncaring as he stared blankly ahead, not saying anything to anybody.

We were at the breakfast table one morning when Dad

rubbed his tired eyes, then informed us of something incredible.

'Cathy, you're not going to believe this, but the lab technicians found something odd in the culture they took from Bart's wound. We suspected rust; they found rust which caused the tetanus, but they also found the very kind of staphylococcus often associated with fresh animal faeces. It's truly a miracle Bart still has both of his legs.'

Looking pale and tired enough to be sick herself, Mom nodded before her head bowed weakly to his shoulder. 'If Clover were still around, I'd easily understand how he might – You know how our Bart is. If anything filthy is within a mile he'll be the one to step on it, crawl in it, or pick it up and check it over. You know, when he kept on raving last night about apples I gave him one I'd bought and he let it fall to the floor, showing no interest.' Mom closed her eyes while he went on stroking her back and talking. 'When I told him we weren't flying East, I could tell he was pleased.' He looked my way. 'I hope you're not too disappointed, Jory. We'll have to wait until next summer to visit your grandmother, or maybe this Christmas I can get away.'

I was thinking mean thoughts. Bart always got what he wanted. He'd figured out a sure way to avoid visiting old graves and old grandmothers. He'd even given up Disneyland. And it wasn't like Bart to give up anything.

Should I run next door and tell the old lady that Bart was all right? She'd be glad he wouldn't lose his leg. However, I figured Emma would tell Marta and Marta would tell John, and John would tell his employer, and so no matter where you went, or how isolated you thought you were, there was always a grapevine.

That evening I was with Bart alone, and Mom and Dad were in the hospital corridor talking to friends. I told Bart about the conversation I'd overheard between the old lady and her butler. 'There they were, Bart, both of them on her terrace. She was so worried about you.'

'She loves me,' he whispered proudly, his voice very faint. 'She loves me more than anybody,' and here he looked thoughtful, 'except perhaps, Apple.'

Bart, I thought, don't think like that. But I couldn't speak and steal his pride in having found love outside his family. With mixed emotions I watched his expressive face, my own emotions a tumble of uncertainty. What kind of kid brother did I have? Surely he had to know his parents would love him more than anyone else.

'Grandmother is afraid of the old butler,' he said, 'but I can handle him good. I've got hidden powers, real powerful.'

'Bart, why do you keep going over there?'

He shrugged and stared at the wall. 'Don't know. Just wanna go there.'

'You know that Dad would give you a dog, any kind you want. All you have to do is ask, and he'll give you a puppy just like Apple.'

His fierce angry eyes drilled a hole in me. 'There ain't no other dog like my puppypony! Apple is special.'

I changed the subject. 'How do you know that woman is scared of her butler? Did she tell you?'

'She don't have to tell me. I can jus' tell. He looks at her mean She looks at him scared.'

Scared, the same way I was beginning to look at just abou everything.

HOMECOMING *Bart*

Nice the way Momma kept fussing over me. She'd change as soon as I got well. Wouldn't last. Two long long weeks in this stinking hospital that wanted to take my leg and burn it in their furnace. Made me happy to look down and see my leg still there. Boy, just wait until I went back to school and I told them how I nearly had an amputated leg. Gee. They'd be impressed. It was made of good stuff that refused to rot and die. And I hadn't cried. Was brave too.

I remembered how Daddy hovered over me, looking sad and worried. Maybe he really did love me even if I wasn't his own true son. 'Daddy!' I cried when I saw him. 'You got good news, I can tell!'

'It's nice to see you bright and happy-looking.' He sat on the side of my bed and pulled me into his arms before he gave me a big kiss. Embarrassing. I winced. 'Bart, I have great news. Your temperature is normal. Your knee is healing nicely. And being a doctor's son has a few advantages. I'm signing you out today. If I don't I fear you'll fade away to nothing. Once you're home, I know Emma's delicious food will soon put some meat on those bones.'

He looked at me in the kind way, like I really mattered just as much as Jory; it made me want to cry. 'Where's Momma?' I asked.

'I had to get away early, so she stayed home to arrange a special homecoming party for you – so you really can't mind, can you?'

I could so. Wanted her here! Bet she didn't come 'cause she had to fiddle around with that little old Cindy, putting ribbons in her hair. I kept my silence and allowed Daddy to carry me out to his car. It felt good to be out in the sun, going home.

In the foyer Daddy stood me on my legs which trembled. I

stared at Momma who went first to Daddy and kissed him on the cheek – when I was there, wanting to be kissed first. I knew why she'd done that. She was afraid of me now. She saw my skinny body, my bony face that was ugly. She was forcing herself to smile when she looked my way. I cringed when finally she came my way to do her duty to her son who hadn't died. Look at her fake happiness. I knew she didn't love me, didn't really want me any more. And there was Jory too, smiling and pretending he was happy for me to be home again when I knew, really knew, all of them would have been glad to see me dead. I felt like Malcolm when he'd been a little boy, unwanted and unneeded, and so darn miserable.

'Bart, my darling!' said Momma, 'why do you look unhappy? Aren't you glad to be home?' She gathered me in her arms and tried to kiss me, but I yanked away. Saw her hurt face but that didn't count. She was only pretending, like I had to pretend all the time.

'It's so wonderful to have you here again, sweetheart,' she went on with her lies. 'Emma and I have been busy all morning planning just what we can do to make you happy. Since you complained so much about the awful hospital food, we have made all your favourite dishes.' She smiled again and reached once more to hug me, but I wasn't gonna let her get under my skin with her 'feminine wiles' John Amos had told me about. Good food and smiles and kisses were all parts of feminine wiles.

'Bart, don't look so sceptical. Emma and I did prepare every one of your favourite dishes.' I stared at her. She turned red then said with an effort, 'You know, the ones you like best.'

She went on forcing herself to be nice as Daddy came up and gave me a short cane. 'Bear most of your weight on that until your knee is stronger.'

Kinda fun hobbling around like an old man, like Malcolm Foxworth. I liked having them fuss over me, worried when I wouldn't eat. None of the presents they had for me were as good as what my grandmother next door would give.

'Good gosh, Bart,' whispered Jory during dinner, 'do you have to act so ungrateful? Everybody went to an awful lot of trouble to please you.'

'Hate apple pie.'

'You said before apple pie was your favourite kind.'

'Never said that! I hate chicken too, and mashed potatoes, green salads – hate everything.'

'I believe it,' said a disgusted brother who turned his back and ignored someone as picky as me. Then he reached to take a chicken leg from my plate. 'Well . . . as long as you don't want it, it shouldn't go to waste.' He ate every last piece of the chicken. Now I couldn't sneak into the kitchen late at night and stuff myself when they weren't watching. Let 'em all worry about me fading away to skin and bones, ending up in a damp cold grave. Let 'em find out how much they missed me.

'Bart, please try and eat a little something,' pleaded Momma. 'What's wrong with the pie?'

I scowled then slapped Jory's hand when he reached to take my slice of pie. 'I can't eat pie without ice-cream on top.'

She smiled at me brilliantly, then called, 'Emma, bring in the ice-cream!'

I shoved my plate away and slouched in my chair. 'I don't feel so good. Need to be alone. Don't like people making such a fuss over me. Spoils my appetite.'

Daddy looked as if he were losing patience with me. He didn't scold Jory for taking my pie either. That's all it took – one hour and they were tired of me and wishing again I had died.

'Cathy,' said Dad, 'don't plead with Bart any more. If he doesn't want to eat he can excuse himself. He'll eat when he's hungry enough.'

Stomach was rumbling right now. I couldn't eat that stuff in front of me – now that Jory had taken away what I wanted most. There I sat starving while everyone forgot me and began to talk, laugh and act like I was still in the hospital. I got up and hobbled towards my room. Daddy called, 'Bart, I don't want you playing outside until that leg has time to heal thoroughly. Take a nap with your leg propped up. Later on you can watch television.'

TV. What kind of homecoming treat was that? Appearing obedient, I entered my bedroom and stood near the doorway so I could shout to those in the dining room. 'Don't nobody disturb my rest.'

Kept me two weeks in that hospital, and now I was home they were gonna keep me locked inside some more. I'd show 'em. Nobody was gonna keep me inside for another rotten week. But somebody kept an eye on me night and day before finally I could escape through the window after six whole days of being kept a prisoner. Already I'd missed too much of summer, and my Disneyland trip. Wasn't gonna miss anything else.

The big old tree by the wall was not friendly, making it harder for me to climb. By the time I was next door my leg would ache. Pain wasn't nearly as good as I'd thought it would be. Being normal wasn't so hot. Jory sprained his ankle once and went right on dancing, ignoring the pain. I could ignore pain too.

When I was on top of the wall I looked behind to see who might be following. Nobody. Nobody cared what I did to hurt myself. Began to sniff – what was that rotten stinking smell? Coming from out of the hollow oak tree. Ah, I could just remember. Something dead in the hollow tree. What was it? Couldn't remember good any more. Mind was fuzzy, full of mists that rolled like the fog.

Apple, better to think of Apple. Forget the stiff and aching knee by pretending it belonged to some frail old man like Malcolm grew up to be. My young leg wanted to run but my old one controlled all of me, taking over my mind, forcing me to lean heavily on my cane.

Oh! What a pitiful sight it would be to see poor Apple lying dead in the barn. A pitiful bag of fur, skin and bones. I'd cry, scream, hate those who'd tried to force me to fly East and abandon the very best friend I had. Animals were the only ones who knew how to really love with devotion.

A hundred years had come and gone since last I came this way before. Years passed it seemed while I limped to its doors. Get a grip on yourself, I thought. Steel your spine, like Malcolm steeled his. Prepare your eyes for a grisly sight, for Apple loved you too much, and now he had to pay the price by dying. Never, never again would I find such a true friend as the puppypony who'd been my Apple.

My balance, never good, swayed me from right to left, from front to back, and made me feel hazy and crazy. I sensed something was behind me. I peeked over my shoulder and saw no one there. Nothing but those frightening animal shapes that were only green shrubs. Stupid gardeners should have something better to do than waste their time snipping at bushes when real money was out there waiting for real brains to pick it up. Thinking now just like Malcolm, John Amos would be pleased. Had to hunt up John Amos so he could smarten up my brains some more.

Suspecting the worst, I approached the place that Apple liked most. Now I couldn't see. Gone blind! My cane tapped the ground ahead of me. Dark. Why was it so dark? I inched along, peering this way and that. All the barn shutters were closed. Poor Apple, left in the dark to starve. A lump rose in my throat while I cried inside for a pet who'd loved me more than life itself.

I had to force myself to take another step forward. To see Apple dead would scar my soul, my eternal soul which John Amos said had to stay clean and pure if I was to get to heaven's pearly gates where Malcolm had gone.

One step more. I stopped. There was my Apple – and he wasn't dead! He was in a stall with the window open and he was chasing a red ball, swatting it with his huge paw-like hoofs – and there was plenty of food in his dish. Clean water in his bowl too. I stood there shaking all over as Apple ignored me and went on playing like I wasn't even there – *why, he hadn't missed me at all!*

'You! You!' I screamed. 'You've been eating and drinking, and having a good time! And all the time I was at death's door and you didn't care. And I thought you loved me. And I thought you'd miss me a whole lot. And now you don't even bark-whinny to tell me you're glad I'm back. I hate you, Apple! Hate you for not caring enough!'

Apple saw me then and ran to me, leaping to put his huge paw-hoofs on my shoulders as he slurped my face. His tail wagged furiously, but he wasn't fooling me. He'd found someone else to take care of him better – for darn if I'd made his coat look so pretty. 'Why didn't you die from loneliness?' I shrieked. I glared hatred at him, wanting him to wither away and disappear. He sensed my anger and dropped to all fours and stood with his tail between his legs and his head hanging down, his eyes rolled slantwise.

'You get away from me! You need to suffer as I suffered! Then you'll be glad to have me back!' I took all his food, his water, and threw them in a wooden barrel. I picked up his red ball and hurled that so far he'd never find it. All the time Apple stood there, watching, not wagging his tail. He wanted me back now, but now it was too late.

'You'll miss me now,' I sobbed, stumbling away, locking him in the barn with all the windows closed and the shutters too. 'Stay in darkness and die of hunger!' I'd never come back, never.

No sooner was I in the sunlight that I thought of the nice soft hay he had inside to lie on. I went into the barn again, seized a pitchfork and raked all the hay away. He was whimpering now, trying to nuzzle up to me. I wouldn't let him. 'You lie on the cold hard floor! It will make all your bones ache, but I don't care, for I don't love you now!' Why was I crying? Angry, I wiped the tears away and scratched my face.

In all my life I'd made only three friends, Apple, my grandmother and John Amos. Apple had killed my love, and one of the other two had betrayed me by feeding him and stealing his love. John Amos wouldn't bother – had to be grandmother.

Drifted home in a daze. That night my leg ached so badly Daddy came in and gave me a pill. He sat on the side of my bed and held me in his arms, making me feel safe as he spoke softly about falling into sweet dreams.

Fell into ugliness. Dead bones everywhere. Blood gushing out in great rivers taking pieces of human beings down into the oceans of fire. Dead. I was dead. Funeral flowers on the altar. People sent me flowers who didn't know me, telling me they were glad to see me dead. Heard the sea of fire play Devil music, making me hate music and dancing even more than I had.

The sun came in my window and fell on my face, stealing me from the Devil's grasp. When I opened my eyes, terrified of what I might see, I saw only Jory at the foot of my bed, looking at me with pity. I didn't need pity. 'Bart, you cried last night. I'm sorry your leg still hurts.'

'Leg don't hurt at all!' I yelled.

Got up to go limping into the kitchen where Momma was feeding Cindy. Blasted Cindy. Emma was frying bacon for my breakfast. 'Coffee and toast only,' I yelled. 'That's all I want to eat.'

Momma winced, then looked up with her face strangely pale. 'Bart, please don't yell. And you don't drink coffee. Why would you ask for coffee?'

'Time I started acting my age!' I barked. Carefully I eased myself down into Daddy's chair with arms. Daddy came in and saw me in his chair but he didn't order me out. He just used my armless chair, then poured coffee into a cup until it was half-full. He filled the cup to an inch of the brim with cream and then gave it to me.

'I hate cream in my coffee!'

'How can you be so sure when you haven't tried it?'

'Just know!' I refused to drink the coffee he'd spoiled. (Malcolm liked his coffee black – and so would I from now on.) Now all I had before me was dry toast – and if I had to be like Malcolm and grow smart brains – I couldn't spread butter and strawberry jam on my toast. Indigestion. Like Malcolm had to worry about indigestion.

'Daddy, what's indigestion?'

'Something you don't need to have.'

Sure was hard trying to be like Malcolm all the time. Seconds later Daddy was down on his knees, checking over my bad leg. 'It looks worse today than it did yesterday,' he said as he lifted his head, met my eyes, and scowled suspiciously. 'Bart, you haven't been crawling on this bad knee, have you?'

'No!' I yelled, 'I'm not crazy! The covers rubbed off some of my skin. Rough sheets. Hate cotton sheets. Like silk ones best!' (Malcolm wouldn't sleep on anything but silk.)

'How would you know?' asked Daddy. 'You've never had silk sheets.' He continued to care for my knee, washing first, then he sprinkled on some white powder before he covered my wound with a sterile gauze pad held on with sticky tape. 'Now I'm serious, Bart. I warn you to stay off that knee. You stay in the house, out of the garden, or sit on the back veranda – no crawling in the dirt!'

'It's a patio!' I scowled to let him know he didn't know everything.

'All right, a patio – does that make you feel happy?'

No. Never was happy. Then I gave it more thought. Yes, I was happy sometimes – when I was pretending to be Malcolm, the all-powerful, the richest, the smartest. Playing the role of Malcolm was easy and better than being anything or anyone else. Somehow I knew if I kept it up I'd end up just like Malcolm – rich, powerful, loved.

The longest kind of dull day dragged on endlessly with everybody keeping a close eye on me. Twilight came and Momma got busy making herself prettier for Dad who was due home any minute. Emma was fixing dinner. Jory was in his ballet class, and I slipped off the patio unseen. Down into the garden I hurried before anybody stopped me.

All the little humming buzzing creatures of night came out and swarmed about my head. I fanned them away. I was going to John Amos. He was sitting alone in his room, reading some magazine that he hid as quickly as I entered without knocking. 'You shouldn't do that!' he said sourly, not even smiling to say he was glad I was alive, with two legs.

It was easy to put on Malcolm's glum look and scare him to meekness. 'Did you give Apple water and food while I was sick?'

'Of course not!' he said eagerly. 'It was your grandmother who fed him, and cared for him. I told you women can never be trusted to keep their word. Corrine Foxworth is no better than any other women with their wiles to trick men into being slaves.'

'Corrine Foxworth – is that her name?'

'Of course, I've told you that before. She is Malcolm's daughter. He named her after his mother so he'd always be reminded of how false women are, how even a daughter could betray him – though he loved her well, too well in my opinion.'

I was growing bored of tales of women and their wiles. 'Why don't you get your teeth fixed?' I asked. I didn't like the way he hissed and whistled through teeth too loose.

'Good, you said that just like Malcolm. You're learning. Being sick has been good for your soul – as it was for his. Now listen carefully, Bart. Corrine is your real grandmother and was once married to your real father. She was Malcolm's most beloved child and she betrayed him by doing something so sinful she has to be punished.'

'Has to be punished?'

'Yes, punished severely, but you are not to let her know your feelings for her have changed. Pretend you still love her, still admire her. And in that way she will be made vulnerable.'

I knew what vulnerable meant. Another of those words I had to learn. Weak, bad to be weak. John Amos went for his Bible and put my hand on its worn black cover, all cracked and peeling. 'Malcolm's own Bible,' he said, 'he left it to me in his will . . . though he could have left me more . . .'

I realized that John Amos was the one person in the world who had not yet disappointed me. Here was the true friend I needed. Old – but I could be old too when I wanted. Though I couldn't take my teeth from my mouth and put them in an ivory-coloured cup.

I stared at the Bible, wanting to pull my hand away, but afraid of what might happen if I did. 'Swear on this Bible that you will do as Malcolm would have wanted his great-grandson to do – wreak vengeance against those who harmed him most.'

How could I promise what he wanted, when a little of me still loved her? Maybe John Amos was lying. Maybe Jory had fed Apple . . .

'Bart, why do you hesitate? Are you a weakling? Have you no spine? Look again at your mother, at how she uses her body, her pretty face, her soft kisses and hugs to make your father do anything she wants. Take notice of how late he works at night, how tired he is when he comes home and ask yourself why. Does he do it for himself – or for her? So he can buy her new clothes, fur coats, jewellery, and give her a big fine house to live in. That's how women use men, making them work while they play.'

I swallowed. Momma had a job. She taught ballet dancing. But that was more fun than work, wasn't it? Did she ever buy anything with her money? Couldn't remember.

'Now you go in to see your grandmother, and be like you were before, and soon you will find out who betrayed you. It wasn't me. You go in and pretend you are Malcolm. Call her Corrine – watch the guilt and shame flood her face – watch her eyes show fear, and you will know which one of us is loyal and trustworthy.

I had sworn to hurt those who had betrayed Malcolm, but I wasn't happy with myself as I limped on to the front parlour she liked best of all. I stood in the doorway and stared at her, my heart pounding, for I wanted so much to run to her arms, and sit on her lap. Was it right for me to pretend to be Malcolm, when I hadn't given her a chance to explain?

'Corrine,' I said in a gruff voice. Oh, the game was so good, I couldn't be just Bart and feel secure. When I was Malcolm I felt so strong, so right.

'Bart,' she cried happily, rising to extend her arms. 'You've finally come to see me! I'm so glad to see you well and strong again.' Then she hesitated. 'Who told you my name?'

'John Amos told me,' I said, frowning at her. 'He told me you fed Apple and gave him water while I was away. Is that true?'

'Yes, darling, of course I did what I could for Apple. He missed you so much I pitied him. Surely you aren't angry?'

'You stole him from me,' I cried like a baby. 'He was the best friend I ever had; the only one who really loved me, and you stole him away so now he likes you better.'

'No, he doesn't. Bart, he likes me, but he loves you.'

Now she wasn't smiling and pleased looking. Just like John Amos had said, she knew I was on to her wiles. She was gonna tell me more lies.

'Don't speak to me so gruffly,' she begged. 'It doesn't become a boy of ten years. Darling, you've been gone so long, and I've missed you so much. Can't you even show me a little affection?'

Suddenly, despite my promise I was running into her arms and throwing my arms about her. 'Grandmother! I really did hurt my knee bad! I was sweating so much my bed was wet. They wrapped me in a cold blanket and Momma and Daddy rubbed me down with ice. There was a mean doctor who wanted to cut off my leg, but Daddy wouldn't let him. That doctor said he was glad I wasn't his son.' I paused to take a breath. I forgot all about Malcolm. 'Grandmother, I found out my daddy loves me after all – or else he would have been glad for that doctor to cut off my leg.'

She seemed shocked. 'Bart, for heaven's sake! How can you have the slightest doubt that he loves you? Of course he does. He'd have to love you, and Christopher was always a kind, loving boy . . .'

How did she know my daddy's name was Christopher? I narrowed my eyes. She was holding her hands over her mouth like she'd given away some secret. Then she was crying.

Tears. One of the ways women had to work on men.

I turned away. Hated tears. Hated people who were weak. I put my hand on my shirt front and felt the hard cover of Malcolm's book against my bare chest. That book was giving me his strength, transferring it from the pages to my blood. What if I did wear a child's weak imperfect body? What difference did it make when soon she'd know just who was her master?

Home, had to get home before they missed me. 'Goodnight, Corrine.'

I left her still crying, while I still wondered how she knew my daddy's name.

In my garden I checked my peach pit again. No roots yet. I dug up my sweet peas again. Still not sprouting. I didn't have luck with flowers, with peach pits, with nothing. With nothing but playing Malcolm the powerful. At that I was getting better and better. Smiling and happy, I went to bed.

THE HORNS OF DILEMMA *Jory*

Never was Bart in our yard where he should be. I climbed the tree and sat on the wall and then I saw Bart over in that lady's yard, down on his knees crawling. Sniffing the ground like a dog. 'Bart!' I yelled, 'Clover's gone, but you can't take his place.'

I knew what he was doing, burying a bone and sniffing around until he found it. He looked up, his eyes glazed and disoriented – and then, he began to bark.

I yelled to set him straight, but he went on playing like a frolicking puppy before suddenly he became an old man who dragged his leg. And it wasn't even the leg he'd hurt. What a nut he was. 'Bart, straighten up! You're ten, not a hundred. If you keep walking crooked you'll grow that way.'

'Crooked days make crooked ways.'

'You don't make good sense.'

'And the Lord said, "Do unto others as they have done unto you".'

'Wrong. The correct quotation is: "Do unto others as you would have done unto you".' I reached to assist what seemed to be an old man. Bart scowled, panted, grabbed at his chest, then cried out about his bad heart that shouldn't have to endure tree-climbing.

'Bart, I'm fed up with you! All you do is make trouble. Have some sympathy for Mom and Dad – and me. It's going to be embarrassing having you for my brother when we go back to school.'

He limped along behind me as I headed towards home, still panting, muttering in between moans about how already he was a master of finances. 'Never was born a brain more clever than mine,' he mumbled.

He has really gone crazy, was all I could think as I listened to him. When he'd scrubbed his filthy hands with a brush as if he really wanted to get them clean, I gasped. That wasn't like Bart at all. He was still pretending to be someone else. Soon he had his hands clean and was in bed. I ran fast to where I could eavesdrop on my parents who were in the living-room dancing to slow music.

As always, something sweet, soft and romantic stole over me to see them like that. The tender way she looked at him; the gentle way he touched her. I cleared my throat before they did anything too intimate. Without changing their positions both looked at me questioningly. 'Yes, Jory?' said Mom, her blue eyes dreamy.

'I want to talk to you about Bart,' I said. 'I think there are a few things you should know.'

Dad looked relieved. Mom seemed to shrink into herself as quietly she sat beside Dad on the sofa. 'We've been hoping you would come to us with Bart's secret.'

None of it was easy to say. 'Well,' I began slowly, hoping to find the right words, 'first you should know Bart has lots of nightmares in which he wakes up crying. He pretends too much, such as hunting big game and normal kid stuff like that, but when I catch him crawling around sniffing the ground, then digging up a nasty old bone and carrying it between his teeth, only to bury it somewhere else, that's going too far.' I paused and waited for them to say something. Mom had her head turned as if she was listening to hear the wind. Dad leaned forward watching me intensely.

'Go on, Jory,' he urged. 'Don't stop now. We're not blind. We see that Bart is changing.'

Dreading to tell more, I hung my head and spoke very low. 'I've tried several times to tell you before. I've been afraid I'd cry and embarrass myself, then too, you've both been so worried about Bart, I couldn't speak.'

'Please, don't hold anything back.' Dad said.

I looked only at my father, unable to meet my mother's fearful gaze. 'The lady next door gives Bart all sorts of expensive gifts. She's given him a St Bernard puppy he calls Apple, a miniature electric train along with small village and mountain settings – the complete works. She's had one huge room of hers turned into a playroom just for him. She would give me gifts too, but Bart won't let her.'

Stunned, they turned to one another. Finally Dad said, 'What else?'

I swallowed and heard my odd husky voice. This was the worst part, the part that really hurt. 'Yesterday I was in the backyard near the wall . . . you know, where that hollow tree is. I had the hedge clippers and was pruning like you showed me, Dad, when I smelled something putrid. It seemed to come from that hole in the tree. When I checked . . . I found . . .' again I had to swallow before I could say it. '*I found Clover*. He was dead and decaying. I dug a grave for him.' Hastily I turned my back to wipe away tears, then I told them the rest, 'I found a wire twisted around his neck. Somebody deliberately murdered my dog!'

They just sat on the sofa looking appalled and shocked, and also scared. Mom blinked back her tears, she too had loved Clover. Her hands trembled when she reached for a handkerchief. Next she locked her nervous hands together and kept them on her lap. Neither she nor Dad asked who had killed Clover. I figured they thought the same as I did.

Before he went to bed, Dad came into my room and talked to me for an hour, asking all sorts of questions about Bart, what he did with his time, where he went, and about the woman next door. I felt better now that I'd warned them. Now they could plan what to do with Bart. And I cried that night for the last time over Clover who had been my first and only pet. I was going on fifteen, almost a man's age, and tears were only for little boys – not for someone almost six feet tall.

'You leave me alone!' yelled Bart when I asked him not to go next door. 'You stop telling tales on me or you'll be sorry.'

Each day took us closer to September and school days. As

far as I could see Bart wasn't responding to the tender loving care my parents gave him. They were too understanding in my opinion.

'You listen to me, Bart, and stop pretending you're an old man named Malcolm Neal Foxworth, whoever he is.' But Bart couldn't let go of his pretend limp, his fake bad heart that made him gasp and pant. 'Nobody is waiting for you to die to inherit your fortune. Dear little brother, you don't have any fortune.'

I smiled, but charm had never worked on Bart and never would, I'm sorry to say.

'Got twenty billion, ten million, fifty-five thousand and six hundred and forty-two cents!' He used his fingers to tally up. 'But I can't remember how much I have in stock and bonds, so I guess you could triple that figure. A man isn't rich if he can name what he owns.'

I hadn't known he could even name a figure like that. Just when I would say something sarcastic, Bart let out a yelp and doubled over. He fell to the floor and gasped. 'Quick . . . my pills. I'm dying! My left arm is going numb. Save me, send for my doctors!'

That's when I left the house and went outdoors, and on the lawn I fell and pulled out a paperback novel to read. But he was getting to me, really getting to me. It was like living with Jekyll and Hyde. If he had to act, why the heck didn't he choose some role better than a lame old guy with a bad heart?

'Jory, don't you care if I die?' Bart came out and asked me.

'Nope.'

'You've never liked me.'

'I liked you better when you acted your own age.'

'Would you believe Malcolm Neal Foxworth is the father of the lady next door, and she is my real grandmother, truly my own grandmother?'

'She told you that?'

'No. John Amos told me some, she told me more. John Amos

tells me lots of stuff. He told me Daddy Paul and Daddy Chris were not brothers, that my Momma only said that so we wouldn't find out her sin. He says a man named Bartholomew Winslow was my real daddy and he died in a fire. Our Mother seduced him.'

Seduced? I gave him a long searching look. 'Do you know what that word means?'

'Nope – but I know it's bad, real bad!'

'Do you love our Mother?'

Worry tormented his dark eyes. He sat heavily on the ground and contemplated his sneakers. He should have answered quickly, spontaneously. 'Bart, do me a big favour and yourself too – go into the house and tell Mom and Dad what's bothering you. They'll understand anything. I know you think Mom loves me best, but it's not so. She has room in her heart for ten children.'

'Ten?' he screamed. 'You mean Momma is gonna adopt more?' He jumped up and ran then, haltingly, as if pretending to be old had made him lose what little agility he had. That hospital stay had robbed him of a great many things, in my opinion.

It was sneaky of me and not quite honourable, but I had to hear what Bart told our mother when they were alone. She was on the back veranda, Cindy was on her lap, dozing as Mom read a book. When Bart ran up she quickly put the book down, then shifted Cindy on to a nearby chair as Bart stood staring at her, mutely pleading with his eyes.

Then, of all things, he asked, 'What's your name?'

'You know my name,' she said.

'Does it begin with a C?'

'Yes, of course it does.' Now she looked disturbed.

'But, but,' he stumbled, 'I know someone who cries after you go away. Someone little like me who is locked in closets and other scary places by his father who doesn't like him any more. Once the father put him in the attic for punishment. Big, dark, scary attic with mice and spooky shadows and spiders everywhere.'

She seemed to freeze. 'Who told you all of that?'

'His stepmother had dark red hair until he found out that she was only his father's paramour.'

Even from where I hid I could hear Momma breathing hard and fast, as if that small boy she lifted on her lap had suddenly turned dangerous. 'Darling, you don't know what a paramour is, do you?

He stared ahead into space. 'There was a lady slender and fair who had red in her dark-dark hair. And she wasn't even married to his father who didn't care what he did, how he cried, or even if he died.'

Her lips trembled but she forced a smile. 'Bart, I believe you have some poet in you. All that has a cadence, and it rhymes too.'

He scowled, turning dark burning eyes on her. 'I despise poets, artists, musicians, dancers!'

She shivered and I can't say I blamed her. He scared me too. 'Bart, I have to ask you this, and you must give me a truthful answer. Remember no matter what you say you won't be punished – did you hurt Clover?'

'Clover done gone away. Won't come back to live in my doghouse now.'

She pushed him away then, and quickly got up to leave the patio, then she remembered Cindy, and rushed back to pick her up. None of what she did made me feel better as I watched Bart's eyes.

As always, soon after one of his mean attacks, Bart grew tired and sleepy and went to bed without his dinner. My mother smiled, laughed, dressed to attend a formal celebration in honour of my father who had been voted chief-of-staff of his hospital. I stood at the window and watched Dad lead her proudly to his car.

Late, way after two, I heard them come in. I had yet to fall asleep, and could hear their conversation in the living-room.

'Chris, I don't understand Bart at all, the way he talks, the way he moves, or even how he looks. I feel afraid of my own son, and that's sick.'

'Come now, darling,' he said with his arm about her shoulders, 'I think you exaggerate. Bart will grow up to be a great actor if he keeps this up.'

'Chris, I know that high fevers sometimes leave a child with brain damage. Did the fever destroy part of his brain?'

'Look, Cathy, Bart tested out just fine. Don't go getting notions just because we gave him that test. All high-fever patients have to undergo such examinations.'

'But did you find anything unusual?' she persisted.

'No,' Dad said firmly, 'he's just an ordinary little boy with lots of emotional problems, and we, if anyone can, should understand what he's going through.'

What did that mean?

'But Bart has everything! He isn't growing up as we did. He should be happy. Don't we do everything we can?'

'Yes, but sometimes even that isn't enough. Each child is different, each has different needs. Obviously we are not giving Bart what he needs.'

Mom was given to hot quick answers, yet she sat on, silent and still, as I waited for more information. Dad wanted her to go to bed immediately, easy enough to see from the way he kissed her neck. But she was deep in thought. Her eyes were fixed on her silver sandals as she spoke of how Clover had died.

'It couldn't have been Bart,' she said slowly, as if to convince herself as well as Dad. 'It had to be some sadist who tortures animals – you know how we read the animals in the zoo were being crippled? One of them must have seen Clover.' Her voice died away for so seldom did we ever see a stranger on our road.

'Chris,' she added, while that horrible look of fright was still on her face, 'today Bart took me completely by surprise. He told me about a little boy who was locked in cupboards and in the attic. Later on he told me that little boy's name was Malcolm. Could he know about him? Who could have told him that name? Chris, do you think somehow Bart has found out about us?'

I jerked. What was there to know about them that I didn't already know? I knew they had some terrible secret. I crawled away, then raced to my room and threw myself on my bed. Something awful was wrong with our lives, I felt it in my bones – and Bart must have sensed it in his too.

THE SNAKE *Bart*

Sun and fog were playing games, keeping each other company. I had to sit alone in our garden. For fun I stared down at the thick scabs on my knee. I'd been warned by Daddy not to pick them off or they'd leave scars – but who cared about scars? I began to carefully lift the edges of the crust just to see what was underneath. I didn't see a darn thing but red tender-looking flesh, ready to bleed again.

Sun won the game in the sky and shone hot on my head. Almost heard my brains frying. Didn't want fried brains. I moved to the shade. Now my head was aching. I bit down on my lower lip hard enough to draw blood. Didn't hurt but later it would swell up so big, Momma would have to feel worried. That would be good. She should be worried about what was happening to me.

Used to be Momma's little boy who got lots of attention until that dratted little girl came to take my place. Soon Momma and Jory would return from ballet class. That's all they cared about – dancing and Cindy. I knew about the important things in life, what really counted most – money. Having lots of it, then you didn't have to think about needing it, or how to get it. John Amos and Malcolm's book had taught me that.

'Bart,' said Emma who'd stolen up behind me, 'I'm so sorry you missed your birthday trip to Disneyland. To make up for that I've made you a little birthday cake of your very own.' She held in her hands a tiny cake with one candle in the middle of the chocolate. Was not just one year old! I struck that cake from her hands so it fell to the ground. She cried out, looking hurt enough to cry as she backed off. 'That wasn't very grateful, or very kind,' she said in a choked way. 'Bart, why do you have to act so ugly? We all try to do our best.'

I stuck out my tongue. She sighed and left me alone.

Later Emma came out again with that bratty girl in her arms. She wasn't my sister. Didn't want any sister. I hid behind a tree and peeked around. Emma put Cindy in the plastic swimming pool. She began to kick and splash in the shallow water. Dumb, dumb, dumb . . . couldn't even swim. See how Emma laughed and enjoyed all her baby-doings when I could stand on my head. Now if I sat in that pool and splashed with my hands and feet she wouldn't think it was cute.

I waited for Emma to go away, but Emma pulled up a chair, sat down, and began to shell peas. Plop, plop, plop went the green peas in the blue bowl. 'That's it, deary,' Emma encouraged Cindy, 'splash the water, kick your pretty legs, flap your sweet arms, and make your limbs strong so soon you'll be swimming.'

I watched, waited, each pea she shelled told me soon Emma would have to get up and go into the kitchen. Cindy would be left alone. All alone. And she couldn't swim. Cats crouched down low like me when they wanted to catch a bird. Wish I had a tail to swish.

The last green pea fell. Emma rose to leave. I tensed my muscles. Just then Momma drove up in her bright red car and pulled to a stop by the garage. Emma waited to say hello. First it was Jory bounding over the lawn. 'Hi, Emma!' he called, 'what's for dinner?'

'You'll like my dinner no matter what,' answered Emma, all grins for him, her handsome darling. Not like she treated me – the brat! 'As for Bart,' she went on, 'I know he'll hate the peas, the vegetable casserole, the lamb chops and the dessert. Lord knows that boy is hard to please.'

Momma stopped to talk to Emma like she wasn't a servant, then she ran to play with Cindy, kissing and hugging her as if she hadn't seen the dummy in ten years. 'Mom,' sang out Jory, 'why don't we both put on swimsuits and join Cindy in her pool?'

'I'll race you to the house, Jory,' agreed Momma, and off they ran like little kids.

'Now you be a good little girl and keep on playing with your rubber ducky and boat,' said Emma to Cindy. 'Emma will be right back.'

My head lifted before I began to wriggle on my belly on the ground. The brat in the pool stood up and took off her bathing suit. Stark naked and bold she hurled her wet suit at me, then teased and laughed and tormented me with her bare flesh. Then, as if bored with my reaction, she sat again in the shallow water and stared down at herself with a secret little smile. Wicked! Shameless! Imagine her showing her private parts to me.

Mothers should teach their daughters how to act decent, proper, modest. My mother was just like Corrine, just like Corrine whom John Amos had said was weak and never punished her children enough. 'Yes, Bart, your grandmother ruined her children, and now they live in sin and flaunt God and his moral rules!'

I guess it was up to me to teach Cindy a lesson about modesty and shame. Forward I wriggled. Now I had her attention. Her blue eyes opened wide. Her rosy full lips parted. At first she seemed happy that finally I was gonna play kiddy games with her. Then, something wise put fright in her eyes. She froze and made me think of a timid rabbit scared by a vicious snake. Snake. Much better to be a snake than a cat. Snake in the Garden of Eden doing unto Eve what should have been done in the beginning. *Lo, said the Lord when he spied Eve in her nakedness, go forth from Eden and let the world hurl their stones.*

Hissing and flicking my tongue in and out, I edged closer.

Was the Lord who spoke and I who obeyed. Wicked mother who refused to punish had made me what I was, an evil snake willing to do the Lord's bidding, even if it wasn't my own way.

I tried to flatten my head with willpower and make it small, flat and reptile-like. Sinister, had to look sinister, for sinister was the word for today. Meaning evil, threatening harm. Tears came to Cindy's huge scared eyes, and she began to bawl as she tried to wriggle over the rounded rim of the wading pool. The water wasn't deep enough for a little girl to drown in, or else Emma wouldn't have left her alone.

But if a boa constrictor from Brazil was on the loose – what chance did a two-year-old have?

I wriggled over the side and squirmed in the water. She screamed, 'Barr-tie! Go way, Barr-tie!'

'Hsss . . . ssss,' I went. My s's longer than John Amos's. I coiled my body around her small one and hooked my legs under her neck enough to drag her down to the water. Couldn't really drown but the Lord above had to warn those who sinned. I'd seen jungle snakes unhinge their jaws on TV. I tried to unhinge mine. Then I could swallow Cindy whole.

All of a sudden another snake had me. I yelped and released my grip on Cindy to keep from drowning or being eaten alive. *Lord, why hast thou forsaken me?*

'What the Devil do you think you're doing?' yelled Jory, red with rage as he shook me until my head rolled. 'I watched you wriggle your way along to see what you had in mind. Bart – did you try to drown Cindy?'

'No!' I gasped. 'Just punishing her a little, not much.'

'Yeah,' he sneered, 'like you punished Clover a little.'

'Never did nothing to Clover. I take good care of Apple. I am not a bad boy . . . I'm not, not, not.'

'Why are you crying if you are so innocent? You killed him! I see it in your eyes.'

I glared hard at Jory, fury washing over me. 'You hate me! I know you do. ' I lunged forward and tried to hit him. Couldn't. So I lowered my head, backed up, and ran forward to butt him squarely in the stomach. Down he went, all doubled over, crying out from the pain. Before he could kill me, I kicked him but didn't know it would end up where it did. My aim was never good. Gee . . . that must hurt a lot.

'Unfair to kick in the groin,' he groaned, his face so pale he seemed on the edge of a faint. 'That's dirty fighting, Bart. Gross too.' Meanwhile Cindy had recovered enough to scramble from the pool, and naked she tottered off towards the house, howling at the top of her lungs.

'Wicked sinful girl!' I screamed, 'all this is her fault. Her fault!'

From the back door Emma came on the run. Her white apron fluttering, her hands covered with flour. She was closely followed by Momma who had put on a skimpy blue bikini. 'Bart, what have you done?' screamed Momma. She swept Cindy up in her arms, then swooped to pick up a towel Emma had dropped.

'Mommy,' sobbed Cindy. 'Big snake came . . . big snake!'

Why, imagine that. She'd known what I was. Not so dumb after all. Momma wrapped the towel about Cindy and stood her on the ground. She glared at me, I who had my foot raised to kick Jory as he panted with pain. 'Bart . . . if you dare to kick Jory again you will regret it!'

Emma glared at me with hatred. I looked from one to the other. Everybody hated me, would be glad to see me in my grave. Sore and full of pain, Jory tried to rise, not so graceful now. Just as awkward as me. He wasn't so handsome now. Still he could shout: 'You're crazy, Bart! Crazy as a loon!'

'Bart, don't you dare throw that stone at your brother,' cried Momma when she saw me swoop to pick up one.

'You dreadful boy! Don't you throw that,' screamed Emma.

I whipped around and ran to pound on Emma with my fists. 'You stop calling me names,' I yelled. 'I'm not dreadful! I'm not bad!'

Momma raced towards me then, and grabbed me. 'Don't you ever throw another stone as long as you live, or use your fists on another woman,' Momma shouted as she pinned my shoulders to the ground.

Red rage entered my mind, making me see her as all women with beguiling curves and wiles. Malcolm knew about them all, told everything about how he'd wanted to pound all their breasts flat. I filled my eyes with Malcolm's malicious hatred, and it worked. Momma trembled as she held me down. 'Bart, what's wrong with you? You don't know what you're saying or doing. You don't even look like yourself.'

I bared my teeth as if to bite her – and tried to. She slapped me then, hard, repeatedly, until I began to cry.

'You go up into the attic and stay there, Bart Sheffield, until I come up and see what has to be done to set you straight.'

Scary in the attic. I sat on the edge of one of those little beds and waited for her to come in. She'd never spanked me. A few slaps, and the ones on my face today was all the punishment I'd had up until now . . . and now she was doing to me just what had been done to Malcolm. I was just like Malcolm.

The door into the attic opened and I heard her climbing the steep, narrow stairs. Her mouth was set in a grim line as she towered above me, staring downwards, as if forcing herself to look at me. I never thought she could look so mean.

'Pull down your pants, Bart.'

'No!'

'Do as I say or your punishment will be much worse.'

'No! You can't hurt me. You lay one hand on me and I'll wait until you're in your old ballet class and then I'll get Cindy – and Emma won't be able to stop me. I can be in a thousand places before she can move to one – and the police won't put me in jail because I'm a minor.'

'Bart, I'm losing patience with you.'

'That won't be all you'll lose if you hit me!' I bellowed.

She paused three feet from where I sat on the bed. Her small pale hands rose to her throat and she said quietly. 'Oh, God . . .' and it was just a hoarse whisper, 'I should have known a child conceived under such circumstances would turn out like this. Bart, I'm so sorry your son is a monster.'

A monster? Was I a monster?

No – she was the monster! She was doing to me just what Malcolm's mother had done – the cause of him being put in the attic and punished. I hated her then, just as much as I'd loved her before.

I screamed it out: 'I hate you, Momma! I hope you drop dead.'

That's when she backed away, tears in her eyes, then she turned and ran. But before she went down the stairs she locked the door to keep me up in that miserable dry attic that I hated and feared. She was going to make me strong like Malcolm, and mean too. Some day she'd pay. I'd make her pay for doing this to me, when I wanted to be good, and wanted her to love me just a little more than Cindy or Jory. I began to cry. Nothing ever worked out the way I wanted it to.

It was Daddy who spanked my bare bottom after he came home and heard all they had to tell him about me. I admired him for ignoring the way I pleaded, and apologized.

'Did you feel any of that?' he asked when he was finished, and I pulled up my pants.

I smiled. 'No. To hurt me you got to break my bones and then the police would throw you in jail for child abuse.' He studied me with those stern blue eyes.

'You think you have the best of us, don't you?' he asked in his calm rational way. 'You think because you are a minor there is no law that can touch you, but you are wrong, Bart. We live in a civilized society where people are expected to conform to the rules. No one is ever beyond the control of the law, even the President. And one of the worst punishments for a child to endure is being locked away so he cannot come and go at his own free will.' He looked sad then. 'That can be a very traumatic experience.'

I didn't say anything. He spoke again. 'Your mother and I have decided we can no longer tolerate your behaviour. So as soon as I can arrange it, you will go once a day to a psychiatrist. If we have to, if you persist in defying us, we will leave you in the care of doctors who can help you to learn how to behave normally.'

'You can't make me,' I gasped, terrified some shrink would have me locked away behind bars forever. 'If you try and force me I'll kill myself!'

He looked at me sternly. 'Bart, you won't kill yourself. So don't you sit there and think you can outwit your mother or me. Your mother and I have faced up to bigger and better than a ten-year-old boy – remember that.'

Later that evening when I was in my bed, I heard Momma

and Daddy really yelling at each other, yelling out like I'd never heard them before.

'Why did you send Bart into the attic, Catherine? Did you have to do that? Couldn't you just have ordered him to stay in his room and wait until I came home?'

'No! He likes being in his room. He has everything in there to make it a pleasant place to be – and as you know well, the attic is not pleasant. I did what I had to.'

'What you had to? Cathy – do you realize whom you sound like?'

'Well,' she said with ice in her voice, 'haven't I been telling you all along that's what I am – a bitch who cares only about herself?'

They took me to a head shrink the very next day, and shoved me down in a chair and told me to stay there. They sat beside me until a door opened and we were called inside. A woman doctor was behind a big desk. At least they could have chosen a man. I hated her because her hair was slick and black like Madame Marisha's hair when she was young and posing for pictures. Her white blouse bulged in front so I had to turn my eyes away.

'Dr Sheffield, you and your wife can wait outside, we will talk later.' I watched my parents go out the door. Never had I felt so all alone as when that woman turned to me and looked me over with her kind eyes that were hiding mean thoughts. 'You don't want to be here, do you?' she asked. I wouldn't give her the satisfaction of letting her know I heard. 'My name is Dr Mary Oberman.'

So what?

'There are toys over on that table . . . help yourself.'

Toys, I wasn't a baby. I glared at her. She turned her head and I knew she was uncomfortable though trying not to let it show. 'Your parents have told me you like to play pretend games. Is that because you don't have enough playmates?'

Didn't have any. But darn if that idiot woman was gonna know. I'd be a fool to tell her John Amos was the best friend I had. Once it had been my grandmother, but she had betrayed me.

'Bart, you can sit there and be silent, but you only succeed in hurting those who love you most, and you are hurt more than anyone else. Your parents want to help you. That's why they brought you here. You have to co-operate and try. Tell me if you're happy. Tell me if you feel frustrated, and if you like the way your life is going.'

Wouldn't say yes, wouldn't say no. Wouldn't say anything and she couldn't make me. Then she talked about people who kept themselves locked up, and how that could ruin them emotionally. All her words were like rain on the windowpane I made myself into.

'Do you hate your mother and father?'

Wouldn't answer.

'Your brother Jory, do you like him?'

Jory was okay. He'd be better if he was more clumsy than me, and ugly too.

'Your adopted sister, Cindy . . . what do you think of her?'

Maybe my eyes told her something, for she scribbled away on her notepad. 'Bart,' she began when she put her pen aside, her face trying to look motherly and kind, 'if you refuse to co-operate, we will have no choice but to put you in a hospital where many doctors can try to help you regain control of your emotions. You won't be mistreated, but it won't be as nice as being home. You won't have your own room, your own things, your own parents except once a week for an hour. So don't you think it would be much nicer to try and help yourself before this goes any further? What is it that changed you from the boy you were last summer?'

I didn't want to be locked in some crazy house, with lots of nuts who might be bigger and meaner than me, and I wouldn't be able to visit John Amos and Apple.

What could I do? I remembered words from Malcolm's book, and how he made people think he was giving in and all the time he went his own way. I'd cry, I'd say how sorry I was, and when I did just this I even thought I was sincere when I said, 'It's Momma . . . she loves Jory more than me. She loves Cindy better too. I don't have anybody. I hate not having anybody.

It went on and on. Even after I really blabbed, she told my parents I'd have to continue seeing her for a year or more. 'He's a very confused little boy.' She smiled and touched my mother's shoulder. 'Don't blame yourself. Bart seems programmed for self-loathing, and though he might seem to hate you for not loving him enough, he doesn't like himself Therefore he believes anyone who does love him is a big fool. It's a sickness all right. As real as any physical disease, and worse in many ways, for Bart cannot find himself.'

I was hiding, eavesdropping, surprised to hear her say what she did.

'He loves you, Mrs Sheffield, with an almost religious love. Therefore he expects you to be perfect while knowing he is unworthy of your attention, and still, paradoxically he still wants you to see him and acknowledge him as the best son you have.'

'But I don't understand,' said Momma, leaning her head on Daddy's shoulder. 'How can he love me and want to hurt me so much?'

'Human nature is very complex. Your son is very complex. The good and the bad are fighting to dominate his personality. He is unconsciously aware of this battle and has found a very intriguing solution. He indentifies the evil side of himself as an old man he's named Malcolm. Just another of the many characters who enable him to like himself better.'

Both my parents sat very still with wide eyes, looking sort of helpless.

Hours later before I said my bedtime prayers I crept down the long hall and listened outside my parents' bedroom. Momma was saying, 'It's as if we will always be in the attic, and never never set free.'

What did the attic have to do with Malcolm and me? Was it only because both of us had been sent up there for punishment?

On my hands and knees I stole away down the hall and crept into my bed and lay there quietly, scared of myself and my subconscious.

Beneath my pillow was Malcolm's journal which I was absorbing day by day, night by night. Growing stronger, growing smarter too.

GATHERING DARKNESS *Jory*

In the living-room the next evening, Mom and Dad settled down before the fire I'd kindled, then lit. Forgotten by them because I said so little, I crouched down on the floor near the doorway, hoping they wouldn't see me there, and they'd think I'd gone away as I should have. I didn't feel good about deliberately deceiving them, but sometimes it was better to know for a certainty, than to keep on guessing.

At first Mom didn't say anything much, then she brought up the visit to Dr Oberman. 'Bart hates me, Chris. He hates you too, and Jory and Cindy. I think he's got Emma on his list too, but more than anyone, it's me he despises. He resents me for not loving him exclusively.' He pulled her closer to his chest, and held her there as they talked. When they mentioned slipping into Bart's bedroom and seeing if he was there, I quickly scurried into a nearby closet and waited for them to pass on to Bart's room.

'Has he eaten dinner?' asked Dad.

'No,' and she said this like she wanted him to stay asleep so she could avoid the problem he was when awake. But just them being there, staring down at him brought Bart out of his nap, and without a word to respond to their affectionate greeting, he followed them into the dining room. Meals had to be eaten even when a ten-year-old boy sat silent and scowling, refusing to meet anyone's eyes.

It was a terribly awkward meal. No one was comfortable, so appetites were small, and even Cindy was cross. Emma didn't speak either, only performed her duties silently. Even the wind that blew incessantly died down and the trees stood still, their leaves hanging as if frozen. All of a sudden it felt so cold, making me think of the graves Bart was always talking about.

I sat wondering how Mom and Dad could force Bart to go to Dr Oberman's sessions. How could anyone force him to talk when he could be so darn stubborn? And Dad was busy enough without taking time off from his patients – why, that alone should show Bart who cared enough.

'Going to bed now,' said Bart coldly, standing without asking permission to leave the table. 'I hate your meals, Emma. I don't think anything you're cooking is as good as it used to be.'

He left the dining room. We sat on, caught in some kind of spell Bart had cast.

'Shouldn't we punish him for saying that to Emma?'

'No, Cathy. The boy isn't himself. Obviously something is bothering him so much he can't even eat. We have to find out what it is.'

'Mom,' I said, 'I think if you went in and sat on Bart's bed first tonight, and stayed a long time with him, and didn't come into my room or Cindy's, that might make up for a lot.'

She gave me a strange long look, as if not believing it could be that simple. Dad agreed with me, saying it wouldn't do any harm.

Bart was faking sleep, easy to see that. I backed away and stood near Dad in the hallway, in the shadows where Bart couldn't see us. I was ready to spring forward and save Mom if Bart turned mean. Dad kept a restraining hand on my shoulder, and whispered softly, 'He's just a boy, Jory, a very troubled little boy. A bit smaller than most ten-year-old boys, a bit thinner too, and maybe that's part of the problem. Bart is having more trouble growing up than most boys do.'

Tensing, I waited for him to say more. 'It's amazing how he could be born with so little grace, when his mother has so much.'

I looked to where Mom stood gazing down on Bart who looked darkly sullen in sleep – if he was asleep . . . then she came running from his room, throwing Dad a wild distraught look. 'Chris, I'm afraid of him! You go in! If he wakes up and yells at me as he did before, I'll slap him! I'll feel like putting him in the cupboard, or up in the attic.' Both her hands rose to clamp over her mouth. 'I didn't mean that,' she whispered weakly.

'Of course you didn't. I hope he didn't hear you. Cathy, I think you'd better take two aspirins and go to bed, and I'll tuck Bart and Jory into bed.' He gave me a big joking smile as I grinned back. Our night-time talks were the kind of tucking in he gave to me, advice on how to handle difficult situations. Man-to-man stuff a woman didn't have to know about.

It was Dad who had the nerve to approach Bart and with ease he perched on the side of his bed. I knew Bart always slept lightly, and when Dad sat down, the depression he made rolled Bart's slight figure on to his side. That would awaken even someone like me, who used to sleep deeply and sound.

Cautiously I stole closer, wanting to see for myself if Bart was faking. Behind his closed lids his eyeballs were jerking spasmodically, as if he watched a tennis game or something much more terrifying.

'Bart . . . wake up.'

As if Dad had fired the words from a giant cannon put near his ears, Bart jolted wide awake. He bolted upright, his dark eyes bulging and terrified. He stared at Dad.

'Son, it's not eight o'clock yet. Emma has made a lemon pie for dessert that she had to leave in the fridge to set. Don't tell me you don't want a slice. It's a beautiful evening. I used to think when I was your age, that twilight was the best time of all to play outside. Hide and seek, or red light, green light . . .'

Bart stared at Dad as if he spoke in a foreign tongue.

'Come, Bart, don't sulk alone. I love you, and your mother loves you. It doesn't matter if sometimes you move less than gracefully. There are other things that count more, such as honour and respect. Stop trying to be what you aren't. You don't have to be anyone super-special, for in our eyes, you already are super-special.'

Bart just sat on his bed and stared at Dad with hostility. Why couldn't Dad see him as I did? Could a man as smart as Dad be blind when it came to seeing his son honestly? Had Bart opened his eyes when Mom was in the room, and had she seen the hatred there? She could always see more than Dad, even if he was a doctor.

'Summer's almost gone, Bart. Lemon pies get eaten by others. What you don't take today may not be there tomorrow.'

Why was he being so nice to that boy who looked at him with daggers that could kill?

Obediently, when Dad turned to leave the room, Bart tagged along behind him. I was Bart's unseen shadow. Suddenly Bart ran ahead of Dad who was on the back porch now, and he skipped backwards until he nearly tumbled down the steps! 'You aren't my father,' he growled, 'and you can't fool me. *You hate me and want me dead!*'

Heavily Dad sat in a chair close to the one where Mom was sitting with Cindy on her lap. And Bart went to the swings to sit on one, not pushing with his feet, just sitting and holding fast to the ropes, as if he might fall off the wooden slat.

We all ate a slice of Emma's delicious lemon pie, all but Bart, he just sat where he was and refused to budge. Then Dad was getting up and saying he had to check on a patient in the hospital. He threw Bart a worried glance and spoke softly to Mom. 'Take it easy, darling. Stop looking so troubled. I'll be home soon. Maybe Mary Oberman isn't the best psychiatrist for Bart. He seems to hold a great deal of hostility towards women. I'll find another psychiatrist, a man.' He leaned to kiss her upturned face. I heard the soft moist sound of their lips meeting. Then they stared deep into each other's eyes and I wondered what they saw. 'I love you, Cathy. And please stop worrying. Everything will work out fine. We will all survive.'

'Yes,' she said dully, throwing Bart a doubtful look, 'but I can't help worrying about Bart . . . he seems so confused.'

Straightening, Dad cast Bart a long, hard, observant look. 'Yes,' he said without doubt. 'Bart's a survivor too. See how fast he clings to the ropes, and he's less than two feet from the ground. He just doesn't trust or believe in himself. I think he seeks strength in pretending to be older, wiser; his security is in something else. As a ten-year-old boy he is lost. So it's up to us to find the right person to help him, when it seems we cannot.'

'Drive carefully,' she said, as she always said, watching him depart with her heart in her eyes.

Very determined to stay up and protect Mom and Cindy, I still found myself growing sleepy. Every time I checked I saw Bart still on the swing, his dark eyes staring blankly into space as very gently he moved the swing an inch or so, no more than the wind could blow his weight.

'I'm going to put Cindy to bed now, Jory,' Mom said to me, then she called to Bart. 'Bedtime . . . I'll be in to see you in a few minutes, so clean your teeth and wash your hands and face – and we saved you a slice of lemon pie to eat before you brush your teeth.'

No reply from the swing, but he did get up awkwardly, pausing to glance at his bare feet, stopping to stare at his hands, to finger his pyjamas, to glance up at the sky, at the distant hills.

Inside the house Bart wandered aimlessly from object to object, picking it up, turning it over and staring at the bottom before he set it down. A small Venetian glass sailing boat held his attention for a moment, and then he seemed to freeze as his eyes found a lovely porcelain ballerina in arabesque position. It was a figurine my Mom had given to Dr Paul after she married my father; in many ways the dancer was like Mom must have looked when she was very young.

Gingerly he picked up the delicate figure with its fluffy frozen froth of lace tutu, and frail pale arms and legs. He turned it over, stared at the information imparted on the bottom. *Limoges*, it said, for I'd read that too. Next he touched the golden hair, parted in the middle and drawn softly back in waves and held in place with pink china roses, pale pink roses.

Then, deliberately, he let it slip from his hands.

It fell to the floor, where the rug didn't cover, and broke into several large pieces. I dashed forward thinking I could glue them back together and maybe Mom wouldn't notice – but Bart put his foot on the ballerina's head and ground it fiercely with his bare foot.

'Bart!' I cried out, 'that was a hateful thing to do. You know Mother prizes that more than anything else. You shouldn't have.'

'Don't tell me what I shouldn't and should do. You leave me alone, and say nothing about what you just saw. It was an accident, boy, an accident.'

Whose voice was that? Not Bart's. He was pretending to be that old man again.

I ran for a broom and a dustpan to clean up the shards of what had been a lovely ballerina, hoping Mom wouldn't notice it was missing from the shelf.

When I remembered Bart again, I hurried to find him slyly watching Mom as she held Cindy on her lap brushing her hair.

Mom glanced up and happened to catch Bart watching. I saw her blanch and try to smile, but something she saw made her smile fade before it even shone.

In a flashing streak Bart ran forward and shoved Cindy from Mom's lap! Cindy squealed as she fell on the floor – then jumped up to howl. She raced to Mom who picked her up again, then rose to tower over Bart.

'Bart, why did you do that?'

He spread his legs and stared up into her face, scornfully. Then he left the room without looking back.

'Mom,' I said as she calmed Cindy down and put her into bed, 'Bart's very sick in his head. You let Dad take him to any shrink he wants, but make him stay there until he's well.'

I heard her sob, but it wasn't until later that she broke down and cried.

This time it was I who held her; my arms that gave her comfort, and I felt so adult, responsible.

'Jory, Jory,' she sobbed, clinging fast to me, 'why does Bart hate me? What have I done?'

What could I say? I didn't know any of the answers.

'Maybe you should try to figure out why Bart is so different from me, for I would die rather than make you unhappy.' True words I sincerely meant.

She held to me, then stared into space.

'Jory, my life has been a series of obstacles. I feel if one more horrible thing happens, I may break and I can't allow that to happen. People are so complicated, Jory, especially adults. When I was ten, I used to think that adults had it so easy, with all the power and rights to do as they wanted – I never guessed being a parent was so difficult. But not to you, darling, not you . . .'

I knew her life had been full of sadness, losing her father, then Cory, and Carrie, my father and then her second husband too.

'The child of my revenge,' she whispered as if to herself. 'All the while I carried Bart, I suffered from the guilt I felt. I loved his father so much . . . and in a way I helped kill him.'

'Mom,' I said with sudden insight, 'maybe Bart senses your guilt when you look at him – do you think?'

PART THREE

MALCOLM'S RAGE *Bart*

Sunlight fell on my face and woke me up. When I was dressed, suddenly I didn't feel so old like Malcolm, and in a way I was glad, but in another way I was sad, for Malcolm was so dependable.

Why didn't I have friends my own age, like other boys? Why was it only old people liked me? It didn't matter that my grandmother said she loved me, now that she'd stolen Apple. I had to face up to the fact that only John Amos was my true friend.

I went outside and crawled around before breakfast, sniffed at the ground, smelled the wild things that were scared of me in daylight. Little rabbit ran like crazy and I wouldn't hurt it, wouldn't.

They kept watching me at the breakfast table like they expected me to do something awful. I noticed that Daddy didn't ask Jory how he was today, only asked me. I pouted my lower lip and scowled down at my cold cereal. Hated raisins! Looked like little dead bugs.

'Bart, I just asked you a question.'

I knew that already. 'I'm okay,' I said without looking at Daddy who always woke up in a good mood and never looked glum like me – and Momma. 'I just wish you'd hire a really good cook. Or better if Momma would stay home and cook our meals like other mothers. Emma's stuff ain't fit for man nor beast to eat.'

Jory stared at me hard and kicked my leg under the table like he was trying to warn me to keep my mouth shut.

'Emma didn't cook your cold cereal, Bart,' said Daddy. 'It comes that way in a box. And until this morning you always liked plenty of raisins. You used to want Jory's. But if raisins offend you in some way this morning, don't eat them. And why is your lower lip bleeding?'

Was it? Doctors were always seeing blood 'cause they were always cutting up people.

Jory took it on himself to answer. 'He was playing wolf this morning, Dad, that's all. I guess when he jumped at the rabbit and tried to bite off its head, he bit himself.' He grinned at me as if pleased with my stupidity.

Something was up. I could tell because nobody asked why I would play wolf. They just looked at me as if they expected me to act crazy.

Heard Momma and Daddy whispering beyond the pantry – talking about me. I heard doctors mentioned, new psychiatrists. Wouldn't go. They couldn't make me.

Then Mom was back in the kitchen and talking to Jory as Daddy went on to the garage and started his car.

'Mom, are we really going through with the performance tonight?'

She threw me a troubled glance, then forced a smile and said, 'Of course, I can't disappoint my students, their parents, and the other guests who have already bought their tickets.'

Fools and their money were soon parted.

Jory said, 'I think I'll call Melodie. Yesterday I told her the show might be cancelled.'

'Jory, why would you tell her that?'

He looked at me, as if I were to blame for everything, even shows that weren't cancelled – and I wouldn't go. Not even if they remembered to ask me. I didn't want to see no sissy-silly ballet where everybody danced, and said nothing. They weren't even going to dance *Swan Lake*, but the dumbest, dullest ballet of all – *Coppelia*.

Daddy came back into the house then, having forgotten something as usual. 'I guess you'll be the prince,' he said to Jory who turned on him with scorn.

'Gosh, Dad, don't you ever learn? There isn't a prince in

Coppelia. Most of the time I'm only in the *corps*, but Mom will be terrific in her role. She's choreographed it herself.'

'What are you saying?' roared Daddy, turning to glare at Momma. 'Cathy, you know you're not supposed to dance on your trick knee. You promised me you would never dance professionally again. At any moment that knee could give way and down you'd go. One more fall and you may end up crippled for life.'

'Just one more time,' she pleaded as if her whole life depended on dancing again. 'I'm going to be only the mechanical doll, sitting in a chair – don't get so worked up over nothing!'

'No!' he stormed again. 'If you go on tonight and don't fall, then you'll think your knee is fine. You'll want to repeat your success and one more time might see your knee permanently damaged. Just one serious fall and you could break your leg, your pelvis, your back . . . it's happened before, you know that!'

'Name every bone in my body,' she shrilled back at him, and I was thinking, thinking if she broke her bones and couldn't dance again, then she'd have to stay home with me all the time.

'Honestly, Chris, sometimes you act like I'm your slave. Look at me! I'm thirty-seven years old, and soon I'll be too old to dance at all. Let me feel useful, as you feel useful. I have to dance – just one more time.'

'No,' he repeated, but less firmly. 'If I give in it won't be the last time. You'll want to do it again . . .'

'Chris, I'm not going to plead. There is not a student I have capable of playing the role – and I am going on whether or not you like it!' She threw me a glance, as if she worried more about what I thought than what he thought. I was happy, very happy . . . for she was going to fall! Deep inside me I knew I could make her fall with my wishes. I'd sit in the audience and give her the evil eye, then she'd be my playmate. I'd teach her how to crawl around and sniff the ground like a dog, or an Indian, and she'd be surprised at all that could be found out from sniffing.

'I am not talking of a trifling injury, Catherine,' said that hateful husband. 'All your life you have given your joints a great deal of stress, and disregarded the pain. It's time you started realizing that the good health of your family depends on your wellbeing.'

I scowled at Dad, sorry he'd forgotten something, and had to come back and hear too much. Momma didn't even seem surprised he'd forgotten his wallet again. And he was a doctor who was supposed to have a good memory. She gave him his wallet which had been left beside his breakfast plate, and smiled at him crookedly. 'You do this every day. You go out to the garage, start your car, and then remember you don't have your wallet.'

His smile was just as crooked as hers. 'Yes, of course I do. It gives me the opportunity to come back and hear all the things you don't tell me.' Satisfied, he stuffed the wallet in his hip pocket.

'Chris, I don't like to go against your wishes, but I can't allow a second-rate performance, and it's Jory's big chance to show off in his solo . . .'

'For once in your life, Catherine, listen to what I say. That knee has been X-rayed, and you know the cartilage is broken and you still complain of chronic pain. And you haven't danced on stage for years. Chronic pain is one thing – acute pain another. Is that what you want?'

'Oh, you doctors!' she scoffed, 'all of you have such dreary notions of how frail the human body is. My knee hurts, so what? All my dancers complain of aches and pains. When I was in South Carolina, the dancers complained, in New York they complained, in London . . . so what is pain to a dancer? Nothing, Doctor, absolutely nothing I can't put up with.'

'Cathy!'

'My knee has not hurt seriously in more than two full years. Have you heard me gripe about pain? No, you haven't!'

With that, Dad strode from the kitchen, through the utility room, and on into the garage.

In a flash she was running after him, and I was running after her – hoping to hear more of this argument – and hoping she'd win. Then I'd have her for my very own, my own dear Momma!

'Chris,' she cried, throwing open the passenger door and slipping inside his car where she threw her arms about his neck. 'Don't go away angry. I love you, respect you, and I vow on my word of honour, that this will be the very last time I perform. I swear I will never, never dance on stage again. I know why I should stay home . . . I know . . .'

They kissed. Never saw people who liked to kiss so much. Then she was pulling away and looking softly into his eyes, and stroking his cheek as she murmured: 'This is my first chance to dance professionally with Julian's son, darling. Look at Jory, how much he resembles Julian. I've choreographed a special *pas de deux* in which I'm the mechanical doll and Jory is a mechanical soldier. It's the best thing I've ever done, I want you out in the audience watching, feeling proud of your wife and son. I don't want you sitting there worrying about my knee. Honestly, I've rehearsed, and it does not hurt.'

She stroked him, and kissed him some more and I could see he loved her more than anything, more than us, more than himself even. Fool. Damned fool to love any woman that much.

'All right,' he said. 'But this must be the last time. Your knee cannot take years and years of practice. Even in teaching, you use that knee too much, so much so that other joints could become impaired.'

I watched her turn from him and leave the car, her voice so sad when she spoke. 'Years ago Madame Marisha told me there would be no life for me without dancing, and I denied this was so – now I'm going to have the chance to find out.'

Good!

Just the words he needed to hear to make him come up with a new idea. He leaned and called to her: 'Cathy, what about that book you said you were going to write? This is a good time to start . . .' He gave me a long look, and I felt like a clear windowpane. 'Bart, remember you are very loved. If you feel resentment about anyone, or anything, all you have to do is tell me, or tell your mother. We are willing to listen and do what we can to make you happy.'

Happy? I'd be happy only when he was gone from her life. Happy only when I had her all to myself – and then I remembered that old man . . . two old men. Neither one of them wanted her to stay alive . . . neither one . . . I wanted to be like them especially like Malcolm, so I pretended he was in the garage, waiting for Daddy to drive away, and I'd be alone. He liked it when I was alone, when I felt sad, lonely, mean, angry . . . and right now he was smiling.

No sooner had Momma and Jory driven away, shortly after Daddy left, than Emma was at me again, pestering me, hating me.

'Bart, can't you wipe that blood from your lip? Do you have to keep on biting down? Most people refrain from deliberately hurting themselves.'

What did she know about being me? I didn't feel pain when I chewed on my lip. Liked to taste the blood.

'I'll tell you one thing, Bartholomew Scott Winslow Sheffield, if you were my little boy you'd feel the sting of my hand on your bottom. For I believe you like to torment people, and do every mean thing you can just to gain their attention. It doesn't take any psychiatrist with ten diplomas to know that!'

'Shut up!' I yelled.

'Don't you dare yell and tell me to shut up! I've had all I am going to take from you. You are responsible for all the terrible things going on in this house. You broke that expensive figurine your mother prized. I found it in the dustbin, wrapped in newspaper. You may sit there and scowl at me with your black, ugly eyes, but I'm not afraid. You are the one who wrapped that wire around Clover, and killed your brother's pet. You should be ashamed. You're a mean hateful little boy, Bart Sheffield, and it's no wonder you don't have any friends, no wonder at all. And I'm going to save your parents thousands of dollars when I turn you over my knee and paddle your bottom until it's black and blue, and you won't sit comfortably for two weeks.'

She towered over me, making me feel small and helpless too. I wanted to be anybody but me, anybody who was strong.

'You touch me and I'll kill you!' I said in a cold voice. I rose stiffly, planted my feet wide apart, put my hands on the table to steady my balance. Inside I was boiling with rage. I knew now how to turn into Malcolm and be ruthless enough to get what I wanted, when I wanted.

Look at her, afraid now. Now her eyes were big and scared. I snarled my upper lip and showed my teeth, allowing both lips to curl into a sneer. 'Woman, get the hell away from me before I lose control of myself!'

Silently, Emma backed away, and then she was running into the dining room, heading for the hall so she could protect Cindy.

All day I waited. Emma thought I was hiding in my hole in the shrubs, so she left Cindy alone in her sandbox under the shade of a huge old oak tree. Had a pretty little canopy too. Nothing too good for Cindy, and she was only adopted.

She tittered when he saw me limping up, as if I looked funny and was only pretending to be an old man. Look at her smile and try to charm me. Sitting there half naked, nothing on but little green and white shorts. She'd grow up and become more beautiful, and be like all women, sinfully enticing men to be their worst. And she'd betray the man who loved her, betray her children too. But . . . but . . . if she were ugly what man would want her then? She wouldn't make babies if she was ugly. Wouldn't be able to charm men then. I'd save all her children too, from what she'd do later on. Save the children, that was important.

'Barr . . . tee,' she said, smiling at me, sitting cross-legged so I could see her lacy panties beneath her play shorts. 'Play, Barr-tee? Play with Cindy . . .?'

Plump little hands reached for me. She was trying to seduce me. Only two years old and a few months and already she knew all the wicked ways of women.

'Cindy,' called Emma from the kitchen, but I was down low and she couldn't see me behind the bushes, 'are you all right?'

'Cindy's playing sand castles,' answered little nobody as if to protect me. Then she picked up her favourite red sand bucket and offered it to me – and the red and yellow shovel too.

In my hand I gripped the handle of my pocket knife tighter. 'Pretty Cindy,' I crooned softly as I crawled closer, putting a sweet smile on my face that made her giggle. 'Pretty Cindy wants to play beauty parlour . . .'

She clapped her hands. 'Ohhh,' she trilled. 'Nice.'

The blonde hair in my hand felt silky and warm. She laughed when I tugged at her hair and took the ribbon from the pony-tail. 'I'm not going to hurt you,' I said, showing her my pearl-handled knife. 'So don't you scream . . . just sit quietly in the beauty parlour until I've finished.'

In my room I had my list of new words. I had to pronounce them, practise spelling them, and use them at least five times in that same day – and from then on. Had to know big words in order to impress people, make them know I was smarter.

Intimidating. Got that – meant to make people scared of you.

Ultimately – had that down too. Meant sooner or later my time would come.

Sensuous – bad word. Meant thrills you got from touching girls. Had to do away with sensuous things.

I grew tired after a short while of big words I had to learn in order to gain respect. Grew tired of pretending to be Malcolm – but the trouble was – I was losing the real me. Now I wasn't Bart all the way through. And now that he was slipping away, suddenly Bart didn't seem nearly as stupid and pitiful as once he had.

I re-read a certain page in Malcolm's book when he was the very same age I was. He'd hated pretty blonde hair, like his mother's, like his daughter's – but he didn't know about his little Corrine when he wrote:

> Her name was Violet Blue, and her hair reminded me of my mother's hair. I hated her hair. We attended the same Sunday School class, and I'd sit in back of her and stare at that hair which would beguile some man some day, and make him want her, as that lover had wanted my mother.
>
> She smiled at me one day, expecting a compliment, but I fooled her. I said her hair was ugly. To my surprise she laughed, 'But it's the same colour hair you have.'
>
> I shaved off all my hair that day – and the next day I caught Violet Blue and threw her down. When she went home crying, she was as bald as I was.

All that pretty blonde hair that used to be Cindy's was blowing on the wind. She was crying in the kitchen. Not because I'd scared her, or hurt her. It was Emma's shriek that told her something had gone wrong. Now Cindy's head looked like mine. Stubby, short and ugly.

THE LAST DANCE *Jory*

'Jory,' called Mom in relief when she saw me come in, 'thank God you're back! Did you enjoy your lunch?'

Sure, I said, fine lunch, and she didn't pay much attention if I didn't elaborate, for she was much too busy with last-minute details. This was the way it went on performance days; class in the morning, rehearsal in the afternoon, and the performance at night. Rush, rush, rush, all the while making yourself believe the world would stop turning if you didn't dance your role to the best of your ability. When the world wouldn't stop . . .

'You know, Jory,' gushed Mom happily, the two of us were using the same dressing-room, only she was behind a screen, and we really couldn't see one another, 'All my life the ballet has thrilled me. But this night will be the grandest of them all, I will be dancing with my own son! I know you and I have danced many times together, but this night is special. Now you're good enough to dance solo. Please, please, do your best so Julian in Heaven can be proud of his only son.'

Sure, I'd do my best, always did. The footlights went on, the overture ended; the curtain lifted. There was a moment of silence before the first act music began. Mom's kind of music and mine – taking us both to that happy Never-Never land where anything could happen, even a happy ending.

'Mom, you look wonderful – prettier than any of the other dancers!' She did too. She laughed joyfully and told me I certainly knew how to please a woman, and if I kept it up I'd be the Don Juan of the century.

'Now listen carefully to the music, Jory. Don't get so absorbed in counting you forget the music – that's the best way to catch the magic, by feeling the music.'

I was so keyed up and tense I'd likely burst in another second or two. 'Mom, I hope that the father I love best is sitting front row centre.'

That's when she ran to where she could peek out and see the audience. In certain places the footlights didn't blind your eyes. 'He's not there,' she said dismally, 'nor Bart either . . .'

No time for me to answer. I heard my musical cue and danced out with the other members of the *corps*. Everything went just fine, with Mom up on the balcony as the beautiful doll Coppelia, life-like enough to inspire love from afar.

But when the first act was over she was left gasping and panting for breath. She hadn't told Dad she was also dancing the role of the village girl, Swanhilda, who loved Franze even as he fell foolishly in love with a mechanical doll. Two roles for Mom – difficult roles too as she had choreographed them. Dad certainly would have forbidden her to dance if he had known the full truth about her last dance. Had I been wrong to help her deceive him?

'Mom, how's your knee feeling?' I asked when I saw her grimace a time or two between acts.

'Jory, my knee is fine,' she said sharply, once more trying to see Dad and Bart in their seats. 'Why aren't they out there? If Chris doesn't show up to see me dance for the last time, I'll never forgive him!'

I saw Dad and Bart just before the second act started. They were sitting in the second row, and I could tell Bart had been brought along forcibly. His lower lip pouted sullenly as he glared at the curtain that would lift and display beauty and grace – and he'd frown more. Beauty and grace did not light up Bart's life as it did mine.

Third act time. Mom and I danced together, dolls wound up by huge keys attached to our backs. Woodenly we began, limbering up our squeaky joints. The huge room where Dr Coppelius kept his inventions was mysteriously dim, and made more dramatic by blue lights. Even so I could tell Mom was having trouble, but she didn't miss a step as we both kept time to the music and turned on all the other mechanical toys that came alive to dance with us. 'Mom, are you okay?' I asked in a whisper when we were close enough.

'Sure,' she said, still smiling, never doing anything but smiling for it was supposed to be painted on.

I felt scared for her even as I admired her courage. I knew out in the audience Bart was looking at us and thinking us stupid fools and feeling jealous of our grace.

Suddenly I could tell from Mom's tight smile that she was in terrible pain. I tried to dance closer, but one of the clown dolls kept getting in my way. It was going to happen, I knew it would – just what Dad feared.

Next came a series of whirling pirouettes which would take her in a circle around the stage. To do these she had to know precisely where everyone else was located, and all the props too. When she spun near me I reached out to keep her on balance before she whirled on by. Oh, golly, I couldn't stand to watch. Then I saw she was going to make it; pain or not, she'd dance without falling. Joyfully now, I bounded into the air and landed on one knee as I playfully proposed marriage to the doll of my dreams. Then my heart jumped. One of the ribbons of her points had come undone.

'Your ribbons, Mom, watch out for your left shoe ribbon!' I called above the music, but she didn't hear. The dragging ribbon was stepped on by another dancer. Mom was thrown off balance. She put out her arms to steady herself, and might have succeeded in doing this – but I saw her painted-on smile turn into a silent shriek of pain as her knee gave way and down she went right in the centre of the stage.

People in the audience screamed. Some stood up to see better. We on the stage went right on dancing as the manager came out and carried Mom backstage. Her understudy whirled on to the stage, and the ballet went on.

At last the curtain descended. I didn't want to take any bows. I couldn't get to Mom fast enough. Terribly afraid, I raced up to where Dad held her in his arms, and ambulance men in white suits were feeling her legs as if they feared one or both might be broken.

'Chris, did I do all right?' she was asking, though pain had made her face very pale. 'I didn't really louse up the show, did I? You did see Jory and me in our *pas de deux?*'

'Yes, yes,' he said, kissing her face all over, and looking so tender as he helped lift her on to a stretcher. 'You and Jory were magnificent. I've never seen you dance better – and Jory was brilliant.'

'And this time I didn't have to bleed on my feet,' she whispered before she closed her eyes wearily, 'I only had to break a leg.'

What she said didn't make much sense. I turned my thoughts to the look on Bart's face as he stared at her. He seemed to be glad, almost gloating. Was I being unfair to him? Or was it guilt I saw in his eyes?

I sobbed as Mom was lifted on to a stretcher and put in an ambulance that would drive her and Dad to the nearest hospital. Melodie's father promised he'd drop me off at the hospital then drive Bart home safely. 'Though I'm sure Melodie wishes it was Jory who'd go home, and Bart who'd insist on staying with his mother in the hospital.'

Much later Mom awakened from the sedatives given her to stare at the flowers filling her room. 'Why, it looks like a garden,' she breathed. She smiled weakly at Dad, stretching out her arms to embrace him, and then me. 'I know you're going to say I told you so, Chris. But until I fell, I did dance well, didn't I?'

'It was your slipper ribbon,' I cried, anxious to protect her from his anger. 'If it hadn't loosened you wouldn't have fallen.'

'My leg isn't broken, is it?' she asked Dad.

'No darling, just torn ligaments and some broken cartilage that was repaired during the operation.' Then he sat on the edge of her bed and gravely told her every detail of her injury which wasn't as minor as she wanted to believe.

Mom reflected aloud: 'I really can't understand how that ribbon could come loose. I always carefully sew on the ribbons myself, not trusting anyone else . . .' she paused, and stared into space.

'Where are you hurting now?'

'Nowhere,' she flared as if annoyed. 'Where's Bart? Why didn't he come with you?'

'You know how Bart is. He hates hospitals and sick people, just as much as he hates everything else. I'm taking good care of him and Cindy. But we want you home soon, so do what your doctor and nurses tell you – and don't be so damned stubborn you won't listen, or obey.'

'What's wrong with me?' she asked, alerted as I was. I sat up straighter, feeling something was about to slam down on all of us.

'Your knee is in bad shape, Cathy, without going into specifics. You are going to have to sit in a wheelchair until some torn ligaments heal.'

'A wheelchair?' Stunned looking, she said that like it was an electric chair. 'What's really wrong? You're not telling me everything. You're trying to protect me.

'When your doctors are sure, you will know. But one thing is certain, you can never dance again. And they have told me too, you cannot even demonstrate to your pupils. No dancing whatsoever, not even waltzing.' He said it so firmly, but compassion and pain were in his eyes.

She looked stunned, not believing that such a small fall could have done so much harm. 'No dancing . . .? None at all?'

'None at all,' he repeated. 'I'm sorry, Cathy, but I warned you. Think back and count the times you have fallen and hurt that knee. How much damage do you think it can take? Even walking won't be effortless as it used to be. So cry your heart out now. Get it out of your system.'

She cried in his arms and I sat in a chair and sobbed inwardly, as bereft as if it had been me who had lost the use of my leg in the way I preferred to use my legs.

'It's all right, Jory,' she said when she had dried her tears and put on a faltering smile. 'If I can't dance, I'll find something better to do – though Lord knows what it will be.'

ANOTHER GRANDMOTHER *Jory*

In a few days Mom was feeling much better, and that's when Dad brought to the hospital a portable typewriter, a thick stack of yellow legal pads, and other writing utensils. He stacked everything on the table that rolled over Mom's bed and gave her one of his big charming smiles. 'Here,' he said, 'this is a fine time to finish that book you began so long ago. Look at your old journals, and let it all loose – and be damned to those you might hurt! Hurt them as you've been hurt, as I've been hurt. Stab a few times for Cory and Carrie too. And while you're at it, throw in a few blows for me, Jory and Bart, for they too are affected.'

What was he talking about?

They looked at each other for long moments, then unhappily she took an old memorandum book from his hands and opened it so I could see her large girlish handwriting. 'I don't know if I should,' she murmured with a strange look in her eyes. 'It would be like living it all over again. All the pain would come back.'

Dad shook his head. 'Cathy, do what you think you must. There must have been a good reason for you to have started those books in the first place. Who knows, perhaps you'll be on your way to a new career more satisfying than the last.'

It didn't seem possible to me that writing could ever replace dancing, but when I visited her in the hospital the next day, she was scribbling away like crazy. On her face I saw a strange intense look, and in a way, I felt envious.

'How much longer?' she asked Dad who had driven me to see her.

We were all there waiting, Emma with Cindy in her arms, and me holding fast to Bart's hand. Dad lifted Mom out of the front seat and put her in the folding chair he'd rented. Bart stared at that rolling chair with repulsion, while Cindy called out 'Mommy, Mommy!' She didn't care how Mom came home, as long as she did, but Bart hung back and eyed Mom up and down, as if he were looking at a stranger he didn't like.

Next Bart turned and headed for the house. He hadn't even said hello. An expression of hurt passed over Mom's face before she called, 'Bart! Don't go away before I've had a chance to say hello to you. Aren't you glad to see me? You just don't know how much I've missed you. I know you don't like hospitals, but I wish you had come just the same. I know too you don't like this chair but I won't be using it forever. A lady in the physical therapy class showed me how much can be done while sitting in this kind of chair . . .' she faltered because his dark ugly look didn't encourage her to go on.

'You look funny sitting in that chair,' he said with his brows knitted together. 'Don't like you in that chair!'

Nervously Mom laughed. 'Well, to be honest, it's not my favourite throne either, but remember it's not a permanent part of my life, only until my knee heals. Come, Bart, be friendly to your mother. I forgive you for not visiting me in the hospital, but I won't forgive you if you can't show me a little affection.'

Still frowning, he backed away as she wheeled forward. 'No! Don't touch me,' he cried out in a loud voice. 'You didn't have to dance and fall. You fell because you didn't want to come home and see me again. You hate me now for cutting off Cindy's hair. And now you want to punish me by sitting in that chair when you don't need to.'

Wheeling around, he raced for the backyard, using the stepping stones. He'd covered two when he tripped and fell. Picking himself up, he ran on again, and bumped into a tree so he cried out, and I could see his nose was bleeding. Boy, talk about awkward!

Dad made light of Bart's rebellion as he pushed Mom into the house with Cindy delighted to ride on her lap. 'Don't worry about Bart . . . he'll come back and be contrite . . . he's missed you very much, Cathy. I've heard him crying in the night. And his new psychiatrist thinks he's getting better, working out some of his hostility.'

She didn't say anything, just kept running her hand over the smooth cap of Cindy's short-short hair. She looked more like a boy in her coveralls, though Emma had tried to tie a ribbon in a short tuft of her hair. I guessed Dad had told Mom what Bart had done to Cindy, for she didn't ask questions.

Later on in the evening when Bart was in bed, I ran for a book I'd left in the family room, and heard Mom's voice coming from her room. 'Chris, what am I going to do about Bart? I tried to show love and affection for him, and he rejects me. Look what he did to Cindy, a helpless child, who trusts that no one will hurt her. Did you spank him? Did you do anything to punish him? Does he show respect to any of us? A few weeks in the attic might teach him a thing or two about obedience.'

Hearing Mom talk like this made me feel so sad that I had to hurry away and hurl myself on to my bed and stare at the walls, the posters of Julian Marquet dancing with Catherine Dahl. This wasn't the first time I'd wondered what my real father had been like. Had he loved my mother very much? Had she loved him? Would my life have been happier if he hadn't died before I was born?

Then there was Daddy Paul, who came after that tall man with the dark hair and eyes. Was Bart really Dr Paul's son or was he . . . ? I couldn't even finish the question, it made me feel so disloyal for doubting.

I closed my eyes, feeling in the air around me a dreadful tension, as if an invisible sword were held, ready to hack all of us down.

Early the next evening, I cornered Dad in his study and burst out with all I'd held back until now.

'Dad, you've just got to do something about Bart. He frightens me. I don't see how we can go on living with him in the house, when it seems he is going mad – if he isn't already there.'

My dad bowed his head into his hands, 'Jory, I don't know what to do. It would kill your mother if we had to send Bart away. You don't know all she's been through. I don't think she can take too much more . . . another child gone would destroy her.'

'We'll save her!' I cried passionately. 'But we have to prevent Bart from going to visit those people next door who tell him lies. He goes over there all the time, Dad, and that old lady holds him on her lap and tells him stories that make him come home acting queer, like he's old, like he hates women. It's all her fault, Dad, that old woman in black. When she leaves Bart alone, he'll go back to where he was before she came.'

He stared at me in the strangest way, as if something I'd said had triggered thoughts in his head. As always he had places to go and patients to see, but this time he called up his hospital and told them he had an emergency at home. And he did, you bet he did!

I often looked at my mother's third husband and wished he were my own blood father, but at that moment when he cancelled his appointments to save Bart – and Mom, I knew in all the ways that counted, he was my true father.

That evening, shortly after dinner, Mom went to her room to work on her book. Cindy was in bed, and Bart was out in the yard when Dad and I donned warm sweaters and slipped out the front door.

It was murky with fog, cold with damp as we strode side by side towards the huge shadowy mansion with its impressive black iron gates. 'Dr Christopher Sheffield,' said Dad into the black box attached to the side of the gates. 'I want to see the lady of the house.' As the gates swung silently open, he asked why I'd never learned the woman's name. I shrugged, as if she didn't have a name, and as far as I was concerned, didn't need one.

At the front door Dad banged the brass knocker. Finally we heard shuffling noises in the hall, and John Amos Jackson admitted us.

'Our lady tires easily,' said John Amos Jackson, his thin long face hollow-cheeked, gaunt-eyed, his hands trembling, his narrow back bent. 'Don't say anything to upset her.'

I stared at the way Dad looked at him, frowning and perplexed, as the bald-headed man shuffled away, leaving us to enter a room whose door he'd opened.

The lady in black was seated in her rocking chair.

'I'm sorry to interrupt.' said Dad, staring at her intensely. 'My name is Dr Christopher Sheffield and I live next door. This is my eldest son, Jory, whom you have met before.'

She seemed excited, nervous as she gestured us in and indicated the chairs we were to use. We perched tentatively, not intending to stay very long. Seconds stretched by that seemed like hours before Dad leaned forward to speak: 'You have a lovely home. It seems I've been here before.' He glanced around again at all the elaborate chairs and other fine furnishings, and stared at the paintings too. 'I have the strangest sense of *déjà vu*,' he murmured as if to himself.

Her black-veiled head bowed low. Her expressive hands spread expansively, supplicating, it seemed, for his understanding for her lack of words. I knew she spoke English perfectly well. Why was she faking?

Except for those aristocratic hands with all the glittering rings she sat so still, but her hands fluttered, knotted the pearls I knew she wore beneath her black dress. His eyes shot her way, and quickly she sat on her hands!

'You don't speak English?' Dad asked in a tight voice.

Vigorously she nodded, indicating she could understand English. His brows knitted. He looked puzzled again. 'Well, to get to the point of our visit, my son Jory has told me you and my youngest son Bart are very familiar. Jory says you give Bart expensive gifts, and feed him sweets between meals. I'm sorry Mrs . . . Mrs . . . ?' he paused, waited for her to give her name, but when she didn't he went on: 'When Bart comes again, I want you to send him home unrewarded. He's done a number of ugly things that deserve punishment. His mother and I cannot have a stranger coming between Bart and our authority. When you indulge him here, we face the consequences.' All this time he was doing his darnedest to see her hands – as she did her best to keep them hidden.

What was this all about? Why did Dad want to see her hands? Was it the rings, all those fabulous rings that held his fascination? I'd never guessed he liked things like that since Mom had an aversion for jewellery of any kind but earrings.

And then when Dad seemed to be looking towards another of her original oil paintings, her hands came into view, to flutter up near her throat and the magnet of her hidden pearls.

His head jerked around. Dad spoke then out of context, startling me, startling her. 'Those rings you wear – I've seen those very rings before!'

When she too obviously shoved her hands inside her full sleeves, Dad jumped to his feet as if thunderstruck. He stared at her, spun around once more to survey the sumptuous room again, and once more nailed her with his eyes. She cringed.

'The . . . best . . . . that . . . money . . . can . . . buy,' Dad said slowly, separating each word. I caught his bitterness, though I didn't understand. It seemed lately I never understood anything.

'Nothing too good for the elegant and aristocratic Mrs Bartholomew Winslow,' he said. 'Those rings, Mrs Winslow, why didn't you have the good sense to hide them away? Then your disguise might have worked, though I doubt it. I know your voice and your gestures too well. You wear black rags but your fingers sparkle with your status symbols. Do you forget what those symbols did to us? Do you think I've forgotten those endless days of suffering from the cold or heat, from the loneliness – all our pain symbolized by a string of pearls and those rings on your fingers?'

I was shocked, bewildered too, never before had I seen Dad so upset. He wasn't easily provoked and who was this woman he knew, and I didn't? Why had he called her Mrs Bartholomew Winslow – the very name of my half-brother? Could it be true she really was Bart's grandmother and Bart might not be the son of Daddy Paul?

Dad railed on, 'Why, Mrs Winslow, why? Did you think you could hide here and we wouldn't find out? How can you fool anyone when even the way you sit and hold your head betrays your true idenity? Haven't you done enough to hurt me and Cathy? Do you have to return to create more havoc? I should have guessed that you were behind Bart's confusion – behind his weird behaviour. What have you been doing to our son?'

'Our son?' she asked. 'Don't you mean more correctly, her son?'

'Mother!' he raged before he looked at me guiltily.

Looking from one to the other of them, I thought, how wonderful and how strange. At last his mother was free from the loony bin and she really was Bart's grandmother after all. But why did he call her Mrs Winslow? If she was his mother and Dr Paul's mother, then she'd have to be Mrs Sheffield – wouldn't she?

I was thinking all of this even as she said, 'Sir, my rings are not that exceptional. Bart has told me you're not his real father, so please leave my home. I promise never to admit Bart again. I didn't come to harm him – or anyone.' It seemed she gave my father a warning look. I guessed she was giving him a road out on account of me.

'My dear mother, the game is up. I know that emerald and diamond ring you wear is the very same ring Cathy tore from her hand the night Foxworth Hall burned to the ground. She tore off all the fine jewellery she'd taken from your safe and she hurled it in the snow . . . but I guess your ever loyal John Amos Jackson picked it all up and returned it to you.' He laughed as if the joke were on him. 'I see you still wear your pearl necklace.' She was unconsciously fingering it, dragging her high neckline down a bit so the lustre of the pearls could be seen under her veil. 'I can't count the times I've heard Cathy say she hoped every last jewel you owned burned in that fire.'

She sobbed, then covered her veiled face with her hands. He shot out with no regard for her tears, 'When did your doctors release you?'

'Last summer,' she whispered. Her hands lowered so she could use her voice better for pleading. 'Even before I moved here I had my lawyers do what they could to help you and Cathy buy whatever piece of land you selected. I ordered them to keep me anonymous, knowing you wouldn't want my help.'

Dad fell into a chair, bent over to rest his elbows heavily on his knees.

Why wasn't he happy to see his mother free from that place? She was living nearby, and he'd always wanted to visit her. Didn't he love his own mother? Or was he afraid she might go crazy any moment? Did he think Bart might have inherited her madness or her insanity might infect Bart like a physical disease? And why didn't my mother like her? I looked from one to the other, wanting answers to my unspoken questions, and so afraid I might learn Paul wasn't Bart's father at all.

When Dad lifted his head I could see his drawn face, the deep lines that etched from his nose to his mouth. Lines I'd never seen before.

'I cannot in good conscience call you Mother again,' he said dully. 'If you helped buy the land my home sets on, I thank you. Tomorrow I'll see a *For Sale* sign is put up, and we'll move far away if you refuse to move first. I will not allow you to turn my sons away from their parents.'

'Their parent,' she corrected.

'The only parents they have,' he said in return. 'I should have known you'd come here. I've called your doctor and he told me you'd been released, but he didn't say when, or where you went.'

'Where else do I have to go?' she cried pitifully, wringing her bejewelled hands like pale limp rags. It was as if she reached out and touched him then, even as she restrained herself from reaching for him. Each word she said, each look she gave him said she loved him, even I could tell.

'Christopher,' she pleaded, 'I have no friends, no family, no home – and nowhere to go but to you and yours. All I have left is you and Cathy and the sons she bore – my grandsons. Would you take them from me too? Each night I pray on my knees that you and Cathy will forgive me and take me back and love me as you did.'

He seemed made of steel, so unreachable, but I was on the verge of crying.'

'My son, my beloved son, take me back and say you love me again. And if you cannot do that, then just let me live where I can see my grandsons now and then.'

She paused then, waiting for him to respond. When he refused, she went on:

'I hoped you could be lenient if I stayed over here and never let her know who I was. But I've seen her, heard her voice, heard yours too. I hide behind the wall and listen. My heart throbs. My chest aches with longing. Tears fill my eyes from holding back my voice that wants to cry out and let you know I'm sorry. So terribly sorry.'

Still he didn't say anything. He wore his detached, professional look.

'Christopher, I would gladly give ten years of my life to undo the wrong I've done. I'd give another ten years just to sit at your table and feel welcomed by my own grandchildren.'

Tears were in her eyes, in mine too. My heart cried for my father's mother even as I wondered why he and Mom hated her.

'Christopher, Christopher, don't you understand why I wear these rags? I cover my face, my hair, my figure, so she won't know. But all the time I keep hoping, praying, that sooner or later both of you can forgive me enough to let me become a member of your family again. Please, please, accept me as your mother again. If you do, perhaps then she can too.'

How could he sit there and not feel the same pity for her that I did. Why wasn't he crying like I was?

'Cathy will never forgive you,' he said tonelessly.

Strangely, she cried out happily, 'Then you will? Please say it, you forgive me!'

I trembled and waited for him to speak.

'Mother, how can I say I forgive you? By saying that, I would betray Cathy, and I can never betray her. Together we stand and together we will fall, still believing we did right, while you stand guilty and alone. Nothing you say or do can undo death. And every day you stay on here sees Bart more and more deranged. Do you realize he is threatening our adopted daughter Cindy?'

'No!' she cried out fervently, shaking her head so the veils swung violently. 'Bart would not hurt his sister.'

'Wouldn't he? He hacked off her hair with a knife, Mrs Winslow. And he has threatenened his mother as well.'

'No!' she yelled more passionately than before. 'Bart loves his mother. I give Bart treats because you are too busy with your professional life to give him all the attention he needs. Just as his mother is too busy with her life to care if he has enough love. But I cater to his needs. I try to take the place of the peers he doesn't have. I do everything I can to make him happy. And if feeding him treats and giving him gifts makes him feel better – what harm can I do? Besides, once a child has all the sweets he can eat, soon he loses the taste for them. I know. Once I was like Bart, loving ice-cream, candy, cookies and other sweets . . . and now I cannot tolerate them at all.'

Dad got up and motioned to me. I stood and moved to his side as he looked at his mother with pity. 'It's a terrible shame you came too late to try to redeem your actions. Once I would have been touched by any sweet word you said. Now your very presence shows how little you care if we are deeply hurt again, as we will be if you stay.'

'Please Christopher,' she begged. 'I have no other family, and no others who care if I live or die. Don't deny me your love when to do so will kill the very best part of you, the part that makes you what you are. You've never been like Cathy. Always you could hold on to some of your love – hold fast to it now, Christopher. Hold so fast and so true, you can eventually help Cathy to find a little love for me too.' She sobbed and weakened. 'Or if not love, help her find forgiveness, for I admit, I could have served my children better.'

Now Dad was touched, but not for long. 'I have to think of Bart's welfare first. He's never had much confidence in himself.

Your tales have disturbed him so much he has nightmares. Leave him alone. Leave us alone. Go away, stay away, we don't belong to you any more. Years ago we gave you chance after chance to prove you loved us. Even when we ran, you could have answered the judge's summons and spared us the pain of knowing we weren't loved enough for you to even appear and show some interest in our futures.

'So get out of our lives! Make another life for yourself with the riches you sacrificed us to get. Let Cathy and me live our lives we've worked hard to achieve.'

I was baffled – what was he talking about? What had his mother done to her two sons, Christopher and Paul – and what did my mother have to do with their youthful lives?

She rose too, standing tall and straight. Then, slowly, slowly, she removed the veil that covered her head and face. I gasped. My dad gasped. Never before had I seen a woman who could look so ugly and so beautiful at the same time. She still had the scars as if a cat had scratched her face. Her jowls sagged with age; her pretty blonde hair was streaked with grey. I'd been terribly curious to see what she hid under her veil up close – now I wished I hadn't.

Dad bowed his head. 'Did you have to do that?'

'Yes,' she said. 'I wanted you to see what I did so I would no longer look like Cathy.' She gestured to her wooden rocker. 'See that chair? I have one in every room in this house.' She indicated all the comfortable chairs with fluffy soft cushions. 'I sit in hard wooden chairs to punish myself. I wear the same black rags every day. I keep mirrors on the walls so I can see how ugly and old I am now. I want to suffer for the sins I committed against my children. I despise this veil, but I wear it. I can't see well through the veil, but I deserve that too. I do what I can to make the same kind of hell for myself as I made for my own flesh and blood, and I keep on believing that there will come a time when you and Cathy will recognize how I am trying to atone for my sins, and then you can forgive me, and return to me and we can be a whole family again. And when you and Cathy can do that, I can go peacefully into my grave, and when I meet your father again, perhaps he won't judge me too harshly.'

'Oh,' I cried out spontaneously, 'I forgive you for whatever you did. I'm sorry you have to wear black all the time, with that veil over your face!' I turned to Dad and tugged on his arm. 'Say you forgive her, Dad, please don't make her suffer more. She is your mother, and I could always forgive my mother, no matter what she did.'

He spoke to my grandmother as if he didn't even hear me. 'You were always good at persuading us to do what you wanted.' I'd never heard him speak so coolly, in such a detached manner.

'But I'm not a boy any more,' he went on. 'Now I know how to resist your appeal, for I have a woman who has never let me down in any important way. She has taught me not to be so gullible, as once I was. You want Bart because you think he should have been yours. But you cannot have Bart. Bart belongs to us. I used to think Cathy did wrong when she sought revenge and stole Bart Winslow from you – but she didn't do wrong – she did what she had to do. And so we have two sons instead of one.'

'Christopher,' she cried, looking desperate, 'you don't want the world to know of your indiscretion, surely you don't.'

'Yours too,' he responded coldly. 'If you expose us, you expose yourself as well. And remember we were only children – who do you think a judge and jury would favour – you or us?'

'For your own sakes,' she called as we stepped from her parlour and headed towards the double front doors, pushing me ahead of him, for I was holding back, pitying her, 'love me again, Christopher! Let me redeem myself, please.'

Dad whirled about, furious and red-faced. 'I cannot forgive you. You think only of yourself. As you have always thought only of yourself. I don't know you, Mrs Winslow. I wish to God I had never known you.'

Oh, Dad, I thought, you're going to be sorry. Forgive her, please.

'Christopher,' she called once more, her voice so weak and

thin it sounded old and brittle, 'when you and Cathy can love me again, you'll find better lives for yourselves and for your children. There is so much I could do to help if only you would let me.'

'Money?' he asked with scorn. 'Are you going to use blackmail? We have enough money. We have enough happiness. We have managed to survive, and managed to love, and we have not killed anyone to achieve what we have.'

Killed? Had she killed?

On the way home from her mansion I said to him, 'Dad, it seemed I could smell Bart in that room. He might have been hiding and listening. He was there, I'm sure of it.'

'All right,' he answered in a tired way. 'You go back but do not remain.'

'Dad, why don't you forgive her? I believe whatever she did to make you hate her she's truly sorry for – and she is your mother.' I smiled and tugged on his arm, wanting him to go back with me and say he loved her. 'Wouldn't it be nice to have both my grandmothers here for Christmas?'

He shook his head, and strode away, leaving me to race back to the big house. He'd taken only a few steps before he turned: 'Jory, promise not to tell your mother anything about tonight.'

I promised, but I was unhappy about it, unhappy about everything I'd heard. Had I heard the full truth about my dad and his mother, or only part of a long, long story never told to me. I wanted to run after Dad and ask why he hated his mother so much, but I knew from his expression that he wouldn't tell me, and in some odd way, I was glad not to know more.

'If Bart is over there, you bring him home, and sneak him into his room, Jory. Please, for God's sake, don't ever mention to your mother anything about the woman next door again. I'll take care of her. She'll go away, and it will be just like it was before she came.'

Being what I was, I believed, though I felt sorry for his mother. I didn't owe her the loyalty I owed him.

Still, I couldn't keep the most important question from my

tongue. 'Dad, what did your mother do that makes you hate her so much? And if you hate her, why did you always insist upon going to visit her, when Mom wouldn't?'

He stared off into space and as if from a far distance his voice came to me. 'Jory, I fear you will know all of the truth soon enough. Give me time to find the right words, the explanation that will satisfy your need to know . . . but believe this, your mother and I were always going to tell you. We were only waiting for you and Bart to grow up enough, and when you hear our story, I think you will understand how I can both love and hate my mother. It's sad to say, there are many children who feel ambiguous about their mothers or their fathers.'

I hugged him, even if it was unmanly. I loved him, and if that was unmanly too, then darn if being manly was so great.

'Don't you worry about Bart, Dad,' I said, 'I'll bring him home safely.'

I managed to squeeze between the fence and the gate just in the nick of time. Softly they clanked behind me. Then, silence. If there was a more silent place in the world than these spacious grounds, I've never been there.

I jumped and quickly dodged behind a tree. John Amos Jackson had Bart by the hand, and he was leading him away from the house.

'Now you know what you have to do, don't you?'

'Yes, sir,' intoned Bart, as if in a stupor.

'You know what will happen if you don't do as I say, don't you?'

'Yes, sir. Bad things will happen to everyone, even me.'

'Yessss, bad things, things you will regret.'

'Bad things I will regret,' he repeated flatly.

'From woman man is born into sin . . .'

'From woman man is born into sin.'

'And those who originate the sin . . .'

'Must suffer.'

'And how must they suffer?'

'In all ways, by any ways, by death they will be redeemed.'

I froze where I crouched, not believing my ears. What was that man doing to Bart?

They drifted beyond my hearing, and I peeked just in time to see Bart disappearing over the wall, going home. I waited until John Amos Jackson shuffled into the house and turned out all the lights. Then suddenly I realized I hadn't heard Apple bark. Wasn't a dog as old and big as Apple supposed to bark and warn those in the house a prowler was on the grounds? I sneaked into the barn and called Apple by name. He didn't come running to lick my face and wag his tail. 'Apple,' I called again, louder. I lit a kerosene lamp that hung near the door and I shone it into the horse stall where Apple had his home.

I sucked in my breath! Oh. No! No!

Who would be so cruel as to starve a dog like that? Who could then drive a pitchfork into that poor bag of·bones covered by beautiful fur . . . and now he was all bloody. Dark with old blood that had dried to the colour of black rust. I ran outside and threw up. An hour later Dad and I were digging a grave and burying a huge dog that never had a chance to reach maturity. Both of us knew they would lock Bart up forever if ever this got out.

'He may not have done it,' said Dad when we were home. 'I can't believe he did it.' By now I could believe anything.

There was an old woman who lived next door.

Who wore black rags and black covered her hair.

She was Mom's mother-in-law, twice hated, and much more.

And all I could do was wonder, why. Wonder what she had done to my mom and my dad. Though I had found a glimmer of a fuzzy solution – I'd let my emotions run away with me, and for a moment I'd thought she was my grandmother too, for Chris was so much my real father in my heart.

But in reality, it was Bart who was Paul's son, and I knew why his grandmother wanted him so badly, and not me. I belonged to Madame Marisha as Bart belonged to her. It was the blood relationship that called between them, making them love each other. And I sighed to be only a step-grandson to such a mysterious and touching woman who felt she had to suffer to redeem her mistakes. I thought too, I should take better care of Bart, protect him, guide him, keep him straight.

Right away I had to get up and look at Bart who was curled on his side in his bed with his thumb in his mouth. He looked like a baby – just a little boy who'd always stood in my shadow, always trying to live up to what I'd done at his age, and never achieving the goals I'd already set. He hadn't walked sooner, talked at a younger age, and never smiled until he was almost a year old. It was as if he'd known from his birth that he'd always be number two, never number one.

Now he'd found the one person in the world who would let him come first. I was happy Bart had his very own grandmother, even if she did wear nothing but black. I knew once she'd been very beautiful. More beautiful than my Grandmother Marisha could ever have hoped to be when she was young.

Yet, yet, some pieces in the puzzle were missing.

John Amos Jackson, just where did he fit in the picture? Why would a loving grandmother and mother who wanted to be reunited with her son and his wife, and her grandson . . . why would she bring that hateful old man along with her?

HONOUR THY MOTHER *Bart*

He never bothered to look around. He thought I was safely asleep, in that little bed where they liked to keep me. But I saw Daddy leave the house. Was he going to see my grandmother? Wish everybody'd leave her alone, so I could have her back like she used to be, all mine.

Apple was gone. Gone to where puppies and ponies went. 'That great big pasture in the sky,' said John Amos with his glittery pale eyes watching me carefully, like he thought I was the one who stabbed the pitchfork in. 'You saw Apple dead? You really saw him dead?'

'Deader than a doornail.'

I sneaked along the winding jungle paths that were taking me straight into hell. Down, down, down. Caves and canyons and deep pits and sooner or later we'd find the door. Red. The door to hell would be red – maybe black.

Black gates! Magic gates swung wide to let Daddy through. She wanted him. Fine son he was, putting his mother into the loony bin and next he'd put me in one of those funny farms where they laced you up in straitjackets.

The gates clanked together. Knew Mom was back in her room typing away those pages like she really thought it was just as important as dancing. She didn't seem to mind sitting in that wheelchair, didn't seem to mind at all unless she heard Jory playing that dance music. Then her head would lift; she'd stare into space; her feet would begin to keep time.

'What's intricate mean, Momma?' I'd asked when she said Jory had the concentration to learn intricate dances quickly.

'Complicated,' she'd answered, just like a dictionary. She had dictionaries all over the place, little ones, middle-sized ones, a huge fat one that had its own stand that swivelled around.

I had to make my feet do intricate things. I tried as I slipped along behind Daddy who never glanced backwards. I was always looking over my shoulder, staring to the left or to the right, wondering, always wondering. Dratted shoelace – ouch! Down I was – again. If he heard me cry out, he didn't look back. Good . . . had to do all this secret stuff like a good spy. Or a thief, a jewel thief. Rich ladies had lots and lots of jewels. Ought to get in some practice while she was gabbing with her doctor son, crying and constantly asking him to forgive her, have mercy, take her back and love her again. Boring. Didn't like Daddy so much now, back to how I used to feel before he saved my leg from being amputated. Dratted man was trying to drive away the one grandmother I had. What other kid had a grandmother so rich she could give him everything?

'Where you going, Bart?'

John Amos appeared out of nowhere, his eyes glowing in the dark. 'None of your damn business,' I snapped like Malcolm would have done. I had Malcolm's journal flat against my chest, under my shirt. The red leather was sticking to my skin. I was learning how make money out of rage.

'Your father is in that house, talking with your grandmother. Now you get in there and do your job, and report back to me every word they say. You hear?'

Hear? It was him who needed a hearing-aid, not me. Else he would do his own spying through the keyhole. But all he could do was peek, couldn't hear very good. Couldn't bend over much better, and couldn't pick up anything he dropped.

'Bart . . . did you hear me? What the devil are you doing heading for the back stairs?'

I turned to stare at him. On the fifth step I was taller. 'How old are you, John Amos?'

He shrugged and scowled. 'Why do you want to know?'

'Never saw anybody older, that's all.'

'The Lord has ways of punishing those who show disrespect to their elders.'

He gritted his teeth. They made the sound of dishes clinking in the sink.

'I'm taller than you are now.'

'I'm six feet tall – or I used to be. Boy, that's a height you will never reach unless you always stand on stairs.

I narrowed my eyes, and made them mean like Malcolm would. 'There will come a day, John Amos, when I'll stand head and shoulders taller than you. And on your knees you will come begging to me, pleading, pleading; sir, sir, you'll say, please let me get rid of those attic mice. And I will say to you; how do I know you are worthy of my trust, and you will say to me; in your footsteps I will follow, even when you lie in your grave.'

What I said made him smile slyly.

'Bart, you are learning to be as clever as your great-grandfather, Malcolm.

'Now,' John Amos continued in his whispery-hissy way, 'Put off whatever you plan to do. Go back to your father who is with your grandmother this very second. Remember every word you hear, and report back to me.'

Like a spy, I crawled through the dumb-waiter which was hidden behind a pretty oriental screen. From there I could sneak my way to a hidden place behind the potted palms.

There they were, the two of them, doing the same old thing. Grandmother pleading, Daddy rejecting. I sat down and made myself comfortable before I pulled out my pack of roll-my-owns. Cigarettes helped when life got boring, like now. Nothing to do but listen. Spies never got to say anything, and it was action I needed.

Daddy looked nice in his pale grey suit, like I wanted to look when I grew up – but I wouldn't – I didn't have his kind of good looks. I sighed, wishing I was his real son.

'Mrs Winslow, you promised to move, but I look around and see you haven't even packed one box. For the sake of Bart's mental health, for the sake of Jory whom you say you love well too, and most of all for Cathy, go away. Move to San Francisco. That's not too far away. I swear I'll visit you when I can. I'll be able to find opportunities to see you and Cathy will never suspect.'

Boring. Why couldn't he say something different? Why did he care so much what my Momma said about his mother? If ever I was so unlucky as to have a wife, I'd tell her she'd better accept my mother or get out! Get the hell out, as Malcolm would put it.

'Oh, Christopher,' she sobbed, pulling out another of those lacy handkerchiefs to wipe at her tears. 'I want Cathy to forgive me so I can have a small place in your lives. I stay on because I'm hoping eventually she'll realize I'm not here to harm any of you . . . I'm here only to give what I can.'

Daddy smiled bitterly. 'I suppose you are talking again about material things, but that's not what a child needs. Cathy and I have done all we can to make Bart feel needed, loved and wanted – but he can't seem to understand his relationship to me. He isn't secure in what he is, who he is, or where he's going. He doesn't have a career like Jory to guide him into the future. Now he's grasping, trying to find himself and you aren't helping. He keeps his innermost self very private, locked up. He adores his mother, he distrusts his mother. He suspects she loves Jory more than she loves him. He knows that Jory is handsome, talented, and most of all, adroit. Bart is not adroit at anything but pretending. If he would confide in us, or his psychiatrist, he could be helped – but he doesn't confide.'

I had to wipe a tear from my eye. So hard to hear about myself, and what I was, and worse, what I wasn't – like they knew me inside out, and they didn't. They couldn't.

'Did you hear any of what I just said, Mrs Winslow?' Daddy shouted. 'Bart does not like his image because he thinks it reflects only weakness, no skills, no grace and no authority. So he borrows from all the books he's read, from all the TV shows he's watched, and sometimes, he even borrows from animals and pretends he's a wolf, a dog, a cat.'

'Why, why?' she moaned. He was telling all my secrets! And a secret told had no value, none at all.

'Can't you guess why? Jory has thousands of photographs of his father, Bart has none. Not even one.'

That made her bolt straight up! She flared with anger. 'And why should he have his father's pictures? Is it my fault my second husband didn't give his mistress his photograph?'

I felt stunned. *What was this*? Sure, John Amos had told me crazy stories, but I'd thought he made them up, just as I made up stories to chase away boredom. Was it all true that my own Momma had been the bad woman who had seduced my own grandmother's second husband? Was I really the son of that lawyer-man named Bartholomew Winslow? Oh, Momma, how can I ever stop hating you now?

Daddy was wearing that funny smile again. 'Perhaps your beloved Bart thought he didn't need to give her his photograph when she'd have the living man in her own home, and in her bed as her lawful husband. She told him before he died that she was expecting his child, and he would have divorced you to be the father of his child, and have Cathy – I don't doubt that in the least.'

I was in a tight ball, agonized by all I'd heard. My poor, poor daddy who died in the fire at Foxworth Hall. John Amos was a true friend, the only one who treated me like an adult and told me the truth. And Daddy Paul whose picture sat in my bedroom on the night table, he'd been only another stepfather, like Christopher. I was crying inside from losing yet another daddy. My eyes rolled from Daddy to her, trying so hard to know what to feel about him and her – and Momma. It wasn't right for parents to mess up the lives of little babies who weren't even born, mess it up so much I'd never really know who I was.

Hopefully I stared at my grandmother who seemed to be very hurt by what her son had said. Her white hands fluttered up to her forehead that was glistening with beads of sweat, touching it as if her head ached. Oh, how easily she could feel pain, why couldn't I?

'All right, Christopher,' she said when I thought she might never find the words, 'you've had your say, now let me have mine. When it came down to an ultimatum, Cathy and her unborn child, or me and my fortune – Bart would have stayed with me, his wife. He might have kept her on as his mistress until he tired of her, but then he would have figured out some legal way to take possession of his child. My husband would have bowed out of Cathy's life, holding fast to his son. I know he would have stayed on with me, even as he looked around for the next pretty face and younger body.'

My own daddy. My own blood father wouldn't have wanted my Momma after all. Tears stuck to my lashes. My throat hurt, proving I was human after all, not the freak I'd believed. I could feel a different kind of pain. But still I couldn't feel happy, why couldn't I feel happy and real? Then I remembered some of her words . . . my real daddy would have found some legal way to take possession of me. Did that mean he would have stolen me away from my own mother? That thought didn't make me happy either.

Grandmother sat on, unmoving. I shrivelled even smaller, scared, so scared of what I might hear next. Daddy, don't let out any more bad secrets and make me take action. John Amos would force me to take action. I glanced behind me, suspecting he might be listening with a glass held to the wall so he could hear better.

'Well,' said my father, wound up now. 'Bart's psychiatrist shows an incredible interest in you, whom he believes to be my mother only. I wonder why time and again he keeps harping back to you. He seems to think you are the clue to Bart's secret inner life. He thinks you lived a secret inner life too – did you, Mother? When your father made you feel less than human, did you sit alone and plot how to have your own kind of revenge, and make him suffer?'

What was this?

'Don't,' she pleaded, 'please don't. Have mercy on me, Christopher. I did the best I could under the circumstances. I swear I did my best.'

'Your best?' He laughed and sounded like Momma when she

poked mean fun. 'When your father's younger half-brother walked into Foxworth Hall at age seventeen, did you immediately seize hold of an inspiration – the supreme way to punish your father for making you dislike yourself? Did you set out to make our father fall in love with you? Did you? Did you hate him in a way too, because he looked like Malcolm? I think you did. I think you schemed and plotted to wound your father in the one way that would shatter his ego most, so it might never recover. And you succeeded. You eloped and married the younger half-brother he despised, and you thought you'd won in two ways. You had stung him where it hurt most. Now you had power to gain his tremendous fortune through our father – but it didn't work, did it? I haven't forgotten those days when we lived in Gladstone, when I overheard you pleading with my father to sue, to get what was rightfully his. But our father refused to co-operate. He loved you and married you for what he thought you were, and not for the money you couldn't keep from dreaming about.'

Stunned again, I stared at my grandmother. She was crying, her frail body shaking, even her rocking chair seemed to quiver. I was quivering too, crying too – inside.

'You're wrong, so wrong, Christopher,' she sobbed, her chest heaving. 'I loved your father. You know I loved him. I gave him four children – I gave him the best years of my life – and the best I had in me to give to anyone.'

'Your best is so poor, Mrs Winslow, so very, very poor.'

'Christopher!' she cried out, getting to her feet painfully. She spread her hands in a helpless way, stepping closer to look up into his face. The black shroud she wore fluttered as she shook. She threw a fearful glance around the room forcing me to shrink smaller into the dim shadowy corner. She lowered her voice.

'All right, we've said enough about the past. Live with Cathy, but accept me into your lives. Let me have Bart as my own son. You have Jory and that little girl you adopted. Let me take Bart and go away, so far away you'll never see or hear from me again. I swear I'll never let anyone know about you and Cathy. I'll do what I can to protect your secret – but let me have Bart for my own, please, please!'

She fell to her knees and clutched at his hands, and when he quickly moved them out of reach, she pulled on his jacket.

'Don't embarrass me further, Mother.' he said uneasily, but I could tell he was touched. 'Cathy and I don't give away our children. He is not our pride and joy at this moment, but we love him, we need him, and we will do what is necessary to see that he is mentally healthy again.'

'Tell me what to do, and I'll do it,' she pleaded, tears streaking her cheeks as at last she caught hold of his evasive hands and she crushed them to her breasts. 'Tell me to do anything but leave. I need to see him, and watch and admire as he pretends. He's wonderfully gifted.' She began to kiss his hands, as he tried to pull them away, but he must not have tried too hard, for she was able to retain them both with her fragile strength.

'Mother, please . . .' he begged, looking away before he sat down and hid his face.

'He needs me, Christopher, more than any of my own children have ever needed me. He loves me too . . . I know he does. He sits on my lap and I rock him, and I see a look of contentment on his face. He's so young, so vulnerable, so bewildered by things he can't understand. And I can help. I know I can help him.'

'Something inside of me says I won't be here too much longer,' she whispered, and I had to strain my ears to hear. 'Let me have him until then . . . please, as one last gift to the mother you used to love very much . . . the mother of your youth, Christopher . . . the mother who cared for you when you had the measles, the chicken- pox, all those colds from staying outside in the snow too long. Remember? I remember. Without my memories of the good times, I could never have lived through the bad . . .'

She was getting to him. He was staring down at her, his eyes soft.

'You said a while ago I seduced your father and deliberately schemed to hurt my father by marrying him. You are wrong. I loved your father from the first moment I laid eyes on him. I could no more have held back from loving him, than you held back from loving Cathy. There, I have nothing left of my past, I've lost everything.

'John's the only one from my past,' she murmured low, like she was scared. 'He's the only one I have left from the days at Foxworth Hall.'

'He must know who I am then. And who Bart is.'

Leaning forward she stretched to put her pale hand with all the rings on his trousered knee – I saw him shudder at her touch.

'I don't know what John knows. He thinks all my children ran off and were lost somewhere in the world. As far as I know, he doesn't know Bart's middle name is Winslow . . . but then again, he's so sly, he may know everything.' She trembled and withdrew her hand as if she knew it offended him. 'All this land around here belonged to my father. So he thinks it's only natural I would come out here and settle down on an estate that's been in our family for years and years.'

He shook his head. 'And you arranged for me to buy my land cheaper?'

'Christopher, my father owned land everywhere. He was always saying land was the most valuable asset of all. Now I own all of that. But I would give it all away just to have you and Cathy back as my family. No one knows about you and Cathy but me, and I'll never tell anyone who you are. I promise not to shame and hurt you – just let me stay. Let me be your mother again.'

'Get rid of John.'

First she sighed, then bowed her head. 'I wish to God I could.'

'What do you mean?'

'Can't you guess?' she asked, her greying head lifted so her eyes could search his.

'Blackmail?'

'Yes. He doesn't have any family either. He pretends not to know about you and Cathy, but I can't be sure. He's sworn to help me keep my whereabouts a mystery for there are news reporters who would be hot on my heels if they knew where I was. So I give him a good home, plenty of money to keep me safe.'

'Bart is not safe. Jory has seen John Amos whispering to him. I think he knows who we are.'

'But he won't do anything,' she cried. 'I'll talk to him, make him understand. He won't tell . . . I'll pay him off.'

Daddy stood up to leave. For a moment his hand rested lightly on her head. Then looking guilty he quickly withdrew it. 'All right. You speak to John, order him to leave Bart alone. Don't let Bart know you are his natural grandmother – let him keep on believing you are only a kind-hearted woman who needs him for a friend. Can you do this one small thing for me?'

'Yes, of course,' she agreed weakly.

'And please start wearing that veil over your head again. Jory knows you are my mother . . . but, well, you know. And who knows when Cathy might decide to be friendly and visit her new neighbour? She was busy with her dance classes before. Now that she's not so occupied, she'll need to see people. That was one of the hardest things for her to bear when she was young . . . to be kept locked up for what seemed to her centuries, and only her mother and grandmother . . . that made her need even greater.'

Again her head drooped. 'I know. I've sinned and I regret it. I pray to turn back the clock, but I wake up to another lonely day – and I have only Bart to give me hope.'

Oh, gosh, they'd known so much before I came along.

'I have to ask something,' she said in a faint whisper. 'Do you love her as a man loves . . . a wife?'

He turned so she could see only his back. 'That is none of your business.'

'But I'd understand. I question Bart but he doesn't know what I mean. But he's told me you have only one bedroom you share.'

Angry, he flared, glaring at her: 'And one bed. Now, you satisfied?' Once more he spun on his heel and this time he left.

Puzzling, gosh darn puzzling. Why did Momma hate his Momma? And why did my grandmother ask about bedrooms and bed?

I ran home next. Didn't stop to report to John Amos. Momma was at that dratted barre, trying to pull herself out of that ugly wheelchair. I hid and watched. Strange to see her awkward – like me, clumsy like me, but she managed to pull herself to her feet and then she stood shaking all over. Her face in the mirror was pale, her hair a frame of gold. Molten gold, hot as hell, burning as running lava.

'Bart, is that you?' she called. 'Why do you stare at me so strangely? I won't fall, if you're thinking that. Each day I feel better, stronger. Come sit with me and talk to me. Tell me what you do all the time when I can't see you. Where do you go?'

'Teach me to play your pretend games. When I was your age I liked to pretend too. Why, I used to dream about being the world's most famous prima ballerina, and I made that the most important thing in my whole life. Now I know it was never that important. Now I know it's making the ones you love happy that matters most. Bart, I want to make you happy . . .'

I hated her for seducing my real father and taking him from my poor lonely grandmother, who was her own mother-in-law. And she must have been married then to Dr Paul Sheffield, who was Chris's brother but not my real father at all. Look at her, trying to make up to me for her neglect. Too late! I wanted to run and push her down. Hear her bones break, all of them. She was unfaithful to all husbands. But I couldn't say any of this. My legs went rubbery and weak and made me sink to the floor as all the silent screams echoed in my head. Wicked sinful evil woman! Sooner or later she'd run away with some lover – like Malcolm's mother did. Like all mothers.

And why hadn't my grandmother come right out and told me who she was? Why was she keeping it a secret? Didn't she know I needed a real grandmother? She even lied to me about who my daddy was! Only John Amos told me the truth.

'Bart – what's wrong?'

Alarm on her face. She should be alarmed. Never, never did she tell me anything but lies. There was no one I could trust but John Amos. All the while he shuffled along, looking weird and old, he was honest, doing his best to set the world straight.

'Bart, what's the matter? Can't you tell me, your own mother?'

Stared at her. Saw all that mass of hair as golden snares to ruin men. Took all men and made them suffer. Her fault. All her fault. Took my real daddy from my grandmother and seduced him.

'Bart, don't crawl on the floor. Stand up and use your legs. You're not an animal.'

I threw back my head and howled. Howled all the rage and hate I felt. It wasn't fair for God to give me her for a mother. Wasn't fair when he burned my real daddy to death.

Gotta do something. Make it all right.

'Bart, please tell me what's wrong.'

I could barely see her. She tried to take a few steps away from the barre, her hands reached for me, as if she wanted me in her arms.

I'd never let her touch me again. Never, never, never!

'I hate you!' I screamed, jumping to my feet and backing away. 'I hope you never walk again. I hope you fall down and die. I hope your house burns up and you and Cindy too.'

Ran – ran and ran until my sides hurt and my mind was empty.

In Apple's stall I fell down to rest. I kept Malcolm's journal there, hidden under the old hay and I fished it out to read more. Boy, he sure did hate women, especially when they were pretty. Didn't seem to notice the ugly ones. I lifted my head and stared into space. Alicia. Nice name – wonder what made him love Alicia more than Olivia – just because she was only sixteen when she married his old, old father of fifty-five?

Alicia slapped his face when he tried to kiss her. Maybe Malcolm wasn't as good at kissing as his father. Did it take years to learn how to kiss good enough?

The more I read, the more I learned how Malcolm succeeded in everything he did, except in making women love him, proving to me I'd better leave all women alone since I was so much like Malcolm. Over and over I was reading his words so I could turn into him, all powerful.

C names. Wonder why women liked C names so much? Catherine, Corrine, Carrie and Cindy – whole wide world full of C names. Wish I liked my grandmother like I used to. Now that I knew she was my real grandmother it wasn't as good. She should have told me. She was just another lying, sneaking, cunning female. Just as John Amos had warned me.

I could smell Apple faintly. My ears heard him munching his food; I felt his cold nose nuzzling my hand – and I was crying. Crying so hard I wanted to die and join him. But Apple should have missed me more. He made me do it. He was supposed to suffer when I did – and he didn't. He was mine and he let grandmother feed him, give him water – so it was his own fault. And there was Clover, dead too. Strangled and stuffed in the hollow oak.

Bad, I was bad.

Thinking about my badness made me sleepy. Dreamed of Apple who loved me. I woke up and it was almost dark. John Amos was grinning down at me, smirking too. 'Hello, Bart, do you feel lonely in Apple's stall?'

Towering above me, John Amos didn't notice the hay that fell from the loft above and caught on his stringy moustache and made him look gruesome.

'How did Malcolm make all his money, John Amos?' I asked just to see if the hay fell off his moustache when he spoke.

'By being more clever than those who would stop him.'

'Stop him from what?' The hay didn't fall off.

'From getting what he wanted.'

'What did he want?'

'Everything. Everything that wasn't his he wanted – and to get everything that belongs to others you have to be ruthless and determined.'

'What's ruthless?'

'Doing what you have to to get what you want.'

'Doing anything?'

'Anything,' he repeated. Stiffly he bent over to peer in my eyes. 'And don't hesitate to step on those who get in your way, including members in your own family. For they would do the same to you if you stood in their way.' He smiled thinly. 'You know of course sooner or later that doctor who is dissecting your personality bit by bit, will lock you in an institution. That's what your parents are doing – getting ready to remove from their lives a little boy who is proving to be too much of a problem.'

Baby tears got in my eyes.

John Amos scowled. 'Don't show weakness with tears that belong to women. Be hard, like your great-grandfather Malcolm was.' He paused to eye me up and down, 'Yes, you have inherited many of his genes. Some day if you keep going as you are, you will be just as powerful as Malcolm.'

'Where've you been, Bart?' snapped Emma who looked at me all the time like she was disgusted, even when I was clean. 'Never in my life have I seen a boy who could get dirtier more quickly than you. Look at your shirt, your pants, your face and hands! Filthy, that's what. What do you do, make mud puddles and wallow in them?'

Didn't answer. Headed for the bathroom down the hall.

Momma looked up from her desk in her bedroom. 'Bart, I've been wondering where you were. You've been gone for hours.'

It was my own business, none of hers!

'Bart . . . answer me.'

'Was outside.'

'I know that. Where outside?'

'Near the wall.'

'What were you doing there?'

'Digging.'

'Digging for what?'

'For worms.'

'Why do you need worms?'

'Goin' fishin'.'

She sighed. 'It's too late to go fishing, and you know I don't like you to go off by yourself. Ask your father if he will take you fishing this Saturday.'

'He won't.'

'How can you be so sure?'

'He never has time.'

'He'll take time.'

'No, he won't. Never has, never will.'

Again she sighed. 'Bart, try to be understanding. He's a doctor, and he has many very sick patients. You wouldn't want his patients to go unattended, would you?'

I wouldn't care. Rather go fishing. Too many people in the world anyway . . . especially women. I ran to bury my face in her lap. 'Momma, please get well quick. You take me fishing. Now you don't have to dance, you can do all the things Daddy never has time for. You can spend all the time with me you used to spend with Jory dancing. Momma, Momma, I'm sorry about what I said,' I sobbed, 'I don't really hate you! I don't want you to fall down and die. I just feel mean sometimes and I can't stop. Momma, please don't hate me for what I said.'

Her hands were soft and comforting in my hair as she tried to smooth it down and make it stay neat. Hair brushes and hairspray would never work, so how could her hands? I buried my face deeper in her lap, thinking of how John Amos would scold me if he knew, though I'd already told him what I'd said to her before, and he'd smiled, so pleased I was talking like Malcolm. 'You shouldn't have done that, Bart,' he said to confuse me, 'you have to be clever, make her think she's having her way. If you let her know how you feel she'll find a way to defeat our purpose. And we do have to save her from the Devil, don't we?'

I raised my head to stare up into her pretty face, making tears streak my face for the living lie she had to be. Been married three times, John Amos had told me. I didn't really care if she was good or evil, as long as I had her for my own. I'd make her good. I'd teach her to leave all men alone – but me.

To win I had to play my cards just right, and deal out the aces one by one, like John Amos had told me. Fool her, fool Daddy, make them think I wasn't crazy. But I got mixed up. I wasn't crazy, only pretending to be Malcolm. And she'd never take me fishing, nor would Daddy. Momma was in that detestable chair that wouldn't make it to the river and Daddy was always off somewhere taking care of everybody but me.

'What are you thinking, Bart?' she asked, still stroking my hair.

'I've got no playmates. Got none but what I make up. Got nothing but bad genes from inbreeding – and as for my invir – well, that's no good either. You and Daddy don't deserve any children. You don't deserve anything but the hell you have already made for yourself!'

Left her sitting stunned. Glad to make her unhappy, like she was always making me. But why didn't happiness come and make me laugh? Why did I run to my room and throw myself down on my bed and cry?

Then I remembered the one person who didn't need anyone – Malcolm. He knew he was strong. Malcolm never hesitated in making decisions, even wrong ones, for he knew how to twist them about and make them right. So I scowled, hunched my shoulders, stood up and shuffled down the hall, wanting what Malcolm wanted. I saw Jory dancing with Melodie and went in Momma's room to report to her. 'Stop what you're doing!' I yelled. 'Sinning is going on between Jory and Melodie – they're kissing – making a baby.'

Her flying fingers paused over the typewriter keys. She smiled. 'Bart, it takes more than hugging and kissing to make a baby. And Jory is a gentleman and won't take advantage of an innocent young girl who is decent and wise enough to know when to say stop.'

She didn't care. All she cared about was that damn book she was writing. I didn't have any more chance with her now than I'd had when she was a dancer. Always, always she found something better to do than play with me.

I clenched my fists and hit at the door frame. There'd come a time when I was her boss, and she'd listen then. She'd know who she'd better play with. She'd been a better mother when she taught ballet classes! At least she had a free moment once in a while. Now all she did was write, write. Mountains and mountains of white paper!

Again she stopped paying attention to me, reloaded her typewriter as if she had a shotgun to kill the world. She didn't even notice when I took a box she'd filled and put aside as she began to fill another with her words on paper.

John Amos would be interested in what she'd written. But before he read a sheet, I'd read them first. Even if I had to use a dictionary every minute I struggled to understand some of the longer words she used. Appropriate . . . knew what that meant. I think.

'Goodnight, Momma.'

She didn't hear me. Just went right on as if I weren't there.

Nobody ever ignored Malcolm. When he spoke people jumped to do his bidding. I was gonna make myself over into Malcolm.

A week later I was spying on Mom and Jory. They were before the long mirror and Jory was helping Momma use her bad leg. 'Now don't think of falling. I'm right at your back and I'll catch you if your knee gives way. Just take it easy, Mom, and soon you will be walking just fine.'

She didn't walk just fine. Every step she took seemed to hurt. Jory kept his hands on her waist to keep her from even tottering, and somehow she made it to the end of the barre without falling. Weakly she waited for him to push up her chair so she could sit down again. He turned the foot rests into position as she held up her legs. 'Mom, you're stronger each day.'

'But it's taking so long.'

'You sit and write too long at a time. Remember your doctor said to get up more often, and sit less . . .'

She nodded, looking exhausted. 'Who was that long distance call from? Why didn't they want to speak to me?'

His face breaking into a smile, Jory explained: 'It was my grandmother Marisha. I wrote and told her about your fall, and now's she's flying West so she can replace you in your school. Isn't that great, Mom?'

She didn't look happy even a little bit. As for me, I hated that old witch.

'Jory, you should have told me before.'

'But Mom, she wanted it to be a surprise. I wouldn't have told you today, but I think it's not very polite for people to drop in out of the blue. I knew you'd want to get ready, look pretty, tidy up the house . . .'

Funny kind of look she gave him. 'In other words I don't look my best now, and my house is messy?'

Jory smiled with all that charm I hated. 'Mom, you're always pretty, you know that, but too skinny, and too pale. You've got to eat more and get outside a little more each day. After all, great novels aren't written in a few weeks.'

Later on that same day I followed Jory out into the yard, then I hid in my special hideaway place to spy on Momma and Jory as both took turns pushing hateful Cindy in her baby swing. Never let me swing Cindy. Nobody trusted me. Head shrink wasn't getting anywhere, so why couldn't everybody give up and leave me alone?

'Jory, it's sometimes a torment to hear your ballet music and not be able to dance and express all the emotions I feel. Now when I hear an overture begin, I tighten up and cringe inside. I yearn to dance and the more I yearn, the harder I have to write. Writing saves me, but it seems Bart resents my writing as much as he used to resent my dancing. It seems I am never going to have the ability to please my younger son.'

'Aw heck, Mom,' said Jory with his dark blue eyes sad and worried too, 'he's only a little boy who doesn't know what he wants. I know something weird is going on in his mind.'

I wasn't weird. They were the weird ones, thinking dancing

and stupid fairy tales mattered, when all others with sense knew money was king, queen and God Almighty.

'Jory, I give as much of myself to Bart as I can. I try to show affection and he pulls away. Then he's running away from me, or to me, and putting his face in my lap and crying. His psychiatrist says he's torn between hating me and loving me. And I'll tell you this in confidence, his behaviour isn't helping me recover from my accident.'

I left then. Heard enough. Good time to sneak into her bedroom and steal some more of her book pages. Stuffed in my shirt drawer I had the ones John Amos had read and returned, so I put those back and took some new ones.

In my little green cave made of hedges I sat down to read. Stupid Cindy was laughing and squealing while her two adoring slaves pushed her into the air. Boy, wish I had the chance to swing her. I'd push so hard she'd sail right over the white wall and end up in the swimming pool next door. The pool that never had any water.

Reading Momma's book was very interesting. 'The Road to Riches', was the title of one of her chapters. Was that girl really my own mother? Were she and her two brothers and one sister really going to be locked up in one bedroom?

I read on until the day grew old, and the fog came in and smothered me.

Got up and went inside the house thinking about another title in her book. 'The Attic'. What a wonderful place to hide things. I stared at Momma who was kissing Daddy's lips, teasing him, asking him about his pretty nurses, and had he found someone to replace her yet. 'A beautiful young blonde of twenty or so?'

He appeared hurt. 'I wish you wouldn't make a joke out of my devotion. Cathy, don't provoke me with silly remarks like that. I give all I can to you because I love you with a passion I recognize as idiotic.'

'Idiotic?' she asked.

'Yes, it is when you don't respond as passionately as I do. I need you, Cathy! Don't let this writing come between us.'

'I don't understand.'

'You do understand! Our past is coming alive. You're living it again as you write. I peek in and see your face, watch the tears streak your face and fall on the paper. I hear you laugh and say aloud the words that Cory said, or Carrie. You're not just writing, Cathy . . . *you are reliving*.'

Her head bowed down and her loose hair fell and covered her face. 'Yes, what you say is true. I sit at the desk and relive it all again. I see again the attic gloom, the dusty immense space; I hear the silence more terrifying than thunder. Loneliness that knew me well then, comes and burdens my shoulders, so I look up startled to see where I am, wondering why the windows aren't heavily covered over, and wondering when the grandmother will come in and catch us with windows not covered. Sometimes I'm startled to look up and catch Bart standing in the doorway staring at me. First I think he's Cory, then I can't account for his dark hair and his brown eyes. I look at Cindy and think she should be larger, as old as Cory with the dark hair, and I'm confused, not knowing the past from the present.'

'Cathy,' he was worried, 'you've got to give this up.'

Yes, yes, Daddy . . . make her give it up.

She sobbed as she fell into his arms, and tightly he cradled her to his heart, murmuring sweet love words in her ears that I couldn't hear. Rocking back and forth, standing and swaying like true wicked lovers, they looked like the couples I spied on sometimes, the ones on the lovers' lane which wasn't so far from my grandmother's mansion.

'Will you put the book away, wait until the children are grown and safely married . . . ?'

'I can't!' Even I could hear the agony in her voice, as if she'd like to if she could. 'That story is in my brain screaming to get out, to let others know how some mothers can be. Something intuitive and wise tells me that when I have it down, and it's sold to a publisher, and made into a book for everyone to read – only then will I be set free from all the hate I feel for Momma!'

Daddy couldn't speak. Just went on holding her, rocking, and his blue eyes that stared into space above her head that was pressed against his chest, seemed tormented by his dilemma.

Dilemma. Was another of those words I'd just looked up in her dictionary. I was getting smart quick.

I stole away to play alone in the garden. Jory's old witch grandmother was coming. Didn't want to ever see her again. Momma didn't like her either; I could tell from the way she grew tense and careful around her, as if afraid her quick tongue would betray her.

'Bart my darling,' called my own grandmother softly from her side of the thick white wall, 'I've been waiting for you to come over all day. When you don't come I get worried, and then I'm unhappy. Darling, don't sit alone and pout. Remember I'm over here willing to do anything I can to make you happy.'

I ran. Fast as my legs could take me. I climbed the tree, and she had a stepladder waiting there for me so I could get to the ground safely. It was the same ladder she used to peer over at us.

'I'm going to leave the ladder there for you to use,' she whispered, hugging me, covering my face with her kisses. Lucky for me she took off that dry veil first. 'I don't want you to fall and hurt yourself. I love you so much, Bart. I look at you and think of how proud your father would be. Oh, if only he could see his son. His handsome brilliant son!'

Handsome? Brilliant? Gee . . . didn't know I was either one. It felt good to be told I was wonderful. She made me believe I was every bit as good-looking as Jory, and every bit as talented too. This was a grandmother. The kind I'd always wanted. One who loved me and no one else. Maybe John Amos was wrong about her after all.

Again I sat on her lap and let her spoon ice-cream into my mouth. She fed me a biscuit, a slice of chocolate cake, then held the glass of milk for me to drink. With a full stomach I snuggled more comfortably on her lap and rested my head on the softness of her full breasts that smelled of lavender. 'Corrine used to use lavender,' I mumbled sleepily with my thumb in my mouth. 'Sing me a lullaby . . . nobody ever sang me to sleep like Momma sings to Cindy . . .'

'Lullaby and good night . . .'

Funny. As she sang softly, seemed I was only two years old, and a long, long time ago I'd sat just like this, on my mother's lap, and heard her sing that very song.

'Wake up, darling,' she said, tickling my face with the edge of her sleeve. 'Time for you to go home now. Your parents will be worried – and they have suffered enough without having more anxiety about your whereabouts.'

Oh! Over in the corner John Amos had overheard her speak. It was in his watery pale blue eyes that gleamed dangerously. He didn't like my grandmother or my parents or Jory or Cindy. He didn't like anyone but me and Malcolm Foxworth.

'Grandmother,' I whispered, hiding my face so he couldn't see my lips move, 'don't let John Amos hear you say you have sympathy for my parents . . . I heard him say yesterday they didn't deserve sympathy.' I felt her shiver and try not to let him know she was aware he was there.

'What does sympathy mean exactly?'

Sighing, she held me tighter. 'It's an emotion you feel when you understand the troubles of others, when you want to help, but there's nothing you can do.'

'Then what good is sympathy?'

'Not much good in any meaningful way,' she said with her eyes looking sad. 'It's only good is letting you know you are still human enough to have compassion. The best kind of sympathy moves one into action to solve dilemmas.'

'I know what dilemma means.'

'Of course you do.'

John Amos whispered as I sneaked out into the evening shadows: 'The Lord helps those who help themselves, remember that, Bart.' Gravely he returned the pages of my mother's manuscript I'd given him to read. 'Put these back exactly as you found them. Don't get them soiled. And when she's written more, bring those – and you will be able then to solve all your own problems. Her book is telling you how. – Don't you understand, that's why she's writing it.'

EVER SINCE EVE *Bart*

She was coming now, coming from Greenglenna, South Carolina, where the graves grew like weeds. Any day I could expect to look up and see her ugly mean face.

My own grandmother was a thousand times better! Sometimes lately she left her face unveiled. She'd wear a little make-up to please me – and it did. Sometimes she even put on a pretty dress – but never, never did she let John Amos see her in anything but that black robe and the veil over her face. Only for me was she pretty.

'Bart, please don't spend too much time with John.'

He'd warned me many times she wouldn't approve. 'No, ma'am. John Amos and me don't get along.'

'I'm glad. He's an evil man, Bart, cold, cruel and heartless.'

'Yes, ma'am. He don't like women much.'

'He told you that?'

'Yep. Tells me he gets lonely. Tells me you treat him like dirt and refuse to speak to him for days on end.'

'Leave John alone. Avoid him all you can – but keep on coming to see me. You're all I have now." She patted the soft sofa cushion, inviting me to sit beside her. I knew by now that she sat in comfortable chairs whenever John Amos had gone into the city.

'What does he do in San Francisco?' I asked. He went there often.

Frowning, she pulled me into her arms and held me close against the soft silk of her rose coloured dress. 'John is an old man, but still he has many appetites that must be satisfied.'

'What does he like to eat?' I asked, curious about an old man who had false teeth and great difficulty chewing even chicken, much less steak. Mush, jelly, bread sopped in milk, that's what John Amos usually ate.

She chuckled and kissed the top of my hair.

'How's your mother? Is she walking well now?'

Changing the subject. Didn't want to tell me what he ate. I shifted away. 'Bit by bit she's getting well, so she tells my daddy, but she's not so hot. When he's not home sometimes she gets a cane and uses that, but she doesn't want Daddy to know.'

'Why not?'

'I don't know. All she wants to do now is play with Cindy, or write. That's all she does, honest Injun. Writing books is just as exciting to her as dancin' . . . sometimes she gets all hot and bothered-lookin'.'

'Oh,' she murmured weakly, 'I was hoping she'd give it up.'

So was I. But it didn't seem likely. 'Jory's grandmother is coming soon, real soon. Think I might run away if she decides to stay in our house.'

Again she said 'oh' as if surprises were stealing her tongue. 'It's all right, Granny,' I said. 'Don't like her like I like you.'

I went home around lunchtime, chock full of ice-cream and cake. (Really was beginning to hate sweets.) Momma was at the barre, doing exercises before the long mirror, and I had to be careful she didn't spot me when I ducked behind a chair. I guess we had the only family room in the world with a barre at one end, and a ten-foot-long mirror in back of it.

'Bart, is that you hiding behind the chair?'

'No, ma'am, it's Henry Lee Jones . . .'

'Really? I've been looking for Henry Lee for some time. I'm glad you've finally been found around the corner, around the bush . . . always looking for Henry Lee.'

Made me giggle. It was the game we used to play when I was little, real little. 'Momma, can you take me fishin' today?'

'I'm sorry. I've got a full day planned. Perhaps tomorrow.'

Tomorrow. It was always tomorrow.

In a dark corner I hid myself, crouched down so small I felt nobody could see me. Sometimes when I was following Momma in her chair, I tiptoed with my back hunched, making myself into the way John Amos said Malcolm looked when he was old and at his peak of power. I stared and stared at her, morning, afternoons, nights, trying always to decide if she was as bad as John Amos said she was.

'Bart.' Jory could always find me no matter how I hid, 'what are you doing now? We used to have fun together. You used to talk to me. Now you don't talk to anyone.'

Did so. I talked to my grandmother, to John Amos. I smiled crookedly, sneering my lips in the way John Amos curled his lips as I turned to watch Momma who was walking just as clumsy as me now. Served her right for getting out of that chair too soon, and just to catch Cindy and keep her from drowning in her pool.

Jory went away and left me to amuse myself, when I didn't know how to any more except by playing Malcolm. Was Momma really so sinful? How could I talk to Jory like I used to, when he wouldn't believe Momma told lies about who was my real father? Jory still thought it was Dr Paul, and it wasn't, wasn't.

Later on at dinner, while Momma and Daddy were exchanging glances, and saying silly things that made them laugh, and Jory too, I sat and glared at the tablecloth which was yellow. Why did Daddy want Momma to use a yellow tablecloth at least once a week? Why did he keep saying she had to learn to forgive and forget?

Then Jory spoke up.

'Mom, Melodie and I have a date tonight. I'm taking her to a movie, and then to a supper club that doesn't serve hard liquor. Will it be all right if I kiss her good night?'

'Such a momentous question,' she said with a laugh, while I sat in my corner. 'Yes, kiss her good night, and tell her how much you enjoyed the evening . . . and that's all.'

'Yes, Mother,' he said mockingly, grinning. 'I know your lesson by heart. Melodie is a sweet, nice, innocent girl who would be insulted if I took advantage of her, so I'll insult her by not taking advantage.'

She made a face at him – he just smiled back. 'How's the writing going?' Jory sang out before he returned to his room to moon over Melodie's picture he kept on his nightstand.

Stupid question. Already she'd told him writing absorbed her every wakeful moment, and new ideas woke her up at night, and Daddy was complaining she kept him awake with her light on. As for me, I couldn't wait to read what was going to happen next. Sometimes I thought she was making it all up, and it hadn't happened to her, it hadn't. Pretending, the way I did.

'Jory,' she asked, 'have you been bothering my script? I can't find some of my chapters.'

He sounded indignant 'Gosh, Mom, you know I wouldn't read what you write without your permission – do I have your permission?'

She laughed. 'Some day when you are a man, I'm going to insist you read my book, or books. It keeps growing and growing, so it may end up two books.'

'Where are you getting your ideas?'

Stooping, she picked up an old spiral-bound book. 'From this book, and from my memory.' She quickly flipped through the pages. 'See how large I wrote when I was twelve? As I grew older my writing became more precise, and much smaller.'

Suddenly Jory snatched the spiral-bound book from her hands, then ran to a window where he could read a few lines before she had it back in her hands. 'You misspelled a few words, Mom,' he teased.

I hated their relationship; they were more like friends than mother and son. Hated the way she kept scribbling on lined paper before she typed those words up. Hated all her junk, her pencils, pens, erasers, and the new books she'd bought for her new project. Didn't have a mother any more; didn't have a father. Never had a real father. Had nobody, not even a pet.

Summer was getting old now, like me. My bones felt old and brittle, my brain wise and cynical. And I thought, as Malcolm wrote in his journal, that nothing was as good as it used to be, and no toy gave me the pleasure I thought it would before I had it. Even my grandmother's mansion didn't look as huge as it had.

In Apple's stall, which was my special place for reading more of Malcolm's journal, I fell on the hay and tried to read the ten pages a day John Amos had assigned me. Sometimes I hid the book under the hay, sometimes I wore it next to my skin. As I began to read I chewed on a piece of the hay, finding my place marked with one of Momma's little leather bookmarks:

> I remember so well the day when I was twenty-eight and came home to find my widowed father had finally remarried. I stared at his bride whom I later found out was only sixteen. I knew immediately a girl so young and beautiful had married him only for his money.
>
> My own wife, Olivia, had never been what anyone would call a beauty, but she'd had some appealing aspects when I married her, and her father was very wealthy. Suddenly I found out after she'd borne me two sons, she had no appeal for me whatsoever. She seemed so grim compared to Alicia, my stepmother of sixteen . . .

Good golly, I'd read this mushy love junk before. I'd lost my place, gosh darn it. But I had a way of flipping through the book and reading here and there, especially when boring stuff like kissing came into Malcolm's story. It seemed so odd as much as he hated women that he'd want to kiss them.

Now, here it was, where I'd left off.

> Alicia was giving birth to her first child whom I hoped desperately would be a girl, but no, it had to be another son to compete with me for my father's fortune. I remember standing and looking at her, and the baby she snuggled at her side in the big swan bed, and I hated them both.
>
> I said to her when she smiled up at me innocently, and so proud of her son, as if I'd welcome him as much as my father

did, 'My dear stepmother, your son will never live long enough to inherit your husband's fortune, for I am alive to prevent that.'

She annoyed me then so much I could have slapped her beautiful cunning face. 'I don't want your father's money, Malcolm. My son won't want it either. My son will earn his way, not inherit what money other men have made. I'll teach my son the true values in life – the values *you* know nothing about.'

Wonder what she'd been talking about? What were values anyway – sale prices? I turned my attention to Malcolm's journal again and found he skipped a great many years before he wrote again. Why had he skipped *fifteen* years?

My daughter, Corrine, grew more and more like the mother who had abandoned me when I was only five. I saw her changing, beginning to develop into a woman, and I'd find myself staring at her budding young breasts that would soon entice some man. She saw me once staring there and blushed. I liked that – at least she was modest. 'Corrine, promise that you will never marry and leave your father when he's old and sick. Swear to me you won't leave me *ever*.'

Her face grew very pale, as if she feared I might send her back into the attic if she refused my simple request. 'All my fortune, Corrine, if you promise – every cent I will leave to you if you never leave me.'

'But, Father,' she said, inclining her head and looking miserable, 'I want to get married and have babies.'

She swore she loved me, but in her eyes I could see she'd leave me at the first opportunity.

I'd see to it she had no boys or men in her life. She'd attend a school for girls only, a strict religious school that would allow no dating.

I closed the book and headed home, full of all the strange

notions Malcolm had about women, mothers, wives and daughters. To my way of thinking Malcolm should never have married Olivia and had any children – but then, as I thought about it more, I would never have known my grandmother. And even though she was a liar, and had betrayed me, still I wanted to love and trust her again.

Another day I was in the barn reading about Malcolm when he was fifty. He wasn't so regular now about writing in his journal.

> There's something sinful going on between that younger half-brother of mine and my daughter. I've done what I can to catch them touching, or looking at each other in a suggestive way, but they are both very clever. Olivia tells me my fears are groundless, that Corrine could never feel anything for her half-uncle, but then, Olivia is just another woman, true to her devious sex. Damn the day she talked me into taking that boy into our home. It was a mistake, perhaps the most grave mistake of my life.

So, even Malcolm made a few mistakes, but only with those people who were members of his family. Why was it he couldn't stand for his sons to be musicians – for his daughter to marry? If I'd been Malcolm, I'd have been glad to get rid of her, just like I wished day after day that Cindy would disappear.

I hurled Malcolm's journal to the floor and kicked hay over it, then stomped towards the mansion, wanting Malcolm to write about power, and how to get it, and money, and how to earn it, and influence, and how to demand it, and all he did was write about how miserable his two sons, his wife and his daughter made him, to say nothing of that young half-brother who liked Corrine..

'Hello, darling!' cried my grandmother when I limped into her parlour. 'Where've you been? How's your mother's knee?'

'Bad,' I said. 'Doctors say Momma will never dance again.'

'Oh,' she sighed, 'how dreadful. I'm so sorry.'

'I'm glad she won't dance again,' I assured her. 'She and Daddy can't even waltz any more and they used to do a lot of that in the living-room which they don't want us to use.'

She looked so sad. Why should she look so sad? 'Grandmother, my Momma don't like you.'

'You should watch your grammar, Bart,' she choked as she wiped away her tears. 'You should say, she doesn't like you – and how can you say that, when she doesn't know I'm here?'

'Sometimes you sound like her.'

'I'm so sorry I'll never see her again on stage. She was so wonderfully light and graceful she seemed a part of the music. Your mother was born for dancing, Bart. I know she must feel lost and empty without it.'

'No, she doesn't,' I answered quickly. 'Momma's got that typewriter and her book to work on all day and most of the night, and that's all she needs. She and Daddy lie in bed for hours and hours, especially when it rains, and they talk about some big old house in the mountains, and some big old grandmother who wore grey dresses all the time, and I hide in the closet and think it's just like some dumb fairy tale.'

She appeared shocked. 'Do you spy on your parents? That's not very nice, Bart. Adults need privacy – everyone needs privacy.'

I smiled and felt good to tell her I spied on everyone, even her, sometimes.

Her blue eyes grew wider and she stared at me for a long time before she smiled. 'You're teasing me, aren't you? I'm sure your father has taught you better than that. Bart, if you want people to love you and respect you, you have to treat them as you would want to be treated. Would you like me to spy on you?'

'No!' I roared.

Another day, another trip to the office of that grey-haired old doctor who made me lie down and close my eyes so he could sit behind me and ask dumb questions.

'Are you Bart Sheffield today or Malcolm?'

Wouldn't say nothing.

'What is Malcolm's last name?'

Was none of his business.

'How do you feel about your mother now that she can't dance any more?'

'Glad.'

Took him by surprise. He got busy scribbling down notes, getting real excited so his face was red when I opened my eyes and turned to take a peek. I thought I'd give him more to get excited about. 'I wish Jory would fall and smash both his kneecaps. Then I could walk faster than him, and run faster than him, and do everything better too. Then when I come into the room everyone will look at me, not him.'

He waited for more. When nothing else came he said gently. 'I understand, Bart. You fear your mother and father don't love you as much as they do Jory.'

Rage took me over. 'Yes she does! She loves me better! But I can't dance. It's the dancing that makes her laugh with Jory, and frown with me. I was going to grow up and be a doctor – but now I don't want to. 'Cause my real daddy wasn't a doctor like they told me. He was a lawyer.'

'How do you know that?' he asked.

Wouldn't tell him. None of his business. John Amos told me. Heard Grandma telling Dad, too. Lawyers were smart, real smart. That would make me smart too. Dancers didn't have good brains, just good legs.

'Is there anything else you would like to tell me, Bart?'

'Yeah!' I snapped, jumping up from the couch and grabbing his letter opener, 'last night the moon was full. I looked out of the window and heard it calling to me. I wanted to howl. Then I needed to taste blood. I ran like crazy into the woods, and on into the hills, when out of the night appeared a woman who was beautiful, with long, long golden hair.'

'And what did you do?' asked the doctor when I paused.

'I killed her, then ate her.'

He scribbled away, and I picked up several of the lollipops he kept for his younger patients. Then I took about six more, thinking my grandmother might want one, at least.

When I was home I hurried over to Apple's stall and flipped backwards through the pages of Malcolm's journal, I needed to find out something – and I'd skipped some mushy pages before. I wanted to know what drew him towards women whom he despised.

> It was fall again, and all the trees wore brilliant autumn colours. I followed Alicia into the woods as she rode her horse with admirable skill. I had to spur my horse to make him gallop and give chase. She was so enchanted with the beauty of the season she didn't seem to hear the beat of my horse's hoofs. For a brief second I lost sight of her when she disappeared into a thicket. That's when I suspected she might be headed for the lake where I swam when I was a child. One last swim before summer was gone, and winter turned the water icy.

Cherry-flavoured lollipops were my favourites. I licked and licked until I could stick out my tongue and see it red as blood. Good to read and eat sweet stuff as I skimmed through the sickening glop that followed for pages on end. Gee, Malcolm must have started making money and gaining power when he was much older.

> Just as I suspected, she was in the pool, her glorious body as flawless as I'd guessed it would be. And to think my father was enjoying all of that while I had to endure the frigid body of a woman who could only submit, never enjoy.
>
> Dripping and shimmering she stepped from the lake to the grassy bank where her clothes lay waiting. My breath caught as I beheld her in sunlight. The spill of her glorious hair caught red, gold, with dark amber shadow, and the floss between her thighs curled wet and dark.

She saw me then and gasped. I hadn't realized I'd stepped out of the shadows.

Thank God she slapped him, and told him off. Now, now, he was getting to be like the Malcolm I knew him to be; mean, hard, ruthless and rich.

'You'll pay for this, Alicia! Both you and your son will pay, and dearly pay. Nobody rejects me after leading me on, and letting me believe – '

Closed the book and yawned.

MADAME M *Jory*

Another letter had come from my grandmother Marisha to announce that she was on her way to take over my mother's ballet class, 'And I'll have the chance to see my grandson more often, and give him the benefit of my experience.'

Mom was none too happy since she and Madame M did not have a close or warm relationship, and this had always bothered me. I loved them both, and wanted them to love each other.

We were all waiting for Madame to show up, all starving because already she was an hour late. She'd telephoned to say she didn't want anyone to meet her, as she was independent and not accustomed to being waited on. Nevertheless, Mom had helped Emma prepare a gourmet meal, and now it was growing cold.

'Lord, but that woman can be inconsiderate,' complained Dad after looking at his watch for the tenth time. 'If she had allowed me to meet her at the airport, she'd be here by now.'

'Isn't it strange,' asked Mom with a mocking smile, 'when she always insisted that her students be punctual.'

Finally, an hour after Dad ate alone and hurried off to do his hospital rounds, Mom retired to her bedroom to work on her book until my grandmother arrived. 'Bart,' I called, 'come on and play some game with me. Checkers?'

'No!' he bellowed, keeping to his dark corner, his eyes black and mean as he crouched there, almost unblinking. 'I'm wishing for that old lady to fall from the sky.'

'That's mean, Bart. Why do you always say such hateful things?'

He refused to answer, just sat on staring at me.

The doorbell rang. I jumped up and ran to open the door,.

My grandmother stood there smiling, and looking rather dishevelled.

She was at least seventy-four, I knew that, crinkled, old and grey. Sometimes her hair was jet black, and sometimes it had two inches of white near the roots. Bart said it made her look like a skunk or an old black seal. He thought her hair was so slick she kept it oiled. But I thought she looked wonderful when she threw her arms about me, and hugged me close, and tears streaked her rouged cheeks. She didn't even give Bart a glance.

'Jory, Jory, how handsome you are,' she said. Her bun of hair was so huge I guessed it might be false.

'Can I call you Grandmother when we're not in class?'

'Sure,' she agreed, nodding like a bird. 'But only when nobody else is around, you hear?'

'There's Bart,' I said to remind her to be polite – which she seldom was. She didn't like Bart, and he didn't like her. She gave Bart a brief nod, then casually dismissed him as if he didn't exist.

'I'm so glad to have a few moments alone with you,' Madame gushed, hugging me again. She pulled me to the family-room sofa, and together we sat while Bart stayed in his dim corner. 'I tell you, Jory, when you wrote and said you weren't coming again this summer, I felt ill, really ill. I made up my mind then and there that I'd had enough of this once a year grandson, and I was selling my own dance studio and coming out here to help your mother. Of course I knew she wouldn't want me, but so what? I cannot endure two long years of longing to see my only grandchild again.

'The flight here was ghastly,' she went on. 'Turbulence all the way. They searched me too before I boarded, like some criminal. Then we had to circle round and round the airport, waiting our turn to land. It made me sick enough to vomit. Finally, just before our plane ran out of fuel, we landed – bumpiest landing, I thought my neck would break. Great God in heaven, you should have heard what that man wanted for his rented car. He must have thought I was made of money. Since I've come to stay, I decided then and there I'd buy a car of my own. Not a new one, but a nice old one that Julian would have loved. Have I told you before your father loved to tinker around with old cars, and fix them up so they'd run?'

Boy, had she told me that before.

'So, I paid those crooks the exorbitant price of eight hundred dollars, and stepped into my new red car and took off for your place, reading a map as my car choked and chugged along. I felt so happy to be on my way to you, my beloved grandson, Georges' only heir. Why it was just like it used to be when your father was an adolescent, and he'd rush home so proud to take me for a spin in his new car made out of old junk he salvaged from the city dump.'

Her sparkling jet eyes seemed young, and she won me again with her affection, her praise, the vibes she sent out telling me I was wonderful and special. 'And like old ladies everywhere, you've to understand once I get started thinking backwards all sorts of memories are triggered. Your grandfather felt so happy the day Julian was born. I held your father in my arms and stared up at my husband who was so handsome, like Julian, like you, and I could have burst with the pride I felt to give birth at my age for the first time with so little difficulty. And such a perfect baby your father was, so wonderful from his very beginning.'

I wanted to dare and ask how old she was when my father was born – but I didn't have the nerve. Somehow the question must have shown in my eyes. 'None of your damn business how old I am!' she snapped, then leaned to kiss me again. 'My, but you are even better looking than your father was at your age, and I didn't think that possible. I always told Julian he would have looked better with a healthy suntan, but he'd do anything to defy me, anything – even keep himself unnaturally pale.' Sadness clouded her eyes. To my surprise she glanced then at Bart who was listening too – and another surprise, he seemed interested.

She still wore the same black dress that seemed stiff with age, and over that she wore an old leopardskin bolero that had seen its better days. 'No one really knew your father, Jory, just as no one really possessed him. That is, no one but your mother.'

She sighed, then went on as if she had to say it all before my mother appeared. 'So, I've determined I have to know my Julian's son better than I knew him. I've decided too you have to love me, because I was never sure Julian ever did. I keep telling myself that the son born of the union between my son and your mother would have to make the most wonderful dancer, with none of Julian's hang-ups. Your mother is very dear to me, Jory, very dear, though she refuses to believe that. I admit I used to be nasty to her sometimes. She took that as my true feelings, but I was only angry because she never seemed to appreciate my son.'

Uncomfortable with this sort of talk, I shifted away from her; my first loyalty was to my mother, not to her. She noticed my attitude but went on regardless:

'I'm not trying to take you away from your parents, just that I'm lonely. I need to be near you, near her too.' Remorse like evening shadows came to darken her eyes, putting additional years on her face. 'The worst thing about growing old is being lonely, feeling so alone, so purposeless, so used up.'

'Oh, Grandmother!' I cried, throwing my arms about her. 'You don't ever need to feel lonely or purposeless again. You have us.' I hugged her tighter, kissed her again. 'Isn't this the most beautiful house? You can live here with us. Have I told you before my mother designed it herself? She says this is the the very same type of house she grew up in way back in Gladstone, Pennsylvania.'

Madame looked with great curiosity around the family room. 'Yes, this is a lovely home, so like Catherine. Where is she?'

'She's in her room writing.'

'Writing letters?' She looked hurt, as if Mom should be a better hostess and not attending to trivialities.

'Grandmother, Mom is writing a book.'

'A book? Dancers can't write books!'

Grinning, I jumped up and did a few practice steps out of habit. 'Madame Grandmother, dancers can do anything they set their minds to. After all, if we can endure the kind of pain we do, what else is there to fear?'

'Rejections,' snapped Madame. 'Dancers have sky-high egos. One rejection slip too many and Mommy will come crashing down.'

I smiled, thinking that was a good one. She'd never come crashing down even if she got a thousand rejection slips.

'Where's your father?' she asked next.

'Making his evening rounds at his hospitals. He said to give you his apologies. He wanted to be here and welcome you to our home, but you didn't show up on schedule.'

She snorted, as if that were his fault somehow. 'Well,' she said, getting up and looking around the room somewhat more critically, 'I guess it's time I went in and said hello to Catherine – though certainly she must have heard my voice.' Certainly she should have, it was shrill enough. 'Mom gets very engrossed, Grandmother. Sometimes she doesn't even hear her name spoken from a foot away.'

'Har-rumph!' she snorted again. Then she followed me down the hall. I rapped softly on Mom's closed door, then cautiously opened it when she mumbled something like . . . 'Yes . . .'

'You've got company, Mom.'

For a second it seemed I saw dismay in my mother's eyes before Madame stalked arrogantly into her bedroom. Grandmother flung herself down, without an invitation to sit, on the lush rose velvet chaise-longue. Dad had given it to Mom for an anniversary of some miserable summer both remembered well, but wouldn't explain when I asked for details.

'Madame M!' cried Mom. 'How wonderful to see you again. At last you've decided to come and see us instead of the other way around.'

Why was she so nervous? Why did she keep glancing at the portraits on her nightstand? Same old portraits of Dad, and Daddy Paul. Even my father was there, but in a small oval frame, not wide silver ones.

Madame glanced at the nightstand too – and frowned.

'I have many wonderfully framed portraits of Julian,' Mom hastily explained, 'but Jory likes to keep them in his room.' She sounded so apologetic.

Again Madame snorted. 'You're looking well, Catherine.'

'I'm feeling well, thank you. You look well too.' In her lap her hands worked nervously, just as her feet kept the swivel deskchair in constant motion.

'Your husband, how is he?'

'Fine, fine. He's making hospital rounds. He waited for you but when you didn't show up . . .'

'I understand. I'm sorry I'm late, but people in this state are robbers. I had to pay eight hundred for a piece of junk – and it dripped oil all the way here.'

Mom ducked her head. I knew she was hiding a laugh. 'What else can you expect for eight hundred?' Mom finally managed.

'Really, Catherine. Julian never paid much for any car he owned, you know that.' Her strident voice grew reflective. 'But then he knew what to do with the junk and I don't. I guess I let sentiment run away with my common sense. I should have bought a better one, but I'm also thrifty.' Next came her questions about my mother's knee. Was it healed? How soon would she be dancing again?

'It's fine,' said Mom testily. (She hated people to question her about her knee.) 'I only notice a little pain when it rains.'

'And how is Paul? It's been so long since I saw him last. I remember after you married him I felt so angry I never wanted to see you again, and I gave up teaching for a few years.' Again she glanced at the portrait of Dad. 'By the way, does your brother still live with you?'

Silence came and weighed down the air as Mom studied the smiling portrait of my stepfather, Chris. What brother was she talking about? Mom didn't have a brother any more. Why did Madame look at Dad when she asked about Cory?

'Yes, yes, of course,' said Mom, making me puzzled as to what she meant. 'Now tell me all about Greenglenna and Clairmont. I want to hear about everybody. How is Lorraine Duval? Whom did she marry, or did she go on to New York?'

'He never married, did he?' pursued Grandmother with her eyes narrowed.

'Who?'

'Your brother.'

'No, he hasn't married yet,' answered Mom, again testy. Then she was smiling. 'Now, Madame, I have a big surprise for you. We have a daughter now and her name is Cindy.'

'Hah!' snorted Madame, 'I already know about Cindy.' There was a strange gleam in her eyes. 'But still I would like to see and hear more about this paragon of all little girls. Jory writes she may have some dancing abilities.'

'Oh, she does, she does! I wish you could see her in her little pink leotards trying to imitate Jory or me – I mean when I could dance.'

'Your husband must be getting along in years by now,' Madame said, disregarding photographs Mom tried to show her of Cindy who was already in bed for the night.

'Did Jory tell you I'm writing a book? It's really fascinating. I didn't think it would be when I first started, but after I mastered transitions I really surprised myself, and now writing is more fun than work. Just as satisfying as dancing.' She smiled and fluttered her hands about, plucking at lint on her blue pants, tugging down her white sweater, fiddling with her hair, shuffling papers to tidy her desk. 'My room is a mess. I apologize for that. I need a study, but in this house we don't have the room . . .'

'Is your brother making hospital rounds too?'

I sat there, not understanding who this brother was. Cory was dead. He'd been dead for years. Though no body lay in his grave, no body at all. Little headstone beside Aunt Carrie and no body there.

'You must be hungry. Let's go into the dining-room and Emma can heat up the spaghetti. The second time around it's always better . . .'

'Spaghetti?' snapped Madame. 'You mean you eat that kind of

junk? You allow my grandson to eat starches? Years and years ago I warned you to stay away from pasta! Really, Catherine, don't you ever learn?'

Spaghetti was one of my favourite dishes – but we'd had leg of lamb tonight in Madame's honour, fixed the way Momma thought she liked it best. Why had she said spaghetti? I gave my mother a hard look and saw her flustered and breathless, looking as young as Melodie, as if she were terribly afraid something might go wrong – and what could?

Madame M wouldn't eat at our house, wouldn't sleep there either, for she didn't want to inconvenience us and already she'd found a room in town, close to Mom's dance school. 'And though you haven't asked me, Catherine, I'll be delighted to stay on and replace you. I sold out my school the moment Jory wrote and told me of your accident.'

Mom could only nod, looking queerly blank.

A few days later Madame looked around the office that had been Mom's; 'She keeps everything so neat, not like me at all. Soon I'll have it looking my own.'

I loved her in an odd kind of way, the way you love winter when you're hot in the summer. And then when winter was shivering your bones, I wished it would go away. She moved so young and looked so old. When she danced she could almost make you think she was eighteen. Her black hair came and went according to which day of the week it was. I'd learned by now she used some colour rinse that was shampooed in, and soon came out to darken the teeth of her white comb. I liked it best when it was white, silvery under the lights.

'You are everything my own Julian was!' she cried, smothering me with too much gushing affection. Already she'd dismissed the young teacher Mom had hired. 'But what makes you so arrogant, huh? Your momma tell you that you are sensational? Always your momma thinks the music is what counts most in the dance, and is not, is not. It is the display of the beautiful body that is the essence of ballet. I come to save you. I come to teach you how to do everything perfect. When I am done with you, you will have flawless technique.' Her shrill voice lowered an octave or two. 'I come too because I am old and may soon die and I do not know my grandson at all. I come to do my duty by being not only your grandmother, but also your grandfather and your father too. Catherine was a big fool to dance when she knew her knee could fold any second – but your mother was always a big fool – so what's new?'

She made me furious. 'Don't you talk like that about my mother! She's not a fool. She's never been a fool. She does what she feels she must – so I'll tell you the truth and you let her be. She danced that last time because I pleaded and pleaded for her to dance at least one time with me professionally. She did it for *me*, Grandmother, for *me*, not herself!'

Her small dark eyes turned shrewd. 'Jory, take lesson number one in my philosophy course: nobody ever does anything for anyone else unless it gives them even more.'

Grandmother wanted me to love her best. Every word she said and even those she didn't, conveyed her desire, but I couldn't say the words. Her dark eyes weren't soft, they didn't shine or sparkle or light up with joy. Nothing about Madame was sweet, vulnerable . . . and therefore, human.

I smiled to charm her, human or not. I smiled to please her, to give her happiness, but it was Mom I loved best for evermore. Madame fell into the chair that had been my mother's and swept all the little mementoes Mom cherished into the trash can, like they were so much junk. Next she hauled up a huge beat-up satchel, and in minutes had the desk more cluttered with her junk than it had been before.

Immediately I knelt to take from the trash can all the things I knew my mother loved.

'You don't love me like you love her,' complained Madame in a gritty voice of self-pity that sounded weak and old. Startled at the pain in her voice, I looked up and saw her as I'd never seen her before – an old woman, lonely and pitiful, clinging desperately to the only meaningful link to life she had – me.

Pity flooded me. 'I'm glad you're here, Grandmother – and of course I love you. Don't ask if I love you more than anyone else, only be happy that I love you at all, as I'm happy you love me for whatever reason.' I kissed her wrinkled cheek. 'Sure we'll get to know each other better. And I'll be the kind of son you wanted my father to be – in some ways – so don't cry and feel alone. My family is your family.'

Nevertheless, tears were in her eyes, streaking her face, making her lips quiver as she clutched at me desperately. Her voice came cracked and old; 'Never did Julian run to me like you just did. He didn't like to touch or be touched. Thank you, Jory, for loving me a little.'

Until now she'd been just a summer event in my life, flattering me with too much praise, making me feel special. Now I was uncomfortable to know she'd be here always, shadowing all our lives – perhaps.

Everything was going wrong in our lives. Maybe I could put all the blame on that old woman next door. Yet here was another old woman in black, ten times more trying than Bart's pretend grandmother, more dominating too. Bart was a kid who needed some control, but I was almost a man and didn't need more mothering. With some resentment I pulled away from her clutching, claw-like hands and asked with some consideration; 'Grandmother, why is it all grandmothers like to wear black?'

'Ridiculous!' she snapped, 'not all do – ' her jet eyes like stones of black fire.

'But I've never seen you wear any colour but black.'

'You will never see me wear another colour.'

'I don't understand. I've heard my mother say you wore black before my grandfather died, before my father died. Are you in perpetual mourning?'

She sneered scornfully. 'Ah, I see. You feel uncomfortable around black clothes? Makes you feel sad? Makes me feel glad. It makes me different. Anyone can wear pretty colours. Takes someone special to be pleased with only black clothes – and besides, it saves money.'

I laughed and drew away further. It was more the money she saved than anything else I was sure.

'What other grandmother you know who wears black?' she asked, her eyes very narrow and suspicious.

I smiled and backed away more; she frowned and drew closer. My face took on a broader smile as I neared the door. 'It's great having you here, Grandmother Madame. Be especially nice to Melodie Richarme. I'm going to marry her some day.'

'Jory!' she yelled. 'You come back here! Do you think I flew half-way around the world just to replace your mother? I came for one reason only. I am here to see that Julian's son dances in New York, in every major city in the world and achieves all the fame and glory that was due his father. Because of Catherine he was robbed, robbed!'

She made me angry, she made me want to hurt her as her words hurt me, when only a moment ago I'd loved her well. 'Will my fame and glory help a father who lies dead in his grave?' I shouted back. I wasn't putty for her to mould – I was already a great dancer and my mother had done that for me. I didn't need her to teach me more about dancing – I needed her to teach me more about learning to love someone hateful, old and bitter. 'I know how to dance already, Madame, my mother has taught me well.'

Her look of contempt made me blanch, but she surprised me when she got up to drop to her knees and put her hands in prayer position beneath her chin. She tilted her thin face backwards and seemed to stare God straight in his face.

'Julian!' she cried passionately, 'if you are up there looking down, hear the arrogance of your fourteen-year-old son. I make a pact with you today. Before I die I will see your son is the most acclaimed dancer in the world. I will make of him what you could have been if you hadn't cared so damned much for cars and women, to say nothing of your other vices. Your son, Julian – through him you will live to dance again!'

I stared as she fell exhausted and panting into the swivel deskchair again, sprawling her powerful legs before her. 'Damn

Catherine for marrying a doctor years and years older. Where was her common sense – where was his? God knows how he's avoided the grave for so long. Though to give credit where credit is due, he was handsome years ago and appealing enough, but she should have known he'd be old before she even reached her sexual maturity. She should have married a man nearer her own age.'

I stood before her, baffled, trembling, beginning to feel cupboard doors in my mind opening – opening creakily, reluctantly. No, no, my mind kept saying, keep quiet Madame. I watched her jerk upright, her dark stabbing eyes riveting me to one spot so I was unable to leave when what I wanted most was to run, and run fast.

'Why do you tremble?' she asked. 'Why do you look so strange?'

'Do I look strange?'

'Don't answer questions with questions,' she barked. 'Tell me about Paul, your stepfather, how he fares, what he does. He was twenty-five years older than your mother – and she's thirty-seven now. Doesn't that make him sixty-two?'

I swallowed over an aching lump that came to clog my throat. 'Sixty-two is not so old,' I said meekly, thinking she should know that, she was in her seventies.

'For a man it is old, for a woman life is only beginning to stretch out.'

'That is cruel,' I said, beginning to dislike her again.

'Life is cruel, Jory, very cruel. You snatch from life what you can while you are young, for if you wait for better times to come tomorrow, you wait in vain. I told Julian that time and again, to live his life and forget Catherine who loved that older man, but he refused to believe any girl could prefer a middle-aged man to someone as handsome and vibrant as he was, and now he lies dead in his grave, as you just said, and Dr Paul Sheffield enjoys the love that rightly belonged to my son, to your father . . . cry for my son, Jory. Cry for all young men who die too soon.'

I was crying tears she couldn't see. Hot scalding tears of

disbelief. Had my mother lied to Madame and made her believe Daddy Paul was still alive? Why would she lie? What was wrong about marrying Dr Paul's younger brother, Christopher?

'You look ill, Jory. Why?'

'I feel fine, Madame.'

'Don't lie to to me, Jory. I can smell a lie a mile away, see a lie from across three thousand miles. Why is it Paul Sheffield never accompanies his family to his own home town? Why is it your mother always brings only her children and that brother, Christopher?'

My heart was pounding. Sweat glued my shirt to my skin. 'Madame, have you never met Daddy Paul's younger brother?'

'Younger brother? What's that you say?' She leaned forward and peered into my eyes. 'Never heard of a brother even during that awful time when Paul's first wife drowned their son. That was spread all over the newspapers, and no younger brother was mentioned. Paul Sheffield had only one sister – no brother, younger or older.'

I felt sick, ready to throw up. Ready to cry out and run and do something wild and painful to myself, like Bart did when he was hurt and disturbed. Bart . . . for the first time I was feeling what it was to be like Bart. I stood on unsteady ground, afraid everything might crumble if I dared to move.

Through my mind kept running the steady stream of age, years and years of age difference, and Dad wasn't that much older than Mom, only two years and a few months. She was born in April, he was born in November, spring and fall. And so much alike in colouring, in background, in communication without even a word, just a glance and they could speak. Just a touch of the hand and they shivered, felt more than I feared I'd ever feel.

Madame was sitting coiled, ready, so it seemed, to spring upon me – or Mom? Deeper lines etched around her narrowed eyes, her grim, thin lips. She pursed her lips and reached into some hidden pocket of her drab outfit for her pack of cigarettes. 'Now,' she said as if to herself, seemingly forgetting I was still there, 'what was it Catherine gave as an excuse the last time Paul didn't come? Let's see, she called first, long distance, explaining Chris would come with her because Paul was too ill with his heart trouble to travel. She was leaving him in care of his nurse. Thought that odd at the time, that she'd leave him when he needed a nurse, and travel with Chris.' She bit down on her lower lip, chewed it unconsciously. 'And last summer no visit because Bart hated old graves and old ladies – and I suspect, me in particular. Spoiled brat. This summer they don't come again because Bart has driven a rusty nail into his knee and develops blood-poisoning or something similar. Damn kid is more trouble than he's worth – serves her right too for playing around so soon after my son's death. And Paul has heart trouble, on and on he has heart trouble, yet he never has a fatal attack. Every summer she gives me that same worn excuse. Paul can't travel because of his heart – but Chris he can always travel, heart or no heart.'

Abruptly she stopped talking, for I had moved to leave. I tried to make my eyes blank and erase all the milling suspicions I didn't want her to see.

'You know what, Jory?' she asked, sudden rapture lighting her dark narrow eyes, 'it's been my dream to have you for my very own. Just you and me, to teach you as you've never been taught. Oh, to have the chance to give you all the love and admiration I never gave your father. To have a second chance to do it all right, as I should have done it the first time. Thank God for giving me a second chance through you. And it will be me sitting centre row, first aisle, when you rise to your full potential – inherited from all those dancing genes of my son.'

'And my mother,' I whispered to remind her. Never had I felt more afraid than I did at that moment, just watching her scheming eyes, the wheels churning, planning something I knew.

At that moment she jumped to her feet with great agility. 'Put on your coat. I'm going home with you to have a long chat with your mother.'

THE FRAGILE TRUTH *Jory*

'Jory,' began Madame when we were in her ratty old car and driving homeward. 'Your parents don't confide in you much about their past, do they?'

'They tell us enough,' I said stiffly, resenting the way she kept prying, when it didn't matter. 'They are very good listeners, and everyone says they make the best kind of conversationalists.'

She snorted. 'Being a good listener is the perfect way to avoid answering questions you'd rather ignore.'

'Now you look here, Grandmother. My parents like their privacy. They have asked both Bart and me not to talk about our home life to our friends and after all, it does make good sense for a family to stick together.'

'Really . . . ?'

'Yes!' I shouted, 'I like my privacy too.'

'You are of an age to need privacy, they are not.'

'Now you hear me out, Madame. My mother was a celebrity of sorts, and Dad is a doctor, and Mom has been married three times. I don't think she wants her former sister-in-law, Amanda, to know where we live.'

'Why not?'

'My aunt Amanda is not a very nice person, that's all.'

'Jory, do you trust me?'

'Yes,' I said, but I didn't.

'Then tell me all you know about Paul. Tell me if he's as sick as she says, or if he is alive at all. Tell me why Christopher lives in your home, and is the one who acts like the father of you and Bart.'

Oh, I didn't know what to say, and I was trying hard to be a good listener so she'd keep on talking and I'd be able to put the pieces of the puzzle together. Certainly I didn't want her to get the picture before I did.

A long silence grew, and finally she spoke, when I was hopeful she wouldn't. 'You know after Julian died, your mother lived with you in Paul's home, then she took you and her younger sister, Carrie, to the mountains of Virginia. Her mother lived there in a fine home. It seems Catherine was determined to ruin her mother's second marriage. The husband of your mother's mother – was named Bartholomew Winslow.'

That cursed darn lump came back in my throat and ached there. I wasn't going to believe Bart was the son of anyone but Daddy Paul, wasn't.

'Grandmother, if you want me to keep on loving you, please do not tell me ugly things about my mother.'

Her skinny hand reached to squeeze mine. 'All right, I admire you for being so loyal. I just want you to know the facts.' About that time she almost careened off the road into a ditch.

'Grandmother, I know how to drive. If you are tired and can't see the road signs very well, I can take over, and you could sit back and relax.'

'Let a fourteen-year-old kid drive me around? Are you crazy? Are you saying you don't feel safe with me at the wheel? All my life I've been driven around, first in hay wagons, then carriages, then taxis or limousines, but three weeks before I came here, soon after your letter came telling about your mother's accident, I took driver's lessons at the age of seventy-four . . . and you see now how well I learned. This old dog can learn new tricks.'

Me and my big mouth! Wish I'd never written her at all.

Finally, after four near misses, we made the turn into our circular drive. And there out front was Bart stalking some invisible animal with his pocket-knife held like a dagger, ready to thrust and kill.

Madame ignored him as she pulled to a stop. Briskly I jumped out and raced to open her door, but she was out before I got there, and just behind her Bart was stabbing into the air with his knife.

'Death to the enemy! Death to all old ladies who wear black raggy clothes! Death, death, death!'

Calmly, as if she didn't hear and didn't see, Madame strode on. I shoved Bart aside and whispered, 'If you want to be locked up today, keep on with what you're doing.'

'Black . . . hate black . . . gotta wipe off all dark black evil.'

But he put the knife in his pocket after he carefully folded it and stroked the pearl handle he admired. He should. It had cost me seven bucks for that present.

Without waiting for a response to her impatient push on the door-chimes, Madame stalked into our house and tossed her purse on the love-seat in the foyer. The clack of typewriter keys came to us faintly.

'Writing,' she said, 'I guess she goes at that just as passionately as she did dancing . . .'

I didn't say anything, but I did want to run ahead and warn Mom. She wouldn't let me. Mom looked up very startled to suddenly encounter Madame Marisha again in her bedroom.

'Catherine! Why didn't you tell me Dr Paul Sheffield was dead, why?'

Momma's face went red, then white. She bowed her head and put her hands up to cover her face. Regaining her composure almost immediately, she raised her head, flashed angry eyes at Madame, then began to shuffle her papers into a neat pile. 'How nice to see you, Madame Marisha. It would have been nicer if you had called in advance. However, I'm sure Emma can split the lamb chops unevenly and let you have two . . .'

'Don't evade my question with silly talk of eating. Do you think for one moment I would pollute my body with your stupid lamb chops? I eat health foods, and health foods only.'

'Jory,' said Mom, 'in case Emma saw Madame, run tell her not to set another place.'

'What is all this idiotic chatter about lamb chops? I drove miles out of my way to ask an important question, and you talk about food. Catherine, answer my question – is Paul Sheffield dead?'

Mom looked at me, and gestured I was to disappear, but I couldn't. I stood my ground, and defied her. She paled more and seemed appalled that I, her darling, would not obey. Then, as if resigned, she muttered in an indistinct way: 'You never asked me about myself, about my husband, so I took it you weren't interested in anyone but Jory.'

'Catherine!'

'Jory, please leave this room immediately. Or do I have to get up and throw you out?'

I backed out the door just before she reached to throw it shut.

I pressed my ear hard against the other side of the door and I could just hear. 'Madame, you don't know how much I have needed someone to confide in . . . But you were always so cold, so remote, I didn't think you could understand.'

Silence. A snort.

'Yes, Paul died years ago. I try not to think of him as dead but as still alive, though invisible. We brought his marble statues and benches here and tried to make our garden grow like his. We failed there. But still when twilight comes and I'm out in the garden near his statues, it seems I can sense him near, still loving me. We were married for such a short time. And he was never really well . . . so when he died, I was left feeling unfulfilled, still yearning to give him the years of happy married life I owed him. I wanted somehow to make up for Julia, his first wife.'

'Catherine,' said Madame softly, 'who is this man your children call Father?'

'Madame, what I do is none of your business;' I could hear the anger building in Mom's voice. 'This is not the same kind of world you grew up in. You have not lived my life, and been inside my mind. You have not known the kind of deprivations I suffered when I was young and needed love most. Don't you sit there and condemn me with your dark mean eyes, for you can't understand.'

'Oh, Catherine, how little credit you give my intelligence. Do you think me dumb, blind and insensitive? I know now very well who the man is my grandson calls Dad. And it's no wonder you could never love my Julian enough. I used to think it was Paul, but now I see it wasn't Paul you truly loved; it wasn't that Bartholomew Winslow either – it was Christopher, *your brother*. I don't give a damn what you and your brother do. If you sleep in his bed, and you find the happiness you feel was stolen from you long ago, I can rationalize and say that much worse goes on every day than brother and sister who pretend to be husband and wife. But I must protect my grandson. He comes first. You have no right to make your children pay the price for your unlawful relationship.'

What was she saying?

Mom, do something, say something, make me feel good again! Make me feel safe and real again – make it all go away, this talk of your brother you've never mentioned.

I crouched down lower, bowing my head into my hands, not wanting to hear, not daring to leave.

Mom's voice came strained and very hoarse, as if she were having trouble keeping tears away. 'I don't know how you found out. Please try to understand . . .'

'As I said before, I don't give a damn – and I think I do understand. You couldn't love my son, as you could never love any man more than you loved your brother. I'm bitter about that. I'm crying inside for Julian who thought you an angel of perfection, his Catherine, his Clara, his Sleeping Beauty that he could never wake up. That's what you were to him, Catherine, the personification of all the dancing dolls of the ballet, virgin and pure, sweet and chaste, and in the end you are no better than the rest of us.'

'Please!' cried Mom, 'I tried to escape Chris. I tried to love Julian more, I did, I really did.'

'No, you didn't try. If you had, you would have succeeded.'

'You can't know,' came Mom's distressed cry.

'Catherine, you and I have travelled the same road for many a year, and little bits and pieces of information you have let drop along the way. And then there is Jory who tries his best to shield you . . .'

'He doesn't know? Please say he doesn't know!'

'He doesn't know,' Madame soothed in what was a soft voice – for her. 'But he talks, and spills more than he knows. The young are like that; they think the old are so senile they can't put two and two together. They think the old can live to be seventy and still not know more than they do at fourteen. They think they have a monopoly on experience, because they see us not doing very much, while every moment of their lives is full, forgetting we too were young once. And we have turned all our mirrors into windows . . . and they are still behind the mirrors looking only at themselves.'

'Madame, please don't speak so loud. Bart has a way of hiding and eavesdropping.'

Her strident voice toned down making it more difficult for me to hear. 'All right, I'll have my say and go. I don't think your home is the proper place for a boy of Jory's sensitivities to grow up in. The atmosphere here is tense, as if a bomb might explode any moment. Your younger son is obviously in need of psychological help – why, he tried to stab me as I approached your home.'

'Bart is always playing games . . .' said Mom weakly.

'Hah! Some games he plays! His knife almost slit my coat. And this coat is almost new. It will be my last coat, the one I'll wear until I'm dead.'

'Please, Madame, I'm not in the mood for talk of death.'

'Did I ask for your pity? If you took it that way, then I reverse positions. I'll wear this coat as long as I live. And before I die I have to see Jory achieve the fame that should have been Julian's.'

'I'm doing what I can,' said Mom wearily, sounding so terribly tired.

'What you can? Hell and damnation! You live here with your brother, risking public humiliation and sooner or later your fragile bubble will pop. Jory will suffer. His schoolmates will taunt him. The reporters will hound you, him, everyone in this house. The law will take your children from you.'

'Please sit down, stop pacing. To watch you makes me tired, and I have a headache.'

'Damn you, Catherine, for not listening. I guessed a long time ago that in time you would succumb to your brother's adoration. I thought even when you married your Dr Paul that you and your brother . . . well, never mind what I thought, but you married a man almost dead. Was it a guilty conscience?'

'I don't know – I used to think it was because I loved him and I owed him. I had a thousand reasons for marrying him, the most important being he wanted me, and that was enough.'

'All right, you had reasons enough. But you hurt my son. You didn't give him what he needed, and I never understood how you could resist. He used to cry, saying you didn't love him enough. Always he said there was some mysterious man you loved more – and I didn't believe him then. Fool, wasn't I? Fool, wasn't he? But we were all fools when it came to you, Catherine. You were so beautiful, so young and so innocent. Were you born old and clever? How did you know so well, so early, all the ways of making a man love you beyond reason?'

'Love is sometimes not enough,' she said dully, while I felt almost paralysed with the dreadful information I was overhearing. Moment by moment, heartbeat by heartbeat, I was losing the mother I loved. I was also losing the only father I'd ever had long enough to love. 'How did you find out about Chris and me?' Mom asked, making me quiver more.

'Does it matter?' shrieked Madame. I was pinning my hopes to her, hoping she too wouldn't betray me. 'I'm not dumb, Catherine, as I said before. I asked a few questions. I listened to Jory's answers, and I added up the facts. It's been years since I saw Paul – but Chris was always there. Bart is on the brink of insanity from what Jory innocently lets out – never intentionally, remember, only carelessly, for he loves you. Do you think I can stand quietly by and let you and your brother wreck my grandson's life too?I refuse to let you ruin his career, his mental health. You give me Jory to take back East with me, where he'll be safe and far removed from the bomb that will explode and splatter your lives on to the front pages of every newspaper in this country!'

I was sick. I'd opened the door a bit, enough to see my mother was paler than death. She began to tremble, as I was trembling – but she didn't have tears in her eyes as I had in mine. Momma, how could you live with your brother when the whole world knows that's wrong? How could you deceive Bart and me? How could Chris do that to us? And all this time I'd thought he was so perfect, so right for you, for us. Sin, sin. No wonder Bart went around chanting about sin and the torments of everlasting hell. Somehow Bart had found out before me.

I sank to my knees and leaned my head against the door, closing my eyes and trying to breathe deeply to stop my stomach rumbling and wanting to rise.

Mom spoke again. It was easy to tell she was trying hard to hold on to her temper.

'To lose Bart for even a few months in some institution is nearly driving me crazy. But to lose Jory as well *would* drive me crazy. I love my sons, Madame, both of them. Though you have never given me credit for having mercy on Julian, I did the best I could for him. He was not an easy man to live with. You and your husband made him what he was, not me. I didn't force him to dance when he would have played ball if given his way. I didn't punish him by making him practise every weekend, so he never had time for fun – you and Georges did that – but it was I who paid that price. He wanted to devour me alive, forbidding me any friends but him. Jealous of every man who looked my way, every man I looked at. Do you know what it is to live with a man who suspects you deceive him when you're out of his sight – and it wasn't I who did the betraying – it was him. I was faithful to Julian. I never let another man touch me, but he couldn't have said the same thing. He wanted every pretty girl he saw. He wanted to use them, discard them, then come back to me and have me hold him in my arms and tell him how wonderful he was . . . and I couldn't say he was wonderful when the stench of some other woman's perfume was all over him. Then he'd hit me, did you know that? He had to prove something to himself. I didn't know then what he had to prove, now I do – he had to find the love you denied him.'

I felt weaker, sicker, as I saw my grandmother blanch. Now I was losing my real father whom I'd adored as a saint.

'You make your points very well, Catherine, and they hurt. But now let me make mine. Georges and I did make mistakes with Julian, I admit that, and you and our son paid the price. Are you going to punish Jory in the same way? Let me take him back to Greenglenna. Once we're there I'll arrange for an audition for him in New York. I have important connections. I did manage to turn out two brilliant dancers, one named Julian, the other named Catherine. I was not all bad, nor was Georges. Perhaps we let our own dreams blind us to what others wanted and we tried too hard to live through our child. That's all we wanted, Catherine, to live through Julian. Now Julian is dead and he has left behind one child, one only – your son. Without Jory I have no reason to stay alive. With Jory I have every reason to go on. For once in your life give, don't take.'

No, no! I didn't want to go with Madame.

I watched Mom bow her head until her hair fell in two soft wings of pale gold. Her trembling hand fluttered to touch her brow, as if another of those terrible headaches was paining. I didn't want to leave her, sinner or not. This was my home, my world, and she was still my mother and Chris was still my step-dad, and there was Bart, Cindy and Emma too. We were a family, rightly, wrongly, we were a family.

Finally Mom seemed to find a solution. Hope rose in my heart.

'Madame, I'm throwing myself on your mercy, and hoping to God you have some. I realize you could very well be right, but I cannot give up my firstborn son. Jory is the one good thing that came from my marriage to Julian. If you take him, you take part of me, a very important part of me which I cannot surrender without dying.

'Jory loves me. He loves Chris as much as he could love his own father. Even if I have to risk his career, I cannot risk losing his love by letting him go away with you . . . so don't ask for the impossible, Madame. I cannot let Jory go.'

Madame stared at her long and hard while my heart thumped so loudly I was sure they'd both hear. Then Grandmother stood up and prepared to leave. 'Hah,' she snorted. 'I'm going to speak honestly now, Catherine, perhaps for the first time I'll give you the full truth. I have since the first day I met you, envied your youth, your beauty, and most of all your genius for the dance. I know you have passed on to Jory your extraordinary skill. You have been a superb teacher. I see so much of you in him, and so much of your brother in him too. The patience Jory has, the cheerful optimism, the drive and dedication – derived from your family, not from Julian. But there is some of Julian in him too. He looks like my son. He has the fire of my son, and the fleshly desires of my son for women. But if I must hurt you to save him, I will do so. I will not spare your brother, or your younger son either. If you do not turn Jory over to me I will do what I can to bring down your house. The law will give me custody of Jory, and there will not be one thing you can do to stop me once I go to them with the facts. And if you force me to do it this way, which is not the way I would choose, I will take Jory East, and never, never will he see you again.'

Mom rose to her feet and stood taller than my grandmother. I'd never seen her look taller, prouder, stronger. 'Madame, our relationship has always been like a raw wound that refuses to heal. Go on, do what you must. I will not give in one inch, and allow you to steal from me what is mine. Never will I give a child of mine away. Jory is mine. I gave birth to him after eighteen hours of striving. If I have to face up to the whole world and its condemnation, still I will stand with my head held high, and hold fast to my children. There is no force in this world, you, the law, anything, that can force me to give up my children.'

Turning to go, Madame glanced around the room, allowing her eyes to linger longest on the thick stack of papers on Mom's small desk. 'You'll see things my way,' she said in a soft cat's purr. 'I pity you, Catherine, as I pity your brother. I pity Bart too, savage as the little monster is. I pity everyone in your household, for all will be hurt. But I won't let my compassion for you, and my understanding of what made you the way you are, hold back my hand. Jory will be safe with me, with my name, not yours.'

'Get out!' screamed Mom who had lost all control. She picked up a vase with flowers and hurled it at Madame's head! 'You ruined your son's life and now you want to ruin Jory. You want him to believe there is no life but in the ballet, dancing, dancing – but I am living. I was a dancer, and still I am surviving.'

Madame looked around the room again, as if she too would like to hurl some object, and slowly she bent over to pick up the broken vase at her feet. 'I gave you this. How ironic that you would hurl it at me.' Something brittle and hard seemed to crack as she looked at Mom with softness, and she spoke with rare humility. 'When Julian was a boy, I tried to do for him what was best, just as you try to do for yours what is best . . . and if my judgement was wrong, it was done with the best of intentions.'

'Isn't everything?' said Mom with bitterness. 'Always the intentions are so right, so reasonable – and in the end even the excuses ride the waves of indignation like that fabled straw everyone tries to grasp to keep from drowning. It seems all my life I've been grasping for straws that don't exist. I tell myself each night before I climb into bed with my brother, that this is the reason I was born, and for every wrong I have done I have consoled myself by saying I have balanced the scales with the right decisions. I have finally given my brother the only woman he can love, the wife he so desperately needed. I have made him happy – and if that is wrong in your eyes, in the eyes of the world, I don't give a damn. I don't give a damn what the world thinks!'

My grandmother just stood there, with conflicting emotions torturing her aged face. I could tell she too was hurting. I watched her thin heavily-veined hand reach to touch my mother's hair, but she drew it away and kept her eyes blank and her voice under control. 'Again I say, I pity you, Catherine. I pity all of you, but most of all I pity Jory, for he is the one with the most to lose.'

Quickly I backed away and hid as she hurled herself out of Mom's bedroom, and strode down the back hall, by-passing Bart who stabbed at her with his unsheathed knife.

'Witch, old black witch!' he snarled, pulling back his upper lip in a frightful way. 'I hope you never come back, never, never!'

I was miserable enough now to want a hole to crawl into and die. *My mother was living with her brother*. The woman I loved and respected all my life was worse than any mother I'd ever heard of. None of my friends would believe, but when they did, I'd be so shamed, ridiculed, I'd never be able to face them. Then it hit me. Dad was my real uncle. Not just Bart's but mine too. Oh, God, what did I do now? Where did I run? It was not a platonic brother-sister relationship, a fake marriage for appearances' sake, it was incest. They were lovers. I knew! I'd seen!

Suddenly everything was too sordid, too ugly, too shocking. Why had they allowed their love to start? Why hadn't they stopped it from happening?

I wanted to get up and go and ask, but I couldn't bear to look at Mom, or Dad either when he came home. In my room I fell on my bed, with the locked door making me feel safer. When I was called to dinner I said I wasn't hungry. Me, who was always starving. Mom came to the closed door and pleaded: 'Jory, did you overhear anything your grandmother said to me?'

'No, Mother,' I answered stiffly. 'I think I'm coming down with a cold, that's all. I'll feel fine in the morning, just fine.' I had to say something to explain why my voice was husky.

Somewhere in all those tears I shed, I lost the boy I was earlier today. Now I had to become a man. I felt old, cold, like nothing mattered very much any more, and for the first time I knew why Bart was so confused and peculiar-acting – he must know too.

I sneaked to watch Mom writing in her fine blue leather

journal, and when I had the chance, I stole into her room and read every word she'd written, as dishonest as that was.

Madame Marisha visited today and brought with her all the nightmares that haunt my days. I have other nightmares for sleeping. When she was gone I felt panic throbbing so loud my heart sounded like a jungle drum beating out the rhythm of the last battle. I wanted to run and hide as we used to hide when we were locked away in Foxworth Hall. I ran to Chris when he came home, and clung, clung, unable to tell him anything. He didn't notice my desperation. He was tired from a long exhausting day.

Then he kissed me, and was off for his evening rounds, and I sat alone in my room, both of my sons silent and locked behind their bedroom doors. Do they know that soon our world is coming to an end?

Should I have let Madame take Jory and keep him safe from the scandal and humiliation? Was I selfish to want to hold fast to him? And Bart, what about Bart? And what would happen to Cindy if our secret were revealed?

Suddenly I felt I was back in Charlottesville, with Chris and Carrie, and again we were on our way to Sarasota. My memory seemed like a movie as that huge black woman struggled to board the slow bus with all her bags and bundles. Henrietta Beech. Dear, dear Henny. It's been so long since I last thought of her. Just to remember her broad beaming smile, her kind eyes, her gentle hands and a certain peace steals over me, like she is taking me again to Paul who would save us all.

But who will save us now?

Tears were in my eyes when I put her journal away. I stole into Bart's room and found him sitting on the floor, in the dark, hunched over like an old-old man. 'Bart, go to bed,' I said. But he didn't get up. He seemed not to hear me.

THE GATES OF HELL *Bart*

Knew it, just knew it. Jory had to spy and check up on what devilry I was up to. Pretended not to notice. Soon as his room was dark, I pulled out the last pages of Momma's story. Knew it was the end for she'd written her initials and address near the bottom of the page.

Didn't know why I was crying. Malcolm wouldn't feel pity for her and my daddy. Now I'd have to grow tough, mean, pretend nothing could hurt me nearly as much as it hurt others.

Morning came and I went into the kitchen where Momma was helping Emma do little housekeeping chores, making cookie dough, talking about cakes. The woman thought evil could go on unnoticed forever. Unpunished forever. She should know better.

I sat in my corner, hunched over on the floor, my knees pulled up under my chin, my shins wrapped with my arms. Bony arms. Getting skinnier by the day. I stared sullenly at Momma, at Daddy, hoping to look into their minds and find out what they really thought of me, of themselves and what they were doing. I closed my eyes. Behind my lids I saw Momma dancing like she used to before she hurt her knee. Last summer, not so long after I came home from the hospital and I had trouble falling asleep. I'd stumbled into the kitchen to rob the fridge while nobody could see. I wanted them all to worry and think about me starving to death. But before I could gobble down all the cold chicken leg, Momma had danced into the family room wearing a little white tutu with hardly any top, and Daddy had trailed along behind as if he was held in thrall – so much he didn't even see me. Couldn't see anybody but her.

She'd looked pretty in that costume, whirling around, always smiling and flirting with the man who stood in the shadows watching her. She teased him by tugging at his tie, pulling him out into the centre of the room, forcing him to turn around and around, and trying to make him dance that ballet stuff. But he'd grabbed her in his arms and pressed his lips down on hers. I'd heard the sound, wet and mushy. Then her arms tightened around his neck. I stared to see him unhooking all those little dark things that held her tutu on! It slipped and fell to the floor at her feet and she was wearing nothing but white leotards that he soon tugged off. Naked. He made her naked. Next he lifted her in his arms, and while her lips were still pressed to his, he carried her off to their room – and all the time he'd been her brother.

Oh, no wonder John Amos said they had to be punished. No wonder. Whore! Bitch! Sinners with my own blood! They wouldn't get away with this. They'd have to burn, burn – burn like my daddy, like my real daddy named Bartholomew Winslow.

I read all her story. I knew how ugly and mean some mothers could be. Hiding her four children, making them stay upstairs in one room, forcing them to play in a hot miserable attic that was freezing in the winters. All those years locked up, whipped too, and starved – and tar in my mother's beautiful golden hair. I hated Malcolm who'd done so many wicked things to his own grandchildren. I hated that old lady next door who put arsenic on their sugared doughnuts. What kind of crazy nut was she? Had she put poison on my ice-cream, my cake and cookies too? I shivered and felt queasy in my stomach. Why hadn't the police locked her up until they dragged her to the electric chair to burn, burn?

No, whispered a sly voice in my head, they don't let pretty ladies die in electric chairs when clever lawyers can call killers insane. They were locked in pretty places like palaces tucked away in green hills. That crazy woman was the same one my daddy had to visit each summer. The mother of my momma too. Oh, the sins of my momma and daddy piled clear up to the sky. Certainly God was going to punish them now – and if he didn't – Malcolm would see that I did.

Went to bed that night and tried to sleep. But I kept thinking. Daddy was really Momma's brother and that made him really my uncle, and Jory's uncle. Oh, Momma, you are not the saint or angel Jory thinks you are. You tell him not to do this, and not to do that with Melodie, and all the time you keep going into the bedroom with your brother and closing the door. Telling us never to enter when that door was shut without knocking first. Shame, shame! Privacy, always needing privacy to do what brother and sister should never do. Incest! God, how I wished I hadn't looked up that word in her dictionary. No wonder Jory was ashamed to go back to school and face up to his friends, knowing he was living with incestuous parents.

Wicked, both of them, just as wicked as I was sometimes. Just as wicked as Jory wanted to be with Melodie, with other girls – doing all the shameful things Eve did with Adam after she bit into the apple. Doing those horrible things the boys whispered about in the rest-rooms. I didn't want to live with them no more. Didn't want to love Momma or her brother.

Jory knew too. I knew Jory knew too – he was going to go crazy like Momma thought I was. But I was finally gaining sense, good sense, like Malcolm's. The children of incestuous parents deserved to suffer as I was being made to suffer, as Jory was suffering. Cindy had to suffer too, even if she was too young and dumb to know big words like incestuous.

Yet, yet, why did I keep praying for God not to let tomorrow come? What was I going to do tomorrow? Why did I want to die tonight, and save myself from doing even worse than incest?

Another breakfast to eat. Hated food that tasted nasty. Stared down at the tablecloth that would soon be soiled when I accidentally knocked something over. Jory looked as lost as I felt.

Days came, days went, and nobody was happy. Dad walked about looking sick. I guessed he knew we knew, and Momma knew too. Now neither one of them could meet our eyes or answer Jory's questions. I never asked any. I heard Momma one day rapping on Jory's locked bedroom door, 'Jory, please let me in. I know you overheard when Madame M was here – let me try to explain how it was. When you understand you won't hate us.'

Yes he would. I'd read that damn book. Wasn't fair for life to cheat us by not giving us honourable parents.

Thanksgiving Day, and old hateful ugly Madame M showed up when she should never have had the nerve to accept any invitation. Momma shouldn't have given her one. I thought she was gloating when she watched Dad carve the turkey and not once did he smile, and then she was looking at Momma whose eyes were red and swollen. Crying, she'd been crying. Served her right. I didn't like turkey anyway, wasn't nearly as good as chicken. Daddy asked me what meat I liked, dark or white. I scowled, not answering, thinking his voice was so husky he must have a cold, but he didn't cough or sneeze, and his eyes didn't look weak like mine when I had a cold.

And Daddy was never sick.

Only Emma was happy, and Cindy, hateful Cindy.

'Come, come,' said Emma with a big cheerful smile that wouldn't do any good, 'it's time for rejoicing – for giving thanks for our many blessings, including having a new daughter to sit at our table.'

Revolting to hear that.

Dad picked up his carving knife and fork again, no smiles, not a word. I looked at Momma who seemed stricken by his lack of doing the right and gracious thing, though I could tell she was trying to pretend everything was still all right. She ate a bit or two of her meal, then jumped up and ran from the dining room. Down the back hall I heard her bedroom door slam. Daddy excused himself saying he had to go and check on her.

'Good Lord, what's wrong with everybody?' asked Emma while old Madame Marisha sat on silently, looking glum too. And she was part of it all. I glared at her, hating her, hating my own grandmother even more – hating everybody and Cindy too, and all the time thinking maybe Emma had done some evil too by keeping her mouth shut and letting all this sinning go on under her long nose. Jory tried to laugh and smile, teasing Cindy to make her laugh – and eat. But I knew he was bleeding deep down in his heart, just as I was bleeding, crying for my real daddy who died in that fire. And maybe Jory was crying for his real daddy too, whom Momma hadn't loved nearly enough because all the time she had a brother who loved her too much.

I wished I hadn't found out. Why did Momma have to go and write that book? I wouldn't really have believed anything John Amos told me about her, for I'd thought he was a liar, a pretender, like me. Now I knew he was the only truthful person in the whole world, the only one who respected me enough to tell the truth.

Sobbing, I got up and left the table, glancing at Cindy who was sitting on Jory's lap and laughing as she played with some little toy he'd given her. Never gave me anything. Nobody but a lying-black-witch-grandmother who didn't count gave me gifts . . . nobody.

Then, there came a Sunday when Momma didn't seem to feel so wretched, maybe because she thought Madame M was gonna leave us alone, and maybe even go back East where she belonged. I knew then Momma could pretend too, like me, like she and Daddy pretended in their marriage game.

I clung to the shadow near her open bedroom door and watched her go down on her knees in prayer. Silent prayers. Wondered if God ever listened.

Back in the family room I crouched in my corner and began to light matches one by one, holding the flames so close to my face I could feel the heat. How awful it was going to be to be purified and redeemed by fire. How awful it had been when my real daddy's soul went up in black smoke. And I was just a tiny thing then, hiding in my momma's womb, called an embryo and not Bart, and maybe I'd even been a girl then too, worst of all.

Wish Daddy wouldn't tell me so much about things I didn't want to understand.

My head began to ache. Made my hand that held the match shake so much I dropped the match. Quickly I had to snuff it out before someone smelled the carpet burning. They'd blame me, like they always blamed me, not even knowing Jory was outside doing something perhaps just as bad.

What was it John Amos kept saying? 'Your mother made all the bad things happen. Every one of the bad things was her fault – that's the way of women, especially beautiful women. Evil through and through, tricky, sinful, beautiful women, out to steal from men.'

Yeah, I thought, my momma, my grandmother, all tricky, beautiful, sinful women. Telling me lies, hiding from me who she really was, showing me her portrait when she was young and beautiful, seducing my real father when he was too young for her anyway. My head ached more. Momma had done the same thing to my real daddy.

I sighed, thinking I'd better get on with my own business of being the angel of the Lord, sent to act in Malcolm's stead. After all, I was his great-grandson, and getting almost as smart as him. Acted like Malcolm more and more, making my bones feel tired; making my muscles sore and aching, getting the true feel of being old like Malcolm had been when he was wisest. Though it did get painful to make my heart throb so fast. Disgusted with all women. Had to fix them all, every one. Momma thought I didn't know, thought only Jory knew . . . but I'd been there too when old Madame Marisha shrilled out loud enough for everyone to hear.

Head hurt worse. Didn't know who I was any more. Malcolm? Bart? Yeah, was Malcolm now, bad heart, weak legs, thinning hair, but so damned clever and wise.

Stupid daughter, hiding her four children on the second floor and thinking I wouldn't find out sooner or later. Fool. She should have known John would tell me everything. She should have known so many things she ignored, or deliberately forgot. So, she thinks I'm going to die soon, and I'll never climb the stairs, but why should I when John will do that for me. Spy, I told John, spy on my daughter, see what she does when she's out of my sight. She thinks I'm going to die soon, John, and I'll change my will and write her back in, but I'll have the last laugh. She's not going to inherit all my hard-earned money. Jingle, jingle, jingle, hear the money in my pockets, like music, the best kind of music. Never too old to outsmart all of them, never too old – and I'll win as I always win in the end.

Was that a child's laughter I heard in the attic? I started and looked up. Could they be happy up there? Why did they decorate an attic that could never look pretty? Depriving me, that's what. Depriving me of my rightful revenge. I'd show them, show them all.

Shuffling my feet along, I headed for their bedroom which smelled of their evil acts of love. I paused just outside their closed door. Inside I felt like a little boy who was quietly sobbing, but I had to be Malcolm – the stronger, older, wiser part that was me. Where were the blue-misted mountains? This wasn't a great house setting high on a hillside. Where were the servants, the grand ballroom, the double staircases?

Confused, so confused. Head ached worse. Knee began to throb. Back pained, heart was going to have an attack.

'Straighten up there, Bart,' said that man who was really my uncle. Scared me. Made me jump and grow more confused. 'You're too young to be hobbling around like an old man, Bart. And your knee is just fine.' He gave me a friendly pat on my head and opened the door to his bedroom, where I could see my mother was waiting for him in the bed, her eyes wide open and staring up at the ceiling. Was she crying?

'I hate you!' I whispered fiercely, trying to stab him with the glare of my eyes. 'You think you are safe, don't you? You think a doctor can't be punished – but God has sent the black angel of his wrath to see that you and your sister are punished for the evil you have done.'

He froze on the spot and stared at me as if he'd never seen me before. Defiantly I glared back. He closed the door to his bedroom and led me down the hall so she wouldn't hear. 'Bart, you go to visit your grandmother every day, don't you?' His face looked troubled, but he kept his voice soft and kind. 'You have to learn not to believe everything you hear. Sometimes people tell lies.'

'Devil's spawn!' I hissed. 'Seed planted in the wrong soil to create Devil's issue!'

This time he grasped my arm so tightly it hurt, and he shook me. 'Never let me hear you say that again. You are never to mention any of this to your mother – if you do, I'll burn your bottom so hard you may never sit down again. And the next time you see that woman next door, you remind her that it was she who planted all the seeds and started the flowers growing. Watch her face when you speak . . . and then guess who is the evil one.'

I shrank back, didn't want to hear what he had to say. I ran off, bumping into a hall table; upsetting an expensive lamp that toppled to the floor.

In my room I fell on my bed, shaking all over, panting and gasping for breath. In my chest was that awful throbbing pain that made iron bands tighten about me, squeezing me, wanting to shut off my air.

Felt like toothpaste being squeezed from the bottom, then I was rolled up tight as a coil. Painfully I rolled over on my back and stared up at the ceiling as I started to cry. Huge fat tears slid off my face to wet my pillow. If I wet the bed for any other reason I'd get spanked, for ten years old was too old for such baby-doings.

Did I want to be ten, or eighty? Who was making me be so old? God? Was it those children hiding in the attic, laughing, laughing, making the best out of the worst that was driving me to prove Malcolm was smarter and they'd never get away even after he was put in the ground.

Momma's gone and left me.
Left me for good this time.
Momma's gone and left me,
Now I don't know how to end what I've begun . . .

Fell asleep and tossed around. The little boy kept right on crying as the old man hurled him in the dustbin, so soon I'd be dumped outside the city limits – fit only for burning.

For sinners of sinners, those born of incest, they had to be punished too, even me, even me who was dying.

RAGE OF THE RIGHTEOUS *Bart*

The rain came down like bullets fired by God. I stood at the back windows and watched the rain batter the faces of those marble statues, punishing them for being naked and sinful. I waited for Jory to come home and look for me.

Bad. We were both bad from living with parents who weren't supposed to be parents.

Behind me Momma came in from a shopping spree, all rosy-cheeked and laughing, shaking the rain from her hair, greeting Emma like everything was okay. She dumped her parcels in a chair, took off her coat and said she felt she might be catching a cold.

'I hate it when it rains, Emma. Hello Bart – I didn't see you there until now. How've you been? Lonesome for me?'

I wouldn't answer. Didn't have to talk to her now. Didn't have to be polite, nice, or even clean. Could do anything I wanted. They did. God's rules didn't mean anything to them. Meant nothing now to me either.

'Bart, it's going to be so nice this Christmas,' said Momma, not looking at me, but at Cindy who needed more new clothes. 'This will be our first Christmas with Cindy. The best kind of families always have children of both sexes, and in that way boys can learn about girls, and vice versa.' She hugged Cindy closer. 'Cindy, you just don't know how lucky you are to have two wonderful older brothers who will absolutely adore you as you grow up into a real beauty – if they don't adore you already.'

Boy, if she only knew. But like Malcolm had said, beautiful women were dumb. I looked into the kitchen at Emma who was not beautiful, and never could have been. Was she wiser? Did she see through me?

Emma's eyes lifted and met mine. I shivered. Yes, drab

women were smarter. They knew the world wasn't beautiful just because they had hold of beauty for a while.

'Bart, you haven't told me what you want Santa Claus to bring you.'

I stared hard at her. She knew what I wanted most. 'A pony,' I said. I took out the pocket-knife Jory had given me and began to pare my nails. That made Momma stare at me, then her eyes moved to Cindy's short hair that was just beginning to look pretty again.

'Bart, put that knife away. It makes me nervous. You might accidentally cut yourself.' She sneezed then, then sneezed again, and again. Always her sneezes came in threes. She pulled tissues from her purse to wipe her nose, then blow it. Contaminating my nice clean air with her filthy cold germs.

Jory didn't come home until way after dark, soaked and miserable-looking as he stalked into his room and slammed his door. I grinned as I saw Momma frown. So, now her darling didn't love her either. That's what came of doing wrong.

Still the rain came down. She looked at me, her eyes large, her face pale, her hair a tangle all around her face, and I knew some men would think her beautiful. I yanked a hair from my head and held one end between my teeth as I pulled with one hand to stretch it taut. Easily my knife sliced it in two. 'Good knife,' I said, 'sharp as a razor for shaving. Good for cutting off legs, arms, hair . . .' I grinned as she looked scared. Powerful. I felt so powerful. John Amos was right. Women were only timid, fearful imitations of men.

Rain came down harder. The wind blew it around the house and made howling noises. Cold outside, dark and cold. All night it rained, next morning it was still coming down. Emma drove away because it was Thursday and she couldn't miss a visit with a friend. 'You take it easy now, ma'am,' she said to Momma in the garage. 'You don't look well. Just because you don't have a fever doesn't mean you won't come down with something. Bart – you behave yourself and don't make trouble for your mother.'

I left the garage and went into the kitchen, and somehow or

other my arm that was really a plane wing knocked several breakfast dishes to the floor. I saw my bowl of cereal with raisins, little bugs on a creamy sea . . .

'Bart, you did that deliberately.'

'Yes, Momma, you always say I do everything on purpose. This time I let you see how right you are.' I picked up my glass of milk, hardly touched, and hurled it at her face. It missed her by inches for she was quick to dodge.

'Bart, how dare you do that. When your father comes home I'm going to tell him, and he'll punish you severely.'

Yeah, already I knew what he'd do. He'd spank my behind, give me lecture on obedience and having respect for my mother. And his spanking wouldn't hurt. His lecture wouldn't be heard. I could tune him out and Malcolm in.

'Why don't you spank me, Momma? Come on . . . let me see what you can do to hurt me.' I held my knife in position, ready to jab it in if she dared to move closer.

Was she going to faint? 'Bart, how can you act so ugly when you know I don't feel well today. You promised your father you would behave. What have I done to make you dislike me so much?'

I grinned meaningfully.

'Where did you get that knife? That's not the knife Jory gave you.'

'The old lady next door gave it to me. She gives me everything I ask for. If I told her I wanted a gun, a sword, she'd get them, for she's like you are – weak, so eager to please me – when there isn't a woman alive who will ever please me.'

Real terror was in her eyes now. She moved closer to Cindy who was still in her highchair, making a big mess with her biscuit and her glass of milk. And she wasn't scolded.

'Bart, go to your room this moment. Shut and lock the door from the inside, and I'll lock it from the outside. I don't want to see you until your father is home. And since you didn't think enough of your breakfast to eat it, then you don't deserve any lunch.'

'You can't tell me what to do. If you dare, I'll tell the world what you and your husband are doing. Brother and sister living together. Living in sin. Fornicating!' (A good Malcolm word.)

Staggering, she raised her hands to her face, wiped at her running nose again, stuffed the tissues in her pants pocket and then she picked up Cindy.

'What are you going to do, harlot? Use Cindy for a shield? It won't work, won't work, I'll get the both of you – and the police can't touch me. I'm only ten years old, only ten, only ten, only ten, only ten . . .' and on and on I kept saying that like I was a needle stuck in the same groove.

In my ears was John Amos's voice, telling me what to do. I spoke as in a dream: 'Once long ago there was a man in London called Jack the Ripper, and he killed prostitutes. I kill strumpets too, and bad sisters who don't know right from wrong. Momma, I'm going to show you how God wants you punished for committing incest.'

Trembling and looking weak as a white rabbit too scared to move, she stood with Cindy half in her arms, and waited as I stalked her . . . closer, closer, jabbing with my knife.

'Bart,' she said, her voice stronger, more under control, 'I don't know who has been telling you stories, but if you harm me or Cindy, God will have his revenge on you too – even if the police don't lock you up, or put you in the electric chair.'

Threats. Empty threats. John Amos had already told me a boy my age could do anything he wanted and the police couldn't do a thing to stop or punish him.

'Is that man you live with your brother? Is he?' I yelled, overcome with flaming anger. 'Tell me a lie and you'll both die.'

'Bart, calm down. Did you know it will soon be Christmas? You don't want to be put away and miss all the toys Santa Claus will put under the tree for you.'

'No Santa Claus!' I shrieked, even more furious – did she think I believed in that nonsense?

'You used to love me. All your life you have held back telling me so in words, but I could see it in your eyes. Bart, what has changed you? What have I done to make you hate me? Tell me so I can change, so I can be better.'

Look at that, trying to win me moments before her death . . . and her redemption. God would feel pity for her when she was butchered, humiliated in every way possible.

Squinted my eyes and raised my razor-sharp blade that my grandmother had not given me – it had been a gift from John Amos, given shortly after that old witch Marisha came.

'I am the dark angel of the Lord,' I said in my quivering old voice, 'and I am here to deal out justice, for mankind has not yet discovered your sins.'

Swiftly she moved Cindy and turned her body so the little girl wouldn't be injured when I thrust. Then while I was watching what she was doing, her right leg shot out and caught my wrist with a hard kick. The knife went flying. I ran to get it, but she moved quicker and kicked the knife under the counter. I threw myself down to feel for it, and in that time she must have put Cindy on the floor, for suddenly she was on top of me, twisting my arm behind me. With a handful of my hair in her other hand, she made me stand up.

'Now we'll see who is boss, and who will be punished.' She shoved and dragged me, and never released my arm or my hair, as she forced me into my room and threw me on the floor. Quicker than I could scramble to my feet, she slammed the door and I heard the key turn. Locked. I was locked in.

'You whore, let me out. You let me out – or I'll set this house on fire. And we'll burn, all burn, burn.'

I heard her raspy breathing as she panted, leaning on my closed bedroom door. I tried to find the stash of matches and candles I'd stored in my room. Gone. All my matches, all my candles, even the cigarette lighter I'd stolen from John Amos.

'Thief!' I roared. 'Nothing in this house but thieves, cheats, whores and liars! All of you after my money too. You think I'll die today, tomorrow, next week or next month – but I'll live to see you dead, Momma! I'll live to see every last one of the attic mice dead!'

Down the hall she sped. I heard the clickety-clack of her satin mules. I'd scared myself, now I didn't know what to do. Hadn't John Amos told me to wait until Christmas night, so everything would coincide with the other fire in Foxworth Hall? Do it the same way, only differently.

'Momma,' I whispered, down on my knees and crying, 'I didn't mean none of that mean stuff – Momma, please don't go away and leave me alone. Don't like to be alone. Don't like what's happening to me, Momma. Why did you have to go and pretend you were married to your brother? Why couldn't you just have lived with him and us, and been decent?' I sobbed, afraid of what I could be when I felt mean.

She didn't need to lock the door when she had Cindy with her, did she? Never could she trust me to do the right thing. But that must be because she couldn't help herself either, no more than me. She was born bad and beautiful, and only through death could God redeem her sinful soul. I sighed and got up to do what I could to save her from the mess she'd made of her life, and ours. 'Momma!' I yelled, 'Unlock my door! I'll kill myself if you don't. I know all about you now, what you and your brother are doing – the people next door told me everything about your childhood. And your book told me the rest. Unlock my door, if you don't want to come in and see me dead.'

She came to my door and unlocked it, staring down in my face, even as she wiped her nose and ran her hand through her hair. 'What do you mean the people next door told you everything? Who are the people next door?'

'You'll find out when you see her,' I said smugly, all of a sudden mean again. Drat that Cindy she had to hold on to all the time. Was me she gave birth to, not Cindy. 'There's an old bent man over there too, he knows about you and your attic days. Just go over and talk to them, Momma, and you won't feel so happy to have a daughter any more.'

Her mouth gaped open, even as a wild look of horror came to

her blue eyes and made them dark, dark. 'Bart, please don't tell me lies.'

'Never tell lies, not like you do,' I said, watching as she began to tremble so much she almost dropped Cindy. Pity she didn't. But it wouldn't hurt if she just fell to the carpeted floor.

'Now you stay here and wait for me,' she said as she headed for the coat cupboard. 'For once in your life do as I say. Sit down and watch TV – eat all the sweets you want – but stay in this house and out of the rain.'

She was going next door. I felt panicky inside, afraid she wouldn't come back. Afraid she wouldn't be saved, afraid maybe after all, this wasn't a game John Amos was playing, not a game after all. But I couldn't speak. For God was on the side of John Amos – He'd have to be since John wasn't sinning.

Dressed in her warmest white winter coat, wearing white boots, Momma picked up Cindy who was dressed warmly too. 'Be a good boy, Bart, and remember always I love you.'

Dumbfounded . . . new word for today . . . I was dumbfounded. How could she love me when I was trying to destroy her? When Malcolm was inside me, etched there with his journal I kept with me night and say.

'I'll be back in less than ten minutes, though heaven only knows what that woman in black can know about me.'

I flicked a quick ashamed glance at her pale, worried face. Momma was going to crack up when she met my grandmother who was her own mother. Momma was going to end up in a strait-jacket and I'd never see her again.

Why wasn't I glad that already God was punishing her, beginning her redemption? My head ached again. My stomach felt queasy. Legs didn't want to obey, but had a leaden weight of their own that knew their mind. Pulling me along with them to the coat cupboard as Momma slammed the front door behind her.

Momma, my soul was crying, *don't go and leave me alone. Don't like to be alone. Nobody will love me but you, Momma, nobody will. Please don't go over there – don't let John Amos see you.* I shouldn't have said anything. Should have known you wouldn't stay here where it was safe. I pulled on my new coat and raced to the front windows to watch her carrying Cindy into the wind and cold rain. Just as if she, a mere woman, could face up to God and his black wrath.

Soon as she was out of sight I slipped outside and began to follow her. Did this new coat mean she really did love me? No, said the wise old man in my brain, didn't mean anything. Gifts, toys, games and clothes were easy things to give – things that all parents gave their children even when they were about to feed them arsenic on sugared doughnuts. Parents held back what was most important, security.

I sighed wearily, hoping some day, somewhere, I'd find the mother who would stay forever, the mother who was right for me – who would always understand I was doing the best I could.

The wind when I was outside blew my slicker against my body and drove the rain into my face. About ten yards ahead I could see Momma was having a rough time attempting to hold Cindy who was trying to wiggle free and run back home as she screamed: 'Don't like rain! Take me home! Momma, don't wanna go!'

Trying to comfort her while she kept her footing and at the same time trying to keep the hood over her hair, she finally gave up efforts to keep herself dry, and settled for keeping Cindy as dry as possible. Soon her golden hair was pasted down flat to her head, as flat as my hair was by now, for never never would I slip a hood over my head – made me scared to look in a mirror.

Momma slipped on the mud that was being washed down from the hills, and she almost lost her footing. But she caught herself and rebalanced, Cindy screamed and beat at her face with small fists. 'Home! I want home!'

Ran fast, for she wasn't looking backwards. All her concentration was on the winding road ahead. 'Stop fighting me, Cindy!'

High walls. Iron pickets. Strong gates. Magic boxes to speak into. Small voice coming back – and hear the wind blow. Privacy didn't mean nothing to God and the wind, not nothing at all.

Heard my Momma's voice as she shouted to be heard above the shriek of the wind and rain: 'This is Catherine Sheffield. I live next door and Bart is my son. I want to come in and talk to the lady of the house.'

Silence, only the wind.

Then my Momma was calling out again: 'I want to see her, and if I have to climb this fence I'll do just that. I'm coming in, one way or another – so open the gates and save me the trouble.'

I stood back and waited, gasping as if my heart truly did hurt. No small voice came back to allow her in, but slowly, slowly, the wide black iron gates swung open.

For a moment I wanted to shriek out, *don't walk into a trap, Momma!* But I really didn't know if there was a trap at all. I just suspected between John Amos and the Malcolm that was inside of me, nothing good would come of Momma's venture into my grandmother's house. Quickly I ducked inside the gates just before they clanged softly closed. Sounded like prison doors.

She trudged on ahead, all the while Cindy was crying out she was cold, wet, sleepy. By the time they reached the door, both seemed soaked to the skin. I was too and I'd had two hands to hold my coat together.

Up the stairs Momma stumbled, clasping Cindy who was still trying to kick free and there she lifted the loose jaw of the brass lion's head and she banged loud.

It was as if John Amos had been expecting her for he swung one side of the double doors open immediately and bowed very low, as if admitting a queen. Ran, ran then as fast as I could so I wouldn't miss a thing. Quickly into the side door, and down the corridor to the dumb-waiter – hoping that she'd be in that room, for behind the potted palms was not such a secure place. Jory had found me there once, and it could happen again.

I crawled into the dumb-waiter after I dropped my coat on the floor, then slid open the door just a slot. Momma was probably still in the foyer taking off her wet coat and muddy white boots.

Then she appeared in the doorway, minus her coat and boots. And I hadn't even had the time to check and see if my grandmother was in her rocking chair – but she was there all right.

Stiffly she rose, facing my Momma, hiding her trembling hands behind her back, the veil hiding most of her face as it hid all of her hair.

Something small, weak and young inside of me wanted to cry as I saw Momma step into her room, still carrying Cindy; only Cindy's outer clothes had been taken off. She was completely dry while Momma's hair stuck to her face and head like strings. Her flushed face looked so feverish I again wanted to cry. What if God struck her dead this second? What if death by hellfires was what He really wanted?

'I'm sorry to burst in on you like this,' said my Momma. I'd thought she'd pitch right into her. 'But I have to have a few answers to my questions. Who are you? What is it you tell my youngest son? He's told me terrible things he claims you told him. I don't know you, and you don't know me, so what can you tell him but lies?'

So far my grandmother hadn't said a word. She kept staring at Momma, then at Cindy.

My grandmother gestured towards a chair, then inclined her head as if to say she was sorry. Why didn't she speak?

'What a lovely room,' said Momma, glancing around at all the fine furniture. She smiled vaguely. There was a troubled look in her eyes, even her smile seemed drawn. She put Cindy on her feet and tried to hold on to her hand, but Cindy wanted to explore and see all the pretty things.

'I'm not going to stay any longer than necessary,' Momma went on, keeping an eye on Cindy who had to touch everything. 'I have a severe cold and want to be home in bed, but I must find out just what you have been telling my son so he comes home and says terrible things. And doesn't respect me as his mother. When you can explain, Cindy and I will leave.'

Grandmother nodded, keeping her eyes lowered, like she truly was some Arab woman. I guessed from the odd way Momma kept looking at her, she was thinking this was a foreigner of some kind who didn't understand English.

Momma sat down uninvited near the fire, as Cindy came to perch on the raised hearth near her legs.

'This is an isolated area, so when Bart comes home and tells me the lady next door has told him this and that, I knew it had to be you. Who are you? Why are you trying to turn my son against me? What have I ever done to you?' Her questions went on and on, for the woman in black wouldn't speak. Momma leaned forward to peer more closely at Grandmother.

Was Momma suspicious already? Was she so smart she could tell despite the disguise of the black veil, the long loose black dress? 'Come now, I've given you my name. Be courteous enough to tell me yours.'

No answer, just a shy nod of the black-veiled head.

'Oh, I think I understand,' said Momma with a perplexed frown, 'you must not speak English.'

The woman shook her head again. Momma's frown deepened. 'I truly don't understand. You seem to understand what I say, yet you don't answer. You can't be mute or you wouldn't have been able to tell my son so many lies.'

Time was ticking away loudly. Never heard the clock on the marble mantel tick so loud before. My granny just rocked on and on in her chair, like she'd never speak or raise her head.

Momma was beginning to be annoyed. Suddenly Cindy jumped up and raced to pick up a porcelain kitty. 'Cindy, put that down.'

Obeying reluctantly, Cindy carefully replaced the cat on the marble table. I'd have dropped the thing. Dratted hands weren't even as good as those of a two-year-old. The minute the cat was out of her hands, Cindy looked around for something else to do. She spied the archway to the next room and ran that way. Jumping to her feet, Momma hurried to prevent Cindy from roaming. Cindy had a way, like me, of wanting to examine everything – though she didn't drop as often as I did.

'Don't go in there!' cried out my grandmother as she too stood up.

As if stunned, my mother slowly turned around, Cindy forgotten. Her blue eyes widened and her flushed face seemed to pale momentarily as she kept staring at the woman in black who couldn't keep her nervous hands from straying up to the neckline of her black dress. Soon she had the rope of pearls and was twisting them between her fingers. Those pearls she always wore beneath her rusty black clothes.

'Your voice, I have heard it before.'

Grandmother didn't speak.

'Those rings on your fingers, I've seen them before. Where did you get those rings?'

Helplessly my grandmother shrugged and quickly released the pearls which dropped down out of sight under her black robe. 'Pawn shop,' she said in a strange raspy foreign way. 'Bargain.'

Momma's eyes narrowed as she continued to stare at the woman who wasn't a stranger. I sat breathless, wondering what would happen when she knew. Oh, Momma would find out – I knew my mother couldn't be so easily fooled.

As if her knees were suddenly weak, Momma sank down on the nearest velvet chair, unmindful that her clothes were still wet, unmindful that Cindy had wandered into the other room.

'You do understand a little English, I see,' she said in a quiet slow way. 'The moment I walked into this room, it was as if the clock had been turned backwards, and I was a child again. My mother had the same taste in furnishings, the same choice of colours. I look at your brocade chairs, the clock on your mantelpiece, and all I can think of is how very much my mother would have approved of this room. Even those rings on your fingers look like the rings she used to wear. You found them in a pawn shop?'

'Many women like this type of room . . . and jewellery,' said that lady in black.

'You have a strange voice . . . Mrs . . . ?'

Another shrug from the black figure.

Momma got up again and went into the other room to fetch Cindy. I held my breath. The portrait was in there. She'd see it. But she must not have looked around for in another second she was back, pulling Cindy, and standing close to the fireplace, keeping tight hold of Cindy's hand.

'What a remarkable home you have. If I closed my eyes I could swear I was looking at Foxworth Hall as I saw it from the balcony.'

Dark, dark were the eyes of my grandmother.

'Are you wearing pearls? I thought I saw pearls when you were fiddling around your neck. Those rings are so beautiful. You show your rings, why not your pearls?'

Again another shrug from Grandmother.

Dragging Cindy along with her, Momma stepped closer to the woman I didn't want to think of as my grandmother any more. 'As I stand here all sorts of memories come flooding back,' said Momma. 'I remember a Christmas night when Foxworth Hall burned to the ground. The night was cold and snowy, yet it lit up like the Fourth of July. I yanked all the rings from my fingers and hurled the diamond and emerald jewellery into the deep snow. I thought no one would ever find it – but Madame, you are wearing the emerald ring I threw in the snow.'

'I am sick too. Go away,' whispered that forlorn figure in black, standing in the middle of her room, avoiding the rocking chair which might trap her.

But she was already trapped.

'You!' cried my mother. 'I should have known. There is no other rope necklace of pearls with a diamond butterfly clasp except yours. How you love to play with it, to finger and twist it – '

'Of course you are sick. What else could you be but sick! I know who you are. Now everything makes sense. How dare you come into my life again? After all you have done to us, you come back again to do more. I hate you, I hate you for everything you have done, but I've never had the chance to pay you back.

Taking Bart from you wasn't enough. Now I have the chance to do more.'

Releasing Cindy's hand, she lunged forward and caught hold of my grandmother who tried to back away and fight her off. But my mother was stronger. Breathless and excited I watched the two women pull at one another.

My grandmother cringed away from the fierce attack. Her fluttering beringed hands didn't seem to know what to do. Then suddenly Cindy let out a howl of fear and began to cry. 'Mommy, let's go home.'

The door opened and John Amos shambled inside the room. As my mother prepared another attack, he reached out to lay a large knobby hand on my grandmother's shoulder. I'd never seen him touch her before.

'Mrs Sheffield,' he began in his whiny-hissy voice, 'you were graciously admitted into this house, and now you try and take advantage of my wife who has not been well for several years. I am John Amos Jackson, and this is my wife, Mrs Jackson.'

Stunned, Momma could only stare.

'John Amos Jackson,' repeated my mother slowly, savouring the name. 'I've heard that name before. Why, just yesterday I was rereading my manuscript, and I had to think of a way to change that name slightly. You are the John Amos Jackson who once was a butler in Foxworth Hall. I remember your bald head and how it shone under the chandeliers.' She swivelled about and reached for Cindy's hand, or so I thought. But instead she snatched off the veil from my grandmother's face!

'Mother!' she screamed. 'I should have known months ago it was you. From the moment I entered this house I sensed your presence, your perfume, the colours, the choice of furniture. You had sense enough to cover your face and body in black, but were stupid enough to wear your jewellery. Dumb, always so damned dumb! Is it insanity, or is it stupidity that makes you think I could forget your perfume, your jewellery?' She laughed, wild and hysterical, spinning around and around so John Amos who was trying to prevent what she might do, was stumbling clumsily around, trying to grab hold of her before she could attack again.

Look at her – she was dancing. All around my grandmother she whirled, flicking out her hand to slap at her mother – and even as she whipped her legs around, she screamed: 'I should have known it was you. Ever since you moved in Bart has been acting crazy. You couldn't leave us alone, could you? You had to come here and try and ruin what Chris and I have found together – the first time we've been happy. And now you've ruined it. You've managed to drive Bart insane so he'll have to be put away like you were. Oh, how I hate you for that. How I hate you for so many reasons. Cory, Carrie, and now Bart – is there no end to what you can do to hurt us?' She kicked and hooked her foot behind my grandmother's knee and threw her off balance, and the moment my grandmother spilled to the floor in a heap of black rags, my mother was on top of her, ripping at that rope of pearls with its diamond butterfly clasp.

Using both her hands, she forced the knotted string to part, and the pearls scattered all over the soft Oriental rug that seemed silently to swallow them up.

John Amos roughly seized hold of my Momma, and pulled her to her feet. There he held her and shook her until Momma's head rolled. 'Pick up the pearls, Mrs Sheffield,' he ordered in a hard, mean voice that was suddenly very strong. I was surprised that he would speak so harshly and handle my mother so cruelly. I knew what Jory would do – he'd run to fight John Amos and save Momma. But me, I didn't know if I should. God was up there wanting Momma to suffer for her sins, and if I saved her, what would God do to me? Besides, Jory was bigger. And Daddy was always saying everything happened for the best – so this was meant to be, despite the miserable way I felt.

But Momma didn't need my help after all. She threw back her head and butted her skull squarely against his false teeth. I heard them crack as she whirled free. Then he went after her with more determination. He was gonna kill her, and be the agent of God's wrath himself!

Quicker than I could move, Momma's knee came up and caught him squarely in the groin. John Amos screamed, doubled over, clutching at himself as he fell to the floor and rolled about moaning: 'Damn you to hell!'

'Damn you to hell, John Amos Jackson,' my Momma screamed back. 'Don't you ever touch me again, or I will dig out your eyes.'

By this time my grandmother had regained her feet, and she stood in the centre of the room swaying unsteadily as she tried to fit the torn veil over her face again. That's when my mother's slap caught her cheek, so Grandmother fell backwards into her rocker. 'Damn you to hell too, Corrine Foxworth! I hoped never to see your face again. I hoped you'd die in that rest home and spare me the agony of looking at you again, and hearing that voice that I used to love. But I've never been lucky. I should have known you wouldn't be considerate enough to die and leave me and Chris alone. You are like your father, clinging desperately to a life not worth living.'

Oh, I hadn't known before my mother had such a terrible temper. She was just like me. I felt shocked, scared as I watched my mother tackle my old grandmother so her chair tipped over and both women fell to the floor, rolling over and over as John Amos groaned and was likely never to recover. In a few moments Momma was sitting on top of my grandmother, ripping off all those glittering expensive rings. Weakly my grandmother tried to defend herself and her jewellery.

'Please, Cathy, don't do this to me,' she pleaded.

'You! How I've longed to see you on the floor, pleading with me as you are. I was wrong a moment ago – this is my lucky day. My chance to have my revenge again for all you've done. You watch and see what I do to your precious rings.' She raised her arm, and with one wild gesture she hurled all those rings into the roaring fire. 'There, there! It's done!' cried my Momma. 'What should have been done long ago on the night Bart died.'

With a gloating expression she picked up Cindy; ran to the

foyer cupboard to yank on Cindy's coat and then reached for her own coat and boots she'd pulled off.

John Amos had picked himself off the floor, muttering to himself about Devil's issue that should have died when she was caged and helpless, that should have been slaughtered before she could create more Devil's issue.

I heard.

Maybe Momma didn't.

I moved out of the dumb-waiter unseen by my grandmother who was crying as she sat on the floor in a broken heap.

Momma had on her boots now, her white coat, though she was shivering as she came to the door and looked in on the woman still on the floor. 'What did you say, John Amos Jackson? Did I hear you call me a hellcat, Devil's issue? Say that again to my face! Go on, say it to me now! Now that I'm an adult and not a frightened child any more. Now that my legs and arms are strong and yours are weak. Don't think you can do away with me so easily – for I'm not old, and I'm not weak, and I'm not scared any more.'

He headed her way, holding in his hand a poker he must have taken from the fireplace. She laughed, seeming to think he was a fool and an easy enemy. Quickly she dodged, then shot out her good leg and kicked his bottom hard so he fell prone upon his face, screaming out his rage as he fell.

I was screaming too. This was wrong. This was not the way John Amos and I had planned for God to have his revenge. He wasn't supposed to hurt her.

Momma saw me then. Her blue eyes widened, her face paled and she seemed to crumple.

I whispered, 'John Amos told me all the things I had to do.'

She whirled on her mother, as if my grandmother had been in on the plot. 'Look what you have done. You have turned my own son against me. And all the time you get by with everything, even murder. You poisoned Cory, poisoned Carrie's mind so she had to kill herself – killed Bart Winslow when you sent him back into the fire to save the life of a wretched old woman who didn't deserve to live – and now you poison the mind of my son against me. And you escaped justice by pleading insanity. You weren't insane when you set fire to Foxworth Hall. That was the first clever stunt you pulled in your life – but this is my time for revenge.' And with those words she raced to the fireplace, picked up the small shovel for ashes, pushed aside the firescreen, and began to pull red hot coals from the fire on to the Oriental rug.

As the rug began to smoke, she called to me, 'Bart, put on your coat, we're going home, and we'll move so far away she'll never find us, never!'

I screamed. My grandmother screamed. But my mother was so busy buttoning up Cindy's coat she didn't see that John Amos had the poker in his hand again. As I froze, my lips parted to scream a warning again – the poker came down on her head. She slumped quietly to the floor like a rag doll.

'You fool!' cried my grandmother. 'You have killed her!'

Things were happening too fast. Everything was going wrong. Momma wasn't supposed to be hurt. I wanted to say this, but the face of John Amos was twisted, his lips snarled as he advanced on my grandmother . . .

'Cathy, Cathy,' she pleaded, down on her knees and cradling my mother's head, 'please don't die. I love you – I've always loved you. I never meant for any of you to die. I nev – '

The thump was so hard that she slumped right over the body of my mother.

Rage was in my head. Cindy was screaming. 'John Amos!' I yelled, 'that wasn't in God's plan.'

He turned, smiling and confident. 'Yes it was, Bart. God spoke to me last night and told me what to do. Didn't you hear your mother say she was going far, far away? She wouldn't take a bothersome boy like you with her, would she? Wouldn't she put you away first in some institution? Then she'd go, and never would you see her again, Bart. Just like your great-grandfather, you'd be abandoned for ever. Just like your grandmother you'd be locked up, and you'd never see her again either! That's the cruel way life treats those who try to do their best. And it's me, only me who is trying to take care of you, and see you escape confinement worse than prison.'

Prison, prison, so much like poison.

'Bart, are you listening? Have you heard? Do you understand I'm doing what I can to save both of them for you?'

I stared at him, not really comprehending.

'Yes, Bart, instead of one, you will have two souvenirs.'

Not knowing what or who to believe, I stared down at the two women on the floor, my Momma, my grandmother who had fallen crosswise over the slight body of my Momma. It came over me in an overwhelming flood, I loved those two women. I loved them more than I'd known I had. I wouldn't want to stay alive if I lost one, much less two. Were they as evil as John Amos had said? Would God punish me if I kept them from being redeemed by fire? Whom did I turn to for truth?

And there he was in front of me, John Amos, the only one who had been fully honest with me from the beginning, telling me from the start who my real daddy was, who my real grandmother was, who Malcolm the wise and clever was.

Helplessly I spread my hands; I looked into his small narrow eyes for instructions. God was behind John Amos or else he wouldn't have lived to be so old.

He smiled and chucked me under the chin, and I shivered. Didn't like people to touch me when I couldn't even feel the touch.

'Now listen to me carefully, Bart. First you are to take Cindy home. Then you make her swear not to tell anything or you will cut out her little pink tongue. Can you make her promise?'

Numbly I nodded. Had to make Cindy promise.

'You won't hurt my Momma and my grandmomma?'

'Of course not, Bart. I'll just put them away where they'll be safe. You can see them whenever you want. But not one word to that man who calls himself your father. Not one word. Remember he too will take you away from your home and have you locked up. He thinks you're crazy too. Don't you know that's why they keep taking you to doctors?'

I swallowed, my throat hurt. Didn't know what to do.

John Amos knew. 'Now you go home with Cindy, keep the brat quiet, lock yourself in your room, play dumb, know nothing. And remember . . . you threaten that kid sister so horribly she'll be scared to let out a squeak.'

'She's not my sister,' I whispered weakly.

'What's the difference?' he snarled irritably. 'You just do as I say. Follow instructions, as God wants men to believe in him unquestioningly and never let out to your brother, or your father, that you know his secret, or that you have any idea where your mother went. Play dumb – you should be good at that.'

What did he mean? Was he making fun of me?

I knitted my brows and turned on my best glower, and imitated Malcolm. 'You hear this, John Amos. The day you can outsmart me will be the day the earth sits on the head of a pin, and I swallow it. So don't you mock me, and think I'm dumb . . . for in the end, I'll win. I'll always win, dead or alive.'

Power swelled up huge within me. Never felt so stuffed full of brains. I looked down at the two women I loved. Yes, God had planned for it to happen this way, give me two mothers to keep for ever as my own . . . and I'd never be lonely again.

'Now you keep your mouth shut, and don't tell Daddy or Jory one word or I'll cut out your tongue,' I said to Cindy when we were home and in our kitchen together. 'Do you want your tongue cut out?'

Her small face was wet with rain and tears, streaked with dirt too. Her lips gaped and her eyes bulged, and whimpering like a baby, she allowed me to put on her pyjamas and put her in bed. I kept my eyes closed all the time so none of her girl's body would shame me into hating her more.

WHERES MOMMA? *Jory*

There was somebody I had to tell off. Somebody who seemed to have started a tornado that was going on for ever and ruining our lives. Finally I could hold in my anger no longer. Dad and I had talked but things were still very tense and I was so confused. What would happen? Why did she have to come and start all this? Soon after ballet class was over, I raced to Madame's office, now full of her clutter, worse than Mom's.

'I hate you, Madame, for all the mean things you said to my mom! Everything's been terrible ever since that day. You leave her alone from now on, or I'll go and never come back to see you. Did you fly all the way here just to make her sick? She can't dance now and that's bad enough.

'If you don't stop causing so much trouble, I'll quit dancing too. I'll run away and you'll never see me again. For in ruining my parents' lives, you have managed to ruin not only theirs, but mine and Bart's too.'

She paled and looked very old. 'You sound so very much like your father. Julian used to blaze his dark eyes at me in the same way.'

'I used to love you.'

'Used to love me . . ?'

'Yes, used to. When I thought you cared about me, about my parents, then I believed that dancing was the most wonderful thing in the world. Now I don't believe.'

She looked stricken, as if I'd stabbed her in her heart. She reeled back against the wall and would have fallen if I hadn't stepped forward to support her. 'Jory, please,' she gasped, 'don't ever run away. Don't stop dancing. If you do then my life has been meaningless, and Georges will have lived for nothing, and Julian too. Don't take everything from those I have loved and lost.'

I couldn't speak, I was so confused. So I ran, ran like Bart always ran when things got too heavy.

Behind me Melodie called out: 'Jory, where are you going in such a hurry? We were going to have a soda together.'

I ran on. I didn't care any more about anyone or anything. My life was all screwed up. My parents weren't married. How could they be? What minister or judge would marry a brother and his sister?

Once I hit the street I slowed down, then went on to a public park where I sat down on a green bench. On and on I sat, staring down at my feet. A dancer's feet. Strong, tough with calluses, ready for the professional stage. What would I do now when I grew up? I didn't really want to be a doctor, though I'd said that a few times just to please the man I loved as a father. What a joke. Why should I try and lie to myself – there was no life for me without dancing. When I punished Madame, my mother, my stepdad who was really only my uncle, I punished myself even worse.

I stood up and looked around at all the old people sitting lonely in the park, wondering if one day I'd be like them, and I thought, No. I'll know when to say I made a mistake. When to say I'm sorry.

Madame M was in her office, her head bowed down into her thin hands, when I opened the door quietly and stepped inside her office. I must have made some noise for she looked up and I saw tears in her eyes. Joy flooded them when she saw me, but she didn't mention all that had happened half an hour ago.

'I have a gift for your mother,' she said in her natural shrill voice. She slid open a desk drawer and withdrew a gold box bound with red satin ribbon. 'For Catherine,' she said stiffly, not meeting my eyes. 'You are right about everything. I was ready to take you from your mother and father because I felt I was doing the right thing for you. I see now I was doing what I wanted for myself, not for you. Sons belong with their mothers, not their grandmothers.' She smiled bitterly as she looked at the pretty gold box. 'Lady Godiva chocolates. The kind your mother was nuts about when she lived in New York and was with Madame Zolta's company. Then she couldn't eat chocolates for fear of adding weight – though she was the kind of dancer who burned off more calories than most when she danced – still I allowed her only one piece of chocolate a week. Now that she won't dance again, she can indulge to her heart's desire.'

That was Bart's phrase.

'Mom has an awful cold,' I explained just as stiffly as she had. 'Thank you for the chocolate and what you just said. I know Mom will feel better knowing you won't try and take me away from her.' I grinned then and kissed her dry cheek. 'Besides, don't you realize there is enough of me to share? If you aren't stingy, she won't be. Mom is wonderful. Not once has she ever told me you and she had any difficulties.' I settled down in her single office chair and crossed my legs. 'Madame, I'm scared. Things are going crazy in our house. Bart acts weirder each day. Mom is sick with that cold; Dad seems so unhappy. Clover is dead. Emma doesn't smile any more. Christmas is coming and nothing is being done about it. If this keeps up, I think I'll crack up myself.'

'Hah!' she snorted, back to her old self, 'life is always like that – twenty minutes of misery for every two seconds of joy. So, be everlastingly grateful for those rare two seconds and appreciate; appreciate what good you can find, no matter what the cost.'

My smiles were false. Underneath I was truly depressed. Her cynical words didn't really help. 'Does it have to be that way?' I asked. Rain, rain, grey everywhere, in my heart most of all.

'Jory,' she said, thrusting her old pastry-dough face closer to mine, 'think about this. If there were no shadows, how could we see the sunlight?'

I sat there in her gloomy office and allowed this kind of sour philosophy to give me some peace. 'Okay, I get your meaning, Madame. And if you can't say you are sorry, then I can.'

She whispered as if it hurt: 'I'm sorry too.'

I hugged her close, and we had come to some sort of compromise.

All the way home I held the gold box of chocolates on my lap, dying to open it. 'Dad,' I began falteringly, 'Madame is sending Mom this chocolate as a reconciliation gift, I guess.'

He threw me a glance and a smile. 'That's nice.'

'I think it's terribly strange Mom is staying sick with that cold for so long. She's never been sick more than a day or two. Don't you think she looks very tired?'

'It's that writing, that damned writing,' he grouched, watching the heavy traffic, turning on the windshield wipers, leaning forward to peer more closely at the traffic signal to the right. 'I wish it would stop raining. Rain always bothers her. Then she's up till four in the morning, next up at dawn to scribble, afraid to use the typewriter for fear of waking me. When the candle is burned at both ends something has to give – and that's her health. First that fall, now this cold.' He gave me another sideways glance. 'Then there's Bart and his problems, and you and yours. Jory, we know you know our secret now. Your mother and I have talked it over, and you and I have talked about it for hours and hours. Can you forgive us? Haven't I managed to help you understand?'

I bowed my head and felt ashamed. 'I'm trying to understand.'

'Trying? Is it that difficult? Haven't I told you how it was with us, up there, all four of us in one room, growing up, finding out in our adolescence that we had only each other . . .'

'But, Dad. When you ran away and found a new home with Dr Paul, couldn't you have found someone else? Why did it have to be her?'

Sighing, he set his lips. 'I thought I explained to you how I felt then about women. Your mother was there when I needed her. Our own mother had betrayed us. When you're young you fix very strong ideas in your mind. I'm sorry if you've been hurt by my inability to love anyone but her.'

What was there for me to say? I couldn't understand. The

world was full of beautiful young women, thousands, millions. Then I thought of Melodie. If she were to die could I go out and find another? I thought and thought about that as Dad turned silent and his lips stayed in that grim line, and the rain came down, down, driving hard. It was as if he could read my mind. For yes, if ever I was so unfortunate as to lose Melodie, if she moved away and I never saw her again, I'd go on living, and eventually I'd find another to take her place. Anything was better than –

'Jory, I know what you're thinking. I've had years and years to think about why it had to be my sister and no one else. Perhaps it was because I'd lost faith in all women because of what our mother was doing to us, and only my sister could give me comfort. She was the one who kept me from falling apart during all those long years of deprivations. She was the one who made of that one room a whole house. She was a mother to Cory and Carrie.

'She made that room seem a home, making the table pretty, making the beds, scrubbing clothes in the bathroom tub, hanging them in the attic to dry, but more than anything, it was the way she danced in the attic that made me love her, and put her in my heart for ever. For it seemed as I stood in the shadows and watched her, she was dancing only for me. I thought she was making me the prince of her dreams, as I made her the princess of mine.

'I was romantic then, even more so than she. Your mother is made of different stuff than most women, Jory. She could live on hate and still flourish, I couldn't. I had to have love or die. When we escaped Foxworth Hall, she flirted with Paul, wanting him to take her from me. She married your father only after Paul's sister, Amanda, told her a lie. She was a good wife to your father, but after he was killed she ran to the mountains of Virginia to complete her plans for revenge which included stealing her mother's second husband. As you have found out, Bart is the son of my mother's husband, and not the son of Paul as we told you, and told him. We had to tell lies then, to protect you. Then, after your mother married Paul, and he died, she came to me.

'During all those long years I waited. I somehow knew eventually she'd be mine as long as I held fast to my faith, and kept the flame of my first love burning. It was so easy for her to love other men. It was impossible for me to find any woman who could compare. She took me for her own when I was about your age, Jory. Be careful whom you love first, for that is the girl you will never forget.'

I let out a long-withheld breath, thinking that life was not at all like fairy tale ballets, or TV soap operas. Love did not come and go with the seasons as I'd kinda hoped it would

The drive home seemed to take for ever. Dad was forced to drive very slowly and carefully. From time to time he flicked his eyes to the dashboard clock. I stared out of the windows. People were beginning to put up their Christmas decorations. Through picture windows I saw gaily-lit Christmas trees. Longingly I stared at the windows we passed, seeing everything in the rain in that indistinct way that made scenes ten times more romantic. I wished it was last year. I wished we had the happiness that had seemed so permanent then. I wished that old woman next door had never come into our lives and messed up what I'd thought was perfect. I wished too that Madame M had never flown here to snoop in their lives, and reveal all their secrets better left hidden. Worst of all those two women had destroyed the pride I had in my parents. Try as I might, I still resented what they were doing, what they had done, risking scandal, risking ruining my life and Bart's, Cindy's too, and all because one man couldn't find another woman to love. And that one woman must have done something to keep him faithful and hoping.

'Jory,' began Dad as he turned into our driveway, 'from time to time I hear your mother complain about chapters she's misplaced. Your mother isn't the kind of woman to be careless in any important work project. I'm presuming you've been slipping her completed chapters out of her desk drawer and reading them . . .'

Should I tell him the truth?

Bart was the one who first stole pages from her script. And yet my sense of morality hadn't kept me from reading them too. Though as yet I hadn't read to the end. For some reason I couldn't force myself to read beyond the time when first a brother betrayed his sister by forcing himself upon her. That this man beside me could rape his own sister when she was only fifteen was beyond my comprehension, beyond my ability to sympathize no matter how desperate his need had been, or what the circumstances had been to drive him to commit such an unholy act. And certainly she shouldn't tell the whole world.

'Jory, have I lost you?'

I slowly turned my eyes his way, feeling sick and weak inside, wanting to hide from the torment I plainly saw on his face. Yet I couldn't say yes – or no.

'I guess you don't need to answer,' said Dad in a tight way, 'your silence gives your answer, and I'm sorry. I love you as my own son, and I hoped you loved me enough to understand. We were going to tell you when we thought you were old enough to empathize with us. Cathy should have locked her first drafts in a drawer and not trusted two sons to remain uninterested.'

'It's fiction, isn't it?' I asked hopefully. 'Sure, I know it is. No mother could do that to her own children . . .' and I threw open the passenger door and was racing to the house before he could answer.

My lips parted to call out to Mom. Then I shut my mouth and said nothing. It was easier for me to avoid her.

Usually when I came home I dashed out into the garden and ran around, doing practise leaps and positions, and on rainy days like this, I spent more time at the barre. Today I threw myself down in front of the television set in the family room, pushed the remote control button, and lost myself in a silly but entertaining soap opera.

'Cathy!' called Dad as he came in, 'where are you?'

Why hadn't he sung out, 'Come greet me with kisses if you love me?' Did he feel silly, guilty saying that now that he knew we knew where that line came from?

'Have you said hello to your mother?' he asked as he came in.

'Haven't seen her.'

'Where's Bart?'

'Haven't looked for him.'

He threw me a pleading look then went on into the bedroom he shared with his wife.

'Cathy, Cathy,' I could hear him calling, 'where are you?'

A few seconds later he was in the kitchen behind me, checking there – and not finding her. He began to race around from room to room, and finally banged on Bart's locked door. 'Bart, are you in there?'

First a long silence, then came a reluctant, surly reply, 'Yeah, I'm in here. Where else would I be with the door locked?'

'Then unlock it and come out.'

'Momma locked me in from the outside so I can't come out.'

I sat on, immersing myself in the show, keeping myself detached, wondering how I was going to survive and grow up normally when I felt so unhappy.

Dad was the type to have duplicate keys to everything, and soon Bart was out and undergoing a third degree. 'What did you do to cause your mother to lock you up and then go away?'

'Didn't do nothin'!'

'You must have done something that made her furious.'

Bart grinned at him slyly, saying nothing. I looked their way feeling anxious, scared.

'Bart, if you have done anything to harm your mother, you won't get out of this lightly – I mean that.'

'Wouldn't do nothin' to hurt her,' said Bart irritably, 'she's the one always hurting me. She don't love me, only Cindy.'

'Cindy,' said Dad, suddenly remembering the little girl, and away he strode to her pretty room. He showed up minutes later with a little girl who had been quickly changed into clean clothes.

'Where is your mother, Bart?'

'How do I know? She locked me up.'

Despite myself, I was losing my ability to stay uninvolved. 'Dad, Mom left her car in the garage a few days ago, and Madame drove us home the rest of the way, so she couldn't have gone far.'

'I know! She told me – something wrong with her brakes.' He threw Bart a long scrutinizing look. 'Bart, are you sure you don't know where your mother is?'

'Can't look through solid doors.'

'Did she tell you where she was going?'

'Nobody ever tells me nothin'.'

Suddenly Cindy piped up: 'Mommy went out in rain . . . rain got us all wet . . .'

Bart whirled around to stab her with his withering glare. She froze and began to tremble.

Smiling, Dad picked up Cindy again and sat down to hold her on his lap. 'Cindy, you're a lifesaver. Now, think back carefully and tell me where Mommy went.'

Trembling more, she sat staring at Bart and unable to speak.

'Please, Cindy, look at me, not Bart. I'm here, I'll take care of you. Bart can't hurt you when I'm here. Bart, stop scowling at your sister.'

'Cindy ran out in the rain, Daddy, and Momma had to chase outside and catch her, and then she came in dripping water, and coughing, and I said something, and she got mad at me, and shoved me in my room and slammed the door.'

'Well, I guess that explains Cindy's tangled damp hair,' said Dad. But he didn't look relieved. He put Cindy on her feet and began to make a series of phone calls to all Mom's friends, and Madame Marisha. My grandmother said she'd drive right over.

Then he was talking to Emma who couldn't return until tomorrow because of the storm. I thought of my grandmother on the road, trying to drive here in the downpour. Even in perfect weather, she wasn't what I'd call a safe driver.

'Dad, let's check all the rooms, even the attic,' I said, jumping up and running towards the linen closet. 'She may have gone up there to dance like she does sometimes, and accidentally locked herself in, or fallen asleep on one of those beds . . . or something.' I concluded this lamely, thinking he was looking at me in an odd way.

When Dad started to follow me up the attic stairs, Cindy let out a loud wail of fright. Quickly he returned to the hall and picked her up as if to take her with us. Bart pulled out a new pocket knife and began to whittle on a long tree branch. It seemed he was going to skin off all the tree bark and make a smooth switch. Cindy couldn't take her eyes off that knife or switch.

Dad, Cindy and me looked our house over, in the attic, in the cupboards, under the beds, everywhere. Mom was nowhere to be found. 'It's just not like Cathy to do anything like this,' Dad said worriedly. 'Especially I know she wouldn't leave Cindy alone with Bart. Something is very wrong, very fishy.'

Yeah, I thought, if there was a fish in the house, it was watching us and whittling away on a branch that should be used on his bare bottom.

'Dad,' I whispered as he stood in the middle of his bedroom again, looking around with bleak eyes, 'why don't we presume Bart knows where she's gone? He's not the most honest kid ever born. You know how crazy he's been acting lately.'

We set off together, Dad still carrying Cindy, and hunted now for Bart. Now we couldn't find him. He was gone.

Dad and I stared at each other. He shook his head.

I stared around, knowing Bart had to be hiding behind a chair, or was crouched down low in some corner that was dim, or perhaps out in the rain, acting like an animal.

But the storm was getting worse. His cave in the hedges wouldn't keep him dry. Even Bart had more sense that to stay out in the cold and wet.

My thoughts in a turmoil, I felt wild inside, like the storm. I hadn't done anything to deserve all this trouble – yet I was in the midst of it, suffering along with Dad, with Mom, with Cindy . . . and maybe Bart too.

'Are you hating me now, Jory?' asked Dad, looking at me squarely. 'Are wheels churning in your head saying your mother and I brought this all on ourselves and we deserve to pay the price. Are you thinking you shouldn't have to pay any price? If that's what you're thinking, I'm thinking the same thing. Maybe your mother's life would have turned out better, and yours and Bart's too, if I had gone away and left her to live in Paul's home until she found another man. But I still loved her. I love her now, tomorrow and for ever. God help me for not being able to think about life without her.'

Dully I turned away. So that was what everlasting burning love was like, destroying everything that got in its way.

On my bed I lay down and sobbed.

Finally, I sat up and wondered again where Mom was. For the first time it really hit me – she might be in danger. She wouldn't leave Dad. Something terrible must have happened or she'd be here, setting the table as she did every Thursday when Emma had her day off. Thursdays were very special to them for reasons I was just beginning to understand.

Thursday, the day the maids of Foxworth Hall went into the city. Thursday, the day Mom and Dad could climb out the attic dormer window and lie on the roof and talk, and as they talked, as they looked at each other in their high and lonely place, they fell mindlessly, uncontrollably in love.

For now I knew why Mom had married one man after another. Trying always to escape the sinful love she felt too.

I got up. Decided. It was up to me to find Bart.

When I found Bart, I'd find my mother.

MY ATTIC SOUVENIRS *Bart*

In the huge kitchen of the mansion John Amos had everything under control. The maids and cook were scurrying about. 'Madame had to leave early,' he told them. 'Now you are to pack up what clothes she'll need for her trip to Hawaii, and be quick about it. Lottie, I want you to drive her bags to the airport and put them on the plane. Don't just stand there and stare at me with your blank face looking so stupid. You understand English. Do as I say!'

Boy, he could act mean when he wanted to. They scattered like scared birds, one this way, one that, and then we were alone and he was grinning at me with his cracked teeth. 'How did your end go?'

Just like the movies, him and me. I swallowed over some lump that stayed in my throat and wouldn't go away. 'They don't know where Momma is. They're worried, and keep asking, where is she?'

'Never mind about them,' he said in his funny old voice that made me wonder why God had chosen him for such a special job, 'I'll take care of everything until God sends his signal that your mother and grandmother have been redeemed, and saved from hellfires. You just go home and keep quiet.'

Fire in my mind, growing bigger, hotter. 'You told me my Momma would be my attic souvenir. And now you won't even tell me where you put her. I've looked in the attic and they're not up there. You tell me where they are, or I'll go home and tell my daddy what you've done.'

'What I've done?' he asked with a curling sneer. 'It's what you have done, Bart Winslow Sheffield. Do you think for one moment, with your violent pyschiatric history, that you can be believed and not blamed? The law will take you and find you guilty, and you will be locked away.'

When he saw the red Malcolm anger in my eyes he tried to smile. 'Come now, Bart, I was only testing you, trying to see if you'd break and lose your courage. But you're strong and full of the righteous power, the same as your great-grandfather, Malcolm. Every power he had you have. And now is your chance to use those powers. For now you'll be in charge of the adults – your mother and grandmother. You will control their lives, and feed them – if you will – or let them starve if you are so inclined. But you have to be careful. You must keep them a secret until . . . well, remember always your father and brother will be suspicious, and they may betray you if you give them the least hint of what you're up to.'

People always suspected me. If something was broken it was always my fault. If the toilet stopped up and overflowed it was always because I'd thrown down too much paper. If Momma lost her jewellery, that was my fault too. Whatever bad thing happened in our house, they said it was my fault. I'd show them now how wrong it was for them not to love me.

'Bread and water,' I said. 'Bread and water is good enough for women who are unfaithful to husbands and sons.'

'Fine, fine,' mumbled John Amos.

Down, down the narrow cellar steps John Amos led me, carrying a small flashlight. Made eerie shadows on the walls, felt clammy. Long time ago when this house belonged to Jory and me we'd found every nook, every cranny. But this was where ghosts lived, where I'd never felt comfortable, so I stayed close at the heels of John Amos, terrified if he moved more than a yard ahead of me.

'They'll look down here,' I whispered, scared of waking up things that might be sleeping. 'No, they won't look where I have them hid,' answered John Amos. He chortled. 'Your father will be sure they are in the attic, and why not? That would be the perfect revenge. But they'll never, never find the snug little cage the workmen made when they put up a new brick wall to reinforce the wine cellar.'

Wine cellar. Didn't sound nearly as good as the attic. Wasn't nearly as scary, but it was very cold and dark down here.

John Amos began brushing away spider webs, then he shoved old furniture aside, and finally came to a board door that was very hard to open. 'Now you go in and peek through the little trap at the bottom of that door over there,' he said. 'We used to have a stray kitten your grandmother took in, but it disappeared shortly after you started coming over here. She had me cut this little door in the larger one so the cat could come and go when it wanted to.'

With the flashlight held beneath his chin he looked like something dead and dug up. Didn't trust him not to slam the door shut behind me, and I'd never be able to wiggle through that little kitty door.

'No! You go in the wine cellar first,' I ordered like Malcolm would. For a moment he didn't move. Maybe he thought I might slam the door behind him. Then he gave me a long look and went slowly into the wine cellar. He put the flashlight on one of the wine racks while he tugged and tugged at the back rack holding many dusty old wine bottles.

Finally it creaked open. Smelled bad in there. I held my nose and stared, and then stared some more. John Amos held his flashlight high so I could see the two women prisoners better.

Oh, oh. Momma, Grandmother – how pitiful my Momma looked, lying on the damp concrete with her head held on my grandmother's lap. Both of them raised their hands to shield their eyes from the bright light come so suddenly into their dark evil cell. I could barely see it was so dim.

'Who is it?' asked my Momma weakly. 'Chris, is that you? Have you found us?'

Was my Momma blind now? How could she think John Amos was my Daddy? If my Momma went blind and crazy too, would God think that enough punishment?

My grandmother spoke up. 'John, I know that's you. You let us out of here this minute. Do you hear me – let us out immediately.'

John Amos laughed.

I didn't know what to do, but Malcolm came in my brain and

told me. 'You give me the key, John Amos,' I ordered sternly. 'You go up the stairs and let me give the prisoners their bread and water.'

Wonder why he obeyed? Did he really think I was as strong as Malcolm? I watched until he was out of sight, then I ran to bolt another door so he couldn't sneak up behind me.

Feeling more like Malcolm than like Bart, I crept on my hands and knees, shoving along the silver tray with its half loaf of bread, and its silver pitcher of water. It didn't seem to me funny to be serving prison meals from a silver tray, for that's the way my grandmother always did things, elegantly.

Big door was shut now. It appeared only another of the wine shelves full of dusty old bottles. Flat on my stomach I reached under the lower shelf and opened the little door that would swing inwards, or outwards – wonder why the kitten liked it back in the darkest part?

'Bread, water,' I said in a hard gruff voice and quickly shoved in the tray. I slammed the little door shut and picked up a brick to wedge it so they couldn't see me if they pushed.

I stayed to spy on them. I heard my mother moaning, and crying out for Chris. Then she surprised me. 'Momma – where has Momma gone, Chris? It's been so long since she visited us, months, months. And the twins don't grow.'

'Cathy, Cathy, my poor darling, stop thinking about the past,' said my grandmother. 'Please hold on, eat and drink to keep up your strength. Chris will come to save us both.'

'Cory, stop playing that same tune over and over. I'm so tired of your lyrics. Why do you write such sad songs? The night will end, it will. Chris, tell Cory the day will begin soon.'

I heard sobs then. From my grandmother?

'Oh, my God!' she cried. 'Is this the way it's going to end? Can't I do anything right? This time I was so sure I could work it out, please, God, don't let me fail all of them, please.' I listened to her pray out loud. Praying for my mother to get well, for her son to come and find them before it was too late. Over and over she said the same words, while my mother asked crazy questions.

I sat and listened for hours and hours. Legs got cramped and uncomfortable, got old and weary inside, like I was locked up in there with them, crazy too, hungry, hurting, dying.

'Goin' now,' I said in a whisper. 'Don't like this place.'

Nobody was home and it was dark. Now I could run to the refrigerator and steal the food. I was stuffing in another ham slice when Madame Marisha opened the door from the garage and stalked into the kitchen. 'Good evening, Bart,' she said. 'Where's your father and Jory?'

I shrugged. Nobody told me nothin'. Didn't know why Daddy and Jory would go off and leave Cindy alone with me.

Then Emma was calling out from another room. 'Hello, Madame Marisha. Dr Sheffield told me you were due here any moment. I'm sorry you went to so much trouble. Once I knew Cathy had disappeared, I couldn't stay away. I have to know what's happened to her, and she was so sick, so feverish, I should have known better than to leave her.' Then Emma saw me. 'Bart! You wicked little boy. How dare you add to your father's worries by disappearing too. You are a bad boy, and I'll bet my life you know something about where your mother is!'

Both old women glared at me. Hating me with their mean eyes. I ran. Ran from knowing soon I'd be crying and I couldn't let anybody see me cry – now that I had to act just like Malcolm – the heartless.

THE SEARCH *Jory*

The night was not fit for man nor beast. It was raining like Noah was building his ark. The wind howled and shrieked and was trying to tell us something, like wild music that would destroy your brain. I kept pace with Dad, though that wasn't easy since I'd yet to grow legs as long as his. His hands were balled into fists. I fisted mine too, ready to do battle with him when the need arose.

'Jory,' said Dad, striding on without pausing, 'how often does Bart come over here?' We'd reached the black iron gates by this time, then he leaned to speak into the box which sent his voice into the house.

'I don't know,' I said miserably. 'Bart used to trust me, now he doesn't trust anybody, so he doesn't tell me what he does any more.'

Slowly, slowly, the black gates swung open. They seemed like black skeleton hands welcoming us into our graves. I shivered, thinking I was getting as morbid as Bart. I had to run then to keep up with Dad. 'I've got to say something,' I yelled so I could be heard above the wind, 'when I first found out you are Mom's brother and our own uncle, I thought I hated you and her too. I thought I could never forgive either one of you for making me ashamed, so disappointed. I thought I'd dry up inside and never love or trust anyone again. But now that Mom's gone I know I'll always love her and you. I can't hate either one of you, even if I want to.'

In the hard driving rain, in the dark, he turned to clasp me against his chest, his hand pressing my head against his heart. I think I heard him sob. 'Jory, you don't know how much I've longed to hear you say you don't hate me or your mother. I always hoped you'd understand when we told you – and we were going to tell you when you were older. We thought, perhaps foolishly, that we needed to wait a few more years, but now that you have found out on your own, and you can still love us, maybe later on you will come to understand.'

I drew closer to Dad as we continued on our way to the shadowy mansion. I felt a new kinship had developed between us that was stronger than what we'd had before. In a way he was more my father, because he had much of my own kind of blood. Blood of my blood, I thought, my own uncle and Bart's, though I'd always thought he was Bart's uncle, and that had made me a little jealous, now I could lay claim to him too. But why hadn't they realized I was mature for my age, and I would have understood when they told me Mom had an affair with Bart's father . . . I would have . . . I think.

We reached the steps. Before Dad could bang on the door-knocker the left side of the double doors swung open and there stood that butler, John Amos Jackson. 'I'm packing,' he said by way of greeting, scowled up and ugly looking, 'and my wife has gone to Hawaii. I have a million things to take care of here without entertaining the neighbours. I plan to join her as soon as I'm done here.'

'Your wife?' bellowed Dad, his astonishment so clear it slapped me too.

Something smug came and went in the butler's watery eyes. 'Yes, Dr Christopher Sheffield, Mrs Winslow is now married to me.'

I thought Dad would fall with shock. 'I want to see her. And I don't believe that. She'd be out of her mind to marry you.'

'I don't lie,' said that grim ugly butler. 'And she is out of her mind. Some women can't live without a man to run their affairs, and that's what I am – someone to lean on.'

'I don't believe you,' stormed my Dad. 'Where is she? Where is my wife? Have you seen her?'

The butler smiled. 'Your wife, sir? I have enough to do

keeping up with my own wife without looking out for yours. Yesterday my wife railed about this terrible weather and took off with one of our maids. She told me to join her later, after I'd arranged to close up this house. And after all the trouble and expense she went to having this place redecorated and refurbished – now she wants to move.'

Dad stood staring at John Amos Jackson. I thought we'd leave then but Dad seemed rooted. 'You know who I am, don't you, John? Don't deny it. I see it in your eyes. You are the butler who made love to the maid Livvy while I lay on the floor behind the sofa and heard you tell her about the arsenic on the sugared doughnuts meant to kill the attic mice.'

'I don't know what you're talking about,' denied the butler, while I looked from him back to Dad. Oh, I should have finished every page of Mom's manuscript. Things were even more complicated than I'd realized.

'John, perhaps you are married to my mother and perhaps you are lying. Regardless, I think you know what has happened to my wife, and now I'm concerned about my mother as well. So, get out of my way, I'm going to search this house from top to bottom.'

The butler paled. 'You can't come over here and tell me what to do,' he muttered indistinctly, 'I could call the police . . .'

'But you won't, and if you want to, go ahead, call them. I am going to search now, John. There's nothing you can do to stop me.'

The old butler shuffled away, shrugging helplessly. 'Go on then, have your way, but you won't find anything.'

Together Dad and I searched. I knew the house much better than he did, all the cupboards, the secret places. Dad kept saying the attic was where they would be. But when we were up there and looking, there was nothing but junk and dusty clutter.

Again we returned to the parlour where the woman he called

mother had her hard wooden rocker which I sat in and found quite uncomfortable. Restlessly Dad prowled the room, then paused in the archway that led to the adjacent room, that parlour where the huge oil portrait hung. 'If Cathy came over here she would have seen that, and she could have come if Bart told her something.'

Rocking back and forth in the chair, I made it walk a little closer to the fire that was guttering out. Something crunched beneath one of the rockers. Dad heard the sound and bent to pick up an object. It was a pearl.

He tested it between his teeth and smiled bitterly. 'My mother's string of pearls with a butterfly clasp. She had always worn them, just as our grandmother always wore her diamond brooch. I don't believe my mother would go anywhere without those pearls.'

Another hour of searching the house, and questioning the Mexican maid and cook who did not understand English very well, and both he and I were frustrated. 'I'll be back, John Amos Jackson,' said Dad as he opened the front door, 'and the next time I'll have the police with me.'

'Have it your way, Doctor,' said John the butler with a tight malicious smile.

'Dad – we can't notify the police – can we?'

'We will if we have to. But let's wait at least until tomorrow. He wouldn't dare harm your mother or my mother, or he'd land behind bars.'

'Dad, I'll bet Bart knows what is going on. He and John Amos are very thick.'

I explained then how Bart was always talking to himself whenever he believed he was alone. He talked in his sleep too, and when he stalked around playing pretend games. It seemed the most important part of Bart's life was spent alone, talking to himself.

'All right, Jory, I understand what you're saying. I have an idea I hope works. This may well be the most important part you've ever played, so pay attention. Tomorrow morning you are

only to pretend you go to school. I'll let you out as soon as we turn the corner on to the highway. You run back home and make sure Bart doesn't see you. I'll try to fnd out if my mother really flew to Hawaii, and if she really married that horrible old man.'

WHISPERING VOICES *Bart*

Questions, questions, all they did was ask me questions.

Didn't know nothing, nothing. Wasn't guilty, wasn't. Why ask me? Crazy kids didn't give straight answers. 'Momma's gone 'cause she always hated me even when I was a little baby.'

That night whores, harlots and strumpets came to dance in my head. Woke up. Heard the rain beating on the roof. Why didn't the rain stop?

I fell asleep again and dreamed I was like Aunt Carrie who didn't grow tall enough. Dreamed I prayed and prayed and one day God let me grow so tall my head touched the sky. Looked down and saw all the little people running around like ants, afraid of me. I laughed and stepped on the ocean, making tidal waves rise up and wash over the tall cities. More pipsqueak screams. All the people I didn't squash were drowned. Sat in the ocean then that came to my waist and cried. My tears were so huge they made the ocean rise up again – and all I could see all around me was my reflection, and how handsome I was now. Now that there wasn't a girl or woman left alive to love and admire me, I was handsome, tall and strong.

I told John Amos about my dreams. He nodded his head and told me he used to dream when he was young about girls and how much he could love them, if only they wouldn't see how long his nose was. 'I had other attributes I couldn't show them, but they never gave me a chance, never a chance.'

Next morning Jory left with Daddy. Easy to slip away from Emma and Madame Marisha, for they had to fool around with Cindy so much. Dratted Cindy.

But it gave me the chance to steal into the mansion next door. I sneaked around to find John Amos. He was packing all the beautiful lamps, paintings and other valuables in boxes. 'The silver should be wrapped in tarnishproof papers,' he said to one of the maids, 'and be careful with that china and crystal. When the movers show up have them put in the best furniture first, for I may be busy elsewhere.'

The prettiest maid was young, and she frowned. 'Mr Jackson, why we go? Thought Madame liked it here. She never say we moving.'

'Your mistress is a woman of changing moods – it's that nutty boy next door. That little one who keeps coming over here. He's gotten to be a real nuisance. He killed the dog she gave him. I suppose none of you know that?'

I stared in the room and saw the maid's lips part in horror. 'No . . . thought dog went over to boy's home . . .'

'The brat is dangerous! That's why Madame has to move – he's threatened her life more than one time. He's under the care of a psychiatrist.'

They looked from one to the other and made circles above their heads. Mad! Mad as hell at John Amos, telling lies about me.

I waited until he was alone, sitting at the fancy desk where my grandmother kept her chequebook. He jumped when I came in. 'Bart, I wish you wouldn't sneak around like that. Make some noise when you enter, clear your throat, cough . . . do something to announce you are there.'

'I heard what you told the maids . . . I'm not crazy!'

'Of course you're not,' he said, his S's hissing as always. 'But I do have to tell them something, don't I? Otherwise they might become suspicious. As it is, they think your grandmother has gone on a trip to Hawaii . . .'

I felt sick inside, standing there, balancing on my sneakers, and staring down at them. 'John Amos . . . can I give my Momma and granny sandwiches to eat today?'

'No. They can't be hungry already.'

Knew he would say that.

He forgot me then. He was reading over her bank books, her savings accounts, her receipts . . . giggling to himself. He found a little key and opened a tiny drawer way back behind another door. 'Stupid woman, thought I didn't notice where she hid her key . . .'

I left him having his fun with my granny's things, and I stole down to where my caged mice were. Made me feel better to think of them as only mice.

My Momma was groaning, half crying from the cold, and as I peeked inside, I saw they had the little stub of candle lit. I'd shoved in the candle along with some matches so I could see what they were doing. Momma looked little and white, and still my granny held her head in her lap, and wiped her face with a rag she must have torn from her slip for it had lace on one ragged edge.

'Cathy my love, my only daughter left, please listen to me. I have to speak now for I may never have another chance. Yes, I made mistakes. Yes, I allowed my father to torment me until I didn't know right from wrong, or which way to turn. Yes, I put arsenic on your sugared doughnuts thinking each one of you would get only a little sick, then I could slip you out one by one. I didn't want one of you to die. I swear I loved you, all four. I carried Cory out to my car where he breathed his last breath just as I laid him on the back seat and covered him with two blankets. I panicked. I didn't know what to do. I couldn't go to the police, and I was so ashamed, so guilty.'

She shook my mother, while I trembled too.

'Cathy, my daughter, please wake up and listen,' she pleaded. Momma had awakened from the shaking and seemed to be trying to focus her eyes. 'Darling, I don't think Bart killed the dog I gave him. He loved Apple. I think John did that hoping Bart would be blamed and considered crazy and dangerous so the police would put the blame on Bart when you and I disappeared. I think John strangled Jory's little pet poodle too, and killed my kitten as well.'

'Bart is a very lonely, confused little boy, Cathy, but he's not dangerous. He likes to pretend he is, and in that way he can feel like he's going to be a powerful man. But it's John who is dangerous. He hates me. I didn't know until a few years ago that if I hadn't returned to Foxworth Hall after your father died, John would have inherited all the Foxworth fortune. My father trusted John as he trusted no one else, perhaps because they were so much alike. But when I came back, he forgot John. He wrote John out of his will and put me back in as his sole heir. Cathy, are you listening?'

'Momma, is that you, Momma?' asked my mother in a small voice that sounded like a child in trouble. 'Momma, why don't you look at the twins when you come in to see us? Why don't you notice that they don't grow as they should? Are you deliberately not seeing – just ignoring them so you won't feel guilty and ashamed?'

'Oh, Cathy!' cried Grandmother, 'if only you knew how much it hurts to hear you say those things after all these years. Did I hurt you so deeply you can never heal, you and Chris too? It's no wonder you and your brother – I'm sorry, so sorry I could die.' But in a moment or so she pulled herself together and went on with a desperate urgency.

'Even if you are delirious and can't fully understand now, I must speak, or I may not live to tell you everything. When John Amos was a young man, about twenty-five, he lusted after me, though I was only ten. He'd hide in corners and spy on me, then hurry to my father and make the worst of innocent deeds on my part. I couldn't tell my parents that John told lies for they never believed me – they believed him. They refused to recognize a young girl is often preyed upon by older men, even older relatives. John was third cousin to my mother, the only member of her family my father could stand. I think my father put it in his head after my two older brothers died, that if ever I fell out of his favour, John would benefit. That was my father's way of extracting the most out of everyone – dangling his sugar-plums that would vanish when reached for.'

'John wanted my mother's wealth too. They encouraged him to think he might inherit. They thought him a saint. He wore a pious look all the time, he acted godly, and all the while he was seducing every pretty young maid who ever came into Foxworth

Hall. And my parents never suspected. They couldn't see any evil but what their children did. Can you understand now why John hates me? Why he hated my children too? He would have been the beneficiary if I had stayed in Gladstone.'

'One day I heard him in the back hall whispering to Bart, your son, that I used my feminine wiles to cajole my father into disinheriting the only man who was his friend, his best confidant.'

Grandmother began to cry then. I shrivelled up tight, hurting deep inside from all I was finding out. Malcolm, were you evil too? Who was I to trust now? Which way should I turn? Was John Amos just as conniving with his masculine wiles as my granny was with her feminine ones? Was everybody just as wicked as my granny and Momma? Was God on my side, on her side, or John's?

'Momma, are you still there, Momma?'

'Yes, darling, I'm still here. I'll stay and take care of you as I never took care of you before. This time I'll be the mother I should have been before. This time I'll save you and Chris.'

'Who are you?' demanded my mother, bolting up again and shoving my grandmother away. 'Oh!' she screamed, 'It's you! You weren't satisfied just to kill Cory and Carrie, now you've come back to kill me too. Then you'll have Chris all to yourself, all yours, all yours,' she broke then and cried, then she began to scream like she was crazy, shrieking out over and over again how much she hated her mother. '*Why don't you die, Corrine Foxworth – why don't you?*'

I went away. Couldn't stand any more of that. They were both evil. But why was this hurting so much?

DETECTIVE *Jory*

Just as Dad and I had planned, early the next morning Dad drove me off towards school, then he let me out on the road that led to our house. 'Now take it easy, Jory. Don't do anything that will endanger your life, and don't let Bart or that butler know what you're up to – they could be dangerous, remember that.' He hugged me close, as if afraid I might be foolhardy. 'Listen carefully to me now. I'm going to see Bart's psychiatrist this morning so I can tell him what has happened. Then I'm checking the airports to see if my mother has flown anywhere though God knows that's not likely. But for both women to disappear on the same day is just too much of a coincidence.'

I had to say it. As much as I dreaded hearing the words come from my own lips, I had to speak. 'Dad, have you considered that Bart might have . . . well, you know. Clover was strangled with wire. Apple was starved and then stabbed with a pitchfork. Who knows what he might do next?'

He patted my shoulder. 'Yes, of course I've thought of that. But I can't picture Bart managing to overcome your mother. She's very strong even if she does have a cold. That's what worries me most, Jory. She had a temperature of one hundred, and fevers do make a person weaker. I should have stayed home to take care of her. How did she ever convince me she could handle Bart and Cindy while Emma enjoyed her day off? A woman is a fool to marry a doctor,' he concluded bitterly, as if he'd forgotten I was there. And all the while his motor was purring softly. He bowed his head down on his hands that held the steering wheel.

'Dad . . . you go on and do what you can to check the airlines. I'll handle everything here.' And I added with a big burst of over-confidence, 'And remember – Madame M is here. And you know how she is. Bart won't pull anything with her around.'

Smiling, as if I'd given him the assurance he needed, he waved goodbye and drove off, leaving me standing there and wondering just what to do. The fierce rain of yesterday had dwindled down to a slow drizzle that was miserable and cold, but not wild.

Home again, and I was hiding behind the shrubbery all wet and dripping, as Bart sat in the kitchen and refused to eat his breakfast. 'Hate everything you cook!' he said sullenly. It was surprising to hear his voice coming to me so clearly. Then I smiled, not feeling spooked as I had before. It was the inter-com system, left on. Often delivery men came to our back door rather than use the special drive that circled the front. Our breakfast nook wasn't too far from the panel on the wall with dozens of buttons. I remembered when our house was being constructed how Mom had wanted music in every room – so housework wouldn't seem such a bore. Then came Madame's strident voice, 'Bart, what's wrong with your cereal?'

'Don't like cereal with raisins.'

'Then don't eat the raisins.'

'They get in the way.

'Nonsense. If you don't eat breakfast, then you won't eat lunch either. And if you don't eat lunch, there will be no dinner – and one ten-year-old boy is going to bed very hungry!'

'You can't starve me to death!' Bart shrieked. 'This is my house! You don't belong here! You get out!'

'I will not get out. I am staying until your mother returns safely. And don't you dare raise your voice to me again or I might turn you over my knee and paddle your behind until you scream for mercy.'

'It won't hurt,' he jeered – and it wouldn't. Spankings never bothered Bart who had skin made of leather, with no surface nerve endings.

'Thank you for telling me,' said Madame with great aplomb. 'I will then think of a better punishment – such as keeping you indoors, locked in your room.'

By this time I was peering in a window. There sat Bart with a secret smile on his face.

'Emma,' ordered Madame, 'take Bart's plate away, take his bowl, his orange juice too. Bart – go straight to your room and don't let me hear another word out of you until you can come to this table and eat your meals without complaints.'

'Witch, old black witch come to live in our house,' Bart chanted as he ambled away. But he didn't go to his room. He bolted out of the garage door when Madame wasn't looking, and from there he headed towards the garden wall, and the old oak tree he could climb to take him over the wall.

I ran as fast as I could, following him. But once I was inside the mansion I lost sight of him. Where had Bart gone? I stared right and left, looked behind me, turned around slowly. Had he disappeared up the stairs or down into the cellar? I hated this house with its maze of long corridors, with so many niches between the walls where Mom could be hidden. Usually a builder used the left-over spaces to make cupboards or put in shelves. But this one, I knew for a fact, had secret doors, only I'd already searched all the secret rooms. Useless to look in them again.

Suddenly I heard a footfall. Bart was right behind me. He looked right through me, his eyes glazed as he stared bleakly at nothing. I couldn't believe he didn't see me.

I followed silently, believing he'd take me to where Mom and her mother were hidden. But, he headed for home. Sickened, disheartened, I trailed along behind, feeling I'd betrayed my father and failed him.

Lunchtime and Dad came home tired and distressed-looking. 'Any luck, Jory?'

'No. How about you?'

'None. My mother did not fly to Hawaii. I checked with all the airlines. Jory, both Cathy and my mother must be inside that house next door.'

I had an idea. 'Dad, why don't you have a long talk with Bart? Don't jump on him, or condemn him, just say nice things. Praise him for being nice to Cindy, tell him how much you care about him. I know he's behind this for he keeps mumbling about the Lord and being His dark angel of revenge.'

Dad couldn't find any words to say as he digested my information. Then silently, he set off to find Bart and do what he could to make an unwanted little boy feel needed – if it wasn't already too late.

THE LAST MEAL *Bart*

Later I went down to the cellar again with John Amos. 'Corrine,' John Amos called softly as he bent over stiffly. Clumsy as me, he got down on his knees and peered through the small kitty-door he opened. 'I want you and your daughter to know this is your last meal, so I made it a good one.' He lifted the lid of the silver teapot and spat inside, then poured the steaming hot liquid into fine china cups. 'One for you, one for your daughter,' he said. He shoved one cup and saucer inside the kitty-door, then the other set. Next he picked up a plate of sandwiches which looked stale and kind of dirty, then managed to drop the plate on the filthy cellar floor.

He picked up the little triangles and wiped them off against his trouser leg, shoved the meat that had fallen out back in, then put the plate of coal-dusted food in through the kitty-door. 'Here you are, Corrine Foxworth,' snarled John Amos in his hissy voice. 'I hope you find these dainty sandwiches to your liking, you bitch! I took your word when you married me, truly believing you'd be my wife – and though you have never been my wife in the way I'd hoped, still I will inherit what is rightfully mine. Finally I have managed to destroy you and yours – just as Malcolm wanted to kill all your Devil's issue.'

Did he have to hate my granny so much? Maybe she wasn't to blame, like me who sometimes did bad things and couldn't help it. Why was everybody doing bad things to everybody else and calling the excuse inheritance?

'You flaunted your beauty before me!' screamed out an enraged old man, 'tormenting me when you were a child – teasing me when you were an adolescent, thinking you could have your fun and I could never harm you. Then when you married your half-uncle and came back to disinherit me, you treated me like I wasn't even there – just another piece of furniture to be ignored.

'Well, are you arrogant now, Corrine Foxworth? Do you feel haughty sitting in your own filth, holding your dying daughter's head on your filthy lap? I have made you crawl at last, haven't I? I have beaten you at your own game, stolen Bart's affection from you, made him mistrust you and trust me. You can't use your charm and feminine wiles now. It's too late. I hate you now, Corrine Foxworth. For every woman I have fantasized was you, I have paid, but no longer. I have won and though I am seventy-three now, I will live on at least another five or six years in luxury enough to make up for all the years I've suffered at your hands.'

My grandmother was sobbing quietly. I was crying too, wondering again who was right, him or her?

Was I born mixed-up and scowling, knowing even when I was a baby that this was ahead of me? That sounded like Jory. Was I a little like Jory after all? For some reason that made me feel a little better. But still I didn't know how to unravel what was going on.

John Amos was saying terrible things. Nasty evil bad words that little boys wrote on bathroom walls. Grown-up old men shouldn't talk like that, and in front of my grandmother and my Momma.

'John!' yelled Grandmother, 'haven't you done enough? Let us out, and I'll be your wife in the way you want, but please do not punish my daughter more. She's very sick. She needs to be in a hospital. The police will call this murder if you let her die and me too.'

John Amos just laughed and walked heavily back up the stairs.

But I couldn't move. I was frozen, so confused I didn't know who was good and who was bad.

'Bart!' screamed my grandmother suddenly, 'run fast to your father and tell him where we are. Run, run!'

Bleary-eyed, I just stood there. Didn't know what to do. 'Please, Bart,' she begged. 'Go tell you father where we are.'

Malcolm . . . was that him over in the corner, his ghost face frowning at me? Passed my smutty hand over my blurry eyes.

Dark, so dark. I pretended to leave, but I snuck back. I wanted to hear more of the truth.

Out of the darkness came my mother's thin voice screaming at that old woman who was her mother, my grandmother.

'Oh, yes, Mother. I understood everything you said. We didn't stand a chance no matter who died and who didn't die when you took us into Foxworth Hall and locked us away. Now, years later, we will die just because that crazy old butler didn't inherit the money he expected, promised to him years ago by a dead man – and if you believe any of that – you are just as crazy as he is.'

'Cathy. Don't deny the truth because you hate me so much. I'm telling you the truth. Can't you see how John has used your son, the son of my Bart. Don't you see how perfect his revenge is – to use the son of the man he hated, the man he felt took his place, when it could have been him who married me if my father could have forced me to do it? Oh, you don't know how Father tried to make me see I owed it to John to marry him, and allow him to have half of his fortune – he didn't guess, or maybe he did, that John wanted it all.

'And when you and I die, it won't be John who is found guilty – it will be Bart! It's John who killed Clover, then Apple. It's John who dreams of having Malcolm's power, Malcolm's wealth. It's not my imagination – I hear him mumbling to himself incessantly.'

'Like Bart,' mumbled Momma, so funny-sounding. 'Bart's always pretending he's old and feeble, but powerful and rich. Poor Bart. What about Jory – has he got Jory? Where is Jory?'

Why did she pity me and not Jory? Got up and left..

Was I crazy too – like him? Was I a killer at heart – like him? Didn't know nothing about myself I was foggy-minded, hazy-seeing, but I did manage to move my heavy legs and somehow I climbed up all those old stairs to reach the outside.

He was the only father I could remember well, and I loved him even more in that relationship. He held out his hand and told me what we had to do, and I followed, as I would have followed blindly anywhere he led. For out of every terrible situation something good had to come, and I knew now how much he meant to me.

With Dad leading the way, we went once more to the house next door. We hadn't seen Bart all afternoon. How stupid of me to let him outsmart me, and sneak away when I had my head turned, watching some cute thing Cindy did as she tried to dance like me.

Mom had been missing a full twenty-four hours.

That old butler let us in, standing back to scowl at us. 'My mother has not flown to Hawaii,' stated Dad, his blue eyes hard and cold..

'So? She is not an organized woman. She may have gone on to visit friends during the holidays. She has no friends here.'

'You smoke expensive cigarettes,' said my father dryly. 'I remember that night when I was seventeen lying behind the sofa while you and Livvy the maid were there . . . and you smoked the same cigarettes – Turkish?'

'Right,' said John Amos Jackson with a sneering grin. 'Old Malcolm Neal Foxworth's tastes gave me the habit . . .'

'You pattern yourself after my grandfather, don't you?'

'Do I?'

'Yes, I believe you do. When I checked this house the last time I opened a closet full of expensive men's clothes – yours?'

'I am married to Corrine Foxworth. She is my wife.'

'How did you blackmail her to marry you?'

Again the old man smiled. 'Some women have to have a man in

the house or they don't feel safe. She married me for a companion. As you can see, she treats me like a servant still.'

'I think not,' said my father with his narrowed eyes sweeping over the butler who was wearing a new suit. 'I think you were thinking of your future when, or if, my mother should die.'

'How interesting,' replied John Amos Jackson, grinding out his stub of quickly smoked cigarette. 'I've made my departure plans. I'm flying back to Virginia where I expect my wife will join me when she becomes tiresome to her hosts. Her daughter ruined her socially in Virginia years ago, which you must know, but still she will go there.'

'Why?'

John Amos Jackson grinned widely. 'She is having Foxworth Hall reconstructed, Dr Sheffield. From out of the ashes, Foxworth Hall shall rise again – like the fabled phoenix!'

Dad faltered, still staring at the cigarette dribbling faint smoke. 'Foxworth Hall,' he said in a haunted voice, 'how far along is it?'

'Almost finished,' answered John Amos Jackson smugly. 'Soon I shall reign as king where Malcolm ruled, and his arrogant beautiful daughter will reign at my side.' He laughed crazily, seeming to enjoy my father's discomfort. 'She'll have her facial scars reconstructed, her face lifted again. She'll colour her hair and make it blonde again, and she'll sit at the foot of my dining-table. Behind me will stand one of my own cousins, where I used to stand. It will all be as it was before.'

Wheels were churning in Dad's head. 'You will never rule anywhere but in prison,' he said before he turned and left.

'Dad,' I said when we were home, 'did you believe what that butler told us? Do you think he has Mom and your mother locked up somewhere?'

'I don't know yet. I do know he's cleverer than I thought. When I was a boy in Foxworth Hall looking down on his bald head, I never suspected he had any power. He seemed just another servant. However, I can see now he laid his plan a long time ago and is now fulfilling his schedule for revenge.'

'For revenge . . . ?'

'Jory, can't you see that man is insane? You have told me that Bart imitates a man he calls Malcolm who has been dead for years. But the man Bart is really imitating is John Amos Jackson who is himself imitating my grandfather Malcolm Foxworth, dead and gone, but still influencing our lives.'

'How do you know? Did you ever see your grandfather?'

'I saw him one time only, Jory,' he said in a sad reflective way. 'I was fourteen, your age. Your mother and I hid in a huge chest on the second floor and looked down in the ballroom, and Malcolm Foxworth was in a wheelchair. He was a far distance away, and I never heard his voice. But our mother used to come to us with descriptions of how he talked about sin and hell, quoting from the Bible, talking about Hell and Judgement Day.'

Night came. We turned on all the lights hoping that would light Mom home and Bart too. Emma and Madame put Cindy to bed early. Emma went from Cindy's room back into the kitchen, but Madame came into the family room and slouched in a chair across from Dad. Bart came in the door and crouched down in a corner.

'Where have you been so long?' asked Dad, sitting up straighter and fixing Bart with a strange long look. Madame M riveted her dark ebony eyes on Bart too. Bart ignored them, and continued to make shadow pictures on the wall by holding his hands in contorted positions.

The TV set behind me was turned on though no one was watching. A choir of boys were singing Christmas carols. I felt exhausted from trying to follow Bart around all day, exhausted more from worrying about Mom, to say nothing about what would happen to all of us . . .

I decided I had to escape by going to bed, and rose to say goodnight, but Madame put her finger before her lips and gestured to Dad so he too would pay attention to what Bart was muttering to himself as he made the eerie picture of an old man talking to a child.

'Bad things happen to those who defy the laws of God,' he

crooned in a hypnotic way. 'Bad people who don't go to church on Sundays, who don't take their children, who commit incestuous acts, will all go to hell and burn over the everlasting fires as demons torment their eternal souls. Bad people can be redeemed only by fire, saved from hell and the Devil and his pitchfork only by fire, fire.'

Weird, really weird.

Dad could control his impatience and rage no longer. 'Bart! Who told you all that hocus-pocus?'

My brother jerked upright, his dark brown eyes went blank. 'Speak when spoken to, said the wise man to the innocent child. The child says in return, unholy people who commit sins will come to a fiery end.'

'Who told you that?'

'Old man from his grave. Old man likes me better than Jory who does sinful dancing. Old man hates dancers. Old man says only I am fit to rule in his place.'

Crap! I thought, but Dad was listening intently. I was remembering what Bart's shrink had advised. 'Play along with the boy, pretend to believe everything he says, no matter how ridiculous. Remember he's only ten and at that age a child can believe in almost anything, so let him express himself in the only safe way he's found so far. When the old man speaks, you are hearing your son speaking of what bothers him most.'

'Bart,' said Dad, 'listen to me carefully. If your mother didn't know how to swim, and she was drowning, and I was there but looking the other way – would you tell me so I could jump in and save her?'

Any son should have said yes immediately, but Bart considered this heavily, frowning, weighing his answer when it should have come spontaneously.

Finally he answered. 'You wouldn't have to do anything to save Momma from drowning, Daddy, if Momma was pure and without sin. God would save her.'

JUDGEMENT DAY *Bart*

Nobody understood me and what I was trying to do. Wasn't no good trying to explain. Had to do it all on my own. I slipped away from Daddy, from Jory, from all those people who saw me as bad and unnecessary in their lives. I had come, and I could go, and it would make no difference to anyone. They didn't know I was trying to help right all the wrongs they'd done before I was even born, and all those done after I was born.

Sin. The world was full of sin and sinners.

Wasn't my fault if Momma had to be punished. Though it did worry me some why God didn't want Daddy included in the punishment.

John Amos had told me that men were meant for better things. Heroic things like going off to war and doing brave deeds. No matter if legs and arms were lost, it was a far, far better way to suffer than what God had in mind for women.

I got to thinking hard on the subject. What if the pearly gates of heaven didn't open to receive my Momma's purified soul? 'Go forth and sin no more,' I'd say if I were God. I stamped my golden staff on heaven's golden floor, and struck a huge boulder far below so it split wide open and I could write on it my twenty Commandments. (Ten weren't enough.) Wonder how I could split open the Pacific and let all the righteous escape the heathens that were fast on their heels?

Gee, thinking like this made me feel bad in my head, in my legs, and it made my hands and feet cold. Momma, why did you have to be so bad? Why did you have to go and live with your brother and put the burden of your death on me?

Jory was outside my door. Spying on me. I knew it was him. Was always him sneaking around, trying to find out what I was up to. I'd ignore him and concentrate on my Momma's last hours. She and Grandmother oughta have good food for their last meal. Been told by someone every prisoner had her favourite meal before the end. Had to do right by my Momma and grandmother. What did they like to eat most? I liked sandwiches best, so maybe they did too. Sandwiches, pie and ice-cream should be just fine. Just as soon as everyone was in bed, I'd slip their last meal over to them.

Black night came. All the lights were turned off. Soon everything was very, very quiet. What was that? Was it snoring I heard across the hall, in the guest room next to Jory's room? Old Madame Marisha snored. Disgusting.

I slapped turkey between slabs of Emma's home-made cheese bread. With two slices of cherry pie and a quart of ice-cream in my sack, I made my way to the white whale of a house, moving as quiet as a mouse.

Down, down, down all the steep stairs into the cellar where rats, mice and spiders roamed, and two women were moaning and groaning and calling for me. Made me feel important. I lifted the kitty-door that was under the wine shelves and shoved in the sack with all the goodies.

The light from the candle stub I'd given them was very dim, flickering, showing pale forms that didn't seem solid at all. My grandmother was trying to calm my mother who raged on and on: 'Take your hands off me, Mrs Winslow. For a while I felt like a child again, and I was glad you were with me in the dark, but now I remember. How much are you paying that butler to do this to me? Why are you here?'

'Cathy, Cathy, John hit me over the head, just like he did you. He hates me too. Didn't you hear all I explained?'

'Yes, I heard. It was like a bad dream, all the same things Chris used to say to me, trying to explain why you acted as you did. Oh, you do have a champion in your son. Even though he pretends to hate you, underneath it all, I've always known he still loved you, despite all you did. He kept a little of his faith in you . . . but he's stupid in his loyalty to women. First you, now me.'

I was glad I knew so many big words, so some day I could

write in my own journal and tell everyone how I saved my Momma from hellfires.

Straw was in her golden hair which wasn't so pretty now. Same old straw that once was in the barn where Apple stayed. They hadn't even thanked me for making their prison softer and warmer with that hay – had shoved it all in while they were both sleeping.

'Cathy, don't you really love your brother? Have you just used him?'

My Momma seemed almost crazy as she struck out at my grandmother. 'Yes, I love him! You made me love him. It was your fault and now we have to live ashamed and guilty, afraid any day our children will find out, and now they have because of you!'

'Because of John,' whispered Grandmother. 'I only came here to help, to be near you, to share just a little in your lives. But stop feeling guilty, make it my shame and my guilt. I accept it as mine, all mine, for you are right. You have always been right in your judgement of me, Cathy. I'm weak, foolish, and manage always to make the wrong decisions. I think they're right when I make them, but never do they prove anything but wrong.'

Momma quieted down. She sank back on her heels and stared at her mother. 'Your face, why did you dig at your face?'

My grandmother bowed her head. She seemed to have aged ten years in one long long day. 'I wanted to die after Bart died. I wanted to destroy my beauty so no man would ever want me again. I didn't want to look in a mirror and see you staring back at me, for I hated you too for a long time. It was Chris, who came each summer and talked to me about you, who made me see your side of your affair with my husband. He told me you really loved Bart, that you should have had Bart's child aborted for your own health, but you wouldn't have it done. You wanted to keep his baby. Cathy, thank you for doing that. Thank you for giving me another Bart, for he is mine as Jory will never be.'

They both loved me. Momma had risked her health to give me

life. Grandmother had stopped hating Momma on account of me. I wasn't nearly as bad as I thought.

'Cathy, please say you forgive me,' pleaded my granny. 'Say it, please say it at least once. I need so to hear you say it. It was Christopher who loved me, who defended me, but it was you who kept me awake at nights, tormenting me even on my honeymoon with Bart – it is your face, the faces of the twins that haunt me still. Christopher will always be mine – and yours, but give me back my daughter.'

My mother screamed. Loud, fierce, crazy, she screamed over and over. She lunged at my grandmother and pounded her with her fists. 'No! I can never say what you want!" She knocked the candle and it turned over and the hay caught fire. Old newspapers they'd used to keep warm soon were ablaze, and my grandmother and mother were beating at the flames with their bare hands, trying to put them out.

'Bart!' screamed my grandmother, 'if you're out there listening to us, run for help. Call the fire department! Tell your father! Do something quick, Bart, or your mother will die in this blaze – and God will never forgive you if you help John Amos kill us!'

What? Was I helping John Amos or God?

I ran like mad up the cellar stairs and out into the garage where John Amos was putting his bags in the last one of the black limousines. The other was gone, driving the maids to safety.

He slammed down the trunk of the car, turned to me with a wide grin, and said, 'Well, tonight is the night. At twelve o'clock sharp – remember that – trip slowly down the stairs and into their place and light the string – '

'That smelly string?'

'Yes. It's soaked in gasoline.'

'I didn't like the smell, so I threw it away. Didn't want their last meal to be eaten in a smelly place.'

'What are you talking about? Have you been feeding them?' He whirled as if to hit me and then out of nowhere Jory sprang upon John Amos. The old man fell on his back, with Jory astride, and then Daddy raced into the garage.

'Bart, we watched you make sandwiches and take the ice-cream – now where are your mother and your grandmother?'

Didn't know what to do.

'Dad!' yelled Jory, 'I smell smoke!'

'Where are they, Bart?'

John Amos yelled out at Daddy, 'Take that crazy kid away from here – him and his matches! He's started a fire. Him and his crazy stunts, like killing that dear little puppy who loved him so much. It's no wonder Corrine panicked and ran without telling me where she was going.' He cried real tears and swiped at his runny nose, 'Oh, God . . . I wish to heaven we'd never come here to live. I told Corrine no good would come of this.'

Lies. He was telling lies on me. Wasn't none of that true.

'You did it all! You are the crazy man, John Amos!' and like Malcolm would, I ran over to kick at him. 'Die, John Amos! Die and be redeemed through death!'

My arms were caught and I was lifted away and Daddy had me in his arms and was trying to calm me. 'Your mother . . . where is your mother? Where is the fire?'

A red haze was in my eyes, but I reached in my pants pocket and gave him the key. 'In the wine cellar,' I said dully, 'waiting for the fire to end them like they ended Foxworth Hall. Malcolm wanted it that way. All the little attic mice to burn and stop reproducing contaminated seed.'

Far away from my body I was standing, watching the stunned amazement in Daddy's eyes as he tried to delve my eyes . . . but I knew they were blank – for I wasn't there. Didn't know where I was. Didn't care.

REDEMPTION *Jory*

Fire. The mansion was on fire.

I straddled John Amos who fought me off – or tried to, but soon he knew who had the best of the battle. 'Yoe can't get away, old man. You've poisoned my brother's mind, made him think awful things. I hope to God you rot in some jail cell for the rest of your life for what you've done.'

While John Amos and I were struggling, Dad sped off to find Mom and his mother, with Bart at his heels screaming out how he could get to the wine cellar.

'Get off me, boy!' yelled John Amos Jackson. 'That brother of yours is crazy – dangerous. He starved that poor puppy then stabbed him with a pitchfork. Is that the act of a sane child?'

'Why didn't you stop him if you saw him do all that?'

'Why, why . . .' sputtered the old man, 'he would have turned on me like a wild beast. The boy is insane like his grandmother. Why, it was my own wife who saw him dig up the skeleton of her pet kitten. Ask her, go on, ask her.'

Some of what he said was getting to me. Bart was irrational. Yet, yet . . . was he a killer? 'Bart talks in his sleep, old man. He repeats everything he hears during the day like a parrot. He quotes from the Bible and pronounces words he wouldn't be able to if someone like you wasn't coaching him.'

'You fool boy! He doesn't know who he is! Can't you see that? He thinks he is his great-grandfather Malcolm Foxworth . . . And like Malcolm he's driven to kill every last living member of the Foxworth clan!'

At that moment I saw my father stumble into the garage carrying my mother in his arms, with the old woman in rags, his mother, following behind. I jumped up and ran over.

'Mom, oh Mom!' I cried, overjoyed to see she was still alive.

But she looked dreadful, dirty, pale and thin . . . but alive, thank God!

She was conscious. 'Where's Bart?' she whispered.

With that question she lost consciousness and slumped in Dad's arms. While looking around for Bart, I noticed that John Amos Jackson was no longer to be seen. 'Dad,' I said to draw his attention, and just then out of the dim shadows of the garage, the butler appeared with a heavy shovel. He brought it down hard on top of Dad's head. Silently, without a groan, Dad slumped to the floor with Mom still in his arms. Again that butler raised the shovel as if to kill Dad – and maybe Mom too. I ran, and I kicked with my right leg as I'd never kicked before. The shovel went spinning away, and as John Amos Jackson whirled to face me, I let him have it with my left foot square in his stomach. He groaned and slumped over.

But Bart – where was Bart?

'Jory,' called the mother of my parents, 'get your parents out of this garage as quickly as you can. Pull them so far away they won't be hurt if the garage blows up when the fire reaches the gasoline in here! Hurry!' I started to object, but she took care of that. 'I'll find Bart. You just keep my son and daughter safe.'

It was easy to pick up Mom and run with her to a safe place and lay her down, but not so easy to drag Dad by his shoulders to lie beside her under a tree – still I managed. The house now smoked from several windows. My brother was in there – and my grandmother too.

Once more I took off for the garage, to find John Amos Jackson had recovered and he too was inside the burning house. In the kitchen I saw John Amos struggling with my grandmother who was so weak she could do little to defend herself – or so I thought. As the two of them staggered into the adjoining sitting-room, he was battering her face with slaps. I ran to rescue her though the smoke was in my eyes. 'You'll never get away with this, John!' she yelled as he tried to choke her. I fell over a chair that had been turned over, and jumped to my feet just in time to see her bring down a heavy Venetian glass ashtray so it struck him on his temple. He slumped to the floor like a bird shot down by a rifle.

That's when I saw Bart. He was in the parlour trying to lug that huge portrait to safety. 'Momma,' he was sobbing, 'got to save Momma. Momma, I'm going to get you out of here, don't you fear, 'cause I'm just as brave as Jory, just as brave . . . can't let you burn. John Amos was lying, he doesn't know what God wants . . . doesn't know . . .'

'Bart,' crooned my grandmother and her voice was so like my Mom's when she spoke softly, 'I'm here. You can save me – not just the portrait.' She stepped forward, limping badly, and I guessed she'd tripped and fallen on that long black robe and sprained her ankle, for at each step she grimaced. 'Please, darling, you and I have to leave the house.'

He shook his head. 'Got to save Momma! You're not my momma!'

'But I am,' said another voice in another doorway. My eyes widened to see my mother standing there, clinging weakly to the door frame as she pleaded with Bart. 'Darling, let go the portrait and all of us will leave this house.' Bart looked from her to his grandmother, still clinging to the huge heavy portrait that he would never have the strength to drag from the house.

'Going to save my momma, even if she hates me,' muttered Bart to himself as he tugged at the huge heavy portrait. 'Don't care no more if she loves Jory and Cindy better. Got to do one good thing and then everybody will know I'm not bad, and not crazy.'

Mom ran to him and covered his small dirty face with kisses, as all around us the room filled with smoke.

'Jory!' called my grandmother, 'call the fire department! Take Bart out of here, and I'll lead your mother out.'

But Mom didn't want to go; she seemed oblivious of the danger of staying in a smoke-filled house, with fire underneath. Even as I dialled for the operator and told her what was going on, then gave her the address, Mom was down on her knees hugging Bart close. 'Bart, my sweetheart, if you can't accept Cindy as your sister and live happily with her, I'll send her away.'

His grip loosened on the portrait as his eyes grew wider. 'No you won't . . .'

'Yes, I swear I will. You are my son, born from my love for your father . . .'

'You loved my real daddy?' he asked unbelievingly, 'You really did love him, even if you seduced and killed him?'

I groaned, then ran to seize hold of Bart. 'Come on, let's get out of here while we have the chance.'

'Bart, you go with Jory,' called my grandmother, 'and I'll take care of my daughter.'

There was the side door Bart used to sneak inside the house, and I dragged him towards that, looking back to see Mom was being pulled along by her mother. Mom seemed on the verge of fainting, so my grandmother almost had to carry her.

As I ran from the house, forcing Bart to join Dad under the tree where I'd left him, I saw Mom had sagged in her mother's arms. When she did, both women tumbled over backwards, and for a moment the smoke obscured my view. Dad, disoriented, was wiping blood from his head injury, as he stared at me. 'Where's your mother?'

'Cathy, come back!' screamed the old woman in black. 'Bart is safely outside. Jory took care of him – you don't have to go back and search!'

'Oh, my God, is Cathy still in that house?' asked Dad, still wiping at the blood which wouldn't stop flowing from the deep gash on the side of his head.

'Momma's going to die, I know it!' cried Bart, racing towards the house and forcing me to run after him. I hurled myself forward and brought him down with a tackle. He fought me like a madman. 'Momma, got to save Momma! Jory, let me, please let me!'

'You don't have to. Her mother is going to save her,' I said, looking over my shoulder as I held him down and prevented him from entering that house of fire again.

Suddenly Emma and Madame Marisha were in the yard, holding on to me, on to Bart, hurrying us both towards Dad who had managed to stand. Blindly, with his hands groping before him, he was headed towards the house, crying out 'Cathy, where are you? Come out of that house! Cathy, I'm coming!'

That's when I ran to keep him from entering the house. That's when Momma was shoved violently through one of the french doors that opened on to the patio.

I ran forward to lift her up and carry her to Dad. 'Neither one of you has to die,' I said with a sob in my throat. 'Your mother has saved at least one of her children.'

But cries and screams were in the air. My grandmother's black clothes were on fire! I saw her as one sees a nightmare, trying to beat out the flames.

'Fall down and roll on the ground!' roared Dad, releasing my Mom so quickly she fell to the ground. He ran towards his mother, seized her up and rolled her on the ground. She was gasping and choking as he slapped out the fire. One long wild look of terror she gave him before some kind of peace came over her face – and stayed there. Why did that expression just stay there? Dad cried out, then leaned to put his ear to her chest. 'Momma,' he sobbed, 'please don't be dead before I've had the chance to say what I must . . . Momma, don't be dead . . .'

But she was. Even I could tell that from the glazed way her eyes kept staring up at a starry winter night sky.

'Her heart,' said Dad with his dazed look, 'just like her father . . . it seemed her heart was about to jump from her chest as I rolled her about.'

JORY

All the shadows that clouded my youthful days, all the questions and the doubts I'd been afraid to speak about, all have been cleared away now, like cobwebs from the corners.

I thought when we came back from the funeral of our grandmother that life would go on as usual and nothing much would be changed.

Some things have changed. Some weight lifted from Bart's shoulders and he became again the quiet little boy who couldn't really like himself very much. His psychiatrist said he would grow out of that gradually, with enough love given him, and enough friends his own age to play with.

He has friends now, lots of them. Even as I write this I can look through the open window and see Bart playing with the Shetland pony our parents gave him for Christmas.

At last he had his 'heart's desire'.

I watch him often, the way he looks at the pony, the way he stares at the St Bernard puppy my daddy gave him too. Then he turns his head and stares over at the ruins of the mansion. He never speaks of her, the grandmother of our lost summer. We never speak the name of John Amos Jackson, nor mention Apple or Clover. We can't risk the health and happiness of one little boy trying to find his way in a world that isn't always like a fairy tale.

We passed a true Arab woman on the street the other day. Bart turned around to stare after her, wistful longing in his dark dark eyes. I know now that whatever else she was, Bart loved her – so she couldn't have been as awful as I think when I read Mom's book. She made Bart love her, even as John Amos took a vulnerable child and warped him.

And so John Amos got what he deserved, and like my grandmother he too lies dead in his grave, way back in Virginia, the home of his ancestors. All his plotting and scheming all for nothing. If, wherever he is, he can think, I wonder what he thinks and feels, knowing what was in the will my grandmother left. Did he turn over in his grave when the lawyer read before us all that our grandmother had left the entire Foxworth estate to Jory Janus Marquet, Bartholomew Scott Winslow Sheffield, and surprisingly enough, Cynthia Jane Nickols too would get her share. And none of us were legally her blood kin – *legally*. All that money held in trust for us, until we reach the age of twenty-five. All held in trust, my father and mother the administrators.

We could live in splendour if we chose – or if my parents chose, but we live on in the same redwood house with the nude marble statues out back, and every year the garden grows more lush.

Bart keeps himself exceptionally clean now. He will not lie down to sleep at night until his room is in complete order, everything precisely placed. My parents look at each other when he insists on doing this, fear way back in the recesses of their eyes, making me wonder if Malcolm Neal Foxworth was exceptionally clean and neat.

He laid down the law to my mother and father one morning soon after Christmas had come and gone, and he had his pony: 'If you are to keep Cindy then you can no longer live together as man and wife and contaminate my life with your sinning. You have to sleep in my room, Daddy, and Momma has to sleep alone for the rest of her life!'

Neither one of my parents said anything, they just looked at him until he flushed and turned away, murmuring, 'I'm sorry . . . I'm not Malcolm, am I ? I'm just me, nobody much.'

Bart is a true Foxworth over and over, for he will rule again, so he says, in the new Foxworth Hall that he will build again. 'And you can dance your head off until you are forty,' he yelled at me when he was angry because I petted his new pony, 'but you won't be as rich as I'll be. At forty, I'll be able to buy and sell you ten times over, for dancing legs won't matter when you grow old, and brains count more, a million times more!'

'I'll be the greatest actor the world has ever known!' he stated arrogantly, turning from meek to aggressive just because he was holding that red book in his hands.

Perhaps he would be the greatest actor, perhaps . . .

'And when I'm done with the stage and screen, I'll turn my talent to the business world, and everybody who didn't respect me as an actor will stand up and applaud my genius for making money.'

Acting, that's all he was doing again, for he was only a little boy who seldom spoke except to himself. And yet, sometimes when I lie awake at night, thinking about all that happened before he and I were born, there must be some reason for all that went before. Out of the ruins should come the roses, right? I worry about all the women Bart would step on to get his way. Would he be as ruthless as our great-grandfather just to obtain an even greater fortune? And how many would suffer because of one eventful year when I was fourteen?

I'll take him by the hand tomorrow, and lead him out into the garden, and together we'll stand before the copy of Rodin's 'The Kiss' and maybe then he'll realize that God planned for men and women to love in a physical way, and it's not sinful, only natural.

I pray that some day Bart will see life my way – that love – no matter what its form, or how it comes wrapped, is worth the price, no matter how high.

Between the choice of love or money I'll take love. But first comes dancing. And when Bart is old and grey and he sits in Foxworth Hall counting his billions, I'll sit with my wife and family content with the happy memories of how it used to be when I was young, graceful, handsome, on stage with the footlights in my eyes, the sound of applause in my ears, and I'll know I fulfilled my destiny.

I, Jory Janus Marquet, will carry on the family tradition.

BART

They don't know or understand me any more than they did before. Jory looks at me with pity, like I'm different from the rest of the human race. He feels sorry that I don't like his kind of music, or any kind of music, and colours don't paint vivid pictures in my brain or make music in the air. He thinks I will never find joy in anything. But I'll find a way to enjoy. I'll know the future that is right for me, for that was the true reason God sent my grandmother to me, wearing black veils over her face, like fate come to lead the way. She came to show me how to save my parents from the everlasting fires of hell.

I watch my Momma and Daddy night and day, and sneak into their room at night, fearing to catch them doing something wicked. But they only sleep in each other's arms, and to my relief her eyes don't move rapidly behind her closed lids. She doesn't have nightmares any more. I see my daddy's eyes at the breakfast table, looking bluer than ever for he has let go of his stranglehold on his sister. I have saved them.

So, Jory pities me. But one day when we're both older, wiser, and I have found the right words, I'll tell him something Malcolm wrote in his book – there has to be darkness, if there is to be light.

EPILOGUE

I remember so much of what went on before we flew to Greenglenna to bury my mother beside her second husband. It was Bart who insistd that his grandmother had to lie in eternal sleep beside his father, his real father, Bartholomew Winslow. We cried, all of us, even Emma and Madame Marisha, and I never hoped to see the day when Madame would cry for a member of my family.

When the first clod of damp earth struck her coffin in its grave, it took me back to when I was twelve years old and Daddy was in his grave, and Momma was holding fast to my hand, and to Chris's, and each twin held an older brother or sister. And only when I heard the dirt hit her mahogany casket did I cry out something I'd withheld for so long – too long. It came from the depths of me, tearing away the years and making me a child again, and needing, so needing to hold on to my parents.

'Momma, I forgive you! Can you hear me now where you are? God, please let her know I forgive her.' I sobbed then and fell into my brother's arms. I would have said more to her on her burial day, but Bart was there, glaring his dark eyes at me, commanding me to be strong, to let go of the man I loved. But how could I, when to do so would destroy him?

We still live in the house next to the ruins of the mansion where my mother died in her efforts to save my life, but it's not like it used to be before she came with her evil butler who gave Bart that journal of Malcolm Foxworth. I love him, God knows I love him, but when I see those dark merciless eyes in the shadows, I cringe and wonder why I needed revenge so much when I had Chris to save me?

Last night Jory and Melodie danced an astonishingly beautiful performance of *Romeo and Juliet*. I trembled to see Bart cynically smiling, as if he'd lived a century or more and he'd seen all this happen before, and it would be he who got everything he wanted in the end, as Bart has always found a way to make himself the centre of attention.

He steals into our bedroom at night, having taught himself how to pick locks, and stares down at Chris and me, while I feign sleep, holding still, breathless, until he is gone, so terribly afraid that the evil that lived in Malcolm will live again in my youngest son. And sooner or later history will repeat itself.

'Today the mail brought a letter from my literary agent,' I whispered to Madame M while Jory and Melodie changed from costumes to street clothes, 'she's found a publisher who's made me an offer on my book, the first one. It's not a fortune, but I'm going to accept.'

Madame gave me another of those long speculative looks that had once made me feel very uneasy and vulnerable, as if she could see through me. 'Yes, Catherine, you will do what you must regardless of the consequences or the protests I make, or anyone makes.'

I knew who she meant, for he glared at me, telling me I should keep my secrets to myself and not let the whole world know. But Bart cannot rule my every action.

'You will be rich and famous in a different way than I expected when you were fifteen,' continued Madame who was now my dearest confidante, 'for everything can come to those who have the desire, the drive, the dedication and the determination.'

I smiled uneasily, afraid to look at Bart again, but fixed my eyes on my eldest son who was the star of the evening. I knew for a certainty that when my books were published, and all the skeletons were out of the Foxworth cupboards, I'd lay the shade and thwart the ghost of Malcolm Neal Foxworth, and never never would he rise up to rule over me again.

Nervously my hands fluttered up to my throat to feel for those invisible pearls that used to adorn my mother's throat, but never mine, never mine. I said again to myself that it wouldn't hurt to give it a try. Evil did thrive in the dark shadows of lies. Evil could not possibly survive in the full bright light of unstinting truth, as incredible as it may seem to some who won't believe.

Shivering, I moved a bit farther from Bart, nearer to Chris who put his arm about my shoulders, as my arm encircled his waist, and I was safe, safe. Now I could look at Bart and smile; now I could reach for Cindy's hand, and try to reach for Bart's . . .

But he drew away, refusing to join the chain I would form of our family, one for all, and all for one.

I'd like to conclude by saying I don't cry any more at night, that I don't have nightmares in which I see my grandmother climbing the stairs to try and witness evil deeds we didn't do. I want to write that I can only be grateful that from all the thorny stems the attic flowers managed to grow and produced at least a few roses, real roses, the kind that blossom in the sun.

I'd like to conclude with that. But I can't. Nevertheless I've grown old enough and wise enough to accept what gold coins are offered, and never never will I turn over anything that glitters to look for the tarnish.

Seek and you shall find.

For some reason I glanced up then. Bart was sitting in a shadowy corner again, holding in his hands a red volume that appeared to be covered in leather with gold tooling. Silently he read, his lips moving as he mouthed the words of a great-grandfather he'd never seen.

I shivered. For Malcolm's journal had burned in the fire. The book Bart held was a cheap imitation of leather and every page was blank.

Not that it mattered.

Virginia Andrews
The Dollanganger Series

FLOWERS IN THE ATTIC
PETALS ON THE WIND
IF THERE BE THORNS
SEEDS OF YESTERDAY
GARDEN OF SHADOWS

When *Flowers in the Attic* was first published, it rapidly became an international publishing sensation, establishing Virginia Andrews as one of the most popular and biggest selling authors in the world.

Her spellbinding story of four children who spent days, and then years, imprisoned in an airless attic – just so that their mother could gain her inheritance – proved so irresistible that it was made into a chilling film, and was soon followed by four more bestselling books continuing the story of those loveless, forgotten children and the terrible effect their harrowing ordeal had on them and their own families . . .